REJECT ME
AN IMMORTAL VICES AND VIRTUES NOVEL

KEL CARPENTER

AURELIA JANE

RAGING HIPPO PUBLISHING

Reject Me

Kel Carpenter and Aurelia Jane

Published by Raging Hippo LLC

Copyright © 2022, Raging Hippo LLC

Immortal Vices and Virtues Universe Copyright © 2022 Kel Carpenter LLC

Edited by:

Amy McNulty

Analisa Denny

Proofread by Dominique Laura

Cover Art by Yocla Designs

Photography by Lindee Robinson

Models featured: Travis Bendall and Nicole Moffatt

All rights reserved.

copyrighted work is illegal. Criminal copyright infringement, including infringement without monetary gain, is investigated by the FBI and is punishable by up to 5 years in prison and a fine of $250,000.

❀ Created with Vellum

About the Authors

Kel Carpenter and Aurelia Jane are the hilarious team behind the international bestselling series, A Demon's Guide to the Afterlife.

They pride themselves in being absolute weirdos, spending hours on the phone coming up with detailed worlds, and laughing about crazy ideas for torturing characters. While they believe they each have the personality of a rabid badger, people still seem to like them okay.

They share a love of coffee, travel, and tacos, and they've made some adorable tiny people with their equally weird husbands. Best friends and work wives, Kel has the audacity to live in Maryland while Aurelia lives in Texas, but they try to see each other as much as possible.

For the women who know their worth.

Stand before the people you fear and speak your mind
—even if your voice shakes.
　　—Maggie Kuhn

ELIAS

Blood dripped slowly from my fingertips, each droplet hitting the ground with a sickening splat. In the fireplace, flickering red and orange flames died down to smoldering embers, the black coals glowing with the last remnants of life.

My bedroom was silent.

The Blood and Beryl grounds were in a hushed state.

If only the echoes in my head would quiet down, but after what I'd done . . . all I heard was noise. The screams of shifters, vampires, and witches dying. The singing of a blade as it sliced through the air. The dull thud as it came into contact with an enemy's head. The squelching sound as weapons cut through bodies.

Thousands died because of the choices we made.

Choices *I* made.

While the blood rage was still pulsing through my veins, and the violent desire to kill was begging for release, it was the witch's words that haunted me.

Her soft brown skin glowed, and her eyes had been as pale as moonlight, yet looking into them . . . I had the feeling she could see into my soul. And what she saw . . .

Dahlia Renfrew had pointed a finger at my chest, uttering her prophecy in a melodic voice.

"You have rage in your heart, Elias Laskaris," she'd said. "But also guilt. Both will guide you as you seek your revenge, but your heart will be lost. On the anniversary of this night in twenty-four years' time, while you mourn, you will find your mate. She will be the greatest vampire queen Blood and Beryl has ever seen. You will *know* she is yours . . . and you will be too late. Her future is marked by death."

Dahlia was never wrong.

What she didn't know was that I had no interest in finding my mate. I'd just lost my sister. I wasn't strong enough to save her. I had no interest in opening myself to that vulnerability ever again. I wouldn't lose someone I loved.

No. If I ever found this supposed mate . . .

I'd reject her.

CHAPTER 1
DANNIKA

They say I was born on a cursed moon.

A night when the sky glowed red as the blood spilled in Portland. Later, we'd call it "the Great Sacrifice"—because somehow, on those blood-soaked streets, peace was found.

Order had been restored.

Or some form of it, perhaps. That was what we were told. It was certainly how the leaders presented it.

I wasn't sure who believed it. I wasn't sure what the truth was. Even with a truce, there was an undeniable strain between the Great Houses. But no one ever mentioned that underlying tension. Not in public, anyway. What I did know was that the world had been irrevocably changed that day.

I'd probably heard the story more times than I

could count, because that night was twenty-four years ago today.

"Cheer up," Adora said. I guessed the firm line of my mouth gave away my gloomy mood, despite the Spice Girls album blasting through my room. Her choice, not mine.

"It's not like I want to go to this stupid party," I groused. "Our birthday is literally the day millions of people died. It's not exactly a day people should be celebrating."

But they did. Every year. They focused on the peace forged instead of the lives lost that day. Lives like my father's.

He'd had to defend the pack while my mother had gone into labor, but he'd never come home. She'd found his body. Brutalized. Claw marks had been gouged deep into his chest. There was no doubt it had been another shifter, but there was also no way to know who—not that we could do much about it even if we *had* identified his killer. What had happened before the Great Sacrifice was supposed to be left in the past.

Even murder.

"It's also the last massacre we've had in twenty-four years," Rowe pointed out. She sat cross-legged on my bed, her wild, red hair falling out of the ponytail that bound it. "That's gotta be worth something."

No. It really wasn't. Not when shifters had only

walked this realm for fifty years, ever since the portal opened in Portland. After that happened, the human governments fell apart. As expected, the people revolted and then *they* fell apart. Turns out there was a whole other world no one had known about. The supernatural one. Nowadays, that was the only one that existed. All over the world, six giant portals had opened up over the past few thousand years, but they had remained closely guarded. Unseen by humans. Each one led somewhere different.

Ours?

It led to a land of beasts.

Shifters crossed over from it and mingled with the population. My parents were both products of that merging. There were other ways people had turned into shifters. Those that lingered too close to portals sometimes changed, absorbing bits of magic. It leaked into our world like a radioactive hazard. The result? Thousands of shifters basically popped up overnight.

So no, considering our kind had only been on this earth for fifty or so years, the last massacre being twenty-four years ago didn't impress me. Not when it had all been senseless violence.

The Houses may rule, but that didn't make them any less corrupt than previous governments.

My silence told them my opinion, and Adora snorted. "Dannika's a Debbie Downer, Rowe, you know that. When has she ever looked on the bright side?"

At my sister's jesting, my lips twisted, trying to hide my amusement. Not the easiest thing to do when she was all of a foot from my face, pointing liquid eyeliner toward my lids, flicking it about like a black magic wand.

"I'm not a downer, asshole. I just don't like to commemorate the day my dad died as one giant party. You know how much Mom has suffered because of it." Her lips pressed together, and she looked away. Shame turned her cheeks a shade pinker.

With the exception of Adora, all the peacock shifters had been wiped out in the Great Sacrifice. My sister had been found the same night I'd been born, abandoned in the woods but unharmed. No one knew what she was, and that secret stayed safe in our family.

My mom had kept her, knowing she wouldn't have survived otherwise. Then she'd stepped down as the Alpha Female of the pack to raise us. While Adora was probably older than I was by a few days, we considered today our joint birthday, since we didn't know hers.

"You know I didn't mean it like that," she whispered.

I sighed. "I know." Now I *did* feel like a downer, and a jackass to boot. "I just hate that we're being forced to go to the commemoration because the Alpha Supreme's son still hasn't found his mate. It's ridiculous he's forcing all unmated shifters to attend when it's not like he's stepping down anytime soon. I get that Markus needs to have a kid—the heir having an heir, and all that—but there's still plenty of time."

"It only takes a moment for things to change," Adora said softly. Not somberly, but she was thoughtful in her answer. "You never know what the future holds. It sucks for us, but if something happened to the Alpha Supreme, Markus would need to be ready to take his father's place—or we'd all be in deep shit." The ruler of the House of Fire and Fluorite had to be prepared for anything. There were always schemes in play to take that power away. The Alpha Supreme used to fight a dozen challenges every year or so until it had become clear he'd always win. If something *did* happen, and Markus took over, things would be chaos. But by Markus having an heir—and by extension, a mate—it meant he could actually be powerful enough to handle the transition. If he didn't, no one in our House would be safe, let alone our pack. The scramble for control would end in bloodshed. I hated that she was right, but I nodded anyway. She frowned, pinching my chin with one hand to hold me still. Oops.

"I wouldn't be as annoyed if he weren't such a douche," I muttered.

"Yes, you would," Adora said, calling me out. From the bed, Rowe laughed, the sound like a witch's cackle. "But he *is* a douche. You won't hear an argument from me. I feel bad for whoever ends up stuck with him."

"You and me both."

Adora capped the eyeliner and gave my shoulder a squeeze.

"It's one night. Just a couple of hours, then we can come back and watch some episodes of *The Vampire Diaries*. 'Kay?" She smiled, and it was brilliant. My sister was absolutely stunning with hair that changed in the light, morphing with shades of blues and greens. People often noticed her small, curvy frame or big, brown eyes. It was her smile I liked best, though.

"'Kay," I repeated, taking a deep breath.

I checked my appearance in the full-length mirror, appraising my outfit. The night was a celebration, but the dress code was never formal, at least not for shifters. Black leggings with a nice tunic and boots were simple and tasteful—and it allowed me to be a wallflower. I applied a quick coat of mascara and swiped my phone off the bathroom counter. Rowe reclined back on my bed, kicking her feet up.

"You good if I hang out here?" she asked. "I can head back to my room if you prefer." Rowe was the only human in our pack, and part of a very small number that our House accepted. At the bottom of the totem pole in the new world order, she existed as the pack janitor—and punching bag on more than one occasion.

It was total bullshit that the others could treat her that way just because she didn't have magic, and almost everyone overlooked it. More than once, Adora and I had taken a hit meant for her. We might have been outcasts too, but at least we had magic. We could heal fast. Rowe? Not so much.

"Go for it. If I'm not back until late, feel free to just crash here. I wouldn't want to be out tonight if I were you."

Drunk shifters? Wayward magic? Loose morals because everyone was too preoccupied with the commemoration downtown?

Yeah, no. It was a recipe for disaster if one of the pack assholes found her on a night like tonight. She was way safer here with my mom and stepmom, Abbey.

"Thanks, Dannika. You're the best," Rowen said with a wink, reaching for the remote.

"No, she's not," Adora called from across the house. We both rolled our eyes, and I flashed her a smile before closing the bedroom door behind me. "I don't know why Rowe inflates her ego like that," she continued, speaking loudly, so her voice carried. The humor in her tone made me smile. "We all know who the best *really* is."

My moms' laughter greeted me as I walked around

the corner and into our living room. It was modest, but it was just what we needed for our family. A navy-blue sofa and coal-colored recliner were the only furniture in the common space. We couldn't fit more. Not with Nova, my wolf.

She lifted her head when I walked in. Her icy-blue eyes were exactly the same shade as my own, and her fur was just as silver as my hair. Eight feet long, from the tip of her nose to the end of her tail, and nearly four feet tall, she was a true Alpha Wolf and the rightful heir of this pack—if not for one little problem.

I couldn't shift.

When other toddlers had been turning into cubs, I'd been cut off from her. I'd known she was there, but not how to bring her forward. Our bond was broken somehow.

But we'd found a way to fix it, however unconventional it may have been.

I still couldn't shift, but she was with me always. The other half of my soul, brought forth with the help of a witch. I wouldn't have had it any other way, even if it made me a freak.

"Oh, honey," Mom said. "You look so grown up now." I sensed the sadness in her voice as she walked up and embraced me with strong arms. Behind her, Adora and Abbey stood at the kitchen counter, watching us.

"No more than I did yesterday," I reminded her.

She was always very emotional on her daughters' birthday. I hated leaving her when I knew the grief had resurfaced. I was so thankful that she'd found the strength to love again when she'd mated with Abbey. It made it easier, knowing that my stepmom was here for her when I couldn't be.

"I love you, baby girl."

"I love you too."

Mom lifted her hand, cupping it around my jaw as she pulled back a few inches. Her dark-brown eyes looked over me like she was committing my face to memory. She always did. It was part of why I hated leaving her for any reason on my birthday. While many years had gone by, this day seemed to take her back in time every year. The pain became fresh. Raw.

It made me even more pissed off about being forced to attend this year's commemoration.

"You get that from your daddy," she said wistfully.

"What?"

"Your steadfastness." She patted my cheek. "He was loyal to a fault, but also fair. Never seemed to have an issue figuring out right from wrong, despite how much the rest of us could struggle with it. He would have been so proud of the woman you've become . . . at how much you've taken care of me, even when you shouldn't have needed to."

I frowned at the water pooling in her eyes.

This was exactly what I'd wanted to avoid, not

because I didn't care—but because I hated seeing her like this.

"Mom," I said quietly, shaking my head. I brought my hand up to cup around her fingers, squeezing gently. "You did the best you could."

Abbey came up behind her, wrapping her arms tightly around my mom. "And you did a damn good job," she said. "Look how well our girls turned out. Scott would have been proud as hell if he were here to see this now." While she spoke to my mom, she made eye contact with me, letting me know she had her. Reminding me it would be okay.

"I just miss him so much sometimes," my mom said apologetically. She turned to hug Abbey back.

"And that's okay. Missing someone when they're gone is the price we pay for love."

Adora came up, wrapping one arm around Mom and one around Abbey. She leaned up on her tiptoes to kiss our moms' cheeks.

"We'll be back late. Don't wait up for us," she said, though we both knew they would.

"You two watch out for each other tonight," Abbey said, speaking to us over my mom's shoulder. While my mother wasn't exactly short, Abbey was quite tall. Just a smidge over six feet, she could easily look at us while embracing my mom. "Stay in No Man's Land. Don't even think about heading northside—"

"We know," Adora said.

"Don't accept anything from strangers—"

"We know." My sister sighed while I squinted at our stepmom. It wasn't like we didn't know any of this. They'd been giving us this talk for over a decade now.

"Use protection, and don't forget your fluorite stones—"

"We *know*!" we both said in exasperation. The fluorite ring on my finger had never left my hand since the day my mom had given it to me. It signified our House, our pack within it, our protection. Shitty as my pack may have been at times, it was better than being without one. "Seriously, Abbey. We'll be safe. I promise," I added. She gave us both a smile and then nodded.

"Then have fun, and happy birthday, baby girls."

I grabbed my keys off the hanger by the front door while Adora held it open for Nova to go out. My wolf brushed up against my side as she did, a comforting graze that conveyed she knew how much I didn't like leaving, and she sympathized with it.

"Rowe's in my room. If any assholes show up looking for her tonight . . ." I trailed off, but they got the gist.

My mom sniffled and lifted her head. "I might not be our pack's Alpha Female anymore, but I can still put a wolf in their place."

I glanced up at Abbey. "I'll make sure she doesn't kill some stupid punk," she said.

Adora snorted, and I just nodded in thanks.

While Abbey would have been the more intimidating of the two if someone met them in an alley, my mom was crazy when it came to protecting her own. Her temper flared the second someone looked at us wrong, and that extended to Rowe since the first night we'd brought her over. It was half the reason I loved Abbey so much. She knew how to bring my mom down with her "calm juju," as we called it. She exuded the peace of a still lake and tempered my mom's fiery personality when needed.

"All right, let's gooooo," Adora said, gently pushing me toward the door. "We'll never leave if I don't make you, and I am *not* getting punished by the Alpha Supreme for disobeying a direct command."

"Yep," I said, following behind her. She dropped the tailgate open on my truck and Nova jumped in, tucking herself under the canvas canopy. I slid into the driver's seat just as Adora closed it up. We were backing out of the driveway in no time, but as we were headed down the road, I couldn't help a feeling that overcame me when I looked in the rearview mirror. The full moon skimmed just above the treetops, painting our house in an eerie light.

They said I'd been born on a cursed moon . . . but they never said what that had looked like. Had it glowed the same as the moon did tonight? What had been different about it? Had it been the color? The size?

Or had it been cursed because of a feeling in the air? An uneasiness that had settled in the blood, gradually seeping in like a potent poison? Or had it violently riled up the magic within us, stirring it into a frenzy that couldn't be denied?

Between the options, I hoped it was simply the way the moon had looked, but something told me it wasn't.

It was the same "something" that had been eating at me all week, ever since the day the attendance order had gone out. It was telling me not to go. To stay home. To run. To be anywhere except the commemoration on the full moon.

I'd ignored the voice, even as it whispered through me that soon it would be time to fight. To disobey. To rise.

Maybe I was crazy . . . or maybe it was a feeling in the air, sending me a warning sign.

Something like a cursed moon.

CHAPTER 2
ELIAS

I had no desire to attend the commemoration. Especially not this one. Year after year, it was the same charade. An event the House Leaders insisted on hosting annually to create the illusion that we were somehow better off now than we'd ever been. That tensions had abated, and the Houses were still at peace.

It was a farce.

My boots smacked the wet pavement while we walked, my hands shoved into my jacket. The rain had stopped earlier in the day, and the clouds cleared out to reveal a haunting full moon.

Ysabeau, my second, kept pace with me while she surveyed the city streets. Always alert, her dark eyes were concealed by the sunglasses she frequently wore, no matter the time of day.

"You know, Dahlia could be wrong," she said as we walked, not turning to face me. "Her foresight could be weak. Witches aren't always right."

I huffed. "This one is."

I'd never known Dahlia to give an inaccurate reading. I'd never heard of anything she'd foreseen not coming to pass. And I was *not* ready for what she'd told me. Finding my mate. A vampire, she'd said. One of my own. It was in my cards tonight. But it was not something I wanted. Oddly enough, fate and mates didn't give a shit what you wanted. It was all some grand plan the universe had for us, and we couldn't escape it.

Mates. They couldn't call it what it really was. Losing the concept of free will when it came to finding someone you wanted to be with. What was the point of dating or any type of relationship when it didn't matter what you wanted in the end?

I shook my head. Tonight of all nights. The commemoration is where I was supposed to find my mate.

Ysabeau sighed. "You already forbid all unmated vampires from attending tonight. That was a heavy move. We could just head home and lock you in the basement or something."

I side-eyed her as we continued on. The building was just up ahead. "Don't tempt me. While I think this event is a joke, it would look bad for Blood and Beryl. I'm not willing to disrespect those we lost."

Ysabeau shrugged as we approached the convention center. Two bouncers stood at the entrance, and they dipped their heads in reverence, opening the doors. They knew who I was. We walked through, then slowed our pace.

"We keep this short tonight," I said. The sounds of supernaturals gathering reached our ears, the noise filtering down the hallway as we approached the double doors. "Make the rounds, listen to the speech. Then we go. The less time I spend here, the better."

Ysa ran her fingers through her short black hair, then cracked her neck. "Got it."

The grand ballroom was decorated from floor to ceiling. Fire and Fluorite hosted this year's commemoration, and their Alpha Supreme made sure all who attended would know it. High-top tables were scattered around the room, covered in sheer tablecloths in every shade of the rainbow. The effect filled the space with a prism of colors. Cast-iron bowls sat as the centerpiece, flames flickering from the small blaze that was lit in each container. A server walked by with a tray of assorted shot glasses. I grabbed two, slamming them back-to-back.

"Feels more like a party than a mourning," I muttered quietly, setting the empty glasses on a table.

"It's why I wear all black." Ysabeau nodded in

agreement, then quietly mouthed, "Incoming, two o'clock." I jutted my chin out to her, telling her to go. She turned on her heel, off to listen to the chatter and report any news back to me.

Knowing who was approaching, I gritted my teeth, the pressure in my jaw pulsing. Turning around, a tall, brooding figure headed toward me. His long white hair was slicked back in a ponytail, contrasting the salt and pepper goatee he kept short and trimmed. An oily smile spread across his face as he closed in. The Alpha Supreme.

"Elias," he said as a way of greeting. He held his hand out to shake. "What a pleasure to see you come out of the shadows to join us tonight."

"Mathis," I said, my tone equally as fake as his own. Glancing down, I flicked my eyes back to him without accepting his gesture. "Forgive me if I don't shake hands."

His eyes narrowed at my snub, and he curled his hand into a fist as he pulled it back, sticking it in his pocket. "You know, I wasn't sure if you would come tonight," he mused.

I suppressed the need to roll my eyes. He threw out the bait, but he wasn't good at it. "Mmm? And why is that, Mathis? Would be a bit odd for a House leader to not show up to honor the memory of the fallen, wouldn't it?" I purposely looked around at the lavish décor, bringing my eyes slowly back to him.

"Even if it looks more like a mating ceremony than a memorial."

Darkness clouded his vision for a moment before he calmed himself. Always such an easy target. He slicked his hair back, trying to cover his emotions. "Yes, well, I can't imagine it's easy for you being here, on tonight of all nights, especially unmated and in such a precarious position." Mathis picked at his nail as he tried to goad me further. "Markus should find his mate tonight, and he'll give me another heir, furthering our line within this House. You"—he brought his gaze to meet mine—"still have no mate, and thus no heir." He pouted mockingly. "So sad."

Another server walked by, and I grabbed a shot glass, knocking it back. "Vampire, remember?" I grinned, extending my fangs slightly. "We don't die as quickly as your kind."

A flicker of fire entered his eyes. "Ah, that's true. But you can be killed."

I raised an eyebrow. "Ambitious. Seeking Blood and Beryl to add to your collection, Mathis?"

His mock laugh made my skin itch. "Goodness, no. Just mere conversation. Pointing out the facts." He sipped his drink, sticking his shoulders back in an attempt to stand taller than me. Mathis's lips curled up, and he was pleased as he thought he'd won our war of words.

"So tonight is the night for your boy, is it?" I said,

waving over a server who was holding a tray of what looked like whiskey.

"It is indeed," he said. An attractive shifter caught his eyes as she walked by, her long legs accentuated by her high heels. His tongue darted out, licking his bottom lip.

"Well, best of luck with that," I muttered, looking for an out.

"There's a lot of tail here tonight, Elias. I've seen plenty of unmated supernaturals. You should be on the lookout and find your mate." Two fae walked by, excusing themselves as they tried to navigate through the crowd. One bumped into me, looking up and paling when she saw my face, quickly muttering her apology and speeding away before I could respond. The encounter made Mathis smile cruelly. "Though it does appear your reputation precedes you. You scare them all off. Even with the females, it would seem."

I sighed. "I'm not interested in a relationship, nor am I as invested in producing heirs as you appear to be."

He chuckled. "Who cares about the relationship? Women are only good for one thing. Breeding. So long as a woman carries my son's heir, that's all I care about." He shrugged.

I may not have had any interest in finding a mate, but the way he'd devalued half the entire population in one sentence made my blood boil.

"It's a good thing if Markus finds his mate tonight. Without the bond being forced upon some unknowing woman, he wouldn't have a chance in hell at getting laid, would he?" I kept my face neutral as Mathis turned a shade of red. "Probably a good thing for you as well. Seeing that you view females as nothing more than livestock, someone choosing to spend their life with you seems unlikely, so I see where your offspring gets it from. I'm sure the missus is thrilled with your performance."

"How *dare* you—"

"Just pointing out the facts," I said, turning his words on him. The server arrived after making other stops in the crowd. He gave me an apologetic look, and I grabbed a whiskey from the tray, patting him lightly on the shoulder to thank him. Mathis schooled his features, letting his cold demeanor take over again. I held my glass up in a toast, then added, "If you'll excuse me, I have somewhere else to be."

As someone from his House was coming toward us, I walked away, leaving him to stew in his anger.

Taking another drink, I breathed heavily through my nose. Off to a great start and ready to leave. I glanced at my watch, disappointed that time wasn't moving faster. My shoulders and neck were tense, the muscles bunching up and tightening as I looked through the crowd. The longer I was here, the more

Dahlia's words whispered in the back of my head, and the more I wanted to get out.

I walked through the throng of partygoers, scanning the crowd to find Ysabeau. Each and every one of the supernaturals got out of my way, doing their best to keep their distance. Fear leaked off them as I passed by, and they tried to avoid making eye contact. Mathis was right. My reputation did precede me. Power had a way of doing that.

"I won't tell you again. Not a chance," an unknown woman's voice said coldly.

"You don't know what you're missing out on, beautiful," a male responded. I recognized him as one of my own, and I turned to see their encounter.

A young woman with flowing, blue-ombre hair crossed her arms as she stared down the vampire in front of her. His name was Kym. A low-ranking soldier in my House. "Bruises and bite marks when you choose to cross the limits set by your partners?" she said. "Being threatened if I choose to tell someone what you've done to me? Being gaslighted into thinking I somehow misled you and gave you the wrong signals?" Kym took a step back, his lips parting slightly. The young woman telling him off looked him up and down in disgust. "No, I know *exactly* what I'm missing out on."

I raised my eyebrows at her candor, and her venom. Her accusations were specific, but it didn't appear they knew each other. Another woman walked up to stand next to her. Her hair was silvery-white, but she was young. High cheekbones and proud shoulders accentuated her air of superiority. With eyes the lightest shade of blue I'd ever seen, she was intriguing. Beautiful and fierce. A knot curled in my stomach, and a flash of worry coursed through me. It wasn't needed. Everyone knew when you found your mate, that was it. Whether it was pheromones or fate, there was no controlling oneself. It was one of the few things in life that when you knew, *you knew*. While the woman in front of me was alluring and had my cock half-hard with a single look, she wasn't mine.

The wolf standing by her side with matching eyes and fur like the woman's hair exuded strength and its commanding presence sent people scattering like rats under a spotlight.

I understood that feeling all too well.

"Is there a problem, Adora?" the woman said, stroking the white wolf's fur. I couldn't take my eyes off her.

Without looking at her friend, she shook her head. "None at all, Danni. This douchebag was just learning what 'no' means."

Kym's dark eyes narrowed, and he stepped into Adora's space. He towered over her by at least six inches. "You don't know what you're talking about," he said in a low and threatening tone. The wolf growled at his proximity, sending a message that the vampire clearly didn't get.

I walked toward them, intending to put a stop to it. On a night where we honored keeping the peace, this was headed in an unpleasant direction. I didn't want to stay to clean up a mess. I wanted to leave.

"That's enough," I said as I approached them.

The one named Danni turned, eyeing me, blinking a few times before turning her attention to her friend.

"Kym, you heard the ladies. Move on. Tonight is not your night."

Adora snorted. "You heard your leader. Move along." She shooed him away, flicking her blue hair over a shoulder dismissively.

Danni suppressed a laugh, but the wolf curled its lip up further, as if sensing this wasn't over. As Adora turned to walk away, Kym grabbed her arm.

Her head whipped back to glare at him.

"Bitch, who do you think you are?" he snarled. I shot my hand out, grasping his wrist tightly.

"Let her go," I ordered, feeling the ulna fracture beneath my palm, warning him I would crush it should he not follow directions.

Adora just smiled at him. "Nova."

It was permission and a command.

The great wolf lunged, snapping her jaws, holding Kym just above the elbow. I let go quickly, and the animal squeezed. A sickening crunch rent the air before she jerked her head to the side, ripping his arm from his body.

Kym screamed, falling to his knees while he held his upper arm, or what was left of it. Blood gushed from the fleshy stump, pooling on the floor. Nova held the severed limb in her mouth, teeth still bared for all to see.

Adora straightened her dress, unfazed, while Danni pinched the bridge of her nose and held her hand out to the wolf.

"Give that to me, Nova," she said, and the wolf dropped her prize unceremoniously into Danni's outstretched palm. Danni looked up at me, holding it out. "Um, I guess this belongs to you."

A crowd had gathered as soon as Kym's screams had pierced the air, but I simply stared in awe. Who was this woman who not only commanded a wolf but stood undaunted by what had transpired? She'd either been through a lot or was crazier than she appeared. Something told me it was the former.

"What is going on here?" Mathis boomed as he stormed toward us.

For fuck's sake. I ripped Kym's other sleeve and balled it up. Gripping the back of his neck, I stuffed the sweat-soaked material in his mouth to muffle the sounds of his wailing. He swayed in my grasp, struggling to stay upright but quickly failed in the balance department.

Danni dipped her head at the Alpha's arrival, and Nova sat back on her hind legs. She was nearly as tall as the white-haired woman beside her, but three times as wide. Adora followed her friend's lead, though reluctantly at best. "Alpha Supreme," they said in unison.

Mathis's eyes flashed in anger as he saw the bloody appendage in Danni's grasp. "You dare cause a scene and attack another when I am the host?"

"We're sorry, sir. We were—"

I reached out, grabbing Kym's arm from Danni's hold. "Just holding that for me. Thanks," I said. I brought my clean hand to my mouth, placing my fingers against my lips, sending a high-pitched whistle into the air. Multiple vampires appeared at the ready. I gestured to Kym, then handed his arm to Ysabeau. "Get him out of here before he bleeds out on the floor."

Ysabeau's confusion would have been hard for anyone to discern, but I knew how to read her. "What should we do with him?" she asked, flicking her gaze to him in disgust.

"I don't care; just follow the rules of the treaty," I answered. "And clean up the mess."

That was something I'd learned long ago. I didn't need to detail whatever punishment I was going to dole out in order to invoke dread and anxiety. Not knowing—imagining and fearing what it could be—

went a lot further. It didn't hurt that Ysabeau was her most creative when given a blank check.

She nodded, then snapped her fingers for vampires to carry out my orders.

Mathis puffed out his chest as the crowd got louder.

"Your existence dishonors Fire and Fluorite, Dannika. But this? To break the treaty on neutral ground?" He shook his head. "The punishment for this will be severe," he declared, making sure his voice was heard.

Adora stepped forward. "She didn't do it, Alpha Supreme. It was me. I called Nova."

His eyes widened in anger, and he backhanded the young woman. Her head jerked to the side, and a small cut appeared from the Fluorite ring on his finger. A single drop of blood dripped down her cheek. She held her ground, turning back to stare at him.

"You will speak when you are spoken to, orphan!" he roared, hatred filling his words.

"My wolf is my own. Not my sister's." Danni raised her voice, Nova standing tall by her side. "But we didn't break the rules, sir."

So she was a shifter. Between her House and having what appeared to be some type of bonded wolf, I'd been fairly certain. While witches with familiars were possible, I hadn't gotten that impression from her. Most of the witches existed in Spirit and Sapphire, whereas Fire and Fluorite probably had over eighty percent of the shifter population. That she was a shifter who existed independently of her world, though . . . I raised my eyebrows and my lips parted slightly. Who *were* these girls?

Just as Mathis began to speak, I interjected.

"They're right," I said, holding my palm out and gesturing to the crowd. "As we all know, the rules state there's to be no death on this night. As King of Blood and Beryl, I take no offense. There has been no death, and therefore, no dishonor."

Mathis sneered. His fingers twitched. "You don't care that some girls have attacked one of your own? How safe your people must feel, knowing how you will defend them."

I raised my chin and spoke loudly so all could hear. Two could play that game. "I know you've only been House Leader a short time, but let me remind you: There is no clause for spilled blood. Only death. These *women* have every right to defend themselves against men that don't understand the word 'no.' If that's a crime in Fire and Fluorite, I pity your House for having gone back in time instead of forward. Kym is at fault and will be punished accordingly." I turned to Danni and Adora. "I thank you for bringing his behavior to my attention."

Danni scrunched her eyebrows and she looked at

her leader, then back to me. "Um . . . you're welcome." Adora went to speak, but Danni elbowed her quickly.

The murmurs in the crowd favored my explanation, and Mathis knew he was cornered. His embarrassment was on display, and he wasn't going to take it lightly.

He lowered his voice, piercing Danni with a vile stare. "Keep that bitch of yours in line tonight." He looked at Adora, adding, "Both of them." He stormed away, yelling for the crowd to disperse.

"Fun party," I said when he'd left. "I don't believe we've met before. I'm Elias—"

"I know who you are, Your Majesty. We're sorry about your man's arm and making a scene. Now, if you'll excuse us," Danni said in a rush. She grabbed Adora's elbow and leaned toward her. "We need to talk. *Now*," she muttered through clenched teeth.

She dragged her sister away with her wolf at her side. Nova turned, her keen eyes meeting mine before she huffed. Shaking her body, she looked away and kept moving.

I had no idea why that wolf had taken an interest in me, but I'd already seen her take an arm off. I had no desire to be the canine's next victim. Unlike Kym, I knew when I wasn't welcome.

CHAPTER 3
DANNIKA

I tugged my sister through the crowd, desperately searching for a dark corner to hide in. Away from the judgmental stares and out of earshot. I just wanted to blend in with the tacky wallpaper and disappear from this cursed night.

Adora grumbled as I dragged her behind me, mumbling that this wasn't necessary. She knew what was coming. Nova sauntered after us, doing her best to slink through the sea of partygoers.

Once we managed to find an exit and lurk in a hallway safely away from people, I stopped, whirling around on her.

"What the hell was that? What were you thinking?" I whispered harshly. With so many supernaturals, I had to be careful. Some had better hearing than others, and no one needed to overhear our conversation. "And don't tell me you don't know what I'm talking about."

Adora pulled her hair over her shoulder, picking at her nonexistent split ends, not meeting my gaze. "He was a prick."

I sighed, knocking her hand down from playing with her hair, making sure she was paying attention to me. Her eyes widened at my boldness. "Stop it, Adora. You know you can't do that. It's not safe."

She put her hands on her hips. "It just came out, okay? I didn't think before I started speaking. I can't help what I saw. It's not like I can turn it off."

Her gift was rare. Unknown to anyone outside the walls of our home. The last peacock shifter, blessed with a magic that leaders would kill for. Something they would weaponize. They called it the *Eyes of God*. She could see into someone's soul. See their secrets. Their truth. Their lies.

Which was why no one knew she had the very power that had led to the slaughter of her kind. To everyone else, she was simply a latent shifter. A little vain. Beauty without brains or brawn. Useless in battle, and with no magic to speak of. They saw what we wanted and needed them to see. Because if they ever found out how brilliant and dangerous she actually was, every House would either want her for themselves or want to kill her if they couldn't have her.

I leveled her with a look, albeit gentler this time.

"Yes, you can turn it off. You have to. We've spent our entire lives pretending. When you let your senses take over, it gets to you, and it clouds your judgment." I pointed to the ballroom nearby. "Like just now. Some dude just got his arm ripped off, and we've royally pissed off Mathis. That's the last thing we need."

Adora huffed in an unamused laugh, reaching up to touch the dried blood on her cheek. "He's hated us for twenty-four years. Our mere existence pisses him off. There's nothing that's going to change that."

I groaned, running my hands through my hair. "And that is precisely why we shouldn't give him any more ammunition. Imagine what would happen to you. To Mom and Abbey. To Nova. To me."

Adora's hard expression turned soft, and she glanced at Nova for a moment. She took a deep breath, pressing her lips together, then nodded. "I know. I'll work on it."

I pulled her into a hug, wrapping my arms around her tightly, and she reciprocated. "All we have is each other, right?" She nodded against my shoulder. "I will always trust your judgment when it comes to someone's character. Just try to minimize your reaction to it."

Letting go, she put on her carefully crafted mask of apathy. "Yeah, yeah. Consider it done." She smiled, looking toward the entrance down the hall. "You think we can leave yet?"

I shook my head and sighed, looping my arm through hers to walk side-by-side back to the commemoration, and Nova trailed behind us. "I wish. Mathis said we have to stay for a few hours. I'm amazed he didn't cast us out tonight."

"Just our luck, right? I call out some creep, Nova rips his arm off, I get slapped, then chastised in public, and I *still* can't manage to get us out of this shindig," she said, annoyance settling in as we turned into the entryway, walking through. "Talk about getting the fuzzy side of the lollipop."

I jerked my head in her direction while laughing. "The fuzzy *what*?" I repeated through my chuckles. Before she could respond, I tripped over my foot, stumbling forward and into someone's chest.

Adora pulled me up, and I found my balance, muttering my apologies, hoping to avoid angering anyone else with my presence. I was still grinning from her comment, and I tried to keep walking, but my sister held firm, a look of concern obscuring her care-free features.

I turned to see whom I'd bumped into and came face-to-face with the one person I never wanted to see. Markus, the son of our Alpha Supreme. Taller than his father, and just as imposing, he'd been graced with his mother's beautiful ocean blue eyes, dirty blond hair, and deep laugh lines when he smiled.

I didn't fear him, and neither did my sister. We just

despised him. He was a bully. My bully, specifically. Entitled—and never held accountable for anything bad he'd ever done in his life. I wasn't even sure he knew right from wrong. He was protected from any kind of punishment. Made to believe he deserved to follow in his father's footsteps. As Mathis's heir, what else could we expect?

He'd tormented me since we'd been children. I was an easy mark. Cursed, my pack would say. My House too. Everyone considered it a bad omen that the *actual* heir had been a shifter that couldn't shift. By the time I'd turned eight, every kid in my pack had been able to shift as easily as they could walk. Me? Through the help of a witch, I had a giant wolf by my side. An extension of myself, but not a wolf within me.

For years, I'd been his favorite target. Adora would defend me, but she wasn't high up on the totem pole, either. We'd learned how to take punches, and we'd learned how to process the emotional abuse. The way Markus could belittle me, the way he could get others to follow his lead and taunt me . . . mock my father's death . . . well, sometimes a bloody nose was a lot easier to recover from.

Once we'd left school, I'd finally gotten the reprieve I'd wanted. I'd avoided functions outside our pack, and any gathering that he'd been involved in, I'd made sure to never attend. I minded my own business, making a living crafting the metal jewelry used for our

House's Fluorite stones. My sister was the better talker, and she knew how to sell the product to the other Houses in No Man's Land. It was quiet and peaceful. I just wanted to live my life away from everyone. I didn't think it was too much to ask. For six years, I'd done just that.

But here we were. Staring at each other.

It wasn't his presence that was concerning. Nor was the fact that I'd physically bumped into him. The problem was how he looked at me. Adora and Nova saw it, and so did I.

There was an intense hunger in his dark blue eyes. His pupils dilated and his nostrils flared. Markus's hands curled into fists at his side, opening and closing as he struggled to maintain control of his wolf. His chest rose and fell rapidly as his breathing increased.

The air changed. A twinge of electricity shot through me, and my sister tightened her grasp on my arm, holding me closer to her. As soon as I realized what the sensation was, I felt the color drain from my face.

"Mine," he rumbled loudly, taking a step toward me.

The surrounding crowd hushed, turning their attention toward us. Everyone had heard it. There was no escaping it. No running off and trying not to be seen as the night passed on. We were here, and this was happening.

My stomach roiled in pure disgust, and Nova whined softly next to me. She knew this was out of our control. Adora gasped, whispering, "No fucking way."

"You're mine," Markus said again, grabbing my arm and pulling me from Adora's hold. My body was in shock. My mind was numb. I stumbled beside him, not fully functioning as I tried to process what was happening.

A bond tickled the back of my consciousness, but everything deep inside me revolted against the very notion.

Not him. Not Markus.

My tormentor.

My bully.

The living, breathing example of everything I hated in this world.

It felt like a mob began to develop around us, their whispers and murmurs traveling through the air, reaching me.

"Markus has found his mate."

"He's going to claim her tonight."

"Can she even be someone's mate?"

"Dannika's mated to the next Alpha Supreme."

"Wasn't she the heir before the Great Sacrifice? Looks like she'll get to be on top after all."

No, no, no, no . . .

The crowds parted as Markus's father came

through. "You have found your mate, my boy!" he said, boasting loudly. "I knew tonight would be—"

Mathis halted, complete shock coloring his features. His mouth dropped open as he looked me up and down, turning to his son as though there had to be a way to explain what was actually happening.

What was *actually* happening?

A sick joke.

The universe. The mate bond concept. This House. Everything. All of it.

That cursed moon. My father's death. My orphaned sister. My widowed mother. Ostracized my entire life by Markus and all his little followers.

Nova's warm tongue gently caressed my hand as it hung limply at my side. Her presence grounded me. I began to get feeling back in my limbs and refocus my eyes on the scene unfolding before me.

"She is *mine*, Father. It's undeniable." The grip he had on me tightened.

"If you're certain—"

"The mate bond snapped into place," Markus said, his voice stern.

"No," I choked out.

Mathis's eyes widened, bulging in anger. "What did you say?"

All eyes turned to me. Every House Leader was here. Hundreds of representatives from each faction were witnessing our moment. Each would go back and share the story and how it had all unfolded. I had to control the outcome.

"I'm cursed," I started, pulling my arm away from Markus, but he wouldn't let go. I tugged harder, looking down where his hand wrapped around my wrist, demanding with my eyes that he release me. "I am *cursed*, Markus. A shifter who can't shift."

"That doesn't matter," he said firmly, refusing to let go.

"It *does* matter," I countered, speaking just as harshly as he was to me. "You're the next Alpha Supreme. You should reject me. Find another mate."

Please, just find another mate. Anyone but me.

"I will not." I stared into his dark eyes, wondering what on earth could have this hold on him. How could the mate bond be this strong for him, after everything he'd put me through? Surely, he could see this was the match made in Hell. Nightmares could have better outcomes. "Broken or not. Cursed or not. You are my mate. I won't give up what's *mine*."

What. Not *who*. Whether he realized it or not, he didn't see me as *me* anymore. He saw me as filling some role that fate had decided I should play. He didn't care that I didn't want it. That I didn't want him. It was the most Markus thing ever, and with the worst timing.

"Reject me, Markus," I urged softly, though my teeth clenched as I spoke. "Do it."

The entire ballroom was hushed. Everyone was silent, waiting with bated breath for what would happen next. Even Mathis kept his mouth shut, though if seething could have made a sound, the volume was set to full blast.

His brows furrowed as he looked down at me, and he shook his head. "I would never reject you."

I recoiled like I'd been slapped. A rush of resentment coursed through me, and flashbacks of my past flooded to the surface. The hateful words. Being ganged up on. Criticized. Insulted. Tripped. Kicked. Bruised. Ridiculed.

Oh, but *now* he would be kind to me? *Now* he wouldn't reject me?

Absolutely fucking not.

I leaned into him, whispering in anger. "You do not get to bully me for years then expect to claim me because of some divine-whatever-this-is. You tormented me. You *hate* me. Now some bond tells you that I'm yours, you bang on your Alpha chest like a feral animal, and all that history between us goes out the window? I'm supposed to forget it ever happened and pretend that you didn't enjoy watching me suffer? It changes *nothing*. We are *nothing*." I looked at the crowd in my periphery before pinning him with an icy glare. "I am not your mate, and you know it. Reject. Me."

Markus's cheek twitched slightly, and his expression softened for a brief moment. His eyes flashed with uncertainty. "I can't," he whispered back.

I breathed out loudly and closed my eyes when I heard his words.

"Fine." I yanked my arm away from him, hard, taking a step back. The distance between us wasn't enough. It needed to span miles. Oceans. But a few feet would have to do.

"Oh, fuck," Adora whispered so silently, I wasn't sure anyone else heard her.

Holding my chin up high, I squared my shoulders and straightened my posture. With a hand on Nova's scruff, I pet her softly, letting her give me some of her solace and strength.

She was everything I needed in my cursed life.

Living in this cursed House.

All because of this cursed moon.

"Markus Del Reyes, I reject you."

CHAPTER 4

ELIAS

I stood in awe. Everyone did.

I hadn't been anywhere close to the ordeal when it had started, but the crowd had grown quickly around the commotion. Once the gossip chain and rumors had made it to someone nearby, I'd overheard the details . . . and I'd been intrigued.

The young woman I'd just met had found her mate, but from the sounds of it, it wasn't a happy union. Understandable, given the bastard she was sentenced to be with. Like everyone else, I slowly filtered toward the group gathering around the happy couple.

Markus was every bit the prick his father was. Call them whatever name you wanted to, they were bullies through and through. Mathis dragged his son everywhere he could, showing him off like a prized stallion.

His heir, he would constantly tell everyone present. Born a leader. Markus would puff up and soak in the praise, playing his part. I hated any House business that involved the two of them.

As the two fated mates argued at the center of an open circle, a brutal history between the two shifters came to light. No matter how quietly Danni spoke to him, we could still hear it. Whatever the details were didn't matter. It was simply enough to know that she had been the target of his menacing nature for more than half her life.

Then the final blow came.

"I reject you."

Dannika's words echoed in the near-silent ballroom. Gasps and murmurs of shock filled the air.

Not me. I chuckled to myself. The woman had a backbone. No matter how much she tried to fade into the shadows, she stood out. Even aside from the giant wolf at her side, her very aura radiated strength and control. Defiance and passion.

I wondered if she saw that in herself. If anyone in the room saw it when they looked at her.

Edging myself closer to the circle that had formed around them, I crossed my arms and waited, just like everyone else. Except I was waiting for something different.

Mathis's booming voice rattled the chandeliers after Danni's declaration had sunk in. "You will pay for this," he roared, storming forward and threatening to strike her down.

While Danni didn't move, preparing herself for the oncoming attack, what she probably hadn't been expecting was her rejected mate moving to stand in between her and his father.

Markus stood a head taller than Mathis, his chest puffed out, breathing heavily. "She is my mate, and *you will not touch her*. She will come around and have my pups. Give it time, Father."

Dannika looked nauseous at the very idea. Mathis's nostrils flared as he seethed. "She has rejected you. She dishonors our House. She's sullied your name. *My* name. If she won't accept you and give you an heir, then she must die. End this now."

And there it was, just as I'd expected. He would call on an antiquated law within the House of Fire and Fluorite. One that hadn't been used in a hundred years.

Rejected mates fight to the death. Or rather, if one party didn't accept the rejection, they were forced to fight to the death. Didn't quite have the same ring to it in so many words.

I rolled my eyes at the drama.

"I don't want to fight him," Dannika said, taking a step back, placing her hands behind her.

"Then you accept him," Mathis demanded, as if those were really the only two options available.

She shook her head. "No, I reject him as my mate, but I won't kill your son, either."

Mathis smiled cruelly. "That isn't your choice, now is it? You're bound by the laws of our House. You accept him, or one of you dies."

Markus looked between her and his father. Dannika closed her eyes and nodded once while exhaling. "Nova," she said softly, and her wolf's ears perked up, her stance changing, ready to fight.

"Your dog isn't invited," Mathis said.

There wasn't much he did that surprised me, and I couldn't say this truly did either, but I was slightly amused that he would push so many boundaries with such a large and diverse audience. Every House was represented here tonight, and the gossip would spread like wildfire. So far, he wasn't being painted in a good light, and now he aimed to control the situation. What Mathis didn't realize was that he was already out of favor amongst some, and he wasn't reading the room very well. His own anger was clouding his judgment, and clearly, he wasn't hearing the whispers of astonishment and condemnation.

Sure, he was willing to kill Dannika for embarrassing him. But he was also risking his son's life, and he didn't seem to think twice about it.

Not until he made sure to handicap one side.

"That's horseshit!" Adora shouted, not holding

back her opinion. "If Nova can't fight, then Markus can't shift!"

Mumbling agreements and disagreements surfed the throng of supernaturals that watched the exchange.

Mathis narrowed his eyes on the blue-haired woman. "You have no standing here, and I suggest you keep your mouth shut before you lose your tongue," he threatened in a quiet tone. Raising his voice, he continued. "If Dannika's mutation fights beside her, it's two against one. She fights without it. It is no fault of anyone here that she isn't a proper shifter."

Dannika's cheeks heated, and I had to admit, even I felt anger on her behalf. The ire Mathis held for her was personal, and his disdain was not hidden. If this was how she'd been treated her entire life, it was no wonder she'd rejected his son without hesitation.

Ysabeau came to my side, quietly leaning in, looking on with bewilderment. "What did I miss?"

"So much," I answered, briefly catching her up to speed.

She side-eyed me, crossing her arms and mimicking my stance. "Did you have anything to do with this?"

I furrowed my brows. "No. Why would you think that?"

She leveled me with a glare. "You have a penchant for causing trouble."

"That's for entertainment." I waved her off. "*This* is not my doing. One of them is about to die. And Mathis made sure to take away the woman's wolf."

Ysabeau snapped her head in my direction. "He can't kill her. Are you—"

I held my hand up. "Watch and wait, Ysa."

"Until when?" she asked through clenched teeth. "She doesn't stand a chance against Markus. All he needs to do is shift. Mathis is setting her up to fail. It's not allowed."

I turned to her slightly. "Let our dear friend dig his own hole. He has the shovel."

It was her turn to look at me with a pinched expression. Ysabeau was a stickler for rules. She lived by them, expected others to, and would put anyone in their place if they didn't follow the laws.

She mumbled her displeasure at my decision to linger for a while instead of stepping in immediately.

Mathis's voice cut through our hushed conversation as he commanded the circle to widen. "Fight. Here and now."

Dannika looked at her wolf, dropping to her knees, and rubbed her behind the ears. Forehead to forehead, they touched, and she pointed to her sister. Nova reluctantly retreated, flicking her tail in protest as she went to stand by Adora.

I couldn't help how captivated I was by this shifter, or whatever she was. Not that I cared whether

Markus lived or died, but I very much wanted to see her win.

Dannika tilted her head to the side, cracking her neck, circling Markus. "C'mon. Let's get this over with."

Markus shook his head. "Don't do this, Danni."

She narrowed her eyes at him. "It's 'Dannika' to you."

"Fine. Dannika." He shook his head, following her lead and circling around her. "We can—"

"Stop talking, Markus. I reject you. Just shift and get this over with. I won't condemn myself to a life as your mate. Not after everything you've done. I know who you are. You know who I am. You should've just rejected me." Dannika's eyes flicked to Markus's legs, likely looking for a weak spot.

He scoffed. "You don't know me. Not even a little bit. But we can change that."

"Are you fucking kidding me right now?" She stopped, cocking an eyebrow and looking at him in disbelief. She shook it off. "This isn't what either of us ever wanted. It's not what's good for your future, either," she said, her eyes darting to Mathis and then back to Markus. "Listen to reason, Markus. Please. Reject me. We can break this bond and you can find a second-chance mate. They exist."

"No," he answered through gritted teeth.

She groaned in annoyance, running toward him

and dropping to her knees in a slide as she whizzed by him.

Markus let out a scream and dropped to the ground in a partial shift, his claws gouging the wooden floor in a resounding screech. It took a suspended moment for all of us to realize she'd pulled out a blade—from where, I didn't know—and sliced the side of his leg as she'd passed him.

Jumping to her feet, she turned to face him. Dannika flipped the knife in her hand, holding the steel side, readying a throw.

Blood dripped from his hind leg, and he struggled to maintain his grip on his human form. "I don't want to hurt you," he said, straddling a line between pleading and threatening.

"Guess you should have thought about that before. That you can even ask me to consider you as a mate is despicable after everything you've done."

"I was mean because I gravitated toward you. Can't you see it now? Fate knew. Look at you: You're fucking gorgeous. You're strong. You don't let anything get to you. But I was the Alpha heir, and you were untouchable—"

"Are you seriously giving me that sorry excuse? You threw rocks at me when we were kids because you liked me? You pushed me down the stairs when I was ten because you thought I was pretty? You broke my nose during the group hike when I was fourteen because you wanted to date me?" She shook her head, spitting at his feet. "I wasn't untouchable. I was an easy target for you to take out your frustrations on. Fuck you and your excuses!" She put the knife between her teeth and met him head-on.

"Come on. It's not like you were totally innocent here, Danni. You've thrown some punches over the years too—"

He tried to grab for her, but she twisted and dropped to one knee. She jerked her head, slashing his thigh, making him twitch. Using the distraction, she picked up his ankle and got to her feet. He reached for her, and she grabbed his shirt. With a single sweep of her leg, she threw him to the floor.

He hit the ground with a loud smack, followed by an *oomph*.

Dannika dropped her knee on his stomach, her eyes hard. She maneuvered her other foot up to pin his free hand to the ground, then opened her jaw. The knife fell and she caught it easily, lowering the blade to his throat.

"I defended myself. I never sought you out the way you looked for me every day. I never cornered you in a hallway or tracked you in the woods. I never asked for this." If lightning could have flashed in those pale-blue eyes, it would have. Shadows cast her face in a severe light, turning her from beautiful to an avenging angel without wings.

"I will never accept you," she thundered, "so stop with the bullshit and reject me!"

When he didn't respond, she pressed the knife in, drawing blood.

Markus's lips tightened in anger. His hands shifted to claws. "I won't be able to control myself if you don't stop disrespecting me."

She laughed under her breath. "If only you'd given me that courtesy the last eighteen years. You'll have to kill me because my answer isn't changing." Markus shifted, and as expected, Danni lost the upper hand. He threw her off with ease before prowling forward, putting his giant paws on either side of her head and snarling—preparing to bite her neck.

To my utter surprise, Danni dropped her weapon to the ground instead of slitting his throat. She turned her head to the side and pressed her cheek to the floor, locking eyes with her wolf.

Love and regret were written all over her face. Nova let out a whine, and Adora held her close. Dannika nodded once, as if to say goodbye.

Ysa nudged me, and I shook my head slightly.

I wouldn't interfere . . . *yet.*

Markus, in wolf form, let out a low growl, then moved to the side, blocking her from where Mathis stood waiting impatiently. He shifted back to human form, standing naked. He reached down, offering a hand to help her up. "I won't kill you, just as you won't kill me."

She threw her head back on the ground with a loud *thunk*. "For very different reasons."

He shrugged, pulling her to a standing position.

It made me wonder what exactly her reason was. She hadn't yet stated why she was opposed to killing him. Even if she could have won, she'd made it clear she wasn't going to do it. Now, *his* reasoning was expected. That made sense. But hers remained a mystery.

I liked mysteries. They were so rare after this many years.

"What are you doing?" Mathis roared.

"I won't kill my mate." He shook his head, refusing to do his father's bidding. "We just need time. She can see reason. She just needs to be convinced."

I stifled a laugh while Dannika rolled her eyes so hard she may have seen the back of her skull. Something told me when she used the word 'never', she meant it. She had her own mind, and it would appear that once it was made up, there was no changing that. Did he not see that she'd rather die than be mated to him? That was a pretty big way to say, "never gonna happen."

"Fine," Mathis said, storming forward. "I'll do it myself."

A vicious snarl erupted from Markus, and I raised

my eyebrows. *Not bad, kid.* Hadn't thought he'd had it in him. Everyone else gasped at his public opposition, while Mathis's menacing growl matched his son's.

"You won't touch her," he said, standing between Danni and his father.

"I am the Alpha Supreme!" Mathis shouted in return. Now it was my turn to roll my eyes as hard as Dannika had. When you had to *insist* on your authority to others, you didn't have any. Snapping his fingers, soldiers then appeared at his sides. "Remove my sentimental son so this bitch can be executed."

As they stepped forward, Markus began to shift. Ysa sighed, getting bored. It was time. Mathis had been digging his hole for long enough. Time for me to push him just enough to fall into it.

"Breaking your own rules, Mathis?" I asked, raising my voice so it echoed and was heard by everyone present. "Shameful." Several shifters winced at the volume as the single word boomed across the vast ballroom.

The hushed silence told me my audience was listening.

Perfect.

"I beg your pardon?" he asked, holding his hand up for his soldiers to stop their descent.

All eyes turned to me. Watching and waiting.

"The Law of Rejected Mates is out of date, but the rules are clearly stated. They fight to the death," I said, pausing for effect. When he was about to speak, I made a point of interrupting. "*Without* interference."

"It's not interfering. They have refused to follow the law," he sneered.

"I'm pretty sure killing one party—the one you aren't related to especially—would be considered interfering," I mocked. Murmurs of agreement reached my ears, and I smiled. "Even if you were able to defend your case, you are Alpha Supreme, as you made sure to remind everyone here. The treaty states that *none* shall be killed on the commemoration of the Great Sacrifice. Yet you've ordered one of them to die tonight, after just threatening punishment for Dannika and Adora for protecting themselves." I waved a hand, gesturing to them. "They didn't even kill anyone, but that didn't seem to matter, did it?"

Mathis's eyes narrowed on me. He balled his hands into fists, and he shook with barely contained rage. It took everything I had to not smile. "They are within my House. I make the rules—"

"Your authority does not supersede the treaty of all Houses, Mathis. Unless you think yourself above *all* other Houses?" Muffled dissent drifted through the throng. Whispers of bedlam and grumbles of disapproval. His eyes shifted back and forth, searching the faces as his guests whispered into each other's ears. Heat crept up his neck. He was backed into a corner, and he was being judged. Mathis's gaze made it back to me, and I winked, mouthing, "So sad" before I imitated his earlier frown.

"Get out," he said softly, though his voice warbled with anger.

"Alpha?" a soldier asked, clearly unsure of what to do.

He spun on his heel, whirling toward Markus and Dannika. "Get. Out," he repeated, louder than before. "You are banished from this House. You have no pack. No protection."

Markus stepped forward; hands outstretched in a calm gesture of surrender. "Father—"

"No. You had your chance, and you disappointed me. You're just like your mother," he spat. "Weak. Emotional." He shook his head in disgust, backing away. He looked at the crowd, raising his voice. "Dannika Kresley and Markus Del Reyes are no longer part of the House of Fire and Fluorite, which means they have no place here. Take their fluorite rings and see them out. Now."

Facing his son, he managed final words through clenched teeth. "You fuck her or kill her. I don't care which. Then, and only then, will you be allowed back here." He turned and stormed into the crowd, pushing several people aside as his soldiers followed him.

Leave it up to Mathis to overreact. Disowning his son and removing both him and Dannika from their pack and their House was a dick move in any playbook. The punishment didn't fit the crime in the slightest. Supes without a House didn't survive. They had a week, maybe two, before they'd be killed. Houses were your safeguard. Without them, the world was lawless.

I preferred to sit back and watch the reactions of the various House members. Listen to the hisses of outrage. Staying quiet allowed me to learn. Knowledge was power, and power was what was needed to stay on top of the food chain.

But I couldn't take my eyes off Dannika as she remained in her spot, dumbfounded by the events of the night. Her sister ran to her, grabbing her shoulders and shaking her body. Nova jumped between her and Markus, giving him the stink eye and a low growl, but he didn't move, equally as stunned.

Shade, Mathis's second, appeared from the sidelines. "You have an hour to collect your things and leave pack lands." He shoved Markus on the shoulder, urging him forward.

Adora whispered something to Danni, then she nodded her head, moving along solemnly. As she passed me, her expression changed. It went hard. For a brief moment, she stopped. Pinning me with a glare, she huffed loudly through her nose, then headed toward the exit, with Shade following them.

I found it somewhat amusing. In all of this, she found my interference to be worthy of her ire.

Ysa elbowed me. "You said you wanted to leave early. Now would be a good time for that," she said quietly, surveying the wandering eyes that kept landing on me.

I hummed in response, and she groaned, dropping her chin to her chest. "What was that for?" I asked.

"I know what that hum means. 'Mm-hmm.'"

"What do you mean, 'you know what it means'? All I did was hum."

She frowned, twisting her lips. "We're not going home, are we?"

A small smile curled up the side of my lips. "This is why you're my second, Ysabeau."

"Yay for me," she mumbled, then sighed. "I'd ask if we were going to follow the banished shifters, but I already know the answer."

"Only one. *Her.* I couldn't care less about the boy."

Off in the distance, Mathis was surrounded by House leaders and arguing with members of his own House. Scanning the north wall, I located a door that led to the staircase. Glancing at Ysa, I tilted my head toward the exit. "After you."

CHAPTER 5
DANNIKA

Exiled.

Houseless.

Banished.

Packless.

Homeless.

Shade had said we had an hour to get our things. I didn't believe it, not even for a second. I suspected the instant we left the neutral ground of the commemoration downtown that Mathis would have me hunted and killed for trespassing on pack lands.

I wasn't stupid. I knew our Alpha Supreme well enough. I'd embarrassed him in front of every single house. I'd publicly rejected his son and then refused to willingly participate in the senseless and barbaric custom of our ancestors. It was as stupid as dueling at dawn when someone's so-called honor had been insulted. He'd taken my rejection of his heir as a personal slight, and I couldn't even understand how. Considering I was the black sheep in the shifter world, I would have thought he'd be mortified to have me mated to anyone in his bloodline. I'd half-expected him to try to kill me on principle the moment Markus had named me his mate. By all accounts, he shouldn't have even wanted me to accept Markus, or vice versa.

Wouldn't his son—his heir—being mated to me have been worse than rejection? The way I'd been treated my entire life, I would have thought that would have been the case.

All of that aside, I couldn't understand why Markus wouldn't just reject me.

"Dannika." My sister's tense voice broke through my train of thought.

I paused outside my truck. The rain was trickling down, and soon it would turn from misty droplets to a downpour. I turned to Adora.

"You have to go home. Warn Mom and Abbey," I said, turning to her and tossing the keys. She raised her hand up quickly, catching them effortlessly. "I can't come with you."

The look on her face was conflicted, and even though I could see the desire to fight and protest, she had to know I was right. I didn't have time to dawdle. Nova looked back and forth between us, waiting.

Sighing, she acquiesced. "He's going to make a

play to trap you. I feel it too." She lifted her head, closing her eyes and taking a deep breath. She shuddered, as though she were ruffling her feathers. "Wolves have left the banquet hall. Their scent is near the east exits. Probably taking back alleys and heading to the outskirts of town to get in position."

"They'll corner me after I go home. Won't let me leave. He's not very creative."

"He's a bastard. That's what he is."

I huffed. "Understatement." I opened the back of the camper in the truck bed and let Nova jump in. Walking to the passenger door, I opened it and climbed into the cab so we could finish talking. My sister walked around to the driver's seat and got in, and we sat in silence for a moment.

"You have to take Mom and Abbey and go stay with another pack. You won't be able to leave Fire and Fluorite, but if you're not on his pack lands while this blows over, maybe we can all make it out alive."

Crossing her arms, Adora's nails dug into her skin. "This is bullshit, Danni."

"I don't disagree with you, but we don't have options here. Complain that it's bullshit all you want, but it won't change the facts. Our family is now in danger. Mathis isn't going to let this go."

She exhaled loudly, hitting the steering wheel for effect.

Her body was tense, and her eyes glistened. Frustration rolled off her in waves. I knew what she was doing. It was easier for her to accept her anger and let that show than it was to admit she was just as scared as I was in this moment. That we didn't want to let each other go. In all reality, I wasn't that different.

Reaching behind the seats, I pulled out one of two bags we kept there. They were our emergency kits. Not first-aid. Survival. My mom didn't take any chances, and she'd taught her daughters to do the same. After what she'd witnessed the night of the Great Sacrifice, after losing my dad and raising me on her own, after finding Adora as an abandoned infant—she was always prepared for the world to go to shit again. The next time it happened, she'd be ready.

We each kept a fully stocked hiking backpack in our vehicles at all times. It had everything we needed. A few changes of clothes. Toiletries. Rain gear and traction cleats. Flint. Matches. Protein bars and packs of dried food. Weapons.

I set it on the seat between us, then leaned over to put my hand on her arm. I stroked it softly, letting her work through her emotions.

"It's going to be okay," I said softly. "We'll figure this out."

She side-eyed me, still sniffling. "Trying to convince me or yourself?"

I snorted. "Bit of both."

"Where are you going to go?" she asked, clearing her throat.

I glanced over and noticed she was fidgeting with the hem of her dress. She was anxious. It was an old habit of hers that she'd never really grown out of. I hated that she was going to leave by herself. Risk traveling through pack lands without me by her side. I knew she'd be okay once she got home, but Mathis's minions would be looking for me, and they would be expecting me to be traveling with her.

"I'm not sure where I'm going," I sighed. "Hell in a handbasket?"

She snorted, then dipped her chin toward the backpack. "You've got supplies if you need to stay on the move, but that's not a long-term plan. They're going to come looking for you. They'll start tracking you as soon as they realize you didn't come home with me."

"I know," I said, nodding. "There are some abandoned buildings I can take shelter in if I need it, but I've got to use the little time I have right now. They're not out looking for me yet, and that's a head start I can't waste."

"What are you thinking?" she asked, the question in her voice turning to suspicion.

"I want to see if the House of Earth and Emerald will take me in."

"Are you kidding?" She looked outside, pointing as

though I didn't know what the weather was. "Even if you can huff it, it'll take you hours to reach their nearest border, and that's without it raining. And you have to—"

"Cross through Blood and Beryl, I know. I'm hoping after the display tonight, my crossing through their land won't cause an issue."

"That's *if* they don't kill you on the spot for being in their territory."

"I'll ask for parley. Clemency. Something to plead my case to their leader so I can just pass through."

She stared at me skeptically. "Elias might still be at the commemoration." She shook her head tightly. "And something was up with him. I couldn't read him very well, but he's deceptive. I don't trust him. You've heard the rumors. Even if they aren't true, they're based on his actions."

"I'm a little low on options, Adora."

She groaned, throwing her head back. "I'm sorry. I just hate feeling helpless. I hate leaving you and not knowing where you'll end up. Or what's going to happen."

"Trust me, I feel the same," I told her. She looked at me with apologetic eyes and pressed her lips together. "But I have to try. Earth and Emerald is my best bet. No Man's Land isn't exactly safe, either. Without House protection, it's open season on us." Turning, I saw my wolf in the back of the truck. Her eyes were fixed on me, feeling every emotion and knowing what this would mean for us.

Adora craned her neck and saw Nova back there, standing under the camper shell in the bed of the truck. A sad smile graced her lips before she spoke.

"This is too weird. It doesn't feel real," she muttered.

"This is as real as it's going to get," I said, looking at my watch. "I need you to go. You've got forty-five minutes. They may not stop you, but they are going to come to the house looking for me when that hour mark is up."

She pulled a knife out from a sheath under her skirt and handed it to me, pointing at the seat. "Cut the seam and reach in under the cushion. You'll need something to trade."

I scrunched my eyebrows in confusion but knew it was just better to do what she'd said. It would be easier than asking questions. I ran the blade along the threads, popping them until it was wide enough to stick my hand in. Reaching through, I felt the material of the cushion, then felt a slit that shouldn't have been there. Pushing past the additional tear, my fingertips touched something cold and hard. I grasped it, pulling it out from the hiding spot. Holding the hidden item up, I inspected it and my mouth fell open. Eight small shifter-blood vials were carefully wrapped, the glass protected by interwoven pieces of thick cloth. They were bound with plastic wrap, keeping them tightly enclosed.

"Where did you get this?" I asked.

"Mom's supply," she answered, unashamed. Shrugging, she added, "She always said to be prepared. You need currency while you're out there. There are some empty vials in the bag, but use them sparingly. You need to be able to run and you can't do that low on blood."

I wanted to laugh, and a small one escaped me. "When did you do this?" Looking down at the torn seat, I shook my head incredulously. "You sewed it in the seats. What if the truck had been stolen?"

"Then we lost the vials, and we lost our bags with it. Worth the risk, and apparently, it's paying off now."

I leaned over, grabbing her shoulders and pulling her to me. I wrapped my arms around her, squeezing her tightly, and she did the same to me. "Thank you." The words came out hoarse and my throat clogged with emotion.

"You always look out for me," she said quietly. "I look out for you too. Just in different ways."

We held each other for what felt like a long time and still not long enough. "You're my sister in every way that matters," I whispered in her ear. "I love you more than anything. But don't think you can snark your way out of this, okay? Mathis is looking for any excuse to punish me and he will use you if you give him any reason."

She nodded against me, holding me tighter.

"Say it."

"I won't be a smartass," she grumbled in my ear.

I chuckled, but it sounded sad. Bitter, even. "Take this seriously. It's life or death now. Take care of Mom and Abbey. Keep Rowe safe. The less she knows about anything, the better."

Adora sniffed, and a stuttered breath followed. I knew the tears were flowing. Letting go, she nodded again, glancing out the window. "Nova, you take care of Danni." My wolf dipped her head, and then my sister looked at me. "Be careful," she choked out, grabbing my hand and squeezing.

"You too." I tucked the vials into my bag, placing them between rolled clothes. My sister gripped the steering wheel with both hands, leaning her temple against it as she watched me. With a final glance, I pressed my lips together and took a deep breath. It was like psyching myself up for a duel in the shifting circle, but this was so much more. I was fighting for my life now. Grabbing the door handle, I got out and slid down to the ground on leaden feet. I grabbed a waterproof hoodie from behind the seat and put it on, zipping it up and pulling the hood over my head to shield the rain and hide my face. I slipped the straps of the backpack over my shoulders, not clipping the front piece. Last thing I needed was a harness for someone to be able to easily grab and hold me.

Walking to the back of the pickup, I opened the tailgate and the camper so Nova could get out. Her heavy paws smacked the wet pavement as she landed. Her ice-colored eyes glowed like headlights in the dark. I closed the truck up, then met my sister's gaze in the rearview mirror while I hit the truck twice, signaling for her to go.

The engine revved as Adora pressed the gas, and she pulled away, turning her headlights on and heading home.

Home.

A place I wouldn't get to see ever again.

I had no idea what the hell to do, and that was the scariest feeling of all.

As I watched my sister's taillights fade from view, I placed my hand on the scruff on Nova's neck, slightly scratching her.

"C'mon," I said to her quietly, tugging the hood over my head a little more. "We need to get moving."

We turned, heading northwest. I figured if the wolves had exited the east side of the building, I needed to keep my scent as far away from that as possible.

There were plenty of abandoned buildings in Portland. I wished I could sneak into one, find a lookout, and sleep with my back against a wall, but it would be useless. They'd track me and find me by midday. I had the cover of dark for the time being and roughly twenty minutes had passed since I'd been given that gracious hour. I had forty minutes before they started tracking me, if I was lucky. I had doubts. I had to get to Blood and Beryl and pray to the gods that they'd allow me passage to Earth and Emerald. It was a tall order.

The raindrops were a little fatter, but the skies hadn't opened up in a full downpour yet. I picked up my pace, trying to keep to the shadows as much as possible, but it didn't matter. I stuck out like a sore thumb. *How hard would it be to track Dannika in the city streets?* Just look for the woman with the giant wolf by her side. Easy enough.

Nova felt my frustration and uneasiness, and she whined, nudging my hip. "It's not your fault," I said. "It's not yours, or mine. It's theirs for being a bunch of shitbags." I glanced down at her and smiled, meeting her eyes. I knew she felt my sincerity, and I never wanted her to feel as though I regretted my circumstances when it came to the two of us.

I passed a few alleys, turning my head slightly to gauge what was down each one. Sometimes it was a makeshift shelter, sometimes it felt more sinister, but the images were unclear. Silhouettes and outlines were all I could see. I looked at the roofline of the urban structures, feeling as though I were being watched.

Footfalls sounded behind me, at a distance. Nova's ears perked up and her hackles rose. They'd come for me faster than I'd anticipated.

"Easy," I whispered to her, looking over my shoulder and assessing the proximity of the person I assumed to be an attacker.

It wasn't.

It was worse.

I stopped dead in my tracks, whirling around to come face-to-face with Markus. Pulling out a knife, I held it up. "What do you want?"

He halted, throwing his hands up in a sign of surrender. "I'm not here to hurt you."

I narrowed my eyes. "That'd be a first, wouldn't it?"

Markus flinched at the scathing tone in my voice. "I deserve that."

"You deserve a punch in the throat," I said, sheathing the blade. "Piss off and stop following me."

"Wait," he said quickly, taking a step toward me. Startled, I threw a quick jab, landing the blow on his nose with a crack. He grasped his face, cursing as blood ran from the injury. "Fuck, you hit hard." He squeezed his eyes, shaking off the jolt of pain. "Any chance this makes us even?"

"Not even close. Now tell me what you want or go away," I said harshly, clenching and unclenching my fist.

He scrunched his face, the ligaments popping lightly as the bloody nose healed. He took a breath, again holding his hands up, palms out. "Why didn't you kill me?"

I stared at him for a suspended moment, my lips separating slightly. "Seriously?"

"You were willing to die, Dannika, but you refused to kill me, and you refused to be my mate. I just want to know why you weren't willing to do it."

"I don't know why you want an answer from me. It doesn't matter. We're both screwed now," I said, turning to walk away.

Markus followed to keep up, and Nova growled. I stopped again. "What are you doing?"

"I, um, I was going wherever you're going," he said, his gaze downcast and sheepish.

"You . . . I'm sorry, what?" I pointed in the opposite direction. "Go that way. Find somewhere else to go, but wherever it is, it's not with me." I started walking again, moving quickly to the edge of No Man's Land.

"I don't have anywhere else to go," he said quietly. "I know you won't accept me, but you're my mate. I need to—"

I whirled on him. "You need to what? Protect me?" I scoffed. "Kiss my ass, Markus. I may not have killed you, but that doesn't mean we're friends. We're in this mess because of you. You refused to reject me. And you're wasting what little time I have to get the hell out of here before your dad's minions track me and kill me."

His eyebrows drew together, and he shook his head. "No, he wouldn't do that. It's the—"

"Commemoration? Yeah, I know. Were you paying attention to how many times he was willing to break the rules tonight? I'm the one who rejected you publicly and now you're a stain on his precious name. My death solves the problem, and your dad has no qualms about making that happen. He even tried to already, and it was only the Blood and Beryl king that stopped him. You know it, and don't pretend otherwise. I'm Houseless now, so I can say it out loud. He's the worst Alpha Supreme Fire and Fluorite has ever had, and he's an even shittier person. You're incredibly naïve if you don't see it." I looked him up and down. "But the apple doesn't fall far from the tree, so I don't expect you to give a shit about anyone but yourself."

His jaw tightened as he clenched his teeth, but then his eyes softened. "I deserve that too."

I was caught off guard. Everything that had happened was like I was living in a parallel universe. I just wanted to wake up and go back to how things had been.

"Great," I said, not knowing what else to say. "Well, now that you've heard all that, it's time for me to go and try to save my life, if you don't mind."

"Can I come with you?" he asked.

"Are you asking *permission* to follow me?" I said, confused.

He pressed his lips together in a thin line, digging his hands into his pockets. He dipped his chin once. "I'm Houseless now too. I don't have protection. I don't have anywhere to go, the same as you." His gaze went to Nova as she stared him down, her ears pinned back. "I'm not asking you to accept me as your mate or be my friend right now. But we stand a better chance of survival if there's the two of us—" Nova growled. "Three of us," he amended.

I crossed my arms and glared at him. Part of me wanted to tell him *no*. The other part of me—the part of me that'd seen him fight when he meant it, the part of me that couldn't deny in this case three was better than two—knew it was in my best interest to let him stay.

"Fine," I said, starting to walk again. I looked over my shoulder at him. "You have to keep up, and full disclosure, I will give you up as a trade to one of the Houses if they offer protection in exchange for the prodigal son of Fire and Fluorite."

His eyes searched me to see if I was kidding. I was not. "Maybe you won't have to. Being heir, maybe I can offer a bargain."

I huffed a humorless laugh. "You're crazy if you think I'm heading somewhere that respects your father, or you by proxy—also, per your own words, you're Houseless now, which means you're no longer heir to anything."

He swallowed hard, not arguing but taking that in. "Where are you heading?" he asked, eventually. "We, I mean."

My footsteps were the only response I gave. *Should I tell him? I mean, he's coming with me. He's bound to figure it out eventually. Besides, if he wants to argue, better to dump him now.*

"Earth and Emerald," I muttered, glancing up at the rooftops. "So fast feet there, princeling. It's a long trek and we're short on time."

He muttered something in response, but I didn't care to ask him what it was. This was not a democracy. I was going, whether he followed or not was of no consequence to me.

"We're crossing through Blood and Beryl," he said softly, keeping pace with me. He adjusted his posture as we strode toward the edge of neutral territory. A distinct clinking sound reached my ears, and I turned to see what he was doing. In his hand, he held four vials. "I can't offer you much, but I at least have currency."

I slowed down, taking in the vials. Two filled with blood. Another filled with sparkling stones. The last had glowing strands of fae hair. I came to a stop.

I squinted, taking in his entire form for the first

time. He had a backpack. A raincoat with the hood pulled over his head. Thick, leather boots.

There was no way in hell he'd had all that packed and ready to go.

Markus was naïve. He didn't plan for another war between the Houses. He planned for his next kegger, and even that was a stretch.

That he was outfitted for this meant he'd gotten it off someone because there was no way he'd gone home and back in the time Adora and I had been saying goodbye.

"Where'd you get that?"

"Well, uh, Andreas helped me out. . . "

I cursed under my breath and Markus looked at me in confusion. I scanned the streets behind us, coming up empty. Andreas was Shade's son—and Mathis's third—and he was awful. There was no way he'd given Markus anything out of the goodness of his heart. He didn't have one. Nova narrowed her eyes, her ears twitching as she listened intently for a sound out of place.

"What are you—" he started.

"You're being tracked," I said, pointing to his bag.

"No, he wouldn't do that. We're cool," he responded, but I could hear the uncertainty in his voice.

"He's your dad's third in command and arguably way more of a douche than Shade. You refused to kill me, Markus. They knew you'd come looking for me." I held my hand out. "Let me have it. Now. Hurry up." The urgency in my voice registered with him and he slid it off his shoulders completely. Not even caring that the pavement was wet, I dumped it out.

"Hey," he protested. The few shirts and boxer briefs that had been packed were getting soaked.

I rifled through his belongings and came up short. I stuffed his items back in, barely able to zip it close. A side pocket bulged. Protein bars. I jammed my hand in another pocket. Socks. Another one. This time, my fingertips brushed something hard. I yanked it out, holding it up. It was heavy and no bigger than a coin, but it pulsed as though it were alive. "What is this?"

Markus's lips separated, and he shook his head, speechless.

I smacked the ground with my hand, standing up and handing him his bag. With all the strength I had, I reached back and then threw the tracking stone as far as I could in the direction opposite of the one we'd been headed in. I'd aimed to have it land on top of a building or a fire escape, hoping that would throw them off.

"We have to move fast," I said, taking off in a run with Nova at my side.

Markus ran beside me, silent.

Betrayal hurt.

I would know.

For a brief moment in our childhood, he'd befriended me. Played nice with the little broken shifter girl who'd lost her dad and didn't have a wolf. If some part of the excuses he gave were true, that would be the brief inspiration for the wild tale. But it didn't take long for him to use that friendship and false sense of safety to hurt me so much worse.

The first time I had ever been hit was because of him. He'd done something shitty to another kid and blamed me. Later, I'd gotten kicked off the monkey bars at an old playground and suffered a concussion for it.

Prick.

Still, *my* family had never betrayed *me*. Privileged or not, that had to sting.

We ran for what felt like miles, but it was just enough to get us out of town. Crossing into the trees, our feet met wet and muddy earth. I refused to slow down. We came up to the border between No Man's Land and Blood and Beryl's territory. An invisible barrier, but the hint of a magic line shimmered in the darkness.

Markus threw out his arm beside me, catching me in the chest, and I came sliding to a stop. Nova did the same, her paws digging into the sludge of the forest floor.

"I hear you, Elina," Markus called out into the darkness, still holding his arm in front of me protectively. I knocked it out of the way, but he kept his guard up, moving closer to me.

Great. Elina was a witch, and I doubted she'd be alone. I couldn't see anyone, but I felt it, and so did my wolf. How had he heard her?

She stepped out from behind a tree that we would have passed had we kept going. A wicked grin marred what would have been a pretty face. "You always did know my sounds," she purred. Looking me up and down in disgust, she *tsked*, shaking her head. "Really, Markus? You're trying to protect her? I thought you had better taste than that."

"Old girlfriend?" I muttered out of the side of my mouth.

"Something like that," he replied quietly.

Of course he'd dated her. I'd always kept my distance from her. I had no problem with witches. I just had a problem with bullies. Shifters started to filter in from behind her, and she cast a sphere of power, bouncing it between two hands like a baseball.

"What does that do?" I asked him, never having stuck around long enough to acquaint myself with her magic.

"Turns to fire."

"Fantastic."

I counted our opponents, trying to form a plan to fight my way through. Four shifters from Mathis's pack and two witches, one who apparently could throw fireballs.

"What do you want?" Markus asked as they approached slowly.

"Dannika and that dog dead," a shifter answered.

Markus's body trembled, threatening to shift. Nova let out a growl that sent the pebbles skittering across the broken concrete street. "You can't touch her. Tonight is—"

The witch laughed. "You think we care? Andreas sent us per the Alpha's order—and now that she's Houseless, we're not breaking any laws. Win-win if you ask me."

Her words echoed in the silence, and I knew Markus was finally understanding the reality of our situation.

He shook his head. "Let us by, Elina. We have no quarrel with you."

She rolled the magic sphere over her hand, not meeting his gaze. "She dishonored our House, Markus. You would understand that if the mate bond weren't . . . affecting you. It's nothing personal. She just needs to die."

They'd formed their semi-circle, ready to strike and force us back. I had a feeling another group of shifters would be arriving shortly, and they'd be coming in behind us.

We were well and truly fucked.

"That sounds personal to me," I said, watching their movement. Nova crouched down, ready to lunge.

"I'm inclined to agree." A new voice entered the conversation, and a group of vampires came out of the shadows, the magic of the Blood and Beryl border wobbling as they crossed it. They split, making room for one to come through.

Elias.

Broad-shouldered and tall, he exuded power in the way he walked. He held a small dagger, twirling it in his hand, practically floating on air as he strode forward.

The shifters looked at each other, uncertain and changing their fighting stances. The vampires present were soldiers, each of them prepared for a battle.

Markus angled his head, looking down at me in question. I shook my head.

"We have no fight with Blood and Beryl," Andreas said, coming out of the shadows.

"On the contrary," Elias said, walking toward me, "Dannika here is under our protection as a member of my House. Under the circumstances"—he gestured to the group that was sent to attack us—"it would seem you do have a fight with me if this continues."

Andreas narrowed his eyes. "Under your protection?" he repeated.

"Isn't that right, Dannika?" Elias stopped in front of me, pinning me with his dark eyes. "You joined us shortly after you were banished. That's why you were headed to our land. We take care of our own."

I met the intensity of his gaze with an equal glare. My sister's words rang in my ears. *"I don't trust him. He's deceptive."*

I had no idea what he was asking for. He wouldn't give me something for nothing.

Not in this world.

There were no kind hearts left.

But I was out of options.

Silence reigned. Raindrops plopped on leaves and earth. The wind rustled through the trees. My heartbeat pounded in my ears.

The vampire king had offered me a way out. All I needed to do was say the words, and I was safe. If I didn't, Markus and I would die in this very spot. *Markus.* I knew he wouldn't make it if I left him now. His father would have him sacrificed just to save face. In my periphery, I saw him watching me as he waited for me to answer. A pang of guilt went through me. I hadn't refused to kill him just to let him get shredded here. I might as well have been the one to put a knife through him if I let them kill him because I was too pissed to save him.

Curse this. I couldn't believe what I was about to do. I just hoped it didn't get me killed.

"Yes. Markus and I joined the House of Blood and Beryl."

CHAPTER 6

ELIAS

Clever girl.

Everything about her. She'd added her rejected mate into this arrangement, not knowing the consequences. *But why?* Why would she try to save him? Internally, I had so many questions. Externally, I barely twitched in response to her boldness. No matter. She would give me what I wanted, and Markus would be dealt with.

A low rumble reverberated through the shifters when Dannika's words hung in the air.

I broke the stare I'd held her in, turning to the group of scorned assholes. I held a finger up, chastising them. "Now, now, boy. Consider that you're outnumbered and if you really want to take this risk—attacking a member of my House on this night of all nights."

Andreas trembled in anger; his claws unsheathed. "Mathis will hear of this. You should consider the risk you take, playing these sorts of games on this night of all nights." He parroted back my words, every bit the bastard his Alpha Supreme was.

I shrugged, outwardly pretending to be unaffected, despite the tension rolling through me. "Can you even make this decision?" Taking a step forward, I sauntered to him slowly, sizing him up with a slow gaze. "What are you now? Third in command? This is above your paygrade, pup." I was taller by several inches, but he was built like a bull. Stockier, packed with muscle and spite. "I'm first; king, if you will. And if I chose to, I could end this now. I could destroy all but one of you, leaving that sole survivor to return to your House to send the message."

Concerned glances passed between the shifters and the witches. Vampires snickered behind me, and Dannika and Markus stood still. When Andreas opened his mouth to speak, I held up a hand.

"I know what you're thinking. That wouldn't be like me, now would it? To *leave* one of you alive." I took a step farther, coming close to Andreas as I looked down my nose at him, purposely reminding him of his place. Lowering my voice, a menacing growl took over, carrying through the forest so they could all hear. "I would rather have my soldiers slaughter all of you, leaving your rotting corpses for the animals to feed on, with nothing left but gnawed bones for your mother to bury when your pathetic leader finds your remains. I know how to send a message, so I suggest you and your puppies turn around and run home, quivering with your tails between your legs so you can tell Mathis that you failed at this pitiful assassination attempt."

Andreas narrowed his eyes, letting my words sink in, but he knew better than to challenge me. With a side glance, he looked to his pack members and jerked his head, signaling for them to turn around. He adjusted his stance, facing the former heir. "You can end your exile at any time. You know what you have to do." Returning to me, he said in a low whisper, "Fire and Fluorite will be watching, Elias."

"King Laskaris, to you. Thanks for the warning. I'll make sure to close the curtains." Turning on a heel, I snapped my fingers over my head. Ysabeau strode forward at my command, staring down the rival House as they headed out of the trees, returning to their own territory.

Stopping in front of Dannika, I appraised her. "That was a risky play you made," I said, shifting my eyes to look at the rejected mate and wolf standing beside her. "What would you have done if I had retracted my offer?"

She held her chin up. "You haven't made one."

I couldn't help but grin. "And yet, here you are. It

would seem I have made an offer, and you've accepted my assistance."

Ysabeau came to my side. "They're gone. I'll leave some of our soldiers to patrol the borders in case they try to come through."

"They won't. Not tonight, but keep everyone on high alert." I glanced over at the giant, white-furred wolf, then to my Jeep. Making a snap decision, I pulled my keys out from my pocket and tossed them to Ysabeau. She caught them midair, then frowned. Making the same assessment I just had, her eyebrows lifted over the large-brimmed sunglasses and a small smile played on her lips. She pulled out the keys to her truck and placed them in my waiting palm.

I dipped my head to Dannika, then motioned toward the truck for her to go first. She looked between us, eyes narrowing. Her distrust made me grin. I wasn't sure why I found it amusing. Maybe it was because she'd chosen the devil she didn't know over the one she did, which said more about Mathis than me. Perhaps it was because she'd thrown herself into my path, had had the common sense to be wary of me and my reputation, but had kept walking. Some would call it stupidity. I knew there was more to it. While I had no doubt I could hold my own against a young shifter and her wolf, she walked with the same confidence that said she could hold her own against me—despite losing the challenge and choosing not to kill Markus.

My interest wasn't just piqued. It was ensnared.

I followed at her side, reaching the passenger door a stride faster to open it. She tilted her head, telling Nova to get into the truck bed while she stood on the runner, throwing her backpack onto the floor and climbing in. The wolf snuffed, shaking her body, then jumped up, scratching the faded paint with her claws. The axles creaked under the added weight of the giant beast, and she lay down, keeping her keen eyes on me.

Markus followed, but I stood between him and the vehicle. "You're riding with Ysabeau."

"I'd rather—"

Flying forward at a breakneck speed, I met him, face-to-face. "Understand this: I don't know why Dannika didn't kill you tonight, and I don't know why she saved you just now, but let it be known that I don't care. I know who you *really* are, and your death would be a convenience for me. For all intents and purposes, you are my prisoner right now. You have no rights. Clear?"

His jaw tightened as he clenched his teeth together, but he said nothing. Good. He understood. I flicked my eyes to Ysa, and she hooked her hand under his arm, tugging him toward the Jeep.

I walked to the driver's side of Ysa's vehicle, getting in the truck and slamming the door. Dannika sat in the passenger seat, arms crossed and looking out the window.

"It's a two-hour drive to my estate. Get comfortable." I was met with silence, and that somehow fascinated me more. This woman was not afraid of me. She knew who I was, but that didn't stop her. She balanced herself on this fine line between respect for me and respect for herself. There was a beautiful defiance to it. An inner strength that drew me in, like a fine piece of art that told a greater story the more you stared at it.

Whereas art had it written in paint or etchings, this woman's story was in the set of her posture, the way she held herself. It was in the fluorite ring that hung on a chain around her neck, the way she fidgeted with it, deep in thought despite the way she'd renounced her old House and joined my own in a matter of minutes. I didn't know whose ring it was. She'd been forced to hand over one when she'd been exiled. I started the truck and pulled out onto the mostly deserted road that led into the mountains.

She remained in that closed-off position for the better part of half the drive. The moon peeked through clouds as they rolled through the sky, making its presence known as it filtered through the dense trees and illuminated our path with intermittent bursts of a white light.

I checked the rearview mirror, catching Nova's intense glare as she remained vigilant and on watch.

Her body jostled as we crossed rough terrain from what used to be Oregon into southern Washington, but she never faltered in her post. She didn't trust me. It would take time to work on that. It was easier to convince people. Animals had a different sense, and I didn't know how she and Dannika worked together. This was her wolf—but how much it was connected to her was unclear.

An audible sigh escaped Dannika's lips, and that was when I knew I'd given her enough time to think. Just as I'd hoped. A slight smile crept up my face.

"What do you want?" she asked, turning her focus to me. Her posturing hadn't changed, but she was at least looking in my direction.

"So many things," I said, keeping my eyes on the road. "A rare steak and a neat scotch. For *Hannibal* to have had a fourth season before the world changed. A good fuck without some poorly concealed aim to raise their status. Or simply, answers to my questions." With the end of my statement, I glanced at her for a brief moment and winked. "Which one can you offer to give me?"

She scoffed, muttering something I couldn't make out before turning away from me once more. "Go ahead and ask your questions."

"I want some insight."

"To what?"

"Your motives."

She side-eyed me. "That's not a question."

I grinned. "I watched an interesting exchange tonight. Instead of attending a memorial, I attended a party I had no desire to be at, thrown by a House leader I don't particularly like or respect. And there I watched a woman reject the House heir, but then refuse to kill him when he wouldn't reject her."

Turning to me, her voice was quiet when she spoke. "You think it should have been a memorial?"

I raised my eyebrows, giving her a sideways glance before answering. "I do."

"Me too," she said, the simple words carrying a heavy burden in her voice that I didn't understand. Her soft features were sincere, but they were marred with a flash of pain she didn't share with me. I wanted to know why. It didn't take a mind reader to figure out she'd lost someone. There were so many who'd died that night, after all. But who was it? What had they meant to her? Much as I wanted to ask those questions, I had to prioritize what we covered on the way to my West Coast estate.

"Why didn't you kill him?" It was important to know. I needed to understand the way her mind worked. Her guard was up, but I wanted to break down the walls and see what was inside. "You had ample opportunity. Even if you can't . . . shift." I glanced to the rearview mirror to find her wolf staring *very* intently. "You had him at knifepoint. You could have easily slit his throat, but you didn't. Why?"

"I don't see why that matters." She sighed, drawing it out in a clearly annoyed manner. "Why did you lie about me being in your House?"

I chuckled at her avoidance but let it go for the moment. "It's not a lie now, is it?"

"You had no way of knowing what would happen," she retorted. "You absolutely lied."

"I knew you would choose Blood and Beryl over death. You may like to save wounded animals, but you aren't stupid," I said in response. "So, no, I didn't lie, and I did know what was going to happen."

"Markus isn't a wounded animal," she muttered, uncrossing her arms and picking at her nails. "Don't mistake him for one."

"Then what is he?" I adjusted my position in the seat, resting my wrist on the steering wheel while we were on a smoother stretch of road. "More specifically, what is he to *you*?"

"A thorn in my side," she said. "He's not alone," she added, looking up from her fingertips and shooting me a dirty look. I hid my smile at her boldness. I kind of liked that about her. Then she shook her head, muttering an apology. "I don't know why I said that. You saved me back there and I don't even know you."

I shrugged, using the opportunity to redirect the

conversation back to where I wanted it. "You know, most people in your shoes would've just killed him and moved on with their life."

"Maybe I'm not like most people," she said simply.

"I'm counting on it." I laughed, taking a turn onto a mountain road that tested the integrity of a truck's four-wheel drive. In my periphery, she studied me. Presumably assessing her situation and figuring out what to say next. What she didn't know was I had already done the same with her. She was different, and not just because her wolf was sitting in the bed of the truck. Something deeper ran in her veins. Thirst and desire battled inside me at the mere thought, but I brushed it aside. I could feel it. I just couldn't name it. She was meant for so much more.

A voice in the back of my mind whispered to me, wondering if the role she could play in my plans was bigger than I'd anticipated. The Houses may have struck an accord, but we certainly didn't sit around the campfire and hold hands. We had our allies . . . and our enemies. We kept the peace on the surface, and we protected our people.

But some thrones were meant to be overthrown.

Fire and Fluorite was at the top of my list. The King of Gold and Garnet and Empress of Sea and Serpentine agreed. I'd veered off course slightly by taking Dannika in, and I imagined I would have a bit of explaining to do, particularly with Vesperus. While the Ocean

Empress, Asbesta, cared little for how I did it, the other vampire king would want to know why I'd deviated from the plan set in place. A small part of me asked the same. Sure, Dannika's existence would likely simplify and speed up the process, but it also would heat up tensions in the immediate. There would be very little manipulation required if I played my cards right here.

"What was your plan tonight?" I asked her, breaking the silence between us. "You came to my border. You were either planning on trespassing, or you were looking for me. Which one was it?"

She barked a laugh, but she didn't elaborate as to why. "I was heading to Earth and Emerald. I was going to ask for parley when I arrived. Just to pass through your land. Nothing more."

"What made you think I'd have allowed it? Or that my border patrols wouldn't have killed you on sight?"

"I was short on options," she said, running a hand through her hair. "Mathis was sending someone to kill me, and I knew it. I had no time. If I stayed in No Man's Land, it was a guaranteed death, and there would be no bartering my way out of their attack. You stepped in earlier when you didn't need to, so I hoped if it came down to it, you might feel bad for me and let us through."

"You do realize I'm a tad harder to manipulate than Mathis, don't you?"

She shrugged, unapologetic in admitting she'd

hoped guilting me would have worked. "If that didn't work, I suspected you might allow it just to piss him off. In a certain way, I was right. That's why you lied, isn't it?" Her brazen appraisal of me was . . . refreshing. I chuckled under my breath.

"Blood and Beryl is your House now," I reminded her once more. "You're free to roam the lands as you wish. You will be protected."

"About that . . ." she said, reaching to the backpack between her legs. Dannika pulled out a small package. I glanced over to see what she had. Blood vials. Shifter blood, no doubt. "I have payment for what you did back there."

"Payment?" I asked casually.

"This isn't the payment you want, is it?" The tone of her voice said she already knew the answer.

I angled my head slightly, extending my fangs and winking at her. "Smart girl."

She placed her hands on her lap, the sound sending a small clap into the air. "Are you going to continue being annoyingly cryptic or tell me what it is that you *do* want?" She gestured around us. "It's not like I have anywhere to go or anyone to tell. As you like to remind me, I'm part of your House now. While it might seem minor to you, my entire life just changed. I was forced to leave my family and my home because of the asshole who treated me like shit my entire life. I'm grateful to you for you taking me in, but I'm not stupid, and I'd really appreciate it if you just got to the point right now."

A flash of sympathy washed over me. While I looked at her and saw this exotic creature I wanted to know, on the surface, plain as day, was a woman still grieving a life she'd lost mere hours ago.

"Sometimes I deal in trade, in which case the shifter blood in those vials you have would prove quite useful. Sometimes I deal in information, and that has its benefits." I pointed up ahead, indicating we were almost to my home. "And sometimes I deal in favors."

"What does that mean?" she asked. Her shoulders tensed, and her voice filled with uncertainty. A part of me prickled. I knew why she recoiled the way she did.

"Relax. I don't trade in sexual favors. That's a consensual matter. This is business." I watched as she loosened slightly, nodding her head in what looked like relief. I flicked my eyes to look at Nova—who hadn't taken her sights off me—before looking back to the road. "You're right that I expect payment. While I sympathize that you were put in a difficult situation, the events of tonight made you a very valuable person for someone like me. I took you out of the line of fire and in return, you are going to be the catalyst I need."

"I'm listening," she said slowly, tucking her hands under her legs. I wondered if it was a nervous habit, or if she was trying to hide something.

"Do you believe in the mate bond, Dannika?" I

watched her carefully, slowing down the truck to give us more time. "I know you believe it exists—clearly. But do you believe *in* it is my question."

Her chin dropped to her chest, and she laughed softly. Her shoulders shook, and she tilted her head back and sighed. "Not for me, I don't. It's a cruel joke. We're pieces on a game board and the gods are moving us, laughing as they poke and jab every single festering wound they've caused. The mate bond is part of that."

"I don't disagree," I said honestly. When she looked at me incredulously, I continued. "A mate complicates things. I have ambitions. Plans. Purpose. None of those include a mate, and certainly not a bond." She squinted her eyes at me, tilting her head in clear curiosity. "But I'm king. It's . . . preferred that I have a mate. That I search for the one I'm supposed to be bonded to for the betterment of my House."

"Okay . . ."

I pulled over to the side of the road, sticking my hand out the window to signal to Ysa and the others to go on ahead. Nova perked up in the back, and Dannika looked at me in confusion. I turned in my seat, giving her my full attention.

"What does that have to do with me?" she asked. Her eyes narrowed slightly. There was a slight tic in her cheek.

I considered her carefully before speaking. "I think

it's safe to assume neither of us is a particular fan of Mathis?"

She frowned. "Obviously. I don't see what that has to do with—"

"I'm making plans to remove him from power. Permanently," I said bluntly. Her mouth dropped open. "The reasons why are beside the point. Removing a leader from power is not a simple thing—"

"You'll start another war," she said, her voice dropping low. Her hands bunched into fists at her side. Nova let out a low growl from the back.

"That's precisely why I need you. Because I need to remove him *without* starting a war. Mathis is prone to making rash decisions in the heat of the moment. Tonight is proof of that. By taking you in, I'm betting he won't be able to stop himself from stepping over the line where I can finally challenge him head-on."

"I don't understand, and I don't think you do, either." She'd relaxed slightly upon hearing I had no intentions of starting another war, but she clearly wasn't completely at ease. "Sure, he'll be pissed you took me in, but honestly, he's more likely to try to create problems within your House than attacking you outwardly here. It's not like it will be hard for him to plant rumors about why you took in his son and me. You're a king. You have very few reasons for why you would do that unless you were trying to stir the pot with Mathis. This won't exactly be a hard story to spin to your people because it's the *truth*."

"Which is why I have a reason that neither my people nor Mathis could ever refute," I said. She stared at me blankly. "I need a mate."

Sort of. What I needed was a logical reason for why I'd taken this woman in beyond the reasons she'd so quickly pointed out. Would her acceptance in my House provoke Mathis? Yes. Did she need to be my mate for that? No, but without a proper excuse, there would be questions I didn't want asked. This was the simplest way forward.

Her mouth fell open, and the sound of her breath hitching echoed in my ears. "You just said you don't want payment in sex—"

"I said sexual favors are consensual. Mate bonds don't give a shit about consent. It works to my advantage here." I looked between her and Nova. "You and I claim to be mates, you get protection in my House, and I have the final nail I need for Mathis's coffin."

"I just rejected Markus, and he won't accept it," she said, pointing to the vehicles ahead where she knew he would be. "It doesn't make any sense that I would end up with another mate when I can't get rid of the one I have."

Lifting a single shoulder, I hummed. "Second-chance mates happen all the time."

Dannika scoffed, crossing her arms. "Not that fast, they don't."

I laughed softly. "Fate is such a fickle thing. It seems to surprise everyone."

She pinched the skin between her brows and sighed. "Even if people *did* believe this—which is a stretch, given how impossible I find it—why on earth would you take me on as your mate when you just said you don't want one? I get that you want Mathis out of power, but aren't there better ways?"

"None that have thrown themselves in my path as perfectly as you did tonight," I told her. Her cheeks flushed. "I'm not going to go into the finer details of why this is the best course of action. For both you and my plans, it is—"

"That's presumptuous."

I paused and desire stirred within me. I loved the pushback. Her unwillingness to agree with me simply because I was king. But this wasn't what I needed. Ignoring my body's response to the way she'd refused to yield, I said, "I don't want a mate that fate chooses for me. This isn't the same. It's a business arrangement." She opened her mouth to surely say something else that would disarm me. I held my hand up, palm out, telling her to stop. "I wasn't asking, Dannika. It's this or become Houseless, and you'll be taken back to No Man's Land, as is customary for the exiled. And before you ask, no—you won't have permission to cross through my lands to Earth and Emerald."

"You're a dick," she muttered. She wasn't wrong. I wasn't making this easy, but as she'd pointed out herself, charity didn't exist anymore.

I shrugged, letting out a small laugh. "Perhaps. But you need—"

She jerked her head up. "I sincerely hope you don't finish that sentence by suggesting I need dick."

I chuckled. "I was going to say, you need me. It's a win-win here. But it's still your choice."

"Answer me this: What will you do when you find your *real* mate?" she asked, her pale eyes staring at me in a way she shouldn't have. "This farce is all well and good for your plans to dethrone Mathis. But what about after? What happens when we're still living this lie and your real mate comes along? I rejected Markus because of our past, but you won't have the same situation. It won't be so easy for you to push that bond away. What happens then?"

Wise. She was incredibly wise and insightful, already asking the questions I had barely thought to consider. It was another reason she would make a good mate. With a level head and not allowing her emotions to rule, she would make not just a good queen, but a great one. Beyond Mathis and everything else . . . "My House needs a queen. There have already been rumors about its longevity if I don't find a mate.

I'm the last of my line. When Mathis is dealt with, that problem still exists, and you are still the solution." I studied her expression, trying to glean anything, even the smallest detail about her from it. "You'll be motivated to play your part perfectly—but you won't be a nuisance. Any woman who *wanted* this position would. A true mate would be a distraction at best, and while I don't have your past with Markus, if I find my 'real' mate, I'll reject her. I won't let fate dictate my life for me, nor will it decide the future for my House."

She put both hands on her temples, shaking her head back and forth in disbelief. "No one will ever believe it."

I smiled broadly, extending my fangs. "Then you better make sure you put on a damn good performance. Your life—and Markus's—depends on it."

She met my eyes, leveling me with an impassive glare. Pressing her lips together in a harsh line, she nodded once.

"Good girl." I dipped my head in return, and her gaze narrowed. I pulled the truck back onto the main road, turning onto and driving up the long, curved driveway.

She cleared her throat with intent, drawing my attention. "Call me 'Danni.'"

I looked at her, raising my eyebrows in question.

Releasing a deep sigh, she said, "If you want them to believe it, people I love call me 'Danni.'"

We pulled up to the West Coast Blood and Beryl estate. Situated in what used to be Mount Rainier National Park, the sprawling estate consisted of smaller buildings that sat on either side of the road leading up to the large manor. A circular rose garden with a fountain sat before the double-door entrance. Large, stone pillars lined both sides while a vaulted stained-glass window sat directly overhead. The red, yellow, and blue panes had been arranged in a simple geometric design that hailed from ancient Greece. The center was a soldier's headpiece with a spear going through it. It was the Laskaris House emblem, dating back over two thousand years.

Out front, several SUVs and a few Jeeps were parked, and doors had been left ajar. Ysabeau was escorting an unruly Markus inside, hurrying him along before he could make a scene. She glanced back at us, and while I couldn't read her expression through the large-rimmed sunglasses, I got the distinct impression she was giving me the look she did when she said, *"I hope you know what you're doing."*

I wasn't sure what the woman at my side was used to, but something told me that her home in Fire and Fluorite was a far cry from what awaited her tonight.

"Welcome home, Danni."

DANNIKA

I sat on the edge of the king-sized bed, cradling my head in my hands. My elbows pressed into my thighs, and I gently massaged my temples, squeezing my eyes shut and wishing I could've done something different. That I could have done something that would have changed the course of the evening. The "what ifs" raced through my mind. The "if onlys".

But there was nothing that I could do now. I wanted nothing more than to be home with Adora, Mom, Abbey, and Rowe, but I couldn't see a world where that would ever be the case again.

Instead, I was in a grand room on the third floor of an obscenely large mansion. A cherry wood sleigh bed was the main centerpiece. It faced huge windows that overlooked the sprawling forest, giving a stunning view of the beautiful firs that stood tall for miles. Raindrops splattered against the glass, leaving streaks as they took their paths downward. A great fire roared from the fireplace centered on the wall, and the warmth spread through the room, taking the chill away. It was bigger than the main living area in my home. Even in its grandeur, the room was somehow cozy and inviting.

That didn't mean it was where I wanted to be.

Nova and I finally had two minutes alone so I could change clothes and process the events of the night. I'd rejected Markus, been ordered to fight him to the death, and refused. I'd been kicked out of the House of Fire and Fluorite, and then lost what protection I had. I was now banished from my home, my pack, and everyone I loved. How could all of this have happened in less than twenty-four hours? I never wanted to attend the commemoration in the first place. I'd had a terrible feeling for the entire week leading up to it. I couldn't explain why everything felt wrong . . . why there was this constant sense of catastrophe looming over me? I just chalked it up to being a Debbie Downer, just like my sister said I was. I'd so wanted that to be the case, for her to be right. I huffed a humorless laugh. Adora would hate knowing she was wrong about something. That's when it hit me—hard.

Adora. Mom. Abbey.

They didn't know I was safe. I cursed under my breath. Getting off the bed, I walked to where I'd dumped my backpack on the ground when Ysabeau had taken me to my room. Digging through it, I pulled out my cell phone and checked its charge. It had about half, but I'd need a charging stone to give it more power soon. I called home and my sister picked up on the first ring.

"Dannika?" Her panicked voice greeted me first, quickly followed by my mom's.

"Baby, are you okay?"

Tears suddenly threatened to take hold and my eyes began to water. Emotion clogged my throat. "Yeah. I'm okay."

I heard my mom's deep sigh of relief. Abbey's soothing words whispered through the phone. I could picture her standing nearby, holding our mom and comforting her, stroking her hair.

"Danni, where are you? What happened?" my mom asked.

I hesitated, not wanting to say it all out loud just yet. For some reason, telling them made it real. Concrete. It wasn't that I was in denial about it, thinking there was some way out. By all means, I was lucky. Elias hadn't killed me, and he had no reason to lie. If anything, he seemed incredibly straightforward. I may be playing a role for the rest of my life, but at least it was a comfortable one where my mom wouldn't have to worry. "I'm safe right now. Adora, did you get followed? Nothing happened to you, right?"

"I'm fine. They stopped the truck as soon as I crossed into pack lands, even before the hour was up. They weren't going to wait. They followed me home and tore the house apart looking for you." Muttering and chastising filtered in, but it wasn't something I could make out. I knew what it meant.

I sighed, looking at the ceiling. "How bad did you get beat up?"

"Black eye and busted lip. I'm healing. It's no biggie. I didn't mouth off. They just went for it when they dragged me outside, thinking you were in the house," she said quietly. "They want you dead, like, *yesterday.*"

"Danni, answer me," my mom interjected. "Where are you?"

The suspense would kill her. She wasn't going to like what I had to say, but it was better than me holding out on her. Or lying.

"Blood and Beryl," I finally admitted.

"For passage to Earth and Emerald, right?" Adora asked, doubt and concern lacing her voice. "Right?"

"No," I whispered. "I'm, um . . . I'm a member of the House now." A collective gasp came from the trio on the other line. My mother choked on a sob. "So is Markus," I added.

My sister began shouting. "What the hell is that douchebag doing there? You didn't agree to the mate bond, did you? Please tell me you didn't."

I filled them in. How Markus had found me in No Man's Land. How he'd followed me like a lost puppy. *Stupid bond.* I explained how I'd ended up in a confrontation with Fire and Fluorite. How I'd ended up getting in a truck with the King of Blood and Beryl.

"Elias?" Abbey said skeptically, slowing down her speech and lowering her voice. "What did he want in return?" My mom muttered curses. She knew his reputation, more so than I did, it would seem. For all the time she kept quiet and out of House politics, she was aware of far more than she let on.

"It's . . . complicated." I exhaled, knowing I couldn't tell them all the details. That was part of the deal. No one could know it was all a ruse. "Look, you're going to hear some rumors real soon. Probably tomorrow. I need you to think critically when you hear them. You know me. You know what I did tonight. You know who I truly am inside. So when the news hits, *think*," I pressed.

After a long pause, my mom said, "As long as you're safe, that's all that matters."

I snorted. "That was essentially my thinking too."

"I can't believe you saved Markus. Twice," Adora muttered. "It's not like he'd do the same for you."

"He did," I pointed out. "Tonight. He refused to kill me, and you know it."

"Whatever. *Once*. He did the right thing *one* time," my sister grumbled in response.

"That one right thing saved Danni's life," Abbey said, chastising her, and my sister apologized.

Adora had been there. She knew. I understood how upsetting this was for her, for those exact reasons. She'd been there almost every time I'd been tormented. Beat up. Humiliated. Bullied. She'd witnessed what had happened tonight. I wasn't mad at her. If our situations were reversed, I would've struggled with it all too.

"What does whatever this agreement with Blood and Beryl is mean for you and Markus?" my mom asked.

"There is no 'me and Markus.' The sooner he sees that, the better off he'll be," I muttered. My so-called mate. I still needed to talk to him. "I don't know how any of this is going to go down. I just know that it's only about to get worse. Mathis is going to blow a gasket. You need to be prepared."

Silence ensued and I could just picture my mom and Abbey giving each other "the look" as they quietly understood what I meant, and no doubt agreed.

Be ready to leave. Fight or flight. In this case, they'd need to choose flight. My mom may have been the Alpha female thirty years ago, but she was one wolf. She might stand a chance against our pack, but the rest of Fire and Fluorite? The witches? The vamps?

She may be the most badass woman I'd ever known, but not even my mom could take on all of them.

A knock sounded at the door, and I called out, telling whoever it was to give me a moment.

"I have to go," I whispered. "I'll call you again, okay? Be safe. I love you guys."

The three people who meant the most to me in this shit world all rushed to say they loved me too, talking over each other. I hung up, then turned to the door, appreciating that Elias was nice enough to knock.

When I swung it open, my already bad mood sank further. It wasn't Elias.

It was Markus.

My expression soured at his presence, but I did need to talk to him.

Sighing, I opened the door all the way.

A look of mild surprise and a muttered thanks followed as he came into my new room. Looking around, he found a chair by the fireplace and sat down. Nova lifted her head from the Persian rug she'd lain on and let out a growl. He had the good sense to look down at his hands as I took a seat opposite him and readied myself for the conversation at hand.

"I didn't expect you to invite me in," he said, breaking the silence.

"Don't read into it, Markus. I don't want you here, but we need to have a talk," I replied, leaning forward with my arms resting on my thighs and my hands clasped together.

He held his hand up, stopping me from continuing. "Before you say anything, I just wanted to thank you for what you did back there."

I stared at him, wondering where this grateful, humble male had come from and what he'd done with the shithead who'd bullied me for years. "Yeah. Don't mention it."

"You know there's something between us. The mate bond didn't want you to let me go—"

There he was.

"Shut up." I shook my head. "Just stop talking. This isn't what you think it is."

"Then what is it?"

I stared at him boldly. "What part of *shut up* did you not understand?" I could feel the irritation roll off him. I had the audacity to speak to him in a way that no doubt made his wolf prickle. When he didn't speak again, I continued. "Right. There's a lot that I want to happen to you, Markus, but death isn't one of them. There is no mate bond between us. I rejected you. For whatever reason, you don't see it. You need to reject me so it can 'let go.' You won't be kicked out of Blood and Beryl if you do. As a matter of fact, it'll really help your case for staying."

Staying alive is what I should have said. But I didn't.

"I . . . I can't do that," he said, looking away, toward the fire.

I sat back, leaning against the chair, letting out a flustered breath. "I don't understand you. You spend our entire youth being a completely horrible asshat, and now suddenly, you want to be mated to me." Shaking my head, I stopped talking. I tried to process what his deal was, but I couldn't figure it out. "Do you even know why? Do you really think I'm your only hope at being mated? Second-chance mates happen all the time," I said, then I mentally slapped myself for using the same words Elias had used on me earlier.

Markus sat up straight, his chest broad and proud. "I know you don't believe this now, but I'd be a good mate for you. I would be good *to* you," he pressed.

I barked a laugh, feeling some of the indignation rise in me. Memories of our childhood flashed through my mind. "What does that look like, Markus? Does being good to someone include standing by when your friends gang up on me and knock me to the ground when we were teenagers? You knew I couldn't let Nova fight back growing up. You knew what would happen to me if I let her retaliate. The one time she did, I had my ass chewed out by your dad so bad, my mom requested we get to change packs. That was denied, of course," I added bitterly, recalling the time Nova had put Markus's best friend, Dru, in his place. He'd come for me when my back had been turned and she'd sunk her teeth into his throat, pinning him to the ground. He'd tried to stab her, and she'd severed the hand from his body. Dru had almost died . . . but thankfully he hadn't. Nova and I had paid the price in the end. We always did. It would have been worse if he hadn't lived. "Nova was ostracized after that. Your dad had you *shave her* in front of the entire pack just to humiliate us." I shook my head, recalling the whole ordeal. Nova had stayed back after that. While she'd body-block for me or pull me out of scruffs and run, she'd never attacked another member of Fire and Fluorite. To do so would have been a death sentence for both of us.

"I was a kid too," he said quietly.

"Screw your 'I was just a kid' defense," I said through clenched teeth. "I wish I could say you didn't know better, but I don't believe that. I think you enjoyed it. I don't think you can handle the fact that I rejected you. It's too much for your spoiled, Alpha, Del Reyes ego to handle. In case you've already forgotten, I would rather *die* than be mated to you. I will *never* change my mind about that. Let that sink in."

Markus narrowed his eyes, my venomous words digging under his skin. "Then why did you save me?"

Why, indeed? That was the question. I didn't owe

anyone an explanation. If there was one thing I'd learned from my family, it was that.

"I don't answer to you. And I never will," I said firmly.

"Then why did you invite me in here when I knocked?" he asked coolly. "You saved me, yet you say you want nothing to do with me."

"If you aren't going to reject me, you need to understand what's about to happen." I rested my arms on the chair and looked into the fire. The flames danced wildly, crackling and popping as embers glowed in angry reds and oranges. Returning my gaze to him, I stared him in the eye. "Do you care if you live or die?"

He scoffed. "Of course I care. I have every desire to live."

"Good. Because our choices are exceedingly limited right now. Your father is out to kill me, and if you don't reject me, he's out to kill you too," I reminded him. "He'll marry your little brother off so fast just to get some poor girl knocked up with an heir, and he won't care if she wants it or not. He won't care that he's fourteen. None of you matters to him. You may not realize what kind of guy he is, but I do."

"I'm starting to see it. He's always been . . ." Markus looked away from me, considering his response. "You opened my eyes. I've had some revelations. I'll leave it at that."

"Good for you," I said sarcastically. "This isn't about him. It's about us. About there *not being* an 'us.'" He returned his gaze to me and began to open his mouth to protest. I held a hand up. "No. You need to listen carefully. Our lives depend on it now. Elias expects payment for allowing us to be here. For taking *both* of us in as members when we have targets from a rival House on our backs."

A crease developed between his brows. "What kind of payment?"

I inhaled deeply. I didn't care that he wanted me to be his mate. Not in the slightest. I didn't care for his feelings or whether or not these words would hurt him. What I cared about was compliance. I needed him to play along. Would he? Or rather, *could he*? That remained to be seen.

"Elias is going to announce that he found his mate." I met his gaze with intensity. When he didn't respond, I knew he didn't get it. "Me, Markus. I'm his mate."

He exploded out of his chair. It tumbled back and hit the ground. Nova curled her lips back and snarled. I shook my head at her. I'd expected this response. Unless he moved to hurt me, neither of us should stoop to his level. Reactionary responses would only escalate the situation.

"WHAT?" he shouted. "You can't—"

"Keep your voice down, and sit," I demanded in a

harsh whisper. When he didn't listen, I got to my feet. "I do *not* belong to you."

We stood in front of each other, face-to-face, as he towered over me. I wasn't a short woman, but against a male Alpha wolf? There was no contest for who'd be taller.

"I haven't rejected you. You can't be mated to someone else," he said, seething. He clenched and unclenched his fists, exhaling heavily through his nose.

"Let's step aside from the fact that you can't seem to wrap your head around the fact that *I don't want you*. Whatever this is"—I took a step back, gesturing between us—"it's not real. Your vision is clouded by some instinct you haven't learned to ignore. But *this*?" I pointed toward the door, then again toward the window. "*This* is our new reality. I'm not throwing out blame because that won't get either one of us back home. This is our home now. And I'd rather survive, thank you very much."

"So that's it?" he asked through clenched teeth. "You won't accept me, but you're going to whore yourself out to the vampire king for payment?"

Crack.

The sound of my hand connecting with his face echoed in the room. I could have sworn Nova chuckled. But I didn't. I stood with my chest heaving and my hand stinging from the brutal slap. My brain didn't register what I'd done until after it was over.

Markus's head had snapped in the other direction, and he returned his gaze to me slowly. Feral eyes met mine. There was the bully I knew. Ready to attack. Filled with cruel words. His body shook with unbridled anger.

"I put up with your shit in Fire and Fluorite because I had to," I said, my voice low and menacing. "But don't presume I'll take it lying down now. Call me a whore again and see what happens."

Whispers were creeping around in my mind, telling me I never should have saved his life. I should have killed him in the banquet hall. I should have taken Elias's deal without throwing Markus into the arrangement. I should have saved myself, cared only about myself, and the world would have been rid of him. But that wasn't me.

As I stared him down, his breathing calmed. He took a step back, darting his eyes away for a brief moment. "I shouldn't have said that."

I suppose that was an apology. Not a very good one, but it was more than I'd ever heard him say.

"Not that it's *any* of your business what I do in my private life, but this is strictly a business arrangement. For appearances. That's what I agreed to in exchange for protection. Elias has a reputation, but he's known for keeping his word."

I hoped.

"And I'm supposed to just stand by and listen to him talk about you as though he's your mate? When you know damn well the bond is still between us because I can't reject you?" he asked. His fists remained in a tight ball, but he was pulling the reins on his emotional reactions.

"Yes." I crossed my arms, shifting my weight to one side. I considered him at that moment. The way he was trying to almost be . . . better. It was new for him. He was doing it because he wanted me to change my mind about us. That wouldn't happen. But I could use it to my advantage. "Do you want to see me dead?"

Markus's eyes flashed. "You know I don't," he said quietly.

"Then we do what Elias says. This is what keeps me alive. And you by extension," I pointed out.

He turned to look at the fire, thinking. After a few moments, he nodded his head. "Fine."

I released a tight breath. "Thank you."

He returned his attention to me, an unknown emotion crossing his features. "I'll do my best to control myself. But you can't ignore me. I *will* change your mind about us. If I do this, you agree to spend time with me too." I opened my mouth to argue, but he cut me off. "You can tell everyone we're . . . friends." He said it like it was a dirty word. I doubt he'd ever had a true friend in his life, and he certainly wasn't mine.

My mouth fell open. How was it I'd ended up in a position to be blackmailed by two men? I'd spent my life avoiding people. Keeping to myself. I didn't talk to strangers. I lived in the woods like a good shifter and read books. Made jewelry and threw knives. Went hiking with Nova and rock-climbed on the rare occasion I was feeling adventurous. I didn't waste my time with dating or relationships. I could barely get laid as it was. But I was good by it. Content. And now I was getting screwed by two guys at once. The irony.

"I'm not changing my mind," I said. "I don't like you, Markus. I didn't want to see you die, but that doesn't mean I hold any affection toward you."

"Do you agree or no?" he demanded, his face stern. He wasn't going to let this go. He'd rather die than watch me with Elias and not get his shot. Like I was a trophy to be won. The thought made my blood boil, but I reined it in.

"As friends. That's it. And only as time allows. I have to keep up appearances, and I don't know what all that entails yet."

He nodded. "You'll change your mind about me."

I sincerely doubted that.

"I can't believe you're manipulating me," I said in disbelief, huffing a small laugh. "After I spared your life. Twice."

"If that's what it takes." He smirked, the arrogance I knew well shining through.

"Get out," I whispered, looking away to watch the dancing flames. "Our 'friend' time for today is up."

Markus turned on a heel and exited quietly, not saying another word. If he looked my way, I didn't know. My eyes had welled up with tears and there was no way I was going to let him see it.

I blinked, and the water spilled over, falling down my cheeks as I remained in the same spot I'd been in.

More than anything, I just wanted to sleep and pretend this horrible day had never happened.

I'd talked to my family, and I'd told Markus what we had to do. The hard part was over. I inhaled deeply and then let it out. No longer panicking and trying to process my situation, I was well aware of the position I was in. I looked around, taking in the opulence of my room with a different perspective. The finishes on the solid woods. The plushness of the rug. Assorted books on a small shelf. The candles were placed on various tables and dressers. It made sense. Vampires didn't care much for intense light. It was painful for them. Even the chandelier above had candles imbued with magic, I was sure. Otherwise, the wax would have been dripping everywhere. A few paintings lined the walls. One in particular caught my attention. A ribcage with a floral arrangement in the center. I scrunched my eyebrows, wondering what it meant.

I strode to the corner of the room where two decanters sat on a small table. I smelled the contents of one, and it sure smelled like whiskey, so I poured whatever was in it into a glass, then tilted my head back and took a big swallow. It burned, and I coughed, pouring another and drinking it again before walking to the bed and sitting on the edge, placing the empty vessel on the nightstand.

I glanced at the clock on the mantel. It was silent, but I could still hear the imagined ticktock of the hands as time crawled on, like it was taunting me. This was my home now. These feather pillows and these ornate vases. The soft blankets piled high on a stupidly comfortable mattress. These crystal glasses and fine decor. This weird art.

It was nice. Decadent. Befitting of a king's mate . . . and completely a lie.

Grabbing a pillow, I pressed it to my face and screamed hard. I screamed until my throat was raw. Pulling it off, I gasped for air, trying to shove down the need to hyperventilate and panic all over again. Nova cocked her head, her concern for me evident, but she just watched me with soulful eyes.

Never once had I asked "Why me?" when I was the only shifter who couldn't shift. But here and now? Today? This entire situation? Indignation and fury coursed through me, shoving down the anxiety that had threatened to take hold only moments before.

I pulled on each end of the pillow. Ripped threads with jagged edges split down the fabric and I tore it apart, tossing it into the middle of the room. Feathers exploded in all directions, as though they were delighted in their escape as they floated in the air.

Why me, damn it? Why?

I grabbed the crystal glass, flinging it at the fireplace, listening to the fragile glass crunch against the stone, shattering into infinite pieces.

What had I done to deserve this? What was so wrong about me that I was meant to endure *all of this*?

I ran to a table and picked up a vase, throwing it at the wall, watching it fracture into chunky shards and fall to the floor with a clatter.

I stared out the floor-to-ceiling windows, the overwhelming anger and desire to be anywhere else but here taking over. I grabbed another one, winding it up over my head to smash through my prison walls—

"Why are you destroying my room?" Elias's voice came from behind me, and his words echoed in my ear.

My room.

I froze, eyes wide. The vase dropped from my grasp, crashing into the floor by my feet and splitting apart with a loud thud. Wincing, I turned to face him. "Come again?" I said weakly.

He looked at the broken item on the floor, and he raised an eyebrow. "That was my favorite vase."

My lips separated slightly, and I felt like the color drained from my face. Nova watched the exchange

with curiosity. "I . . . Ysabeau said this was my room
. . ."

He hummed, closing the door behind him and wading through the sea of down feathers that had consumed the floor. "It is yours . . . because it's mine. Mates don't have separate rooms. I wanted you to get comfortable. It would appear you did." Looking at the destruction I'd caused, he let out a long sigh. "Guess I left you alone too long."

"I, um . . ." It was too much to process. I still couldn't find the words.

Pointing to the vase I'd thrown at the wall, he said, "That was my mother."

I blinked a few times, trying to understand his words. Had he said *it* was his *mother*? Then it hit me, and my stomach sank.

Looking in that direction, I saw a murky gray residue that had exploded on the wall. Following the path down to the broken vase, I saw ashes haphazardly scattered all over the floor.

It had been a damn urn.

I inhaled harshly, then coughed, choking on my own spit. Placing a hand on my chest, I tried to clear it. "I'm . . . so . . . sorry," I cried, gasping for breath.

Then he belted out a laugh, and I looked at him, puzzled as I tried to remember how to function and not die by saliva asphyxiation.

"Relax, it was just my dog." He waved me off.

"You . . . kept the ashes of your dog?" I asked incredulously, finally breathing normally. It didn't seem like something the leader of Blood and Beryl would do.

"Well, I did," he answered, gesturing toward the pile. "Until you decided he needed a better resting place."

"I'm sorry I broke—threw—your dog's urn." I ran my hands through my hair, my fingers getting snagged on knots.

A glint of mischief entered his eye as he smiled, his teeth perfectly straight and a brilliant white. "Better than a vampire's mother."

"I can't believe you said that. It wasn't funny."

He raised a shoulder and laughed lightly. "Maybe not for you. I found the look on your face entertaining. Choking on your spit took it to a new level." Sitting on the edge of the bed, he took off his boots and started to get undressed.

"Um, what are you doing?" I asked quickly, forgetting my egregious blunder and glancing at the door.

He unbuttoned his shirt, then his cuffs, shaking the shirt off and throwing it on the floor. "Going to bed. What's it look like?"

It looked . . . incredible. That was what.

His chest and back were broad, but you'd never know how much. The clothes he wore hid it well. Both arms were sculpted and covered in full-sleeve tattoos, from wrist to shoulder, curving into his back, where the designs merged into a dragon wrapped around a Celtic cross. The intricate line work and knots were part of mesmerizing patterns. It was as though they were in motion as his muscles bunched together and he shifted his weight, leaning forward and tugging his pants off . . .

A shot of desire ran through my body, meeting between my legs, and I pressed them together. Nothing about the way he undressed was sensual, and yet it inexplicably was. Something buried deep inside me called out, wanting his hands on my body. Touching me. Doing things to me I'd only read about—

I reached up, threading my hands through my hair as I grasped the sides of my head, shaking it back and forth. No, no, no.

"We can't sleep in the same bed," I stammered, my voice coming out jagged and lusty. I tried to clear my throat to cover it up, but when he chuckled softly, I wasn't so sure it had worked.

"Why not?" he asked, standing up in nothing but his boxer briefs, then turning around.

Don't look. Don't look.

I looked.

My eyes shot back up, but I couldn't look at him directly, so I stupidly looked up. Like I wasn't a twenty-four-year-old woman. Like I'd never seen a man in his underwear before. I had. Such occasions may have been few and far between, but none of them had looked like this.

When I gave no answer, he laughed softly, pulling back the covers and getting into the bed. "It's business, remember? Nothing is going to happen. Just get some sleep. You've had a long night and we wouldn't want it to be longer yet, would we, *mate*?" He shot me a devilish grin, then pulled the blankets up, turning on his side, facing away from me.

I stood there for a while, my mind racing and my anxiety spiking . . . then exhaustion slammed into me. It had been an emotional roller coaster. The worst day of my life, and that was saying a lot.

Still, I had no intention of getting undressed with him in the room. I'd sleep with my clothes on, and that would be just fine. Nova got up from her spot by the fire and quietly walked toward me. I tilted my head toward the bed, telling her to get up there. With a single jump, she hopped up, dropping herself abruptly at the bottom. She was just as tired, but she didn't sense any danger from the feared and renowned vampire king.

Oddly enough, neither did I.

I crawled up, then slipped under the covers, sticking to my side and as far away from Elias as I could get. His soft and even breathing sounded from the opposite end of the bed. Sleep quickly called to me, pulling me into its warmth and safety.

It had to be approaching dawn soon, and the curtains began automatically closing, covering the wall of windows in a thick, velvet fabric that would block out the daylight. I watched them come together on their own accord, getting one last peek at the moon. It watched me in return, mocking me; our last stare down before it disappeared from view.

I'd thought I'd known what being cursed felt like before.

Turns out, I was wrong.

CHAPTER 8
ELIAS

A gentle hum whirred in the background. I cracked open one eye, watching my drapes pull themselves open to give a view of the overcast sky.

It was late afternoon, but I didn't relish the idea of getting up. It wasn't the best sleep I'd ever had, but probably not the worst. I wasn't accustomed to sharing a bed with a giant wolf, or any other occupant for that matter. I preferred solitude.

This was anything but.

Nova was sprawled out at the bottom of the comforter, taking up the lower half of the bed, her face toward me, ensuring I stuck to my bargain. It appeared she didn't consider stopping her other half from making the same mistake.

Dannika had found her way across the bed at some

point in the night, plastering her body against mine. She'd thrown her arm over my abdomen and wrapped her leg over me, her head resting on my chest. The warmth of her body was strangely welcoming. The apex of her thighs pressed against my skin, and I mentally tried to shake that knowledge from my mind.

Her fingers curled into me, hugging me closer as she grumbled about getting more sleep. The touch, the vibration of her throat, the fact that I'd just woken up . . . it was too much sensory detail at once. My erection throbbed, begging for attention. My body accepted the skin-to-skin contact, and it craved more.

She was beautiful; there was no doubt about it. Another pulse between my legs sent a deeper ache through me, and I inhaled sharply.

Bad move.

The scent of orange and peppermint filled my nostrils, and everything about it was delicious. The desire danced on my tongue, urging me to lick her. Taste her. Bite her. Drink from her. Devour her.

Blood pumped into my cock, demanding a release. Demanding I take her.

I mentally cursed the situation. This was not the arrangement. I groaned, trying to maneuver from under her hold. She stirred, pulling me closer again before her hand splayed out, feeling my stomach, patting it in quick, panicked movements as she realized where she was. Her breath hitched and her eyes shot open.

"Morning, sunshine," I said, my throat scratchy.

She pushed herself away from me in a sudden rush, looking down at her clothed body, then back to my prone form. Her cheeks flushed and her mouth opened, then closed, making little popping sounds, but no words came out. Reaching up, she wiped the edges of her mouth, finding drool around her lips. She wiped it away with the back of her hand, her eyes going wide again as she looked at the wet spot on my chest.

"Nothing happened," I told her, trying to calm her nerves. The sound of her heart rate accelerating called to the predator in me, doing dangerous things when my body was already so hyper focused on her every movement.

She turned on the bed, scrambling off the side, and Nova only bobbed her head, watching the exchange. "I didn't mean to." Dannika put her face in her hands. "Oh my god."

"Didn't mean to take over my bed and trap me into holding you all night?" I crossed my arms under my head, resting my head in my palms, giving her a smirk.

She dropped her hands, placing them on her hips, and a crease developed between her brows. "I did *not* take over your bed," she argued, but there was no conviction behind it. The embarrassment leaked from her voice.

I gave her a deadpan look. "Please. You sleep like a starfish."

She scoffed, dropping her arms to her side. "No, I don't." I looked at the empty part of the bed with skepticism, then returned my gaze to her and twisted my lips. She sighed, the insulted expression leaving her face. "Okay, fine. You're not wrong. But don't knock it till you try it. You don't know what you're missing out on."

"I think what you meant to say was: 'You're right,'" I said, uncrossing my arms and moving to sit up.

"No, I said exactly what I meant to say." She tried not to smile, but a bit of a grin snuck through.

I chuckled. Her snark came off playful, and it was ridiculously cute. She stood proudly, defending her position—even if that position was in the shape of a starfish. This had nothing to do with vanity, and everything to do with sleeping next to me. She hadn't checked her appearance, apparently completely unashamed of what she looked like when she woke up. It wasn't a concern to her. No rushing off to make herself presentable. No embarrassment of morning breath. Her silvery hair was disheveled and tangled, and her clothes wrinkled. It didn't detract from her beauty at all. In fact, the authenticity of it made her even more attractive.

A fact that didn't go unnoticed by my libido.

Another pulse made my erection twitch, bringing my attention back to the fact that I couldn't stand up without it being seen. Well. If we were going to sleep together every night, she'd better get used to what that looks like.

"As much fun as it is to tease you about your sleeping habits, I have a busy day laying the ground-work for our big announcement." I tossed the covers off, standing up and stretching my arms above my head, feeling the muscles loosen up.

She groaned, but then her gaze dropped to my crotch, and her eyes widened before she quickly looked at the ceiling. "You, um . . ."

"Believe me, I'm aware of it." I pointed to a door near a bookshelf. "There is a side room through that door. It's my private study. More like a reading room than anything else, but it has an additional bathroom. I assumed you'd like to get ready on your own. I've taken the liberty of having an assortment of clothes brought up since I'm guessing you packed light. Choose whatever suits you. I'm going to"—I gestured to myself and then toward the door to the main bath —"go take care of things."

"Jesus," she muttered, pinching the bridge between her nose and squeezing her eyes shut. "In one day, I go from no relationship straight to practically being married and having to see your hard-on every morning."

Turning on her heel, she walked toward the side room, and I got a view of what she looked like from behind. She glanced over her shoulder as she exited, then shut the door.

I shook my head.

I knew next to nothing about this woman. I needed to keep my distance. Our arrangement had a purpose. As much as I might have liked to jest, sex wasn't part of that arrangement, and I'd made that clear.

I was a man of my word.

But that didn't stop me from thinking about her while I showered. Hot water poured down my back as I gripped my cock, heavy and aching. I pictured her pale-pink lips wrapped around it. Those mischievous icy-blue eyes staring straight into my soul as she sucked me off and swallowed it down.

The disappointment that gripped me as my release washed down the drain should have told me what some part of me knew already.

It was only the first day, and I was already in too deep. There was no way out now.

Nova's gentle breathing had been replaced by loud huffs as she waited outside the door to the study for Dannika to come out.

I couldn't say I was any different. It'd been almost an hour. I couldn't imagine what was taking so long. In the time it took her to get ready, I'd had the room cleaned, removing all evidence of her tantrum the night before.

When the door finally opened, she came out, and she looked . . . well, she looked perfect. I couldn't imagine her appearing sexier than she did at that moment. She had on a shapely, dark-green sweater, black jeans that showed off her shapely curves. Even her dark hiking boots made her legs look longer. She'd finished it off with a simple side braid. What about that made her so sexy? It was the way she wore it. It was natural.

She gave me a once-over, taking in my appearance. Dark jeans. Black shirt. Black boots. Simple and functional.

"You look nice," I lied. She didn't look nice. She looked hot as hell. "The green is a good color on you. I wasn't sure what your style was. Let Ysa know what worked and what didn't. I'll make sure your wardrobe is brought in and you have space in the closet."

Smoothing out the sweater, she said, "I was a bit surprised to see the assortment in there. When you'd said you were going to show me off, I assumed you wanted me to dress like . . . well, not me."

"You expected me to dress you in corsets and leather pants?" I suggested, knowing full well the stereotype for female vampires.

She huffed a small laugh. "Something like that."

I shook my head. "No, I expect you to dress like you. Whatever makes you comfortable. I don't want to make you something you're not."

"Other than me becoming your mate," she taunted, treading carefully between playful and disrespectful.

"Yes, other than that." I grinned, knowing she still had preconceived notions of what this was. Of who I was. "I know this might come as a shock to you, Danni, but my goal isn't to make you uncomfortable or unhappy. I want you to be yourself and enjoy the things you like. You aren't my prisoner."

She regarded me, dipping her chin down and angling her head. "Aren't I, though? My life depends on acting the part you want me to play. Call it what you want, but you can't call it freedom."

"No, I suppose you can't," I said in agreement. "But I'm not out to hurt you. I know the transition isn't going to be easy for you, and I'm happy to accommodate however I can. Despite what you no doubt have heard about me, I'm not inherently evil."

"No, I don't think that you are. It's just been a difficult transition for me." She held her hands behind her back and headed in my direction. "I don't know how to do any of this yet. I'm completely out of my element."

"We have time to figure that out. Mostly." I checked my watch, then added, "You took longer than I expected, so there isn't much time before I need to go meet with my Court."

Taken aback, she stopped walking and stood completely still. "I didn't realize I was holding you up," she said, gazing at the clock on the mantel.

"I didn't tell you I wanted to have breakfast together before my meetings. It was my error." I waved it off. "You don't need to change your routine. Take as long as you need when getting ready. I'll adjust the amount of time I schedule things for us going forward. I thought I'd give you a few days to settle in before doing the official introductions."

She wrinkled her brow. "Okay, that, uh, works for me . . ." she responded, trailing off. She fidgeted with her hands, looking around the room. "Now what?"

"Have a seat," I said, gesturing to the chair oppo-site me in front of the empty fireplace. She strode slowly, sitting down, clearly unsure of what to do. "Tell me about yourself."

Her face fell flat, and she looked around the room. "Are you being serious right now?"

"Of course. I should know things about my mate,

and she should know things about me." I crossed one leg over the other, resting my ankle just above the knee, and leaned back in my chair.

She adjusted in her chair and shrugged. "There isn't much to know."

I suppressed the need to roll my eyes. "I highly doubt that."

She blew out a big breath. "This feels like a staged dating show. What do you expect me to say? I like candlelight dinners and long walks on the beach?"

I lifted my shoulders. "Do you?"

"Not really, no."

"If you'd rather I ask the questions, I'm happy to do so," I said. She pressed her lips together, not telling me whether it was okay or not, so I just went with it. "Why don't we start with the most pressing one? What do you like for breakfast?"

"Huh?" Confusion filled her features, and her guarded posture relaxed slightly.

"Food. You need to eat," I repeated, pointing to the table beside her. She looked at it curiously, taking the dome off the plate. "I didn't know what you liked, so I had them bring up an assortment. What *do* you like so I can have it brought to you when we wake up? Do you like the same thing, or do you like to change it around?"

She blinked a few times while she stared at me. She picked up a biscuit, taking a bite. She chewed slowly, then swallowed and took a sip of water. "Same thing every day. A couple of eggs. Toast. Fruit if you have it," she said. As I opened my mouth to respond, she interjected. "Not melons, though."

I dipped my head. "Consider it done. And for Nova? I'm afraid I'm not familiar with feeding a wolf, and the last thing I would want to do is offend her by treating her like my dogs."

"She's content hunting. We like to do that together, but if we can't, she'll take whatever's raw." Dannika looked at Nova, who sat beside her, and smiled. "Thanks for asking about her too. I didn't expect..."

"For me to care?" I finished. She looked at me sheepishly, confirming my guess. "She's part of you. I respect her." I gazed at the wolf, and she held my stare, considering me. She understood far more than one realized. I was intrigued by her intelligence and was keen to know how much of her was connected to Dannika's psyche. I'd never met a shifter whose wolf existed outside of them. Had she been born this way? Had it been the consequence of some tragic accident? Was she truly cursed?

I didn't care which, obviously, given it didn't affect her ability to be my queen or fulfill the purpose for which I'd chosen her. My curiosity was simply piqued.

"You'd be the first," she mumbled.

"I pity the supe who makes the mistake of underestimating either one of you." I laughed quietly. "I've already had a front-row seat to Kym's dismembering."

Dannika cleared her throat. "Sorry about that."

"Don't be. He deserved it. His behavior was unacceptable. I'm having his past looked into as we speak to figure out all he's done since your sister brought it to my attention." I steepled my fingers together, resting my chin on them. "How did she know about his indiscretions, though?"

Danni didn't react. Her pupils didn't dilate. Her breathing didn't change. Her body didn't tense. She simply shrugged a shoulder and pursed her lips. "Don't know. She has a sense about people. Can tell when they're assholes. Good intuition, our mom always said."

Her poker face was spectacular. I suspected she was lying. I just couldn't prove it, not until I got the interrogation report from Ysa. Nothing about Danni's demeanor gave her away, but if her sister had intuition, one could say I did too. Adora was a diamond in the rough. There was a hidden talent behind that plain curtain. A power or secret they were hiding. If Danni could keep up that charade for the sake of her family, she was going to do well by my side.

"Hmm." I tilted my head, cocking an eyebrow. "I wonder what she told you about me."

Seconds ticked by in silence, and I let the awkwardness sit heavily in the room. I never took my eyes off Danni, and she did damn well holding her own. She would need this kind of pressure to survive the supes she would have to deal with soon. While I was giving her days to adjust, that was hardly anything in the eyes of the Blood and Beryl High Court. All of them were over a hundred years old, some far more than that.

Danni inhaled through her nose, finally deciding to share. "She said she doesn't trust you."

I laughed. "Smart woman. What about you? Do you trust me?"

She sniffed, breaking eye contact to look at her nails. "I'm undecided at the moment."

"Also smart," I said, causing her to look back at me. I winked.

"And you? Tell me about you," she said, not using a mocking tone, but adding a hint of sarcasm to the words.

"I assume you've heard plenty about me," I said casually, tapping my finger against the armrest. Rumors were the one thing never in short supply. "What is it that you want to know?"

"What was your dog's name?" She jutted her thumb over her shoulder. "The one I . . . yeah."

My eyebrows shot up in surprise. Of all things she might have asked, that was not what I'd expected. "Samson."

She nodded. "What's your favorite color?"

"Ice blue." I kept my tone even, watching her response. Her beautiful eyes narrowed slightly, and she hummed.

"You think you're charming, don't you?"

I grinned. "I *know* I am."

She laughed, shaking her head lightly. "I think you're confusing arrogance with charm."

It was my turn to laugh.

She twisted her lips in amusement, then continued. "What do you like for breakfast?"

I gave her a look that said *really?* and ran my tongue over the tip of my fang.

Heat rushed to her cheeks, and she looked away. "Right," she said quietly. "I knew that. Makes sense."

"Does that bother you?" I asked. It shouldn't have mattered. We had a deal, but a deeper part of me didn't want her to care. We were in a business arrangement, but I didn't want her to be the kind of supe who hated other species. It was a quality I didn't care for.

"No, it bothers me when I ask dumb questions," she said flatly, and I kept the desire to laugh suppressed. "What's with Ysa's sunglasses? I've never seen a vampire wear them at night."

"Probably because you haven't met any two-thousand-year-old vampires."

Danni's eyes widened, almost silently whispering, "Two *thousand?*"

I nodded. "The older we get, the more sensitive we are to light. As old as she is, even indoor light is too much for her."

"Wow, I had no idea. None of the vampires in Fire and Fluorite ever mentioned that," she said, thoughtful in her response. It was less awe, and more sympathetic. "What about you? How old are you?"

"Three hundred and twelve." I watched her response carefully, but she didn't react. It wasn't as impressive as two thousand, but I had at least expected some sort of reaction. She gave none. "Sunny days are bothersome, but overcast and cloudy days are much easier for me to handle."

"So if that's the case, do you like being outdoors at all? Or do you prefer being inside?"

"I like both."

"That's not a fair answer."

"Why not? Some activities are better suited for the indoors. Sex on a beach isn't what it's cracked up to be."

She snorted. "I wouldn't know, but now that you mention it, I don't think it sounds like a great location for that, either. I don't like sand in places it doesn't belong."

Between her thighs. Under her breasts. In the crook of her neck. Buried in the slick folds of her . . .

"Do you have any family?" she asked. Glancing at Nova, a slight hint of sadness crossed Dannika's features. I swallowed a little harder than usual, ignoring my hardening erection as thoughts of Danni that I shouldn't have been having continued to surface. If not for her line of questioning bringing that to a halt, I'd be in another strained position—one I couldn't blame on just having woken up.

I hesitated to answer, and her eyes quickly met mine when I didn't speak immediately. "I did. They're gone now."

"All of them?" Her voice lowered, not to a whisper, but to a softness. It was empathy. Understanding.

I cleared my throat. "My father and sister, yes. My mother might as well be. She remains in Rome. While our family comes from Greece, she couldn't bear to reside there. After their loss . . . well, she moved to Rome and won't leave the Blood and Beryl palace. My brother is an asshole, and we don't speak anymore."

"I lost my father too," she said quietly, reaching to the necklace she kept hidden beneath her clothes and toying at it absentmindedly. "During the Great Sacrifice. I never knew him."

"It would seem we have something in common." I rubbed my thumb over my beryl ring, flashes of my past sparking emotions I didn't need to feel in this moment. I needed to push it down. It did me no good here. Guilt would be wasted on something I couldn't change.

"It's a shitball thing to have in common with

someone," she commented. "Like, possibly the worst club you could join."

A humorless laugh escaped me. "I couldn't agree more."

She huffed, shaking her head. "My sister was right," she whispered, and she smiled softly to herself while she looked at the rug.

I tilted my head, curious. "About?"

"I'm a Debbie Downer," she answered, bringing her gaze up. "I always find a way to darken the conversation."

I shrugged, gesturing around the décor in the room. "Vampire. I like the dark."

She snorted, giving me an appreciative smile. I could very much say I didn't like seeing her that sad. Something in my chest tightened at the sight.

"Realities are sometimes dark, Danni. History is dark. Anyone who says otherwise is trying to sell something in an attempt to rewrite it to their narrative. You don't have to put on a happy face for my or anyone else's sake."

She stayed quiet, but nodded in agreement.

"Do you miss them?" she asked, surprising me with that question. No one, not even my second, had ever asked me that before.

"Every day," I admitted. "I won't keep you from your family."

"Ha," she barked. "You won't, but Mathis will. You

don't know him like I do. Shade is his second, and he offered me an hour to get my things, but they came for me immediately. They assaulted my sister and tore apart my home the moment she entered pack lands. He just wants me dead or mated to Markus." She crossed her arms, sitting back in her chair.

"I know," I said. When she looked at me curiously, I answered, "I had scouts watching."

"Why?" Her brows furrowed.

"I make it a point to know everything about my enemies." I maintained an even voice, pulling back any anger from leaking into my tone. "It's part of why I have great faith that this plan will work."

She uncrossed her arms, moving to sit forward. "Is Markus your enemy too?" she asked with genuine interest.

"That remains to be seen." There wasn't really more of answer I could give her. It was true. I didn't know what the future held for Markus and how I viewed him. She seemed to accept it.

Turning her head, she looked out the window. "I told him last night. About the arrangement."

"And?"

"About what you'd expect." She played with the hem of her sweater, then started bouncing her foot. "But he wants to stay alive as well."

"Then he's already smarter than his father," I stated.

She returned her attention to me. "I'd still like to spend time with him." Something in her voice faltered, and she worked hard to keep eye contact. "When we aren't busy with . . . whatever it is I'm supposed to do for show purposes."

I prickled at the notion. Something dark and ugly unfurled in my chest. "What for?"

"Because he still needs to reject me. That would make it easier for everyone. Mainly for me, if I'm being honest."

"Fair enough." I didn't like it one bit, not that I let her know that. "I can allow that."

She dipped her head in thanks, a firm line pressed between her lips.

A knock came at the door. I called for them to enter, and Ysabeau peeked her head through. "Your first meeting starts in ten minutes. I can postpone—"

"There'll be no need for that." I placed my hands on the arms of the high-back chair and pushed myself up. "I'm sure Dannika would appreciate some time to herself this afternoon." To Danni, I said, "Remember what I said yesterday: You're free to roam the forest or walk the halls if you like. There's a fantastic library I can show you this evening if—"

"That would be great," she blurted out, then she smashed her lips together in an awkward grimace. Behind us, Ysabeau began snickering. Nova looked dead at her and narrowed her eyes. She started to choke, disguising it as a cough. Poorly, I might add.

"It's a date." I took her hand and leaned forward to press a chaste kiss on it. The thrum of her heartbeat through the vein in her wrist made my mouth go dry.

Orange and peppermint . . . She smelled exquisite.

Ysa coughed again, this time as a subtle reminder to hurry up.

I winked at Dannika, then walked away, leaving her speechless.

CHAPTER 9

DANNIKA

"Are you sure we can't practice on some lower-ranking supes first? Low-hanging fruit? My kind of people?" Anxiety coiled in my gut.

Today was the big day. Before my life had been turned upside down four days ago, I would have been saying that about sending Adora to the neutral market with a new piece of jewelry I'd designed, or helping Nova blow out her winter coat after a six-hour long de-shedding session.

Becoming queen of a House kind of gave "the big day" a new meaning.

Ysa snorted, and Elias shot her a look. She straightened her posture and hid her smile. "Afraid not. You had an extended weekend to prepare. We're going in hard and fast taking on the High Court, but if we do it quickly, it will be easier for you."

149

"That sounds like a line some douchebag gives when he doesn't want to use lube," I mumbled, and both Ysa and Elias lost their composure.

They weren't as serious as I figured they would be, at least not all the time. I supposed before I'd been blackmailed into moving here, I wouldn't have thought they would have been so normal. Not because they're vampires, but because of their age and position. Elias was king and had been for well over two hundred years. Judging by what Elias had disclosed about his second, her sharp tongue was just the tip of the iceberg when it came to what Ysabeau St. Clare was capable of.

Sure, in front of others, they played those parts well. Elias was a stoic, dispassionate king who exuded cold confidence and calculation. Ysabeau played his silent second, always there but rarely speaking—and when she did, it was either by Elias's request or because someone was probably going to lose a limb.

They were just masks, though. Empty, hollow facades that both people put on for the world because that was what was called for.

And now, I was going to be wearing a mask too. I glanced down to Nova as she trotted beside me, and we shared a moment of unspoken support.

"Your expression changed," Elias said. "You don't seem as nervous as you were."

My head snapped up, and I pressed my lips together. "Thanks for reminding me."

Approaching the door, Ysa stopped and gripped the handle.

Elias sighed. "That's not what I meant." He grabbed my hand, threading our fingers together. I tensed, then quickly tried to shake that off. He brought our joined hands to his mouth, pressing a kiss on top of my skin. I shivered, trying to shake off the flutters that were definitely not part of this *business arrangement*. There were moments where it was hard to remember that was what this was. When we got lost in conversation or the tension got too thick. I swallowed hard as he whispered. "Mates touch. They hold hands. Follow my lead, and you'll be fine." I hummed, nodding my head up and down in quick motions, and Nova huffed. "You ready?"

"Do I have a choice?" I cracked my neck, letting out a harsh breath.

He reached into his pocket, then nodded in Ysabeau's direction. "Showtime," he mouthed, and I thought I turned a shade green.

"No, wait," I said quickly.

Too late.

The doors opened, and every member of the High Court turned in our direction.

Oh, god.

Follow his lead? What did that even mean?

Panic, that was what.

No, that was wrong. He wasn't panicking. What was he doing?

I glanced at Elias from the side as he walked in with confidence, like he owned the room.

He did, technically. King of Blood and Beryl, and all that.

I was the fraud.

But the same way he pretended to be unfeeling and Ysabeau pretended to be his silent counterpart, my role was to be a dumbstruck woman infatuated with her mate. Without the "dumb" part.

Our footfalls sounded, echoing off the high ceilings in the grand room. Chandeliers with magic candles filled the space, the same as his—our—room. At the end was a dais, only slightly raised. In front of it was an ornately carved U-shaped table. It was the longest walk ever. I wasn't sure if I was marching to my execution, but that was what it sure felt like.

The overwhelming desire to hold my breath took over. I swallowed, feeling a thick lump in my throat. My palms started sweating. My armpits were damp.

Had I put on deodorant? *Aw, shit.* They may not have the same heightened sense of smell that wolves had, but BO was *not* a good first impression for a queen to make.

Twelve pairs of vampire eyes focused on me,

flicking their gazes to where Elias held my hand. Then to my giant wolf, walking beside me.

My stomach twisted.

Elias squeezed my hand gently, sending a smidge of reassurance. Nova nudged her head against my arm, reminding me she was by my side, like always.

The words my sister had told me my entire life replayed in my mind.

"You know who you are. Own it."

I ran my fingers through Nova's fur, regaining my strong posture. Holding my shoulders back, I raised my chin.

We walked silently, and I followed Elias's lead, per his instruction. Past the table and to the raised platform.

My vision swam for a moment. This was his throne room. He'd failed to mention that detail.

In front of us, two thrones were positioned. Not the way they were in castles, raised high above in a show of lordship and rank. They were almost on level, raised only a little bit over everyone else. They were carved wood. High-backed and upholstered in red velvet. Grand, but not ostentatious.

Heads tilted as they took us in, and eyebrows raised, but no one whispered. No one glowered. It was an unusual response. I was used to the opposite.

Elias guided me to the twin seats, then gestured for me to take the one next to him. I did, feeling my knees shake as I sat, and Nova settled herself beside my chair. Her head was up and alert, watching the room so I could focus.

I crossed my ankles, trying to give the impression that this was fine and that I wasn't on the verge of fainting or vomiting—or both. To keep up appearances, Elias reached over, taking my hand in his once more, resting our clasped hands where the two thrones met.

The vampires dipped their heads in respect, then all took their seats. I looked at the double door, and Ysabeau remained at her post, as aloof as ever.

Elias knocked on the arm of his chair, garnering attention—not that anyone wasn't already giving us just that.

"Members of the High Court, thank you for arriving on short notice. I have an announcement I wanted to make."

A woman with jet-black hair, brown eyes, and olive skin smiled. She was stunning. Her painted red lips curled into a grin, showcasing her elongated fangs. "We can see that," she said, appraising me from top to bottom. "No need for the formalities, Elias. Fill us in. Have you taken a consort? She's absolutely delicious." The purr in her voice sent a tingle up my spine.

Murmurs of agreement filtered around from others seated at the table. And yet, still—no one had a negative expression. They all looked at me with awe.

Before my confidence could falter, a whisper in my consciousness reminded me that I was new to them. They didn't know me. They didn't know how Nova had come to be. Right now, they didn't know details, and that meant they were curious.

I could handle curious.

Elias motioned for them to settle down. "Easy, Katie." Squeezing my hand, he glanced at me and winked. "Dannika is new to Blood and Beryl. We don't want to scare her off."

"And what is Dannika doing here?" a regal-looking vampire asked. Her chestnut hair was pulled into a bun, decorated with small blue flowers I didn't know the name of. High cheekbones accentuated a pointed nose and piercing red eyes. She didn't seem to be a day over thirty-five in appearance, but her voice was aged and experienced, and she made no move to hide the coldness of her tone. "We heard that you took in shifters from Fire and Fluorite at the commemoration last Friday. One of which had a great wolf," she trailed off, looking to Nova before back to Elias. "I'd assumed them to be prisoners, not consorts. This is not the case?"

"Marisa asks a question I believe we all want to know the answer to," a male vampire agreed. His gaze flicking to our joined hands, he smirked. "I think we very much want to know about your new . . . guest."

I could speak at this moment, or I could let them

gawk at me. Talk about me as though I weren't there. I could let Elias take over, never saying a word and letting him do all the convincing while I mustered the strength to keep a demure smile on my face.

The thing was, I was anything but demure.

If this was going to be a long-term arrangement, I would have to use my voice. I would have to make myself known. I would have to show them who I was. Or at least, who I wanted them to see.

I hadn't gotten to define myself in Fire and Fluorite. The adults who'd whispered about a little girl who couldn't shift had done that for me before I could understand that I was different. Cursed.

Blood and Beryl may not have been my first choice . . . but I was going to make the most of it. I needed to, for my own sanity and safety.

It was now or never.

I just hoped I didn't throw up while doing it.

"I'm not a guest or a consort. I'm Elias's mate," I said, keeping my tenor even and projecting my statement so it echoed in the room. Elias studied me from his seat on the throne, giving me a twisted grin.

I focused my energy on keeping my heart rate slow and steady, like I was hunting. For all intents and purposes, I was. While they would be forced to accept whatever mate bond their leader claimed to have, I was also seeking their approval in other ways, and to do so, I had to tread carefully toward my target.

Marisa cocked an eyebrow ever so slightly. "His *mate*?" she asked, caution leaking through the chill. Murmurs of surprise and elation were whispered around the table, but she still remained unsure. Glancing at my wolf, she stopped herself from speaking further, realizing she needed to reconsider her words.

"I know who you are," a tall and muscular vampire blurted out. His gray eyes held me in a cold stare. His very presence exuded danger, reminding me of the stories I was told as a child. This was the kind of vampire you didn't want to meet in a dark alley. "You're not even a normal shifter, are you?"

Everyone in the room snapped their heads in his direction.

"Kieran!" one shouted in response. "Manners, for the goddess's sake."

He shrugged. "I meant no disrespect. I'm just asking the question we all want to know." He shifted his gaze from me to Nova. "I get intel for this court. I was there the night of the commemoration. I know of the two shifters our king brought in. You can't shift, Dannika. How can you have a mate? Let alone a *second-chance* mate with our king?"

"How dare—" Elias began, but I cut him off with a raise of my hand. This battle was one I'd fight. It was the hill I'd die on if need be. It was my life, my wolf, and my fight to be had. Not Elias's.

"I'm still a shifter," I said, my voice going cold. This argument was all too familiar. "Magic still runs in my veins. It simply looks different. I exist in two forms at once. Two places at once. Some might say that makes me a stronger shifter." I lowered my hand to Nova's head, and she bared her teeth at the man called Kieran. "Master vampires have gifts that no other vampire does, is that correct?" Several members of the High Court nodded. "Then why is it assumed that I'm less powerful, less worthy, and less valued because of my difference? If I were a vampire, you would see this as my strength."

Kieran opened then closed his mouth, clearly considering my argument. "Apologies, my lady. King Elias is my uncle, and it's my job to question and look closer into things that could threaten my family and House. Your mating with my king just seemed incredibly unlikely after the events of the commemoration. That doesn't mean it's impossible. I should not have insinuated as I did."

I gave a rigid nod, anxiety creeping back in now that the initial anger had faded.

"Dannika is a unique shifter indeed, and our mating is not . . . conventional, but I prefer it that way." He grabbed my hand from the armrest of the throne and squeezed it slightly. "She's perfect," he said, looking straight at me. You'd never know he was putting on a show with how intensely I felt his gaze. "They both are."

One of the vampires sighed. "Look at them."

Please don't. Really.

"She's beautiful. There's no doubt about it," Marisa said softly, admiring Nova as my wolf sat beside me. "Does she have a name?"

"Nova."

"Is this the wolf who . . .?" Katie, the vampire with the black hair, spoke up, pointing at Nova. Then she turned to Ysabeau by the door, looking for confirmation of some sort. When Ysa nodded in response, Katie turned her attention back to us. "Well, you have my support, Nova. Not that you need it, but still. I approve of your methods." A smug smile crossed her face.

"Indeed." Another vampire caught on, chuckling. "I heard Katie's ex was missing an arm. Well done."

My mouth opened, but no words came out. I hadn't been expecting that kind of response to Nova ripping off their fellow vampire's arm. A solider within Blood and Beryl. Possibly someone they knew. I had no idea what to say to it. The condemnation from my former House was the polar opposite of the praise in my new House. All over the same situation.

"We're delighted to see that Elias has finally found his mate, regardless of how or where you're from," Marisa said, warming up slightly.

A tall, handsome vampire with pale skin and light

blond hair stood up. He adjusted the cuffs on his shirt, then looked me straight in the eye as he spoke. "Mathis's son attempted to claim you as his mate. And you rejected him, resulting in your exile. Is that correct?"

My toes curled inside my boots, and I attempted to calm my muscles before they tensed. "That is correct," I said.

He pursed his lips, nodding gently while he drew out the moment in silence. "It was also said that Markus has not rejected you . . ." He purposefully trailed off, making sure to look around at the other members of the High Court to plant the seed of doubt.

It worked.

Careful gasps and light murmurs questioned how this could be.

"He has not," I said through clenched teeth.

Elias shrugged. "What of it, Uriah? Weirder things have happened."

"I've never heard of a second-chance mate happening the same night, much less when the first mate hasn't accepted a rejection," he said bluntly.

Your life—and Markus's—depends on it.

"Nor have I," I admitted. "I don't disagree with you. But just because something hasn't been before doesn't mean it will never be." I gestured to Nova, making my point.

Eleven other vampires smiled when I said that, but

not Uriah. He studied me with narrowed eyes, then dipped his head. "I can't argue with that, now can I?"

"No, you can't," Katie chimed in, crossing her arms and sitting back in her chair. "Though I wouldn't put it past you to keep trying."

Marisa rolled her eyes, then pointed for Uriah to sit down. "It should be known that Dahlia foresaw this, so calm your nerves."

Who? Foresaw what? I glanced at Elias, but he shook his head slightly, as though to say, 'I'll explain later, but not here.'

"What exactly did Dahlia see?" Uriah asked.

Ysabeau left her post by the door, approaching the table and standing in front of the dais to address the room. "She foretold that Elias would find his mate at the commemoration. I was there. I can tell you without a doubt, our king was instantly drawn to Dannika from the moment he saw her." She turned to him, pinning him with a stare, then tilted her head. "His desire to find her only increased once she was exiled, and he set us on a path to intercept her before Mathis could get to her."

"I've never known Dahlia to be wrong," Katie mused, then she glanced at the vampire seated next to her, who nodded in agreement.

Elias smirked, like he knew something no one else in the room did. Or maybe because he'd won an argument while barely speaking.

"But it was *foretold* she'd be a vampire in Blood and Beryl," a woman with thin red lips said. Her black hair cascaded down her back, draping slightly over her shoulder in a long, thick braid. She raised a single brow in dissent, creases forming on her high forehead.

"Prophecies aren't always right," Katie argued.

"Dahlia's are," the other woman said. Her sharp gaze focused on Elias.

Marisa sighed. "What of it, Alaysia?"

She shrugged in response. "Dahlia has never been wrong, and this woman isn't a vampire. Does it not seem suspicious to you that she's the unclaimed mate of Mathis's heir?"

"Consider your words carefully, Alaysia," Elias threatened darkly. "I may be lenient with my Court, but I will not stand for being called a liar."

"My apologies. It was not *you* I was insinuating had done anything wrong. She's not even a real shifter. I merely wonder if she's a witch and has put a spell on our king, but I can see I've overstepped." She bowed her head, though a slight smile played on her lips.

"Get out," Ysabeau said, before either Elias or I responded. When Alaysia looked to Elias, wide-eyed for confirmation, he turned stony. Ysabeau stalked over and wrapped a pale hand around the other vampire's arm. "It is only your surname stopping me from forcibly removing you. Insulting your king or his mate is a dishonor to not only your family, but to our House."

Alaysia didn't budge. Ysabeau's eyes narrowed with warning.

"I will only say it once more; get *out*. I will deal with you later."

Ysabeau's threat worked well enough because Alaysia didn't look to Elias to save her again. Without another word, she turned on her heel and stormed out, her hands shaking either from fury or fear at her sides.

As she went, several members shook their heads in disgust. Marisa had watched Alaysia leave, giving her a death glare until she was no longer in sight. She then brought her eyes to me, lowering her chin in respect. "Forgive the outburst, Dannika. We are overjoyed our king has found his mate *finally*. We were just expecting Elias to find his mate, well, in our own House. Some of us adapt better than others, it would seem."

"I am in Blood and Beryl," I said, shifting in my seat. "Mathis wishes me dead, so you should have no fear that I will carry House business to the other side, even if by accident." Several vampires looked away from me as I spoke, but I didn't care. I had the floor, and I was going to say my piece. "Aside from that, if you've been lucky enough to experience it, you know the bond pulls you toward your mate. The force is indescribable. The loyalty and desire you feel toward your intended partner is insurmountable." I looked to

Elias, placing my palm on top of where we rested our joined hands and making a show of it. "Even if you want to deny it, it's nearly impossible."

I knew my words were true. I was living them. As repulsed as I was at the idea of Markus as my mate—and I would reject him until the day I died—it didn't change the fact that the mate bond was that strong. I felt all of it. An invisible force tugging at my insides, demanding that I go to him. Be with him. Accept the cruelty of that cursed bond.

My conviction was stronger. The pull was there. The want was there. And so was the damage I'd carried for too long. It grounded me. Anchored me. And I'd be damned if I acknowledged the rest of it any further.

I figured I could use that feeling, that experience, to convince the High Court that I felt those things for Elias. The lies were easier to speak if I pretended it was him instead of Markus. They were pretty words, and they worked. I felt tension in the room lift slightly, but the slightest movement on his lower eyelid caught my attention. A twitch. Nothing more.

A few of the vampires nodded their heads as they glanced at one another. Others remained silent, considering further discussions.

I needed them to hurry up. I may have looked calm on the outside, holding myself high like I deserved to be sitting beside Elias, but my insides were a mess. My stomach churned, twisting the very meager contents within.

"This is so exciting, Elias," the one seated next to Katie added. "Your mother is going to be so thrilled."

My heart jumped to my throat. Maybe that was my stomach.

Mother?

I'd been so concerned with my own family and telling them that I hadn't even considered what his mother would think of the fake match. Even though he'd told me she was in Rome, I was too traumatized to think about her being real since I'd thought I'd broken her urn in the midst of my rage-induced pity party.

I had to meet his mother and lie to her at some point.

"Dannika?" Elias's voice brought me from my thoughts.

My eyes were wide as I stared at the floor. "Mmm?"

"Bianca was just saying she would like to help you. Show you the ropes within the House. Our customs and what not," he said.

"Who?" I asked, my mouth drying out more as this charade rolled on.

The woman sitting next to Katie held a hand up like she was bidding at an auction. Her hair was a deep red, intricately braided around the back of her head, the extended plait falling over her shoulder. Her dark skin was flawless, and her purple eyes were piercing. "Bianca Santapaga. A liaison within the High Court."

I nodded absentmindedly. "I'd love that," I muttered, hoping my nausea was coming off as overwhelming gratitude.

"That's settled, then," Elias said, clapping his hands together once and standing up. I rose to follow him.

My stomach gurgled. When several pairs of eyes looked at me, I waved it off with a pained laugh. "Hungry. I skipped breakfast. Too much excitement for one day."

Lies, lies, and more lies.

Marisa stood up, addressing the High Court. "We will announce your union to the House today, sending word to the compounds worldwide." She glanced down Elias's body for a moment before continuing and widening her eyes for effect. "When it has become official, that is."

I didn't know how much more official this could be.

Soon the news would reach every corner of the world. But more importantly, it would reach my family. I dreaded talking to them about it. To keep lying to them. Deep down, they would know the truth, but that didn't change the fact that I couldn't speak freely to them about it.

Elias turned around to face me, reached into his pocket, then pulled out a black box and dropped down to one knee.

"Um . . ." I said in a panic before I considered my audience. I did a quick scan around the room, trying to cover my blunder. I smiled through clenched teeth.

I'd seen movies where the women would shriek and fan themselves. Cry with joy and happiness. Me? I stood there, frozen.

This isn't real, I reminded myself.

I'm just playing a part. A role.

I met Elias's steely gaze. A harsh reminder in the moment to get my shit together for the sake of the show.

I pressed my lips into a smile. "I didn't know this was one of your customs," I whispered, knowing full well everyone could hear me.

Out of the corner of my eye, I could see Nova turn her head away. Even my wolf was embarrassed for me as my awkwardness and emotions leaked into her.

"This makes it official," Elias said casually. He opened the box to reveal a ridiculously large, pink beryl ring encased in a silver setting. Intricate signs were carved into the side, but I had no idea what they meant.

"You shouldn't have," I deadpanned. My gut twisted and rolled. Really. He shouldn't have.

Elias cocked an eyebrow. He held my hand in his,

keeping his gaze fixed on me, his thumb caressing my skin as he slowly slid the ring onto my finger. Time almost stilled. The sensual contact between us elicited a shiver I tried to suppress.

He pressed a kiss onto my hand, sending tingles through my veins. I struggled to keep myself upright.

He winked, standing up, and then held my hand up for everyone in the room to see.

Minor chatter filtered in while I silently prayed to whatever gods existed in this world or the next for all of them to leave.

Marisa smirked. "And so the announcement shall be made."

The High Court left their table, heading toward the exit as they talked amongst themselves. Marisa and Uriah sounded as though they were distributing orders, pointing at individuals, and nodding about things I couldn't make out.

They were almost gone.

I exhaled through my nose at a slow pace, keeping myself grounded.

I would be okay.

I'd made it through this.

Bianca elbowed Katie, the last two to leave as the door shut behind them. I caught a glimpse of the giant grin on Bianca's face, the candlelight reflecting on her shiny fangs. "Look at the two of them," she said, making no attempt to speak quietly. "She's adorably innocent. I can't wait until they have an heir. That baby will have all the good genes."

Baby.

Heir.

What?

My stomach roiled and the door clicked shut.

Nova scrambled out of the way, knowing what was coming. Her hind legs struggled to gain traction, sliding around while she tried to move away from me.

There was no time.

I turned, bolting to the first thing that looked like a trash can. Grabbing the sides, I hovered over it, heaving out the contents of my stomach.

"Wow," Ysabeau whispered.

"I know. I tried to hold it in." I coughed, wiping my mouth with my sleeve.

Elias covered the lower part of his face with his hand, blocking whatever expression was underneath it. His eyes pinched at the corners.

"You just threw up in the sacred baptism basin of our first ancestors," Ysabeau said flatly.

I looked back to the receptacle. It was a bowl, curved at the bottom, deeper than what I would've expected a basin to be, and it looked as though it had been made from onyx. The color drained from my face. My stomach twisted again. "I . . . did what?" I jerked my head to look at Elias. He nodded his head in tight movements. I'd thought it was a trash can . . .

My jaw went slack, and my knees went weak. I stumbled onto the floor, dropping onto my backside unceremoniously. I cradled my head in my hands.

In the past four days, I'd been called to accept a mate bond, exiled, stalked for assassination, and coerced into Blood and Beryl by its king. Then I'd destroyed his dead dog's urn, faced the critique of the High Court, and heard that I was expected to bear an heir. To top it off, I'd defiled a sacred artifact in the throne room.

I should've just killed Markus.

CHAPTER 10

ELIAS

A knock sounded, and Ysabeau walked in, taking a seat in front of my desk, saying nothing.

I sighed. "Speak your mind, Ysa. The look on your face says you disagree with something." Bluntness worked best for her. She didn't like to mince words, and frankly, it wasn't my thing, either. I preferred my time to not be wasted.

"I've been thinking about our new queen." She just jumped straight to it, reaffirming my thoughts. "Particularly what Bianca said the other day."

"About an heir?" She hummed in response, indicating we were on the same page. "Bianca's mention of a baby threw Dannika for a loop, but she hasn't brought it up to me. No one saw her reaction afterward except us."

"I'm not overly concerned about how she responded. Yes, it sent her over the edge, but I don't necessarily blame her for that, although she needs to get a better handle on her surroundings before she goes on another vomiting spree." Ysabeau grimaced, shaking her head. Cracking her knuckles, she kept my gaze and continued. "Bianca makes an excellent point. A point I don't know that you considered in this last-minute plan."

I raised a single brow. That was a bold yet underhanded statement from her. "Do you have something you wanted to say to me, Ysa? And tread lightly."

She crossed her arms. "You didn't make me your second to tread lightly," she pointed out, raising her chin. "And I won't start now." It was fair, though I wasn't in the mood to agree with her. After a week of being around Dannika, sleeping next to her, waking up to her . . . something in me was wound tightly at the very sound of her name.

When I said nothing, Ysa took that as her cue to continue. "You can't deny that you came up with this plan quickly. You saw a conflict not go as Mathis expected, and it played directly into your hand, but the plan you came up with was not thought out carefully and laid out in advance. The opportunity presented itself, and you made the decision on the spot. You are my king. I will support whatever you deem necessary, and you know this. Without question. What concerns me are some of the logistics. Bianca is right. An heir will be expected. How do you plan to address that?"

I kicked my legs up, crossing my ankles and resting them on my desk as I leaned back in my chair. She wasn't wrong, but our very nature was to my advantage. Vampire children were difficult to conceive. Certainly not impossible, but it was never a quick conception. Vampires were easily made, but that wasn't what was expected of me. Noble families and leaders produced children to carry on a pure-blood vampire line. I'd have someone investigate shifter-vampire couplings and see if such pairings extended that time any further. Either way, while the desire to see an heir born would be present, the push for one wouldn't be. "We have plenty of time before that becomes an issue."

Her expression didn't change. "But it *will* become an issue, Elias."

"And I will handle it when the time comes," I said firmly. I would find a solution. I always did. Given the way my body responded to Dannika and hers to mine, an heir may not be impossible, given time and a little finesse. I saw the way she pressed her thighs together when her cheeks flushed. At times, I could smell her desire, and it was everything I could do to keep my hands to myself. My blood heated, but Ysa's bold stare cooled it a fraction.

She took a deep breath, considering whether or

not to say her next piece. I gestured for her to go ahead. We'd come this far with it. "What of your mother?" she asked quietly. "What will you tell her?"

I frowned, scratching my neck. "That's more complicated. At the moment, it's not my highest priority, but I will tell her. Time is on my side."

She scoffed, changing her position to view the landscape outside the window. "For now. It will catch up to us. It always does."

"You are still displeased," I stated.

She returned her sharp eyes to me, pinning me with a focused stare. "You have your *mate*," she started. "One whom you have no intention of bedding. Correct?" I hesitated a moment too long. "Perhaps I underestimated just how half-cocked this plan was. I knew your original intentions, but have they changed?"

I sighed. "It's not a black-and-white situation. I don't know what Dannika will want long term. We may be in a different place months or years from now."

Her eyebrows rose above her wide-rimmed sunglasses. "And you? Are you somehow remaining celibate if Dannika doesn't want to change the arrangement?" She raised both her brows, looking for my answer.

I gave her a brittle smile. "A question I've asked myself as well."

And I had. Mates bonded for life. Eyes only for each

other. I couldn't be seen with another woman leaving my bed chambers, nor could I be caught leaving anyone else's. I'd considered the possibility of glamour to seek out that level of intimacy, but the deceit it entailed wasn't a solution.

No, the obvious one was right in front of us, and I was neither blind nor fool enough to ignore it. The attraction was there. For sex, that was all that was needed. If she wanted children, we *could* have them. I had little to no doubt that I could make her body sing for me. But Dannika was unpredictable, while still being level-headed. I didn't know what she wanted for the future, or what she'd envisioned before this life I'd trapped us both in.

I should ask her.

"You haven't answered it then, I gather?" Ysa continued, and when I didn't respond, she hummed. "I figured as much."

"I had no idea you cared about my sex life," I countered, curious as to where this particular line of questioning was coming from.

Her expression hardened. "I don't care about yours, Elias. Fuck or don't. You make your own choices in this. I only wonder if you've considered *hers*," she said, her tone flat.

"I haven't," I admitted. At least not beyond what it might look like with *me*. If she didn't want to extend the nature of our agreement, though . . . I sat back, releasing a sigh. The silence stretched between us. "She did agree to this arrangement."

Ysa gave me a deadpan glare. "Death or pretend mate?" She barked a laugh. "Yes, I'm sure she had time to consider the future of her life as queen and how any of her physical needs would be met. Don't be an asshole. You're better than that."

My eyebrows shot up in surprise. It was rare that Ysa was this straightforward with me. "I didn't expect you to be concerned about Dannika's well-being. Color me shocked."

Tipping her head to the side, she made no move to react with emotion. "She is to be my queen, whether the truth of your bond is real or not. It's my job to be concerned for her, in all ways." She sniffed, twisting her nose a little as she did. We both knew I couldn't argue her point. "Besides," she said, shrugging a single shoulder, "depriving someone of sex for a lifetime is just cruel, which you certainly can be, but not to those you care about."

"Noted," I said. "I'll take your council under advisement and . . . come up with something."

She couldn't—wouldn't be with another man or woman, physically or otherwise. If she were truly opposed to the only real viable solution, things would get complicated. Messy. Bitter. That was the very situation I was trying to avoid.

But like I'd told Ysabeau, we had time. She may not

have been open to it yet, but months or years from now? Something told me I'd have her beneath me eventually. If the lust riding me wasn't enough, celibacy would do us both in.

Ysabeau nodded once, pushing the sunglasses she wore up her nose after they'd slid down a fraction. She'd made her point and was satisfied she'd put me in my place. I could see that she'd enjoyed that.

"Anything else you'd like to scold me about before we handle the main agenda of the day?" I asked, starting to twirl my pen through my fingers.

She smiled broadly, her fangs on full display. "I think that's enough for now."

"Good. Call Mathis. I've been looking forward to this moment."

Ysa reached into her pocket, pulling out a silver remote and pressing buttons. I crossed my arms behind my neck, cradling my head as I looked at the mounted screen on the wall. Magic buzzed around it, pulling the spell forward that allowed us to make video calls in this dystopian post-human-led world.

Some considered it the downside of magic being revealed to the mundane over time. Their work and technology had slowly disappeared, forcing that machinery to be swapped out with magically imbued replacements. Once the last portal had opened in Portland, the entire world had then known of supernatural existence, and chaos had ensued. The Great Sacrifice treaty had stopped the wars, but what humans were left were truly expendable. What could they offer the Houses? Not many viewed their skills as valuable. Their work and jobs had become worthless. We made up for most of it with magic. I could deal with the changes. I just wished the entertainment industry had continued. So many cliffhangers, and we'd never know the ending. It was a travesty.

Ysa cleared her throat, then tilted her head toward the screen.

Static crackled, and Mathis slowly filtered into view.

His smug face took up most of the screen.

"What do you want, Elias?" he said, annoyance filling his tone.

"It is a pleasant day, isn't it?" I asked, ignoring his question.

His expression remained flat, but his irritation was clear. "Has my son killed that bitch and her dog yet?"

"No, I'm afraid not," I said, shaking my head. "But that is the reason I wanted to call you."

"I know what you did after the commemoration. Andreas passed on your message."

"What a good boy he is," I mocked. "I hope you gave him a treat."

He narrowed his eyes, and his brow twitched. "I know what you're doing, Elias. It won't work."

I chuckled, no longer giving him my attention and

instead looking at the ceiling. "Doubtful, Mathis. Very doubtful."

He sat at his own desk, back straight, hands clasped on the tabletop. "You think I care about you holding them hostage?" He looked at someone off screen and laughed. "You'll get nothing from me, so there's no discussion to be had. You have nothing I want. Unless you're telling me she's mated or dead, I don't want them back."

"I believe you," I said, grinning while still not making eye contact. "That's why I wanted to let you know Dannika *is* mated." From my periphery, I saw his mouth fall open. His hands unclasped and he leaned forward, again looking off screen. Perfect. "To me."

I turned my head, wanting to relish in the way he struggled to process what I'd said.

His face twisted in anger, and he growled. "What did you say?" he asked through clenched teeth.

"You heard me. Dannika is my mate. It's the weirdest thing, I know. So soon after she rejected Markus too." I removed my arms from behind my head, looking down to inspect my nails. "That's why I saved her from your assassination squad. I couldn't lose her. *I won't.*" I looked at him from the corner of my eyes, smiling, and it was real. I was happy to make him squirm in anger. "And you know what that means, Mathis."

It meant he couldn't touch her. He couldn't barter

for her return just to execute her. Every bounty on her head and his team of killer mutts would have to be called off. Finally, he would be forced to acknowledge her position publicly. And there was nothing he could do about it. She was untouchable and out of his reach.

He shook with barely contained rage. His palms lay flat on the desk, his nails extending and digging into the wood. Red crept up his face, and his eyes flashed a bright purple, a sign of a shifter's overwhelming desire to shift. His wolf was desperate to come out and attack.

I winked at him.

Taken aback, he snarled. Then his demeanor suddenly changed. The tension in his expression fell to a cool mask of confidence. His claws retracted, and he ran his fingers through his hair, shaking off the ire. What it meant, I didn't know. Then he dropped it on me.

A glimmer in his eye shone while a cruel sneer appeared. "I thought better of you, Elias. That you would learn from past mistakes." He straightened his tie, cracking his neck. "Remember the last time you played games with me. I don't recall that it worked out so well for you. Or rather, it did, I suppose. Just not so much for your sister."

I dropped my legs from my desk, slamming my hands on the table as I stood up. My fangs shot out and my blood boiled. He smirked. Ysa hissed at me, grounding me and reminding me to keep my cool.

"The Houses know of my mate bond, Mathis. You'd do well to remember *your* place. I know how you got there. One step over the treaty line is all it takes for your world to come crumbling down," I said in a low voice. "Touch her and I *will end you.*"

He shrugged. "Give my respects to your mother. I do hope she gets my flowers every year." He winked in return, then the screen turned to static.

I picked up a crystal ball paperweight and threw it where his face had been. The glass shattered on impact, splintering pieces that flew outward. The sphere went straight through the wall, smashing into the concrete barriers under the drywall.

I shouted, and the volume of my anger shook the windows.

Ysabeau stood wide-eyed, jaw slack. "I can't believe he went there . . ." She paused, unsure what to say.

I shouldn't have been surprised. It was Mathis, after all. I hadn't expected it, but I should have. He knew damn well I knew it had been him. I had no proof, and he knew that too. It was my fault my sister was dead. He may have been the one to do it, but I'd put her in the vulnerable position. I'd put her in that monster's path, and I hadn't been there to stop him.

Guilt, regret, and unbridled rage filled me.

He'd taken her from my family. In so many words, he'd threatened to do the same to Dannika for no other reason than hatred for her. Pissing me off was a bonus.

"He was goading me. I took the bait," I said through gritted teeth.

"He was trying to rattle you." Looking me up and down, she added, "And it worked."

I shot her a glare. "The flowers and my mother. What's he talking about?"

Ysa shook her head. "I don't know."

"Find out," I ordered, and she understood that the urgency in my voice meant I wanted an answer today. I had a feeling I knew. I just wanted to be wrong. "I don't care if my mother tells you or if she wants to tell me, but make it happen."

"Consider it done," she whispered, her eyes downcast and shadowed by sadness that had not been there before. I knew she was thinking about my sister. Claudette had been her friend. Sometimes I'd wondered if there had been more to it than that, but I'd never asked. If Ysa wanted to share that part of her, she would. I wouldn't pry.

I dropped back down into my chair, rubbing my fists against my eyes to put pressure onto the oncoming headache. That hadn't exactly gone according to plan. It didn't mean I'd stop. He'd rattled me, yes, but I'd done the same to him. It was why he'd gone as far as he had. That was how much I had gotten to him with the news of Dannika. And that meant I'd laid the foundation.

A knock came, and Ysa went to the door. She dipped her head, thanking them. Then she turned to me. A grim look covered her face. She crossed the room, heading to the windows, scanning the landscape.

"What now?" I asked.

"Dannika is out with Markus *again*," she whispered, side-eyeing me. "We have to get that under control. This is the third time I've seen them together. She is your mate, Elias. You can't afford for rumors to spread that it may not be real."

Even as displeasure washed over me at the thought, I waved her off. "I agreed to them seeing each other. She has to convince him to reject her. He can't be tied to her forever."

And if she didn't get him to end it amicably, it would only be a matter of time until the pup would give me an excuse to do so otherwise.

Ysa didn't look convinced as she twisted her lips to the side and hummed. "And what do we tell people when the King of Blood and Beryl's mate is off taking strolls into the woods with the shifter who also tried to claim her?"

Inside, I bristled at the notion. Outwardly, I shrugged. "They're friends now. He accepts her rejection and they share memories of Fire and Fluorite. Friends take walks, don't they? It's harmless."

She continued to stare out the window. "He bullied her and now they're believed to be friends? Hmm."

I gritted my teeth. "It's her choice. If I take all of them from her, I'm no better than Mathis."

Ysabeau sighed. "You've put yourself in a difficult position here. Does it bother you that she continues to spend time with him, knowing some of what went on?"

"Yes," I said, waiting for the throbbing in my head to heal itself. "I'd rather throw him in the dungeons or cast him out for his father to deal with . . . but she doesn't want that. I may dislike him, but he tortured her for years. Ultimately, it's only right for her to choose what is done with him. Her heart is simply too good to make the choice she should."

Ysabeau inhaled deeply, making a show of her mannerisms. It was a habit more than anything at this point, to breathe, to move. While not an original vampire, she was one of the closest things to it—something very few knew because she made it so. "And what happens if they get closer during this time they spend together as *friends?*" she asked in a falsely innocent tone.

My brows furrowed. I didn't like what she was implying. *At all.*

The moment I'd seen Dannika at the commemoration, there'd been an unknown allure to her very being. A moment of charged electricity between us that I couldn't quite place. A baser instinct would have said it had been purely physical. She was beautiful and fierce. There was no doubt about it. Even if I didn't understand her reasoning, I still found myself in a strange position of awe and admiration for the way she refused to kill Markus. I certainly would have just ended his life. The way in which she'd stood up to her Alpha Supreme with such conviction and defiance . . . it was undeniably attractive. If ever I wanted to be tied down to someone, I'd want that level of fire within them.

But we were strictly business. That was what she was to me. What she was *supposed* to be.

So why did Ysabeau's insinuation make my fists clench involuntarily?

"They won't become more," I said, my voice grave. "She doesn't even want him as a friend."

She turned to me, uncrossing one arm and pointing out the window. "Then I shouldn't address this?" She cocked an eyebrow.

I flew to the window to see what she was talking about.

Dannika stood on a trail that led from the woods onto the main grounds a hundred yards away. Her back was to me, but I wouldn't mistake that cascade of silver hair anywhere. Markus approached from the other side.

Ysa was wrong about them, and I looked at her, raising my eyebrows to question if this mattered. When she cleared her throat, angling her head back at the window, that was when I saw Markus's face glowering over Danni's as he stared down. Something in me clenched tightly, like a muscle coiled, ready to spring.

She flew backward. Her neck whipped, her temple slamming into the ground as she tried and failed to catch herself. The fury cleared from Markus's face, replaced by false concern. He bent down, stroking Dannika's hair with one hand, while the other cupped the side of her face.

Fire licked at my skin, a burning wrath wrapping itself around my body at what I'd just witnessed.

But what sent me into a rage was when I saw her lean into his touch.

He'd pushed her. He'd hurt her again, and *she'd leaned into him.*

Markus was fucking dead.

CHAPTER 11
DANNIKA

ords swirled in my mind. Words like *Mother-in-law. Heir. Baby.*

Those were very new concepts for me. Things I'd barely had time to consider.

Phrases shouted in response. *What the fuck. This is insane. I can't do this.*

I thanked my lucky stars Elias hadn't made me do another appearance since the throne room. No one except him and Ysa had witnessed my faux pas afterward. I had to expect more situations like that would occur. More bombs would get dropped on me. I needed to figure out how to roll with it.

I was to be a queen, that much was known. What did that entail exactly? I didn't have answers. I'd have to sit down with Elias soon and ask some hard questions.

Like all that business about an heir. I could play my part by his side, pretending he was my mate. I wouldn't have to fake a physical attraction. Now that I wasn't at the commemoration protecting my sister or fearing for my life, I'd had time to settle. Be around him. I couldn't deny that my body was *very* reactive to him. I chalked it up to being the first man I lived in close quarters with. Waking up to a king in nothing but his boxers while he made flirtatious comments . . . Yeah, my inexperience was no match. But that was superficial. There was so much to figure out beyond the physical. Sure, we'd had some dinners together. Learned a bit about each other's likes and dislikes, but it was just the tip of the iceberg for a mated couple. Newfound fated mates were downright obsessive with each other. Jealous and possessive. Infatuated to an unhealthy level. That was what the world expected to see from me.

Staring at the ground as I walked, I kept my hands tucked into my pockets. There was a pleasant chill in the air, but my limbs were starting to get cold. My stomach growled, reminding me I should probably feed myself. The snap of a twig caught my attention, and Nova's hackles raised. We both lifted our heads, catching the scent on the wind. Internally, I groaned. He was the last person I wanted to see right now.

"What do you want, Markus?" I asked, acknowledging his presence.

He strode out from the trees several yards away, then headed toward us.

I took him in. His hair was somewhat messy compared to what he usually looked like. Dark circles hung beneath his eyes. His shirt was wrinkled and untucked, but he walked with an air of confidence.

"When I saw you leaving for a walk alone, I thought we could spend some time together," he said, coming to a stop in front of me.

"Again?"

"You agreed."

I wrinkled my nose at his response. It wasn't exactly like he gave me another choice here.

"Following someone in the woods is creepy," I said, changing the subject as I continued down the path. I knew I wouldn't be able to get rid of him. It was just a matter of dealing with him until we got back. Looking over my shoulder, I added, "I was just about to head back. Are you coming, or did you want to keep lurking in the shadows?"

He fell into step beside me, and I kept my pace brisk. The less time I spent with him, the better. Now, if only he'd just stay quiet — "The whispers in the hallway were louder today," he started, his voice tight. "Apparently, Elias has publicly announced he's found his mate."

"I told you what was coming the night we got

here," I said, wishing I had the power to just teleport away.

"You failed to mention the part about you being his queen." To punctuate his last word, he kicked a rock hard, sending it skipping across the dirt path. "It wasn't something I'd considered."

"Kind of goes hand in hand with being mated to a king." I sighed. "It is what it is, Markus. We're in this situation because you won't reject me, and you won't accept my rejection. This is our home now. I don't know how else to word it, but putting it bluntly, that's the truth of it."

"So you've said," he muttered. "But I can't look at this place as home."

Because it isn't. Not without seeing Adora, Mom, and Abbey. The thought interjected itself, unbidden. I couldn't afford to think that way. Part of accepting this life was changing my reactions. Adjusting my responses. Lamenting the fact they weren't here wasn't going to make it so.

I nodded. "It's new, and it probably won't feel like home for a while, but we'll get there," I said, trying to sound encouraging, if only for myself. "The Pacific Northwest is ours. The smell of the forest and the moisture in the air. At least that feels like home."

"Home wasn't filled with vampires." There was a hint of venom in his tone, and though I knew I shouldn't have been surprised, the meaning of it still caught me off guard. "Just this morning, one of them hit on me. Can you believe that?"

No, but not for the reasons he thought. "So what?" I said defensively. "There's nothing wrong with vampires. Every House is mixed. At one time, Fire and Fluorite was only half shifters."

He scoffed. "The better half."

My jaw fell open, and I stopped in my tracks, crossing my arms. "Really? I thought it was just a show you put on in front of everyone because you were the heir. But it's real? You actually believe yourself to be superior? Stop acting like you're better than everyone else. You're not. No species is." I looked him up and down, thinking about how I'd been treated in our former House and how it was a stark contrast to the meeting with the High Court. None of them had looked at me with disgust. They hadn't looked at me like a freak or a bad omen. Like something was wrong with me. Some of them might have questioned our story and what I was doing there, but whatever they'd seen when they looked at me, it hadn't been because I was different. "Blood and Beryl showed us kindness. Elias didn't have to take us in, but he did."

Markus gave me a deadpan look. "First of all, he made a deal to suit himself. Second, he took *you* in, not me. You did that. A shifter looking out for a shifter."

Nova snorted loudly, shaking her body. I cocked my head. "*Now* you see me as a shifter? That's a first.

When we were kids, you held me underwater until I passed out while saying my mother should have drowned me." I uncrossed my arms, turning on a heel and walking away.

"I shouldn't have done that," he said quickly, covering the few paces to catch up with me. "Or said it."

"And yet you did. Repeatedly," I responded.

I didn't want to hate Markus forever. It had nothing to do with him. It was the hate itself. It was exhausting. The anger and the hurt festered, never allowing the wound to close. I'd just avoided him for so long in an effort to not deal with it. It was easier. And now fate wanted to screw with me. Just because I didn't want to hate him didn't mean I wanted to like him.

"I would never hurt you again." His words ran over my skin, tugging on that stupid invisible line that connected us. It tried to reach within, coaxing at emotions that weren't real. Not for him. *Never* for him.

Nova huffed loudly, adding a slight growl under her breath. He frowned at her, moving away by an inch.

"Markus." I sighed. Looking up, I focused on the damp pine needles of the forest as we walked. "I . . . I appreciate that, but if you're about to start up with the mate thing again, drop it. Please. I have entirely too much on my mind right now."

"The mate thing?" he said, his tone clipped. "The mate thing is why you saved me. It's why I'm here, even if you won't admit it."

True, I'd saved him. It was an action I was beginning to regret in moments like this, but I wouldn't say that to him.

"You're strolling through the forest with me right now to be *friends*, remember?" I argued.

"That's only for appearances while we're here."

I shook my head. "We're not going back to Fire and Fluorite, Markus. At least I'm not. You can try, but I honestly don't think you should."

"My father won't accept me coming home without you," he said harshly. "I'm not welcome otherwise."

"Doesn't that tell you something, then? I mean, what kind of parent acts like that?" I asked, knowing he wouldn't be able to recognize that kind of treatment for what it was. "Why do you want to go back to that? You have a real chance to start over here."

"He's still my father." Although Markus said the words, his voice faltered, and I wondered if he believed his own excuses.

I stopped, turning toward him. Nova slowed, then sensed my emotions and sat at my side. "He didn't treat you with the same courtesy." I saw the sadness in his eyes. He knew the truth, but the inner turmoil must have been immense. I would never be able to understand the feeling. I couldn't relate. I had a family that loved me deeply. "Blood and Beryl accepted us. Forget the reason why. I'm going to make the most of it. We can work on separating the bond, and we can find you some sort of job here. Purpose. It'd be good for you."

"I'm not separating the bond." He scoffed.

"Dammit, Markus," I said under my breath. "I know this will probably come as a shock to you, but I don't want you to suffer. The sooner you reject the bond, the easier it will be. I'm trying to help you. It's only going to get harder for you over time, especially after I . . . formally move to become the . . . queen." I moved the dirt around with my boot, looking down at the pattern it created.

Our conversation brought up another question I needed to ask. How was that going to happen? What was the process for that? My stomach dropped at the idea of some sort of public ceremony. Nova's body jostled, like she was laughing at me. Internally, it made me happy she could lift my spirits. I nudged her side in jest, and she turned her head, sneezing on me, sending some spittle onto Markus's arm.

He glared at my wolf, pointing to her. "Does she *have* to be here? She follows you around like a chaperone. I wasn't aware we needed one."

I narrowed my eyes at him, and Nova snarled. "You don't get it, do you? She isn't my pet. She's a part of me."

"That doesn't even make sense."

Indignation coursed through me. "It doesn't have to make sense. It just *is*. She's what I would be if I could shift my body, but I can't, and we carry a piece of each other. You'd know that if you'd listened to me just one time—and not because some stupid mate bond said I meant something to you," I added, making sure he wouldn't use that to argue with me.

I shouldn't have risen to the occasion. Every part of me knew better. I stormed off and saw the clearing ahead as the trail came to a stop when the tree line met the manicured lawn of the estate.

Markus ran behind us, catching up as we neared the path's end.

"Why are you walking away from me, Dannika?" he asked, his voice low and angry.

Keep going, I told myself. There was no reason to engage. Nova picked up her pace, shaking her head and grumbling loudly.

I started to follow her, but I had walked away for so long. And I was done.

I whirled around, pointing a finger at my chest, then his. "Because *I'm* trying to be nice. I'm trying to make this work, helping *you*. And you . . . ugh. You just make it so hard. This entire conversation feels so forced. You can't even be nice to me. We have a damned mate bond, and you *still* can't find it in yourself to be decent to me. You don't even know me. Your snide remarks and underhanded comments. All of it. So I'm walking away from you and I'm going to go talk to someone who isn't an awful jackass."

"What do you even see in that parasite?" he spat. "It's him, isn't it? That's who you plan to *talk* to."

I threw my hands out, pointing at the mansion behind me. "Elias barely knows me and he's shown me more kindness, more sincerity, and more respect than you've shown me in our entire lives. He respects Nova and understands what she is, not treating us like we're lesser or unworthy. If that's what I've committed my life to by making this deal, then sign me the fuck up."

Shock rippled through my mind as the words left my mouth, surprising me with the accuracy of the statement. It was true. Every bit of it. Even with the supposed desire and pull the mate bond was supposed to have, it didn't matter. Markus was who he was. And my pretend mate—the King of Blood and Beryl—was the polar opposite.

I huffed a humorless laugh, putting my hands on my hips and looking at the ground. "I'm trying to be a friend to you, Markus. I want you to heal from whatever you went through. I'm trying to care." I paused, shaking my head, and I took a deep breath. "And I honestly don't know why. It's more than you deserve."

"He's not your mate," he said through clenched teeth.

"He is now."

Markus ran his hands through his hair, then turned, reaching back, and punched the trunk of a conifer. The wood split with a sickening crack that rent the air. Then he turned to me, walking in long strides.

I backed up in hurried steps. Flashbacks of our youth played in my mind. I'd stayed too long—and just stoked that fiery temper of his.

Nova yelped a warning to me just as the heel of my boot hit something hard, and I fell backward. Instinctively, I reached out for Markus as he held his hand out to catch me, but my fingers never found purchase. I slammed against the ground with a thud, my arms flying up, and my head smacking into something hard.

I groaned as pain shot through me and little white dots exploded behind my eyes, swirling in fast circles.

"Shit, Dannika," he exclaimed, pulling me up to a standing position entirely too fast. "I wasn't going to hit you."

I teetered, feeling dizzy from the sudden motion. "Could have fooled me," I mumbled, scrunching my eyes shut against the throbbing.

He cupped my jaw, and I leaned against it. Something to brace myself against while the world spun. Through my blurry vision, it looked as though he was checking me over. "Hold on. You have pine needles in your hair." He picked at something, flicking it over to the side.

"Stop grooming me," I managed to say, then I attempted to take a step. Nope. I wobbled, grabbing on to his arm as I stumbled into him.

The pounding in my head would heal. I just needed some time. Breathe in, breathe out. Nova whined, leaning against me for support, nudging my side so I knew she would help brace me. After a few minutes, the world came back into focus.

I took Markus's hand off my face, stepping away from him. "I have a dinner to go to," I muttered, removing myself from his proximity.

"I'm s—"

A blurred body *whooshed* by before any other words could leave his mouth. My jaw dropped as I witnessed Elias's incredible speed, just as he slammed Markus into a tree. Markus's feet dangled off the ground and his face turned purple as Elias held him by his throat. Fur sprouted along his exposed skin and his claws lengthened.

"Stop it!" I shouted, running to Elias and grabbing his arms. I tugged, trying to pull him away, but he didn't budge. "Please," I said, my voice dropping as I pleaded with him.

Elias turned to me, and I gasped. His fangs were fully exposed, his hardened features turned razor-sharp and deadly. His eyes were filled with crimson rage, and it evoked a fear response in me that I couldn't control. When I stumbled back, his eyes changed. "Why?" he asked, his voice hard. "I saw what he did to you."

"It's not . . . what you . . . think," Markus managed to squeak out as Elias teetered on the edge of crushing his windpipe.

"You will not speak." Elias jerked his attention back to Markus, squeezing tighter. "Shift, and I'll end you now."

I placed my hand on Elias's arm. "He didn't do anything to me. I tripped over a rock." He looked at the top of my head. With his free hand, he stroked it, coming away with blood. His nostrils flared. Something feral and hungry flashed in his eyes as he stared at the liquid smeared on his fingertips.

"And this?"

"Apparently, I wanted to protect my head from the ground, so a nice, soft rock cushioned the blow," I said dryly. He gave me a deadpan look in return.

"You expect me to believe that story?"

"I do, yes," I answered. "I'd be happy to tell you the rest of it, but you'd have to let him go."

Elias held my gaze, not nearly as amused. He dropped Markus, letting him fall to the ground unceremoniously. Coughing and gagging, the shifter held himself up on all fours while he gasped. Elias leaned down next to him and spoke in a threatening whisper. "Just this once, pup. Just the one time. If you ever put her in harm's way again, I will rip the limbs from your body and beat you to death with them before I set your bloody stump on fire."

Elias stood up, facing me. Nova nudged up against my side. His expression was hard to read. His jaw was set, but his eyes softened. "He doesn't deserve your kindness," he said, his tone still filled with anger, even if that anger wasn't directed at me.

I shook my head. "No, he doesn't," I said. Elias raised his eyebrows in apparent surprise. "But he doesn't deserve my vengeance, either."

"Why not?"

Markus pushed himself to a standing position from the forest floor, wiping the dirt and debris from his pants. He looked at me curiously.

I considered not answering, but I couldn't see the merit in holding anything back.

"I was his punching bag. He was Mathis's." The color drained from Markus's face, and he looked away from us. "I won't stoop to that level. I won't continue that cycle."

A faint smile crept up Elias's face, and he huffed a small laugh. "You are something else, Danni." Tightening his lips, he let out a high-pitched whistle. Ysabeau appeared in the distance. I had no idea where she'd been hiding out and watching our exchange, but it shouldn't have been a surprise to me that she'd been nearby.

She approached us, surveying Markus with a

venomous gaze. "Yes?"

Elias tilted his head toward my rejected mate without breaking eye contact with me. "Take him inside. He and I are going to have a chat."

She dipped her head, signaling for Markus to follow her. For once, he looked ashamed. Where he usually stood proud, his shoulders now slouched. His haughty attitude lost its fuel. For the first time in my life, I watched him walk away with his tail between his legs.

Across the lawn, I saw the spectators. Oh, they appeared to be busy as they talked amongst themselves, pointing at papers or something equally unimportant. Elias and I both knew we had an audience.

I winced. "I'm sorry we made a scene. I know it's not good for appearances."

"They don't know what they saw." He crossed his arms and shrugged. "Perhaps it's not what it looks like."

I barked a laugh. "It really wasn't."

"I believe you," he said. Looking down at Nova, he added, "I've seen both of you in action. I should fully trust that you and Nova know what to do if you feel threatened."

I scrunched my eyebrows. "Um, then why exactly did you just storm out here and try to crush his neck?"

"Knee-jerk reaction."

"To what?"

He didn't answer.

Leaning forward, he pressed his lips to my cheek. "See you at dinner," he whispered.

He turned, walking across the lawn and back toward the grand mansion he called home.

Power and authority radiated off him, and everyone who had been observing us had to have felt it too. As he passed them, they all dipped their heads in respect. Or maybe it was fear—if they had seen his face when he'd been moments away from killing Markus.

A torrent of thoughts and emotions churned through me. Never in my life had someone other than my family stood up for me. Never had someone been willing to kill another just to ensure I wouldn't be hurt. Every part of my being knew this was an arranged mating, but it didn't stop the heat on my skin and the flush that crept up when his lips touched my cheek. It didn't stop the animal in me from savoring the possessiveness that rippled off him in waves, even if it was only an illusion. It didn't stop me from briefly wanting that kind of passion to be real.

It didn't stop me from admitting to myself that I wanted to feel it again.

Nova leaned into me, exhaling loudly as her entire body shivered.

I sighed, letting my hand rest on her.

Same, girl. Same.

ELIAS

Candlelight painted her face in a warm glow. Her silver hair was pulled back in a simple French braid, then twisted in a knot that sat low on the back of her neck, leaving the pale column front and center as it descended to her chest, encased in a beige cashmere sweater. She didn't wear makeup. A healthy glow from her walks in the sun nipped her cheeks, like a bite of wind on a cold morning. It made the frosted glass of her eyes even more vibrant and enticing.

"Tell me about our dinner tonight," she said. A raspy tenor in her voice made my inner predator take notice. I wondered if she realized the way she nibbled on her bottom lip as she surveyed the spread before us. Her canine teeth were more pointed than a human's, but less so than a vampire's. It was a shifter trait. Meant for marking. Claiming.

And killing.

Somehow, the last one didn't even occur to me when I was thinking about Dannika.

"The main dish is called saltimbocca. It's a specialty in Italy. Veal wrapped in prosciutto and sage. On the side is fresh spaghetti, as well as sautéed Brussels sprouts with a balsamic vinaigrette."

Vampires needed blood to survive, but food wasn't off the table, so to speak. Our palates became more refined with age. We didn't quite need the nourishment. It was purely for enjoyment, so nothing less than the best was ever consumed.

It was something I wanted to share with Dannika.

"It smells fantastic." She hummed, loading her plate. Between us, Nova sat on my Persian rug, ignoring us both as she stared into the fireplace—seemingly deep in thought.

"My chef assures me it will be, and he insisted we pair it with this Barbera d'Alba."

I poured us each a glass, then lifted my own in a toast. "To our first week."

"Only forever left to go," she replied with dry wit. While there was a slight barb in her words, she gave me a light smile and inhaled the scent before taking a tentative sip.

Her eyes shuttered, a low hum starting in her throat.

My cock stiffened.

"Or at least until I die." She chuckled, taking a larger sip.

"Not going to happen," I replied, my voice terser than it should have been. She arched one thick eyebrow while cutting into her saltimbocca.

"Shifters don't have the same lifespans as vampires."

"You're not simply a shifter."

She snorted. "Being unable to shift means I don't have the same rapid healing. Sure, it's faster, but without a wolf form, it's unlikely I'll slow down in aging. I don't consider myself as lesser, but there is a reason Fire and Fluorite did."

"I was referring to you being my queen," I said lightly, having to set the crystal glass aside so I didn't grip it too tightly. Aging. I hadn't thought about that in a time. Vampires went through a form of second puberty in their mid-twenties where they essentially stopped aging as they came into their full powers. Shifters were similar, but certainly not the same. They had their wolves through childhood, and both went through puberty in their twenties—at the mating age.

Dannika was not a normal shifter, however, which meant it stood to reason everything I knew about them wouldn't necessarily be relevant.

"That's the thing about time," she murmured. "It waits for no one. King. Queen. Alpha. Empress. We're all equal in that. When my day comes, there's not much you or anyone else will be able to do about it." She set her fork down, staring intently at the wine in her glass, then smiled. I didn't bother telling her that wasn't true. Something in her tone told me we had gone beyond talking about her. "Debbie Downer, remember?"

It wasn't a vampire gesture, to ease over any awkwardness by self-deprecation. I wasn't entirely sure it was a shifter thing, either. It was more human.

"I get the feeling you were thinking of someone in particular."

"My dad," she said. "He died in the Great Sacrifice. My mom always told me what an amazing leader he was. Everyone liked him. Respected him. Fought by his side. Didn't stop that night from taking him." She twisted her noodles and pushed the pieces of veal around in the sauce. It was a thoughtful habit I'd picked up on; she did it when thinking.

"I had a sister. Claudette. I lost her shortly before the war started." I wasn't sure how much to say. How much I could bring myself to say. "We were close despite her being eighty years my senior. She was actually the heir, but she gave it up because she wanted to focus on philanthropic efforts that being the queen of a House wouldn't allow. We were in the process of negotiating a peace treaty with Fire and Fluorite when she died."

Dannika's gaze shifted, softening. "I'm so sorry to hear that." Her eyes pulled me in. Deep. Soulful.

"Her death was part of what led to my decision to enter the war," I said slowly. "I was devastated, and in my own grief, I made a horrible decision that affected so many."

She tilted her head. "Grief makes us strangers even to ourselves."

It wasn't forgiveness. Nor was it blame. It was understanding. I shook my head. I'd expected condemnation or for her to offer weak platitudes about it being okay. She'd chosen neither. As usual, she never ceased to surprise me.

"How old were you when he died?" I asked, swallowing harder than I should have on a small bite. What should have been a savory meal was turning in my stomach.

"It was the day I was born."

My lips parted. *Fuck.*

How? How was she this stoic? This calm? I struggled to grapple with the understanding of her age. I suspected she was younger than me by a good bit, but gods above. She'd never known him, yet she spoke like she missed him. Grieved him.

While I struggled with words, Dannika seemed to have them. "My mother went into labor the night of the Great Sacrifice, and it was a few weeks earlier than expected. My dad had already left to fight, and she had no way to tell him. So she shifted and went into the woods to search for him." Not the most logical thing, but who was I to criticize a pregnant werewolf who'd been alone and was having contractions? "She found his body amongst other dead shifters. There was an orphaned baby there too. Adora. The grief took over, and she gave birth right there. So I was born the night he died—hence the whole cursed thing." She motioned with her hand. "Later, when they learned I couldn't shift, the notion of being cursed stuck pretty hard."

"Your mother didn't birth you *and* Nova?" I clarified.

Dannika's mouth twisted, clearly amused. "If you're curious about how she came to be, you know you can just ask. It's not like I have any reason to hide it. Most of my pack knew at least some version of it."

"I am curious," I admitted. "But I thought your mother had both of you. It seemed the only explanation for how you could have a wolf, but not shift."

She nodded, taking a bite of Brussels sprouts and surveying the side dish with pleasant surprise. "My mother was sick of me being bullied. I used to come home from school and beg her to just teach me at home—not that Mathis would have allowed it. So she focused on what she could control. I had a wolf.

They could sense it. I just wasn't able to let her out. Mom took me to a witch when I was eight. Made a bargain and got her to do a spell to release my wolf." Her eyes slid sideways to Nova, who looked back at her right then. Two halves of one whole. "It worked. Just not the way my mom had expected." She smiled wryly.

"What did the witch want in return?"

"I don't know."

"You didn't ask?"

"I was eight."

"Do you know her name?"

"I was *eight*," she deadpanned, meeting my level gaze. "Who the witch was doesn't matter. The debt was paid, and I got Nova."

I hummed, running my fingers down my jaw over the stubble to curve under my chin. "Your mother must have paid her. She sounds admirable. She must love you very much."

"She does," Dannika said, getting quiet again. "Me, Adora, and Abbey are all she has left."

"Abbey. Older sister?"

"Stepmom," she explained. "She was from a different pack in Fire and Fluorite. She transferred to ours for them to be together."

"Forgive me if this seems callous, but if you didn't get on well with your pack, why didn't your family move to Abbey's pack?"

She smiled sadly. "Mathis. He never lets anyone leave once they're in his pack."

"Until you," I noted.

"Until me," she agreed somberly. "And Markus."

"That's bullshit."

She chuckled. "You won't hear any disagreements from me . . . but I did have something I wanted to ask."

I stilled. "I'm listening."

"When you go through with your . . . *plans*"—she hedged around the word, uncomfortable and stiff in her phrasing—"I want my family back. Here. With me."

I softened. It was such an earnest request. Something she shouldn't even have had to ask for. "I could try to get them out now, you know. It would take some planning, but an extraction team could be put together—"

"No." She shook her head. "Mathis will be expecting that, and he'll look for any reason to brand them traitors. I can't risk their lives that way." She nibbled on her bottom lip. "It has to be after."

I regarded her. So delicate, yet strong. Soft in some ways, yet firm and unyielding in others. Dannika was a survivor, but she didn't let that break her or make herself cold to the world. Somehow, she'd found a way to harmoniously exist in the middle.

Even as I and every other bastard tried to take that peace from her to suit our own ends.

"I swear when this is over, they will have a home at every estate we live in—if that is their choice," I told her. "Family is very important to me and my kind. I won't keep you apart from yours."

Dannika held my gaze for a suspended second, and in that brief moment, her eyes darkened. Her expression sharpened. The expression on her face, it almost looked like . . . hunger.

As fast as it had appeared, it then vanished. She leaned back in her chair and set her fork aside. After draining the remaining wine, the crystal clanked against the wood table when she set it down. "Dinner was lovely," she started, then she paused as she stood up. The legs of the chair caught on a ripple in the rug, making her twist to maneuver out of it. "You'll have to give my compliments to the chef."

I opened my mouth, tempted to ask why the sudden subject change when she flashed me a tight smile and retreated to the bathroom—closing the door firmly behind her, shutting me out.

CHAPTER 13

DANNIKA

"This is the library," Bianca said as we rolled to a stop. "It's part of the larger collection that belongs to our House and also holds pieces from—"

"The Great Library of Alexandria," I finished. Bianca lifted her dark brows, purple eyes appraising. "Elias brought me here last week," I explained. And he'd tried to several times since to bring me back, but I always found a reason to decline. After our dinner the other night, I was keeping my distance. It had become clear to me that while this was a business arrangement, the lines were blurring. We had to show intimacy in public, but in private? Well, I was dangerously close to crossing that line of my own volition. Nova gave me a side glance. She was witness to it, and she felt my emotions and desires leak through.

"Ah." A small smile played on her lips. "Did he tell you that his family actually removed most of the library and has it spread all over different Blood and Beryl estates? The largest and most valuable section is with his mother in Rome."

I nodded. "I look forward to seeing it one day."

"It's magnificent," Bianca said. "I can't imagine you'll have to wait long. Elias always spends Christmas with his mother at the villa."

Of course he did, because Elias, for all his dark and broody nature, was also a good son. A family man. He cared about his mother. He mourned the loss of his father and sister.

Things I would have loved to find in a mate . . . instead of being saddled with Markus. *The boy,* as Elias often called him, was a pain in my side. Even after they'd had a little "chat," Markus still insisted on spending time together every day. His persistence might have been attractive if it weren't completely unwanted and exhausting.

"I look forward to it," I said, genuinely meaning it. "I've never been beyond Portland."

Bianca appraised me. "You poor thing. How old are you, if you don't mind me asking?"

We trailed past the library, down the hall, our steps slow and unhurried, Nova strolling quietly at my side. "Twenty-four," I said. "I was born on the night of the Great Sacrifice. Travel is pretty much impossible for members of Fire and Fluorite. Especially if you're in Mathis's pack ..."

She nodded slowly. "You still have family there, don't you?"

"My parents and a close friend." I tugged at the sleeve of my navy-blue sweater. She gave me a sympathetic smile.

"I'm sorry." I appreciated that she didn't try to tell me it would all be okay. Not when neither she nor Elias could guarantee anything.

Feeling like this conversation was steering toward a direction I didn't feel like discussing, I changed course. "How long have you known Elias?"

"Well, our papas were good friends. Mine saved his during a hunting accident."

"An accident?" I frowned, well aware of how vampires had hunted before the modern era.

Bianca nodded. "Yes. An avalanche. It buried Horatius beneath fifty tons of ice and snow and rocks. My papa spent two days straight digging him out, then nursing him back to health. We were given our position in the Court after that." *That* had been unexpected and not at all what I'd envisioned. "I was actually born a few years before Elias. We were raised like cousins. My parents have not been fortunate enough to have another child, so he became more like a brother to me. Still is, though we haven't been as close since he became king." We came to the end of the hall, where the giant stained-glass window that overlooked the front doors was. "It's understandable. Kings are very busy. There's not much time for anything else—" Her mouth snapped shut, realizing how it sounded. "I didn't mean to imply—"

"It's all right," I said, putting her worries at ease. "None of what you said is untrue." It was part of why he wanted me as his queen. To carry out the role without being a drain on his time and energy.

"He's different with you," she said after a moment. "It may not be a traditional mating where you spend nearly every moment together after finding one another—but I've seen the way he is with you. The effort he goes to making plans for you both. He's always been a great king . . . but if it's not too presumptuous to say, I think he's also trying to be a great mate."

I hesitated to respond. Elias and I were pretending. Bianca only saw what he wanted her to see, and yet . . . he was like her brother. They'd grown up together. If it was all pretend, wouldn't she see it? Then there was the matter of our dinners . . . He did go through a lot of effort to have dinner with me every night and spend time with me after. He said it was for companionship, that even if this was a business arrangement, it didn't need to be an unpleasant one. We could be great friends in time. Still . . . I was pretty sure friends didn't want to be touched the way I wanted Elias to touch me. I doubt friends woke up every single morning glued to each other's bodies after dreaming about them.

I doubt they asked the gods why they were given Markus and not *him* as a mate.

I never dared utter that notion aloud, but I thought it. In the quiet of the night, when he was asleep, and the fire crackled, I thought about how different things could have been if Markus had rejected me the day of the commemoration. Mathis probably would have let my family go. His son's rejection would have been a good enough reason to finally cast us out of the House. Perhaps Elias wouldn't have taken me in, but maybe he still would have. Maybe . . .

No good ever came of wondering what could have been.

"He would be—*is*," I corrected myself. "He is a good mate, a great one."

I smiled lightly, even though inside I wanted to bang my head against the glass window. *Stupid. So stupid. I can't believe I slipped up like that.*

Bianca watched me with deeper interest. Her purple eyes were unreadable, though her lips made her seem amused. "Our parents once hoped that we would be mates," she confessed to me. "That was never going to happen. Not even if the gods decreed it. We simply don't see each other that way. Our parents were so sure we were mates that Elias and I were technically betrothed until we finally convinced them to drop it. There was even a time he was with Katie, but that was short-lived. She was never right for him." I blinked, my jaw slipping a fraction. "Look, marriage can be chosen for you, but at the end of the day, it's still a choice. You can be married, but that doesn't make it a marriage. Do you understand?"

I slowly nodded. "I think so."

"Being mated is not all that different. Sometimes we don't get to choose. Sometimes it's chosen for us. As you are very well aware, that doesn't mean that those people are *true* mates. Not unless they decide to be, and if they don't want to . . . there's nothing stopping them from looking elsewhere." She inclined her head, a secretive tilt to her lips. "Elias is a good man, and he will be a good mate because he has *chosen* to be one. That's all that matters."

Bianca saw so much and yet so little.

While it seemed she might not have actually bought the second-chance mate story after all, she didn't realize the real reason Elias had chosen me. We weren't mates in the truest sense of the word. He wasn't looking for a partner or lover. Elias wanted a business arrangement. A relationship of convenience. A weapon to use against Mathis.

All of it was fake. I was a fraud. This whole thing was an utter sham.

All the while I wanted things that a fraud wouldn't have wanted.

I desired more than a fake relationship.

Blackmailed and developing feelings for the vampire king. It sounded like a romance novel or the butt of a joke.

"Not every mating is decided by love," Bianca added after a moment. "There are many reasons why two people choose to spend their lives together. That doesn't mean that love can't be found. Like a wild-flower on a grassy knoll, sometimes you have to find it. By the looks of you two, though, I doubt you will have to look too hard."

CHAPTER 14
ELIAS

I stood in the forest, spinning a knife in my hand. The metal shimmered as it twirled at a high speed, eliciting a warbling sound. A quick toss in the air, I'd catch it blade side, then throw it at a tree, hitting the same mark every time.

I'd been waiting in this spot for half an hour, passing the minutes with target practice.

Dannika wasn't late. She didn't know I'd be here.

For the last week, she'd been working closely with Bianca, learning the ways of our House. Customs, history, our worldwide locations. And for that week, she'd been mostly avoiding conversation with me. Avoiding eye contact. Every night, we had dinner, sitting at opposite ends of the table and barely speaking. I lacked a topic of conversation that was intriguing enough to pique her interest, though it didn't stop me from trying. She hummed a lot. Gave vague responses. Nova seemed to sigh in annoyance at Dannika's side.

I couldn't read her.

I hated it.

For a week, she'd been this way. Ever since we'd had dinner and shared pieces of our life, and our losses. I had no idea what I'd said to change her demeanor that night, but that was when she'd closed herself to me.

Today would be different.

Tilting my head, I listened. Animals chittering and birds calling. Wind rustling the leaves. Finally, I heard what I was waiting for. Dannika's careful footsteps, and Nova's paws pressing into the soft earth. They stopped, and she called out carefully. "Hello? Who's there?"

I paused for a moment, waiting, but not answering. I stepped out from the trees just in time to hear the whistling of a knife as it sailed through the air. Leaning back, I caught the blade before it hit its target.

"Aiming for my eye?" I asked, then hummed. "Good throw."

"I'm so sorry—" Dannika threw her hands over her mouth, mumbling beneath them. Then she dropped them, balling her fists at her side. Her brows furrowed. "What the hell are you doing here? I could have killed you."

I chuckled. "Not likely. If I had lesser reflexes, it'd take some time for that eye to grow back. Painful, for sure. But not dead." I returned the blade to her. "What if I had been someone else?"

"Then they'd have a knife in their eye, and they'd deserve it for trying to sneak up on a woman and not responding when I asked who was there." She glared at me, tucking it away into a sheath. She rested a hand on Nova's side, and the wolf shook her head, almost as though she were laughing. "What is it with guys wanting to follow me in the woods, anyway?"

My skin prickled at the notion of being categorized alongside Markus in any capacity. Brushing it aside, I pointed north. "Bianca mentioned in passing that you were scoping out rock climbing locations and that you were looking for the waterfall. I thought I'd join you."

"Does she report everything we talk about?" She frowned, her mouth turning down.

I lifted a shoulder, tilting my head to that side. "She would if I asked her."

"And you don't?"

I shook my head. "No. Why should I? You're entitled to privacy." Danni's features softened, and she released a small laugh, clearly relieved that I wasn't spying on her. I wondered how she'd feel if she knew I occasionally scanned the security cameras for her. Not to spy. Just to know where she was. That she was okay. That *the boy* hadn't stepped out of line again. "It was a simple question," I explained. "I saw Bianca in passing and asked her where you were. She said you were hiking to the falls. I wanted to join you."

"You mean you wanted to play games and act all mysterious," she said, pressing her lips into a smile.

"Perhaps." I shrugged, taking a step closer to her. Her scent was everywhere, permeating the air surrounding us. It was truly intoxicating. I wondered if she knew the effect she had on others . . . on me. "Maybe I just wanted you alone where no one could hear us."

Her cheeks flushed, and she stumbled over her words. "Why—I mean, what—um, what does that . . ."

"We have a lot to talk about. And you've been avoiding me."

And I don't like it.

Her mouth formed into an 'O' shape, though no sound came out. "I, um . . . I've just had a lot on my mind." She stepped aside and began walking on the trail toward the waterfall.

"That much is obvious." I wasn't going to let that be the end of our conversation. I reclaimed my place beside her, then pointed to our left. "Turn here. It's a shortcut."

She narrowed her eyes. "How did you get here so fast?"

"Vampire. I'm faster than you," I said lightly. She twisted her lips, considering me. "I also drove," I added, gesturing in the general direction where I'd parked Ysa's truck on the 4x4 trail leading here.

"Cheater," she muttered, and I laughed.

The sound of the roaring falls filtered through the trees. Nova's ears perked up, and she went ahead at a trot. I glanced at Dannika from my periphery, gauging her response to the beauty all around us as we exited the forest and came to the clearing.

Her eyes widened. A smile crept up her face, and she took in a deep breath, closing her eyes while she soaked in the late afternoon sun peeking through the clouds. It shimmered on the water, and the cool mist from the falls' spray filled the air.

When she opened her eyes, she turned to me. "What?" she asked, a hint of pink tinging her cheeks.

"Nothing. Just admiring the scenery." I tilted my head toward the body of water before us. "Are you hungry?"

Her brows furrowed, and she looked in the direction I was signaling to. She spotted the setup waiting on the shore. A large blanket was sprawled out, held down by larger rocks so the wind wouldn't pick up the corners. An indistinct backpack sat on top.

Walking toward it, I moved to sit, waving for her to come over. Speechless, she did, dropping her hiking satchel beside her. After a moment of taking it all in, she finally spoke. "What is all this?"

"Lunch." Grabbing the bag, I opened up, taking out

different items for her to choose from. "I thought it would be nice for us to have a date. Alone. Away from the estate."

"I don't know what to say," she whispered. "A date seems . . ."

"Like something two mates would be expected to do?" I finished for her, raising my eyebrows.

I pulled a raw steak from the backpack and unwrapped it. Holding it out, I offered it to Nova. "You're welcome to hunt these woods. There's excellent prey, especially being close to a water source. But if you'd rather not, I did bring something for you too."

Nova got up, sniffed the meat and then wrapped her jaws around it. She walked over by the water, lying down and devouring her snack. Dannika watched the exchange, and her eyes glazed over for the briefest of moments before they cleared.

"I just didn't expect it. That's all," she said, finally.

"Relax," I said, turning my attention to her. "It's just food. Nothing terrible. No ulterior motive, for the most part. This doesn't have to be awkward."

She barked a laugh, and Nova turned her head in the other direction, finding the trees suddenly fascinating as she ignored us.

"Clearly, you don't know me very well. Everything I do is awkward." She reached for a sandwich, unwrapping it and taking a bite.

"You've deliberately avoided me for the last week,"

I pointed out. "That makes it rather difficult to get to know you very well. What's a guy got to do to get your attention, Danni?"

She coughed, hitting her chest with her hand. Around a mouthful of food, she said, "Guys don't generally want my attention. I've never considered it."

I shook my head. "I find that hard to believe."

She huffed a laugh, but it wasn't genuine. "I was the social pariah in Fire and Fluorite. It's okay. I'm not trashing myself here. Trust me when I say that I am not wanted in most situations." Nova exhaled loudly through her snout, seemingly annoyed by the truth of that statement. She stood up, shaking her body before heading into the woods. Dannika turned, watching her exit.

"I want you," I said. She jerked her head in my direction. Clearing my throat, I added, "Here. I want you *here*."

She tried to suppress a smile. "Now that you have me *here*, what else do you want?"

"Now that is a loaded question," I said, taking a flask out of a side pocket. Untwisting the cap, I wrapped my lips around the opening and tilted my head back, taking a swig. I considered describing in detail what I wanted to do with her, but it wouldn't have the effect I'd imagined.

She hummed in response, taking a sip of water from the canteen. "Well, seeing as you've trapped me in the forest, and as you said, no one will hear us . . ." She left her statement open-ended. The thoughts running through my head went wild. I wanted to fuck her raw. Lick the sweet juices that would coat her thighs after I'd make her scream over and over . . .

"Finish your thought," I commanded lightly, clearing my throat of the dry spot that had developed in it and completely bypassing the fact that she was flirting with me in return. I'd let her decide how far we would push this.

"Why do you *think* I've been avoiding you?" she asked, the question falling from hesitant lips.

"I assumed it had something to do with dinner last week. If I said something that offended you—"

"You didn't. Dinner was lovely," she said, interrupting. "I meant it when I said I enjoy that time with you."

"You haven't been yourself since then. Unless something happened with Markus . . ."

She leaned back on her elbows, legs stretched out in front of her, crossing her ankles. She was the picture of ease, if not for how her jaw tightened. "What do you think happened with Markus?"

"Did something?" My voice had gone flat. The forest stilled, as if it sensed the edge I stood on. Had things changed? Did she want to be his mate now? Was Ysabeau right that she could cave, accepting the bond given enough time with him?

I didn't like the idea of it. Turns out, faced with the reality, I liked it even less.

She busted out laughing, her head falling back and her hair pooling on the blanket. "No! Why would you even think that?"

I shifted my position, uncrossing my legs and leaning back on my hands. "The mate bond is strong. I assumed you saved him because you don't want to let him go. Rejection or not, the bond hasn't been fully broken. I thought some part of it might be reaching you."

"No. Absolutely not. I know some women find a connection to their bullies, bond or no bond. But I'm not one of them." Her tone was harsh and firm. "The possibility that I could've wanted to be with him bothers you, doesn't it?"

Relief spread through me. It had disturbed me deeply when I'd considered the possibility she had felt something for him. "I wasn't keen on it, no."

Understatement of the century.

"Feeling a bit of jealousy for your pretend mate?" she joked.

"Yes, actually," I admitted. Her brows shot up in surprise. "I won't lie. I feel a certain amount of possessiveness around you. Especially when it comes to him."

She blinked a few times, and her ears reddened, and she looked at her feet while she spoke. "Markus is nothing more than a pain in my ass. The very minimal time I've spent with him since has been uneventful. He's trying a hand at different trades, but we don't talk for long. The most time I've spent with him was that day you saw us in the woods. He'd just shown up. I was out there clearing my head. After you introduced me to the High Court, I was drowning. I still am, in a sense. What am I even supposed to do as a queen? That isn't something I was prepared for." She sat up, picking up a pebble and tossing it.

"What do you want to do as my queen?"

"That's how this works?" She looked at me incredulously. "If I said I wanted to do nothing and be fed grapes while I kicked my feet up on a pillow, that's what I'd get?"

"Not quite, but it's a nice suggestion." I tilted my head. "Well, maybe we can do that on Tuesdays," I added as an afterthought.

She smacked my arm playfully. "Be serious. I make my appearances with you, and people assume we're mates and that's all fine and whatnot, but what do I do beyond that?"

"Find your purpose."

"Huh?" Her nose wrinkled.

I chuckled. "Find a purpose. Something you find meaningful, not something I tell you to do. Yes, you make appearances. Yes, we are both present for the hearings in Court. Blood and Beryl is a large House, as

I am sure you've learned with Bianca. Just like any other House, there are those who suffer. Those who need our help."

Lowering her head, she breathed a heavy sigh. "I don't want to do good things for people just for show." She shook her head, locks of hair falling into her face. "I want something *real*." Her emphasis on the word told me a bit about where she was mentally.

"You misunderstand. It's not for show. Whom you choose to involve is up to you. This isn't for celebrity. It's to better the lives of our people."

She stared blankly for a moment, breathing the words, "*our people*."

"They'll be yours, too, Danni. You'll be queen. You already are, from a rank and mate standpoint."

"And this—" She gestured between us. "How will we explain that away? Your court will expect an heir. A baby, Elias." She stared at me, eyes wide. "What am I supposed to do with that?"

I brought the flask up, taking another drink before answering. "I don't suppose you noticed a lot of kids around here. It's hard for vampires to conceive them. Takes a long time. Centuries even. Some never have any. They're quite cherished when we do have them. That's why they're tucked away for safekeeping. Not until they reach maturity do they achieve immortality."

She nodded in understanding. "That explains the

animal crackers I saw in the pantry when I was raiding it last night. I can't even begin to imagine where you got those. Now I feel bad because I've been taking snacks from the kids."

I frowned. "Those are mine. I was wondering who was stealing them."

She grinned an awkward smile, looking away. "Oops."

"Have at it. Just leave me some." I laughed, waving it off. "We have more species than vampires in Blood and Beryl, so naturally, they need to eat as well. But yes, the children only eat regular food until they have their first feed."

"Except your cookie stash, apparently," she said, smirking.

"Anything except that."

She took a deep breath, the smile slowly falling from her face. "My point still stands, Elias. The Court, your people—our people—they're going to have the expectation that eventually you'll have an heir."

"Are you suggesting we try for one?" I asked, raising a single eyebrow.

"What?" she spluttered, shaking her head. "I—no. I mean, I don't know how to handle this. When I agreed to all of this, my only thought was survival. I never really thought about babies until Bianca said it. It's all the Alpha Supreme ever focused on in Fire and Fluorite, so naturally, it's something that makes sense that all Houses would think about it. And Blood and Beryl would be no different. It just brings up a rather large gap in our relationship." She paused, looking up at the sky. A moment later, she snapped her head in my direction. "Wait, you've already thought about this, haven't you?"

"Ysa brought it up to me," I answered, looking down at my fingernails and picking at them. "I know what we have here is . . . let's call it *unconventional*, but I'm not opposed to trying for one in some future state." Again, such a mild, almost borderline lie. If I told her the extent to which I thought about her, though . . .

"Wait, what?"

"We're going to be mated to each other in name, and that means we can't take other partners. There are perks to the arrangement if we wanted to have them."

She stared at me blankly for a moment, her mouth hanging open. "That's . . . a big reversal from not wanting to complicate things. You said you wanted a business arrangement."

"It's a potential risk I'm willing to take," I said, testing the waters further.

"Why now?" she demanded. "We barely know each other," she whispered. She sounded like she was defending her stance, but she didn't have the full weight behind her words. I'd heard her stand up for what she believed in. This? This was different.

There was something there too. I wasn't misreading it.

"Because you intrigue me. I like being with you."

She looked away, almost disappointed. "This isn't *real*. You said it yourself." Again with that word. *Real*. She sighed deeply, then reached for my flask that sat on the blanket between us. "If we're having this conversation, I need a swig of that."

"I wouldn't do that," I said, stretching my arm out to take it back from her.

"Why not? I drink," she stated defensively, bringing it to her mouth.

"Unless you've just developed a penchant for blood and whiskey, I very much doubt you drink this." I ran my tongue over the point of my fang right as her lips wrapped around the opening.

"Oh, shit," she said quickly, trying to move it away from her face as fast as possible. She handed it back to me. "Why didn't you say anything?"

"What do you mean?" I asked, holding the flask up. "I just did."

"A little late," she said, digging through the backpack and looking for another flask. When she found one, she held it up and cocked her head, as if asking if this one was blood-free. I dipped my chin, and she unscrewed the lid, knocking a mouthful back before she swallowed, following it up with a cough. She shook her head, clearing away the burn.

"Maybe this is a conversation for another time." Her discomfort proved I was on the verge of saying the wrong thing, and she gave me a tight smile in return. I cleared my throat, changing course. "Find your purpose within Blood and Beryl, Danni. Focus on taking that role. I have no doubts you'll do well."

Leaning forward, she put her head in her hands, running her fingers through her silvery-white strands. "That brings up another thing," she said, exasperation filling her tone. She stood, walking to the shore at the water's edge. Picking up a rock, she threw it into the lake, attempting to skip it. "When does that officially happen? Do I just start calling myself 'Queen' one day in front of the High Court? Is there like a . . . ceremony? How is that done?"

I got up off the blanket, wiping my hands on my jeans, and headed to stand beside her. "Publicly."

"Well, I assumed so—"

"No, I mean the consummation is public." I picked up a stone, examining the shape of it.

Color drained from her skin. "I—We can't . . . Are you serious?"

"Not in the slightest." I angled my stance, flicking my wrist as I flung the stone. It skipped over the water's surface, hopping from one spot to the next. Turning to her, I continued. "But using humor to deflect seems to be helpful when you get yourself worked up over something."

She narrowed her eyes at me, but her lips curved into a smile.

I winked at her.

She pointed at me in jest, reaching down to grab another rock. "So what is it, if not a public sexfest?"

I snorted. "It's similar to the proposal in the High Court."

"Which you didn't warn me about," she chided. She turned her wrist at a bad angle, throwing the rock. Instead of skipping across the water, the stone plopped in with an audible splash, then sunk.

"I wanted to see how you'd react." Picking up another stone, I placed it in her hand, silently wrapping her index finger and thumb around it. "Here," I said, standing behind her, pressing my chest against her back, curving my arm down the length of hers until my hand was on top.

She stilled. The scent of orange and peppermint filled my senses. It was intense, pushing my thoughts into a new realm. I tilted my head toward her, whispering as my lips grazed her earlobe. "We say some words, you're crowned queen, we make some promises, the day moves on."

I mimicked the slow-motion movement of the toss, our bodies shifting as I imitated the side throw. Her breath stuttered at the friction. "That doesn't sound so bad." She swallowed thickly. "That's all?"

"If we want it to be," I whispered.

Dannika dropped the rock, turning around in my arms to face me, her arms caged between us, palms flat on my chest. "What else would 'we' want?" Her words were breathy, her heart audibly thundering.

So much.

The sound of a wounded animal screaming tore through the air, shredding the moment between us. Nova caught a rabbit on the edge of the clearing, shaking her head violently to silence its cries and end its suffering.

Dannika stumbled back, breaking free of the embrace. Disappointment and longing filled me instantly. We stared at each other, unable to find words, no clear direction for what needed to come next.

Clearing her throat, she shoved her hands in her pockets and started walking at the water's edge as she kept her eyes focused on the falls.

"Um, there's something else I need to tell you," she started, continuing to walk farther away from me. "It's made slightly more awkward considering the context of, uh—our earlier conversation."

I crossed my arms, walking slowly along the shore-line. "I'm intrigued."

"It involves Markus."

"I'm less intrigued."

She glared at me from the side, then continued.

"Once shifters have found their mates . . . females go into heat."

I stopped walking. I didn't like where she was going with this. "Do you have to be bonded for that to occur?"

She huffed a humorless laugh. "Nope."

"What is it that you want from me in this scenario? If it's for me to allow *anything* to happen between you and Markus, the answer is *no*."

I would kill him first. I didn't care that she kept saving him.

Her nose wrinkled in disgust. "Ew, no. Beyond the ick factor, it would be a reversal of my rejection if I had sex with him, even if being in heat is what causes it. But the whole thing is out of my control. I need to be locked away. If Markus hasn't rejected me, he needs to be locked far away from me. He won't be able to stop himself. And . . ." She paused, closing her eyes and inhaling deeply. "And I won't be able to resist it."

I sighed. Blood and Beryl had shifters too. If a female went into heat, we knew all about it. But never once had I been witness to one that was rejecting her mate. This wasn't my first experience with she-wolves in heat, but it was the first one I cared about. "Can you feel how far off yours is yet?"

"I'm not sure, but I know it's supposed to happen soon. A few days, maybe. A week at most." Looking down at her boot, she kicked at the rocks. "I can't believe it's gotten this far, but I don't know what else to do or who to ask for help. It helps we both want Markus to go away and for *our* mate bond to be perceived as real. You're the only one I can talk to about this. The only one I can trust. I just want you to make sure I'm okay. Stay with me."

"Of course," I started, but she cut me off.

"There's more." She winced, clenching her teeth. "I might be, um . . . needy. I'm not sure how far it goes outside of the mate bond. It might make me say things or *ask* for things I wouldn't otherwise." She turned, facing me as I came to stand by her side.

"Oh," I whispered, nodding in understanding. Reaching down, I took her hand in mine, twining my fingers through hers. I brought our hands to my mouth, pressing a soft kiss on top of hers. "I'll keep you safe, if that's all that you want from me."

"I believe you," she said, echoing the same words I'd said to her many times.

There we were again, face-to-face, a moment suspended between us. The orange hues of the setting sun filtered through the high treetops, settling on her skin and giving her a warm glow.

Nova trotted by, huffing as she headed toward the trail, stopping at the tree line. Dannika smiled, preparing to follow her wolf.

"I can drive you back," I offered, keeping stride beside her and jutting my thumb toward the truck. It didn't escape me that she hadn't let go of my hand, and that there was no one here to show off to. "Ysa and I switched vehicles so Nova can fit anytime we want to go somewhere."

"That's thoughtful, but I prefer the walk, actually," she responded, shaking her head lightly. "Nature feels like home to me. I figured out long ago when things become too much, if I just find my place outside, I can clear my head. Now that I'm here, it helps me find what's real again."

As we came to the trail where Nova waited, Dannika turned but didn't say anything. I didn't say anything.

Instead, I listened to her breathing change. The flutter of the pulse in her neck. I felt the slickness of her palm against mine. The moment was frozen in time.

I shouldn't...

The moment her eyes flicked down to my lips and her heartbeat picked up, I came undone. There was no stopping me.

My lips crashed into hers, and she gasped. I pulled back, and she stared at me for a brief moment before she fisted my shirt, pulling me back to her. I angled my head, deepening the kiss as I explored her mouth with my tongue. Grabbing her by the back of the thighs, I hoisted her up. Strong legs wrapped around my waist while her arms curled around my neck. Moving swiftly, I strode forward. Her back hit a tree with a thud, but we never lost momentum.

Her hot center pressed against my cock, and I pushed back into her in return. She let out a growl that was distinctly animalistic and drove me wild. I broke away, grazing my mouth down her neck, feeling the beat of her heart beneath my tongue. She tilted her head, breathing heavily as I kissed and nibbled up the column of her throat.

Dannika moaned, and I found her mouth again, covering it with my own. I skimmed up her thigh and found the hem of her shirt before reaching my hand underneath. She inhaled sharply, and the heat of her skin spread beneath my palms as I traveled up the curve of her waist, over her ribs. Slowly, I ran my thumb over the soft skin beneath her bra line.

Euphoria melted away as she hummed against me, then pulled my head away from hers. "We can't do this," she whispered, her chest heaving with ragged breaths. "This complicates things."

"I wanted to give you something that was *real*. No audience. No motive," I said. Her pulse skipped a beat at my answer. I tilted my head forward, touching it to hers, then closed my eyes as I tried to suppress what my body wanted. Trying to shut down what my mind was saying. "And I'm not sorry."

CHAPTER 15

DANNIKA

Chalk dusted my fingertips.

White smudged my skin in different spots as I brushed my open palms over my face, pushing my hair back from my eyes.

Birds sang in the trees while Nova lay on the bank, sunbathing while watching me with a contented half smile on her face. The open cliff face loomed before me. Instead of fear, adrenaline pumped through my veins at the sight.

This was what I needed.

A nice, quiet day where I dangled over the edge of a massive waterfall that had the potential to break every bone in my body if I fell.

Let it be known that I wasn't a masochist. Nor did I have a death wish. I was just . . . complicated.

When life got hard and I struggled to cope, I'd

climb until my muscles nearly gave out. Something about fear and the thrill made it easier to deal with the day to day. Hanging off the end of a mountain, holding on for dear life. It was a good way of reminding me that no matter how big we think our problems to be, we were all so insignificant in the grand scheme of things. These issues, no matter how big they may have felt, would pass.

Which was why I was standing at the bottom of the waterfall, fingers dusted in white. Ysabeau had gotten me a climbing harness when I asked for one. I didn't use it to knot rope through, only because of the deep waters at the bottom of the falls. Instead, I secured a chalk bag to the side after tying the new climbing shoes. The toes pinched a bit from their newness, but a dozen or so climbs would break them in nicely.

I reached for the uneven rock face, mentally charting my path up by studying nooks and crannies. Water sprayed, making my clothes slightly damp and chilled in the late morning breeze.

My chest squeezed as I let out a breath I'd been holding since my feet had left the ground, the hard material tips of my toes finding purchase in a nice crack that angled toward the falls.

I climbed.

Time fell away, broken down into heaved breaths and skittering pebbles as I ascended the side of the waterfall. My skin was slicked with sweat. It poured down my temple and into my eyes. I wiped it away with the back of my hand and then reached for my chalk bag, reapplying it to my hands.

I didn't think about our moment against the tree last night.

I wasn't replaying every word and touch and kiss, pressing rewind over and over.

I couldn't think about Elias.

About . . . feelings. Emotions. My traitorous heart that was listening to my body instead of logic and reasoning.

Thank the gods I always had my mind.

I was a solid halfway up when Nova's low growl made me stiffen. I twisted, my hands grasping at the narrow crevice I was balancing on. The rock I was perched on cracked.

Oh, shit.

I went airborne. Leaning into the fall, I scrunched my knees to my chest and wrapped my arms around them. My back hit the water. Icy cold swallowed me whole, drenching me from head to toe. When my body stalled in its descent, I uncoiled and started for the surface. A figure appeared mid-kick, swimming crazy fast toward me.

Panic acted like a hand crushing my chest. A physical pain rattled me, and I quickened my feet—aiming for the surface.

When I reached it, I gasped, inhaling a lungful of air before swimming to the side and breaking into a swim-sprint for the shore. The figure swerved, trying to intercept me. As they reached my side, Nova bounded into the water. I reached for the knife strapped to a holster at the small of my back.

Pulling it out in one smooth motion, I brandished the blade while treading water.

The swimmer stopped and lifted their head.

"Markus?" I groaned, lowering the knife. "What the hell, dude?" I yelled, putting it back in its sheath.

"You fell," he spluttered. Water sluiced down his face, hair sticking to his skin. "I was coming to . . ." He trailed off, realizing his error before I said it. The look on my face must have given it away.

"Rescue me?"

"No—I—well—" He sighed. "Yeah, basically."

I rolled my eyes, waving Nova, who was up to her hind quarters in water, back to shore. "I've been rock climbing since I was five."

And with that, I swam to shore. Water soaked what little clothes I wore. I cursed at the ruined chalk in my bag. At least chalk was easy to replace. It was the chance I took, climbing over an open body of water without a lead.

"You fell like sixty feet," he said defensively.

"Over water," I replied. "I'm a shifter. I may not be

able to turn, but give me a little credit here. I'm not *that* fragile."

Markus blew out a frustrated breath. "Fine. I'm sorry for assuming you needed saving."

I paused, looking over at him. "Thank you." He blinked, waiting for me to add a sarcastic remark. When I didn't, his shoulders relaxed.

"Does it really bother you that much that I want to help you?"

"Yes." I trudged up the shore, wringing my braid out. "Because it implies that I can't do it. That I'm weaker. Lesser. It's not that you want to help me. You said it yourself: You want to *save* me. To be the hero. I don't need a hero or saving."

Markus swore under his breath. "Everything is a fight between us."

"One might say we're not compatible," I replied. Nova shook herself, flinging droplets of water on Markus as he emerged from the pool. He gave her a withering stare, lips pressed together. I chuckled under my breath. The cool air nipped my skin.

Markus sighed. "I suppose I was asking for that."

I chuckled again. "To what do I owe the pleasure today?"

"The heat is coming."

I stilled; my muscles went taut. "If you try to force me during it—"

"No." Markus shook his head. "Gods. I'm not ready

to let you go . . . but I don't want to force you. I know you don't want it yet. But that doesn't stop it from happening. I can smell it on you. It's like—" I turned to stare at him, and his pupils dilated. My feet reacted on their own, backing away. He shook his head to clear it. "I need to be confined. Locked up. As far away from you as possible by tomorrow night."

"I don't think it'll start tomorrow," I said quietly. Nova came to stand between us.

"The heat lasts longer than a couple of days. It just peaks for forty-eight hours. By tomorrow night, I don't think I'll be able to control myself." The muscle in his cheek tightened as he looked away. "You see me as a bully—I *will not* be a rapist as well. I've already hurt you too much."

I dipped my chin, accepting his acknowledgement. "I'll speak to Elias. I'm sure Ysabeau will take care of it quickly."

"Good." He looked back toward the trail, stalling. I waited, letting the silence grow awkward, then uncomfortable. "During your heat. . ." I lifted an eyebrow, waiting for him to ask. "Will you be *with* anyone?"

"You want to know if I'll fuck Elias."

It was crass, more than I was capable of most of the time. Markus just brought out the worst, most defensive parts of me.

"Will you?" He stared at me, eyes wide, but a hint

of sadness registered. Regardless of what I told him, he'd already made his mind up about what my "plans" were.

I shook my head, looking away. "Don't ask questions you don't want the answer to."

Markus growled. "I'm just trying to—"

"What?" I snapped, turning back to him. "You're just trying to what?"

He swallowed hard. "Do what you need to do, Danni. I know you don't want me, and as much as I want to kill him for touching you . . . I don't want you in pain."

My lips parted.

For the first time in my life, and possibly his, Markus had grown a conscience.

"You too," I said slowly. Breaking his gaze, I turned toward the trail to begin my hike back. Nova followed suit. I paused most of the way there and glanced back. He was staring at the ground. The look on his face was familiar. It reflected the way I'd felt the night my life had been taken from me. Stolen. The world had been ripped out from under my feet.

Even if Markus was giving me permission to have sex with my own partner—pretend or not—didn't matter to me. It was a huge step for him. It was selfless. While I would never accept him as my mate, I could acknowledge the difficulty he'd gone through to tell me that.

"Thank you, Markus," I said quietly. His head snapped up, his eyes vulnerable. I smiled sadly at him. The journey he was beginning . . . It wasn't an easy one. I didn't know if he'd make it to the other side or fall off on the way. But this—this was a good start.

CHAPTER 16

ELIAS

I stood at the window of my main office, looking out over the main property, hands on my hips, lost in thought. I should have been focused on the correspondence that had arrived from the House of Gold and Garnet. King Vesperus and I had working plans. A strategy in place.

Mathis needed to be dealt with. Dethroned. Eliminated.

I didn't care how.

But to unseat or assassinate him without retaliation from the other Houses required solid proof of his crimes, and that was hard to come by. Mathis covered his tracks well. Finding a crack in his armor required stealth, allies, and focus.

I lacked the latter.

Instead, I read the words ten times over, but they didn't register. Flashes of Dannika appeared in my mind. Up against a tree, her legs around my waist. Stealing glances at dinner when we were with other members of the High Court. The way her lips curved into a sly smile when I caught her watching me. We didn't talk about the kiss. She was in bed asleep every night before I got back to our room.

"Elias," Ysabeau said, cutting into my thoughts. We'd been discussing tactics for an hour, but I couldn't concentrate. My mind was somewhere else.

"Yeah," I answered, my tone flat. "I'll take a look at it. Get you my response to send out."

"Pay attention." She snapped her fingers, and I shot her a look. She pointed to my desk, then held up a phone.

The screen was lit up. Shit.

I picked it up, pressing the green button to answer. "Vesperus," I said by way of answering.

"Elias." The King of Gold and Garnet's gravelly voice filtered through the line. "I assume you've gone over the information I sent?"

"Yeah, I was just looking through it here." I sat at my desk, filtering through the papers. Ysa glared at me, pursing her lips. She gestured harshly to its location, irritation leaking through the motions.

"Do you know who the mole is?" Vesperus asked.

My mouth fell open, and I stared at Ysabeau. The deadpan look I got in return spoke volumes. She was immensely frustrated with me.

I squeezed my eyes shut. *Dammit.* I'd lost focus completely. A leak in our ranks was a problem, one that needed to be dealt with swiftly. Everything could unravel, and I hadn't put this much time and energy into destroying Mathis to let it all go to waste. "I hadn't gotten to that part yet," I answered, clenching my jaw. I opened my eyes, taking time to scan the details of what he had sent me. I cursed under my breath. "Is your intel reliable?"

"Rock solid," he answered from the other end of the line. If he was irritated with me, it was impossible to know. "Any ideas?"

"None off the top of my head." I pinched the bridge of my nose. "Those in the know are few and far between. It won't take long to weed them out." *And rip them out by the roots.*

"Send me what you have as soon as you find out. Read through the reports. We don't know how long he's been a mole, but plan for damage control."

"Count on it," I assured him, dipping my head to my second. "Ysabeau has a knack for sniffing out bad apples."

She smirked in return.

"Find them fast, Elias. You know what this could

do to us. Empress Asbesta has been hands-off enough that she'd find a way to get around any charges from the other Houses. The same is not true for our situations," he pointed out. I knew all too well what was at stake. I hummed my confirmation in response. "You sent word you had something new to discuss with me." Vesperus left his statement hanging as a question.

I nodded. "Word from the Portal Guard is that no one unregistered has come through any portal, but there's something new in the air. A surge of power that wasn't there before. I can sense it increasing as of late. Have you felt it?" A greater part of me hoped he answered *no*.

"Yes," he responded, and he left it at that.

I cursed silently. "I've never encountered it before."

"I haven't either. Not until now."

I dropped into my chair, leaning to the side and rubbing my temples. "Fantastic."

"I'm already looking into it," Vesperus said. "It might reach farther than we know. It would be foolish to assume we're the only ones aware of it."

The unspoken words were there. We needed to find the source before another House did.

Especially Fire and Fluorite.

"I'll find the leak. You find the cause of this energy source."

"Agreed, old friend."

The call disconnected, and I looked at Ysa.

"I want the High Court assembled by the end of the day. I want the rat found *now*." My voice rattled the windows, and I slammed my hand on the desk.

Her brows furrowed. "You don't think it was one of them, do you?"

"They are the only ones who know, Ysabeau. I don't involve anyone else except you." She kept her posture in place, not moving her face at all. "And I know it's not you."

"I wasn't concerned that you thought it was." She shrugged. "I'd be dead already if that were the case." She knew me well. "I'm just not sure who would betray you in the High Court. Treason at that level is . . ."

"Not unheard of," I finished for her. And it wasn't, though I was somewhat surprised. Everyone I had appointed held the same common goals, and the same disdain for Mathis. At least I thought they did.

She nodded, pressing her lips together in a firm line. "There's one more thing . . ." she said, trailing off.

I swiped my hand over one eye to relieve the pressure building. I waved my hand at her, telling her to carry on. "It can't be much worse than this."

She blew her cheeks out in such a long breath that I looked up. "I spoke to your mother," she started. Her hesitation to elaborate was concerning, and the antici-pation of what was coming sent a cold rush through my body. "About the flowers."

My mood darkened further. "And?"

Ysabeau looked away. "Every year on the anniver-sary of Claudette's death, Mathis sends your mother flowers." Her voice was soft, filled with a combination of hesitation and sorrow.

I wished I could say it was anger that filled my core and traveled through my veins. It wasn't. It was so much more than that. It was a need for violence. An overwhelming desire to end his existence in a slow, brutal, and cruel way. Hatred in its purest form.

"I need to be alone," I growled, my jaw clenching so tight it threatened to crack my teeth. When Ysa opened her mouth to speak, I shook my head once. She understood, dipping her chin and leaving my office.

After she left, I stewed. Seething. Plotting his death.

When I found the traitor, they'd get the brunt of my wrath for daring to defy everything I had carefully built for a quarter of a century.

Members of the High Court filtered in. I sat on my throne, watching them, all oblivious and unknowing about the purpose of our meeting. Katie and Bianca chatted, sharing jovial laughs between them. Uriah shuffled along quietly, appearing to be lost in thought. Alaysia walked in slowly, looking down at a clipboard and scratching notes. Marisa ushered in with my step-nephew, Kieran, swiftly and discreetly handing something small over to him that he pocketed wordlessly. A flash of anger struck me. I narrowed my eyes, wondering instantly what it was she was keeping secret. And worse, what my nephew had to do with it. My asshole brother had raised him as a child, but he'd attached himself to me early on. After all these years, would he dare betray me?

They'd be the first to answer my questions.

Drumming my fingers on the arm of my chair, I waited. Impatient. Wrath eating at me slowly.

None of them gave away any signs of worry or discomfort. None of them acted like they were hiding anything. That made it so much worse. How long had they been deceiving me?

Ysabeau came in, Dannika by her side, Nova leading both of them. Dannika met my eyes, smiling, but the corners of her lips fell when she saw me. Concern crossed her features as a tiny crease formed between her brows, and she tilted her head slightly. I shook my head in a single, tight movement.

She quietly took the step up the dais and sat beside me. Her arms rested on the chair, and her hand flinched as though she were going to move it, then she changed her mind and thought better of it. Turning to look at her, I struggled with words. Rage had taken over every emotion I had, but she knew nothing of what it meant. Instead of finding a way to speak to her, I stared.

Whatever our silent exchange meant to her, she reached over and took my hand in hers, lacing her fingers through mine, gently squeezing.

Warmth I couldn't explain spread up my arm, sending a calmness to tame the raging fire inside me. Her touch tempered my anger. That was . . . new.

"There's been a development, and that's why you've been called today," Ysa said, addressing the room after everyone had settled in their seats.

I snapped my head to attention, releasing Danni's hand and standing up. I didn't plan on wasting time.

"Fuck the formalities," I said, projecting my voice across the room. "Each vampire present is privy to knowledge that no one else is. Someone has been feeding information to our enemies, and I'm finding out right now who it is."

Jaws dropped, and audible gasps filled the room. Members of the High Court looked at each other, wide-eyed shock crossing their features.

I stormed off the dais, reaching my nephew in record time. Lifting Kieran out of his chair, I shoved my hand into his pocket. He didn't respond, throwing his hands up slowly in surrender while I searched, my fingers touching the parchment. I knew he wasn't stupid enough to fight me, and testing my patience while I was in this state was unwise.

"Elias," Marisa shouted, backing up from her chair. "What are you doing?"

Paper in hand, I ripped it open, reading silently.

· *Strawberries.*

· *Rock climbing—acquire additional equipment.*

· *Potatoes prepared any way.*

· *Sunrises.*

· *Coffee, the strong kind.*

· *Knives—do we need a private space for throwing? Provide variety, including sheaths.*

· *Size 8 boots, <u>no</u> leather laces.*

· *Also, don't be an asshole.*

My brows furrowed, and I held it up, looking directly at Marisa. "What is this?"

"It's—" Her eyes shot between Dannika's throne, Kieran, and me. Lowering her voice, she added, "It's a list of our future queen's preferences, per Bianca. We were trying to make her feel at home here. Kieran was handling some details and"—she cleared her throat—"I included a reminder for him to use manners when interacting with her."

I took a step back, completely thrown off my guard. Danni flushed, struggling between averting her eyes and remaining focused.

Marisa gestured for me to settle, putting her palms

down midair and pushing them toward the ground. "Elias, please. Tell us what is going on," she said, keeping her voice low and even. "I can't help you if you don't explain what you need."

I ran my hands through my hair as I turned away from Marisa and Kieran. I reclaimed my place on the dais in front of the thrones, but I didn't sit down. I cast my gaze out amongst my Court, wondering who had betrayed their House . . . and their king.

"I've just been informed by one of our allies that critical information was leaked. The source is undeniable." I put my hands on my hips, digging my fingers in to keep myself grounded. "The knowledge within this court has been confidential, and no others have been involved in the strategies in place against Mathis." I shifted my gaze around the room, looking at each of them as I spoke. "One of you has shared details. One of you is a traitor." The final words spilled out in a venomous tone.

Jaws slackened and heads turned as each examined the vampire sitting next to them. I watched the exchange with interest. From my periphery, I saw Ysa and Dannika doing the same. Nova sat, nose bobbing in the air, as though she were tempting to sniff out the culprit.

But no one spoke.

"Uncle," Kieran began, "may I ask if what was passed on will ruin what we have set in place?"

I shook my head. "No, but we also don't know how long he'd been getting information from our side."

Alaysia held her hand up, looking to speak next. "And the messenger?"

"Dead."

Marisa twisted her lips. "Why on earth would they kill him before getting more information out of him?"

"They didn't," Ysa interjected, speaking loudly. "When Vesperus's guard came, he killed himself first. Potion."

A collective grumble passed through the room.

"It doesn't answer my question. Who has betrayed this House?"

Uriah inspected his nails. "We've been here for decades, Elias. And not a word has ever been passed beyond these walls. We have nothing to gain from that." Looking up, he flicked his eyes to Danni, then back to me. Instant fire coursed through my veins. "Perhaps the newest addition to our court speaks to her old House more than she admits. Traitors run deep in Fire and Fluorite."

Nova and I moved at the same time, and I beat her there by a mere second. Gripping Uriah around the neck, my nails extended, piercing into his skin. I held him up, his feet dangling off the ground. The wolf pulled her lips back, baring her teeth as she growled, the rumbling coming from deep in her chest.

"Speak of her that way again, and I will rip your throat out," I snarled through clenched teeth.

"Put him down," Danni said quietly. I turned as she stood up, stepping off the dais and coming to my side. She stroked Nova's fur and placed a hand on my arm while she pleaded with her eyes. The same warmth spread through my limbs, tingling at my fingertips.

I dropped Uriah, letting him fall unceremoniously into his seat. Blood dripped down the column of his neck where my nails had torn into his flesh. Dannika had a habit of saving people when they didn't deserve it. "You are too soft," I said.

"Maybe I am," she said, shrugging. "But you're too brash." Gasps filled the room at her brazen statement. No one had ever spoken like that to me. "Uriah is a dick, but he's not wrong to want to question if it's me."

I huffed once, then smirked. "As you wish," I muttered, walking back to my throne.

Uriah attempted to stand, but Danni placed a hand on his shoulder, pushing him back down. "Sit."

Bianca held a hand over her mouth, trying to cover the grin that had crept up her face.

With Nova by her side, Danni towered over Uriah. The wolf's eyes narrowed, and her jowls trembled with anger. "If you have something you want to say to me, speak your mind, but I am *done* with men who think they can treat me as though I am beneath them.

Disrespect me again and I'll let Nova use your arm as a chew toy. You know *nothing* of my past with Fire and Fluorite, or with Mathis. While the details are none of your business, I will tell you one thing: I have no allegiance to that shifter. That House would be better off with him dead."

She turned on her heel, then strode to the throne next to mine. She sat gracefully, her chin held up high and a slight crease between her brows.

Uriah clasped his hands on the table, refusing to make eye contact with anyone.

Bianca leaned toward Katie, sharing a private conversation while everyone was distracted by Uriah's public shaming. They spoke to each other in low tones and harsh whispers, and I watched with intrigue. Bianca's eyes widened, and Katie clasped her hands over her mouth, shaking her head quickly.

"Speak now," I bellowed, and they both jumped at the volume that echoed around us.

Katie's mouth fell open, and she closed it again, trying to find her voice. Bianca put her hand on Katie's arm. "She's taken a new lover," Bianca started.

I shot my gaze to Katie, gripping the arms of my chair, and the wood creaked under the pressure. "And?"

"I didn't tell him anything," she said before explaining more, the words coming out fast and jumbled. "But I . . . I . . ."

"She talks in her sleep sometimes," Bianca finished for her. "It's usually just random. Asking for oranges, the occasional shout for a pool boy with abs. But she's repeated bits and pieces of conversations before. I didn't think anything of it at the time because it wasn't important. Just repeating dinner talk."

"How do you know this?" Marisa asked, glancing between them.

"Because we've had a few flings together," Bianca replied. "Nothing that would have an effect on our duties in the High Court. Just a few threesomes . . . foursomes . . . you know how it is. Falling asleep in a pile of bodies . . ."

Marisa rolled her eyes slowly, resting her forehead in her hands. "This isn't happening," she muttered.

"Name. *Now*," I shouted, standing up.

"Jordan Westpoint," Katie answered, hanging her head in shame. "I swear, I didn't know . . ."

Bianca rubbed her hand over Katie's back, soothing her, but the look of panic on both their faces didn't escape me.

I turned my head to Ysa. "I want him found. Casual. Empty his pockets. Gag him. Whatever it takes to stop him from killing himself like the other rat. Bring him to me when you do. I want to talk to him."

"Elias, I—" Katie started.

"Will be sleeping alone from now on," I said coolly. She shut her mouth and swallowed thickly, nodding in short, quick movements. "If someone so much as breathes a word about this, I will kill you myself—I don't care who you are—and *no one* will stop me. Now get out."

After a suspended moment of continued shock, every member of the High Court silently stood up, shuffling out the double doors with haste. Ysa followed, making eye contact with me, saying nothing. She knew what she needed to do. The door closed in slow motion, leaving me with Danni and Nova.

I scrubbed my hands down my face, letting out a growl of frustration.

The sounds of something shuffling to my side caught my attention. Danni stood up, wiping her palms on her pants and straightening her sweater. "I'll leave you to—"

I stood up quickly, startling her. She took a step back and winced, and I instantly hated the way she reacted. "I'm sorry," I managed, knowing it wasn't enough.

"Don't be. You didn't do anything," she said, fidgeting with her hands.

I stepped toward her, reaching out to grasp her hands in mine. I turned them over, skimming my thumb over the tops. "You flinched because too many times someone has taken their anger out on you. I wasn't going to, but I need to consider your experiences. I'm sorry you thought for even a moment I would harm you."

"I didn't think you would. It's just instinctive, that's all." I cocked an eyebrow at her in disbelief, and she tilted her head toward Nova. "See?"

Nova sat next to the throne, completely unfazed by our conversation and encounter. I huffed a small laugh, a measure of relief filling me. "I understand now. Neither of you saw me as a threat."

She pressed her lips together in a tight smile. "Hope that doesn't damage your ego."

"Quite the opposite," I said with a grin. "I'm actually relieved." I released one hand, stepping into the space between us. Cupping her jaw, I traced a thumb over her bottom lip and leaned in to kiss her.

It was soft. Gentle. I didn't linger. I didn't know if I should.

"What was that for?" she whispered, clearing her throat.

"I don't need a reason," I said in return.

She hummed, twisting her lips and looking toward the door. "I was going to go so you could process what happened, or deal with . . . whatever it is you deal with now. But if you want me to—"

"Stay," I said, my tone firm. "I want you to stay."

"Sure," she said, smiling. As she sat, she wobbled, her balance seeming off. I grabbed her arm to steady her.

"Are you okay?" I asked, searching her body for signs that something was wrong. She closed her eyes, nodding, inhaling deeply and exhaling slowly. After several cycles of breathing, she opened her eyes. "What was that about?"

"The beginning phases of the heat have started." She grimaced, wiping sweat from her brow. "I wanted to tell you. I had some things I wanted to talk about, but then this whole thing happened." She waved her hand around the room.

"What things? Markus?" Concern filled me as I watched her cheeks flush. I needed to know where he was. He needed to be locked up.

"No." She laughed lightly, staring down at her hands while she spoke. "But it would be good to send him away now."

"Are you worried?"

She shook her head, bringing her eyes up to look at me. The depth of her icy-blue irises almost swirled as she concentrated. "You said you'd take care of me. Make sure I was safe," she said. I nodded, humming in agreement. "There might be more . . ."

"You've said as much. I believe the term you used was *needy*." As serious as we were both attempting to be, it was hard to conceal my amusement.

Danni averted her gaze, popping her lips as she said, "Yup."

"And?"

She sighed. "I just wanted to set perimeters around it."

A crease formed between my brows. "What for? I said I would keep you safe. There's no breaking that. I gave you my word."

"The heat will go by faster if I give into it instead of pushing it away." She wrung her hands before placing them under her thighs and sitting on them. "And I'd be lying if I said I didn't want some of it, but I did want to put those hard lines out there before anything happens. I'm going to be in a foggy place, and I am going to ask for things beyond what I say now. That woman, future Danni, she's not me."

"And what does current Danni want?" I asked, keeping my voice low. I knew acting on the impulses would push her through the heat faster, but I wasn't going to propose anything. I wanted her, yes, but I also didn't want her in pain. This kind of arrangement would need to be entirely her idea, no outside influence. Especially not mine.

"Current Danni wants to not feel so awkward saying these things," she muttered, running her hands over her forehead, over her hair, and holding onto the sides of her neck before she let her arms come down.

"I told you I would keep you safe. From Markus, from yourself. That includes me. If you give me a line, I won't cross it," I said, coaxing her. "But you do have to say the words."

She pressed her lips together and groaned, taking her time before she finally spoke again. "No sex. No anal. That's a hard line."

I nodded, shifting my seating position as my length stiffened. My mind immediately went to imagining her writhing in pleasure.

"Fingers, mouth, tongue, I'm good with." She blew out a breath, shaking her shoulders and straightening her body.

"Toys? Cuffs? Bondage?"

Her eyes grew wide. "I hadn't . . . um, I don't know, no, and maybe?"

"Choking, knife play, clamps?"

"Kind of heavy for a first date, don't you think?" she quipped.

"I like to plan ahead," I responded, tapping my temple.

"Hard pass on metal objects. But you should talk to my sister," she said.

"I don't want your sister," I said. She shot me a look, and I grinned, fangs hanging over my lips.

"Oh, and no biting." She winced, an apologetic look crossing her features.

I inclined my head. "That's a given," I said. "But it's always worth stating out loud."

"Do you have any thoughts?" she asked, her brows pinching together.

"About what I'm going to do to you?" I teased.

"Absolutely."

She smacked my arm. "Be serious."

"I *am* being serious. Would it be better or worse for you to know that I find this entertaining?" I propped my elbow up on the armchair, resting my cheek on my fist while I watched her.

She huffed. "I'm not entirely sure at this point. It might be one of the most bizarre conversations I've ever had. And you find it funny."

I shrugged. "Your innocence is showing, and it's honestly adorable."

"I'm not *that* innocent," she argued, annoyance filling her tone. I couldn't help but chuckle, and she sighed. "Okay, I don't have a lot of sexual history to go on here, so it's just weird having such a straightforward conversation about consent when it's so . . . detailed."

"Details are good. They tell your partner what you want"—I flicked my eyes down, following the length of her body—"and *where* you want it. *How* you want it. Makes for a much better experience." I held her gaze until her cheeks tinged pink.

"I do know that much is true," she replied, her voice scratching as the words came out. "This is going to be new for me. Being in heat, I mean. Are you okay with this, Elias? For real? I'm going to scream for more. Beg you. Demand it, probably." Her voice wavered, struggling to keep her composure as she laid out how it would go. "But what I say while in heat isn't real. I know what I'm asking of you, and it seems unfair. I just want to make sure you're okay with it."

"I'd be lying if I said I wasn't looking forward to it," I replied. "And I don't find it unfair."

Her eyes flicked down to the bulge that was showing beneath my pants. "I'd disagree."

I lifted a shoulder in a side shrug, though the pulsing between my legs was distracting. "This is about you. I'm a man of my word."

Danni tilted her head, lifting an eyebrow, smirking. "Then I suppose I'd be lying if I said I wasn't looking forward to seeing what that looks like."

I chuckled. This woman. This pretend mate of mine. She played flirtatious games with me as much as I played them in return. Playful banter could be just that, but knowing what was about to happen, I hoped it was more.

I wanted her. *Gods*, I wanted her.

"If you're feeling the effects now, I'll have *the boy* locked away. You should go. Keep yourself in our room. Take a bath. Relax. You'll be safe with me." I stood up, leaning over her, resting my hands on the arms of the chair and caging her. Her breath hitched as I closed in. "The heat might make you want these things. It might make you feel things you wouldn't otherwise. But everything I'm going to do to you? What I'm going to make you feel when you come?" I nipped at her lips, smiling against her mouth, lowering my voice as I spoke. "That's going to be real."

She shuddered, letting out a shaky breath. "Promise?"

I winked, turning around and walking toward the exit. I had a few things I needed to take care of first.

CHAPTER 17

DANNIKA

Elias's words rang in my ears.

Everything he'd make me feel would be *real*.

I pressed my thighs together as another pulse of desire coursed through me. Water sloshed around the sides of the tub, and I dug my fingers into my legs.

He was making me feel things, all right. Too many to list. But the trouble was that my mind was starting to get cloudy, and I couldn't piece together what thoughts were my own and what was being conjured by the damn universe demanding I screw Markus to complete our bond.

I'd caught Elias stealing glances ever since I'd arrived. Watching me. The subtle way he'd caress his thumb over my hand when he held it, or the random soft kisses when no one was around. That wasn't for show. I wanted those touches more and more. I found myself looking for time alone with him, even though I shouldn't have.

I ran my fingers over my wet hair, groaning in frustration. I was about to have time alone with him, and I'd pushed the hard line of where things had to stop.

Another ache at my center, and a flush crept further over my skin.

I meant it. I wasn't going to go all the way with him. I wanted to. By the gods, *I wanted to.* But I didn't know what that meant. I didn't want to be friends with benefits, no matter what this arrangement entailed. So, was this desire strictly lust? Or was I convincing myself there was something there simply because we were in this for life? A long, completely fabricated existence together as mates? Fake mates who kissed in private. Flirted relentlessly. I was losing track of what was real and what wasn't.

I didn't want to complicate things . . . and at the same time, I couldn't stop imagining what that might look like if I did.

I took a deep breath and dropped beneath the water, submerging my entire body. Then I screamed. Bubbles popped all around me, drowning out the sound, and I came up, sucking in air.

I wanted more time to think, but I knew I was closing in on the finish line. I was in heat, the first of many. There were no two ways about it. The seconds ticked on, each one bringing me closer to a place I wouldn't be able to escape. I just had to hold out for as long as I could. Trust that Elias could satiate the frenzy my natural instincts would undoubtedly create.

The bathwater cooled, but it was all too sudden. My temperature rose, a literal heat ascending alongside a figurative. A hazy mist settled around me and it consumed my senses.

It was here.

I cursed to myself, climbing out of the tub and not bothering to drain it. I had to find Elias. My legs wobbled in their weakened state, and another throb sent overwhelming *need* through me. Dropping to the ground, I landed on all fours, trying to steady my breathing. Nova scratched at the bathroom door, pushing it open and coming to my side. She whined, nudging her snout under my arm so I could find it in me to stand. I pulled myself up using her for balance. With every stride across the bedroom, electricity shot through my body. With every moment that passed, my previous thoughts drifted away.

The hunger was staggering. Hazy as my vision was, an energy I didn't know I had filled me. My skin was on fire, begging to be touched. Itching to be worshiped. Devoured. Bonded. Ravaged. Anything. Everything.

I lifted my head, looking for the one my body was calling to. I walked toward the door with purpose, and

Nova surprised me when she threw her head back and howled, long and loud.

I knew what I needed.

I knew what I wanted.

A whisper in my subconscious tried to say a name, but I shook my head, holding my temple and pressing my palm into it. A primal response within drove me forward, and I flung the door open, ready to track the one being kept from me . . . but Elias stood in my way. His hair was disheveled. His jeans hung low on his hips, his shirt unbuttoned and hanging open. A warmth spread through me as his delicious spicy scent filled my nostrils.

He was what I wanted.

Needed.

Elias's heated gaze studied my naked body, then he moved into my space. I backed up, and he used his foot to kick the door shut. The whirring of a magical lock I didn't know existed sounded.

The whispering voice got louder. *Fuck him.*

I stepped forward, grabbing his shirt and pulling him to me. Our mouths met in a hardened kiss, and I inhaled sharply, ripping the fabric down his arms and tossing it to the side.

His hand pressed into my lower back, his other cupping my face as his tongue explored my mouth, sucking on my bottom lip as he let go.

"Touch me," I breathed, hitching my leg around his waist as I clawed across his back.

He groaned against my mouth, his erection pressing into my center. Bouncing off my toes, I wrapped my other leg around him, and he caught me just as I rolled my hips, gasping at the contact and how intensely I felt it. Elias walked us back until we hit the bed, but I wasn't going to let him go.

"Lie back," he said, his voice heavy. I dropped my arms, and he set me on the mattress. I scooted as he climbed onto the bed after me, then reached for the back of his neck to keep him close.

Pulling his face to mine, I kissed him again, drinking in his scent. I moaned into his mouth, feeling a heat between my legs that screamed for release. Reaching between our bodies, I grabbed the edge of his pants, but he shook his head, breaking our contact. I tried to sit up. Follow him. But he put his palm on my chest, pushing me down as his mouth skimmed down the curve of my breast.

"This is about you," he mumbled against my skin, taking a nipple between his forefinger and thumb and toying with it softly. "Only you."

Threading my fingers through his hair, I held tightly. "Then show me what that means," I said through a husky tenor, nudging his head lower.

He grinned and chuckled darkly, settling between my legs as I opened myself to him.

Elias grazed his tongue up one side, the cool air tickling the wet trail he'd left, and my legs twitched. Then down the other side, and my breath caught in my throat. I angled my hips, unable to help myself.

Placing his hands on my inner thighs, he spread me further, holding me down. With one long swoop, he licked me from ass to clit, stopping at the sensitive nub and flicking it with his tongue.

I arched and moaned at the sensation, and he wasted no time pressing his mouth against my center, rolling his tongue against me, then sucking my flesh into his mouth. My fingers threaded through his hair, and I shamelessly ground against his face, speeding up the friction and bringing me to the verge of exploding.

He hummed a groan of desire against me, and the added vibration tipped me over the edge. My legs shook, and I cried out as an orgasm tore through me. I slapped my hands onto his upper back, digging my fingertips into the muscle, desperate to pull him closer to me. Tingles shot through my limbs, and spots of white dotted my vision as I kept moving against his mouth, dragging out the pleasure as I rode the waves.

Just as it subsided, he drew away, repositioning himself. The lost contact made my body flush instantly, the demand to satiate increasing with each passing second. I sat up, looping my arms beneath his, inching my body forward and pulling him to me at record speed.

His eyebrows shot up in surprise, but he met my impassioned kiss, flattening his palms against my back.

"I need you closer," I said, the words coming out mumbled between our lips. "Inside me." Reaching down, I rubbed against his erection, feeling it throb at my touch.

He growled in frustration, trying to stop me from stroking him. "This isn't what you want, Danni," he said against my mouth. "It's—"

"I want you . . ." Flashes of fire burned my skin, but there were no flames. My lips parted, and heavy breaths came in ragged bursts. I needed release. I needed *more*. I twisted my body, using my legs as momentum and a strength I didn't know I possessed, rolling us on the bed until I was on top of him. My nails dug into his chest, and he gripped my hips. "To fuck me."

I punctuated my words by grinding against him, spreading my thighs more, dragging my wetness over his jeans.

"You don't want me to fuck you," he said through clenched teeth. He threw his head back into the mattress twice. "Not like this."

A primal instinct told me to leave. Nature warning me that only one thing could quench this undeniable thirst, and I had to have it. I narrowed my eyes at him. "If you won't fuck me, I'll find someone who will."

Lifting my leg to get off him, he held me firmly on top, something deep and feral flashing in his eyes. "You're not going anywhere."

"Make me stay," I challenged, rolling against him.

Elias reached up, grabbing my jaw and tugging me toward him. With my hands by his shoulders, I leaned into him. I met his stare before he flicked his gaze downward. He licked inside my mouth, holding me in place with a firm grip, sucking my lip when he let go.

"I promised I would keep you safe, Danni." Sliding a hand between us, he turned my face to the side, hovering over my ear. "I promised I wouldn't cross any lines." Rough, thick fingertips separated my folds, gliding back and forth and eliciting a shaky moan from me. "And I promised to make you come." Two fingers thrust inside me, and he shoved me back so I was seated on his hand.

I let out a harsh sigh of relief, tilting my head back. Elias held my leg, coaxing me to rock back and forth, fucking the hand he held between us.

With his arm at an odd angle, he couldn't do much, but what he did made me see stars. I rode on top of him, his fingers pushing deeper, rubbing against the sensitive pillowy patch of flesh inside me. I dragged my fingers through my wet strands of hair, the rising climax coming on fast as I sped up my pace.

He grunted, biting into his bottom lip and drawing

blood. I watched in fascination, reaching down between my legs to rub my clit with fervor.

My legs tightened, my next orgasm ripping through me. A scream tore from my throat, and I poured onto his hand, riding the peaks and spasms as my body cooled momentarily.

"Fuck," he ground out, removing his soaked arm from between us. I whimpered when the contact was gone, the insatiable heated hunger increasing almost instantly. Gripping behind my legs, he nudged them, attempting to shimmy his body lower while moving me up. "I want you to do that on my face."

I grinned, positioning myself over him, gripping the headboard, never before having felt so sexy, adored, or happy.

"What do you want next?" he asked with his mouth pressed against my dripping wet center.

"I want it all. Please," I begged, ready to fuck his face with wild abandon.

He took my clit into his mouth, eating me out until the world came crashing down around us once more. Waning blissfully in and out of consciousness from one orgasm to the next, I lost track of time and reality when I imagined Elias whispering to me through the haze. "I'd give you everything if you'd let me."

I hummed in contentment, falling asleep to a howling far off in the distance.

CHAPTER 18
ELIAS

Danni lay next to me, curled against my side with her arm slung over my abdomen. With her breasts pressed to my ribs and her cheek against my chest, I watched as her eyelids fluttered in her dream state.

For almost two days, she'd demanded endless attention. She'd collapse in bouts of exhaustion, napping for a short reprieve before the temperature of her body spiked again, needing more from me to get her through the pain caused by her mate bond. Her lapse in consciousness was enough time for me to take care of my own release before servicing her again, and the gods knew I needed it.

My jaw ached from the hours spent between her legs, my wrists equally sore from overuse. Supernatural powers could barely heal me fast enough. There was almost no downtime, and I kept repeating the damage to my joints, tendons, and muscles. As the last of her desires had been sated, and her body ran the course of the heat, she finally drifted off to a full sleep. Sleep was a recovery for both of us, allowing my abilities to drain the last bit of discomfort away.

She was worth all of it.

Visions replayed over in my mind. Memories of the way she'd tasted. The way she'd come on my face. The way she'd screamed and begged me to fuck her. I wanted nothing more than to give into her demands. Bend her over and take her again and again. But I'd given her my word, and I kept it. Even when my baser instincts had told me not to.

Gazing at the clock on the mantel, I knew I needed to get up. For the duration of her heat, I couldn't leave her. Blood and Beryl still needed me, and I had no idea what had occurred in my absence. I shifted sideways and out of the bed, tucking her arm over a pillow I'd left in my place.

I couldn't help but stare. Her silvery-white hair was in absolute shambles, wrecked from hours of twisting and turning her head against the mattress. Lips slightly parted, she breathed through her nose, snoring softly. A sticky sheen of sweat had dried on her skin, leaving a dull shine. Honestly, she looked absolutely brilliant, and I wanted to see her that way time and time again.

The sound of footsteps down the hallway caught my attention. Grabbing a shirt, I pulled it over my head, treading lightly toward the door and opening it. Ysabeau stood on the other side. I brought my index finger to my pursed lips, then looked back to make sure Danni was still asleep. Nova's ears twitched, and she didn't move.

Ysa stepped to the side so I could come out, closing the door behind me without a sound. I held my hand out, gesturing for her to walk, and I took my place beside her.

"It's good to see you've survived," she said, holding her hands behind her back as we strode toward the east wing staircase. The side-eye she gave me would have had more effect had it not been for the slight smirk on her face.

"Barely." Running my fingers through my hair, I could only imagine what I looked like. "Her hunger was endless."

Ysa snorted. "Well, I can tell you her screams were heard by everyone and there were no doubts about what was happening behind those closed doors." She glanced at me, raising her eyebrows knowingly.

Right. Dannika and I had put on a performance that no one could see. Another win for making our supposed status as mates known.

Except it wasn't supposed to be a show for everyone else. It had been meant for . . . I internally sighed. It had been meant to protect her. There was no other significance behind it, and the reality of that irked me. Questions flooded my brain, firing off left and right.

What would she think of this when she woke up? Would she have any memory of it? Of the things she'd said or done? Of what she'd felt? *Had* she even felt anything besides relief, or had it all affected her differently? Had there been any emotion behind what we'd just experienced together?

The prospect that it could have all been meaningless to her didn't sit well with me, and I refused to believe that was the case. We had shared other moments, and it could be easily argued the intimacy of what we had revealed to each other was deeper than several days of heat-induced lust. We'd discussed our families and our losses. Shared things that were painful to talk about. I didn't open up with just anyone, and I got the impression it was the same for her. I'd found myself seeking more time with her, and it had gone both ways as we'd begun to spend more time together. When we were alone, I stole kisses whenever I got the chance, and she kissed me in return. Passion wasn't something that could be faked, and when no one was looking, there was no reason to act. The moments in private were the ones that counted, were they not? What we did when no one was looking, that was *real*.

I was sure of it.

I'd never wanted to accept a forced mate bond, and I'd never wanted to complicate my reign. I hadn't wanted love. I'd wanted power. I'd wanted justice. Now, everything swirled in a haze, clouding those visions I'd had of the future. When it came down to it . . . fuck it all, *I wanted her*. A real version of us together, and not the falsehood of one we had originally agreed to.

"Elias?" Ysa asked, her voice rising in question. "Are you listening to me?"

"Hmm?" I shook my head, realizing she'd been speaking to me. "No, sorry. Thinking about some plans I need to make. I need you to do a few things for me."

"Such as?"

"Send a scout through all our territories that have mountains, cliffs. That kind of terrain. I want a list of locations to take Danni rock climbing. She likes it." I angled my head to meet Ysa's gaze. She appeared stunned, her lips separating, but no words escaping. "Oh, and reach out to Empress Asbesta. I imagine there are cliff sides on the ocean that we could scale, if Dannika is up for that sort of thing."

She exhaled in exasperation, giving me a tight nod.

"What the hell was that sigh for?" I asked, turning to her and stopping our trek.

She halted, crossing her arms. "You're distracted."

I lowered my voice to a low whisper. "I've been a little busy. What's your point?"

Matching my tone, she said, "Your being *busy* is not an issue, Elias. We both knew why you had to be behind that door. But daydreaming of your lover while I'm trying to discuss matters of territory and rule—"

I narrowed my brows. "I am not daydreaming, and she is not my lover, Ysabeau."

"Of course. My mistake. I meant to say the one you loved," she deadpanned. When I opened my mouth to refute what she'd said, she continued. Looking me up and down, she said, "Go ahead, argue with me. Tell me you don't love her. You are many things, Elias, but you can't lie to me."

I clenched my teeth, the muscle in my jaw throbbing at the tension. "Get to the point."

"I already did." She smirked. Ysa was just as bad as I was. She loved being right. "And good for you, by the way. She tempers your rage. But right now? Right now, I'm talking to my king about a rat who's been found, and he's off in dreamland thinking about rock climbing with his lady love." She pointed at me, then at herself. "I will delegate and get someone to look for what you want, but you didn't make me your second to search the world for picnic spots. You made me your second because I get shit done. I dragged in a traitor, and I've held him for twenty-four hours. Jordan Westpoint is waiting for you."

Shock filtered through me. "You found him?"

She nodded, giving me a tight-lipped smile. "Do I have your attention now?"

Hate filled me. I wanted answers, and I wanted to pry them from him.

"Yeah. Let's go." I dragged my hand over the scruff on my face and jaw, taking the stairwell down to the subterranean level in silence. Our footfalls echoed through the dark concrete hallway. The scent of damp earth and moss filled my nostrils. As we approached the dungeon door, I turned to Ysa.

She sighed. "I know, I know. Overstepped my boundaries."

"Yes, you did." I cocked an eyebrow, but she respectfully held my gaze, not shying away. "And you are the only one who can. Anyone else would have lost their tongue. I made you my second for more than your ability to get shit done. Remember that."

I trusted Ysabeau with my life. She bore the scars that proved her loyalty to my family. To my sister. Ysa wasn't often wrong, and a good king knew when to listen to those he'd chosen to advise him, even if that person treaded a thin line when they did it.

Her features remained neutral as she dipped her head. When I turned and opened the door, she whispered, "You and Dannika complement each other." I smiled to myself, appreciating the sincerity. "And honestly, you're insufferable most of the time, so we can only hope she balances that out too."

And there it was. The type of jab I would expect from one of my oldest friends.

I shook my head and huffed as I entered the holding chamber. Dim candlelight provided visibility, and the dank scent of water and dirt permeated the air, thicker than before.

I reached into my pocket and pulled out large sunglasses, putting them on. Ysa perpetually wore them. I flipped a switch, and an intensely bright light filled the room.

Jordan Westpoint groaned at the sudden assault to his senses, sharply inhaling through his nose.

I walked toward him slowly. He hung from the ceiling in chains, arms stretched high over his head, his biceps pressed against his ears. His ankles were cuffed, shackling him to the floor. A ball gag stopped him from talking, drool pouring from the corner of his mouth.

"You know why you're here, Jordan," I started. He squinted, trying to open his eyes, but the light was entirely too painful on his retinas. "And you know who I am."

A muffled sound came from behind the gag, but whether it indicated a yes or a no, I wasn't sure. I glanced at the table Ysa had nearby. On display were assorted tools and other objects I would need to help procure the answers I wanted.

Everyone talked under torture. They'd say anything to make the pain stop, but it was only useful when you knew you had the right captive. I didn't want false confessions. Start slowly. Ask the right questions. Gauge the responses. Listen for the heartbeat. Watch the pupils. Then proceed accordingly.

"Nod or shake your head, Jordan. Do you know who I am?"

He nodded sharply.

"Good. Good." I circled him, watching him shiver. The sounds of my boots scraped against the damp floor as I walked behind his fixed location. "Do you know why you're here?"

He shook his head, his breathing picking up.

"I hear you've taken to sleeping in Katie's bed," I said, not giving him anything more. He gave me a single nod. "I've also heard you've taken the time to make some friends within Gold and Garnet, yes?"

A pause, then a nod.

"In fact, you've stretched that circle of friends to include someone in Fire and Fluorite as well?"

He shook his head.

I sighed. "You've disappointed me, Jordan. A little bird told me you've been sharing secrets."

Shaking his head again, he hummed a "no" sound, squinting so he could try to see.

I tutted. "Let's try again." I unbuckled the clasp on the gag, letting it drop to the floor. Jordan coughed, closing his mouth and opening it again, trying to stretch his jaw. "Your loudmouth friend in Gold and Garnet is dead," I said, looking to see his reaction, but he gave none.

"I don't know what you're talking about," he wheezed, his voice scratchy. His heartbeat remained elevated but steady. Except one little skip when he'd learned his friend's fate. A tiny twitch in his cheek. A slight fidget in his fingers.

He'd given himself away, and I smiled. I continued to pace around his form, out of sight, then in his periphery, stopping right in front of him again and again as I questioned him.

"I think you do." I held my hand in front of him, flicking my wrist, conjuring a knife that formed from the magic beneath my skin. *My* magic. *My* gift as a master vampire. And it elicited fear from whomever witnessed its becoming. It slid into my palm effort-lessly, and I grazed the sharp edge down his cheek, tracing the jawline, traveling down the length of his neck, over the collarbone, around the pectoral muscle. His breath hitched, and I stabbed the short blade into the muscle, then twisted.

Jordan cursed and growled in pain. Through a tense voice, he managed to grind out, "If this is about Katie, you can have her."

"Wrong answer."

Ysa snorted, and I grabbed his jaw, prying it open, holding it in a firm grip while he struggled to keep calm. I pointed a new blade at his gums, then burrowed the steel into the soft and tender flesh while his muted screams filled the air. Carving around the tooth and digging into the root, I cut out a fang and threw it down by his feet.

Blood poured from his mouth, and he moaned, gasping for air and coughing simultaneously.

"Strike two," I said, kicking the tooth across the floor. Taking a step back, I observed his movements.

Jordan shook his head, inhaling deeply, trying to recover and let his body heal. "I would never betray my House." He looked at me, hate flashing in his eyes. It was at that moment I saw how deep his deception went. He wasn't mine. Maybe he never had been.

"Ah. I see now. How long?" I asked, crossing my arms and shifting my weight to one foot. No answer. "This is a question of mere curiosity. You've been playing both sides. How long have you been in Fire and Fluorite?"

Jordan squeezed his eyes shut, taking in sharp, ragged breaths. "I don't answer to you," he ground out.

I chuckled, tilting my head as I looked at him. "You will."

I had been waiting for proof. Desperate to find it.

Mathis had covered his tracks so well. Yes, King Vesperus and Empress Asbesta knew of his treachery. They wanted him dead as much as I did. Other Houses merely tolerated him, but I knew some were on his side. I couldn't make a move on him without proof. It would start another war. Too many lives would be lost. Too many souls shattered, and families broken. I would take him down, but I would go about it the right way. I would prove to the other Houses what he was, and with the treaty, they would back me. What I had working to my advantage was that no one wanted a war. Not even Fire and Fluorite's allies.

Ysa reached my side, touching my arm lightly in warning. "Elias." She shook her head slightly. "I'll get Kieran. We need Jordan alive."

"Oh, I know." I cracked my knuckles. "I have no intention of killing him."

She was right. I needed him alive. I could get the truth from him. It was a power only a few knew I possessed. But it came with a great cost to the one I used it on.

Death.

Jordan wouldn't get that from me.

His chest rose in rapid shudders as he started to laugh, the sound exhaling through his nose. "You think you know what's going on, but you have no idea." He sniffed, then spat out a mouthful of blood on the floor, tilting his head up to look at me.

"Is this the part where you allude to your evil plans, throwing out idle threats and expecting me to react?" I asked while sifting through the various items on the table. The usual. Pliers, electrodes, other sharp objects. Oh, a cattle prod. I held it up, shaking it in his direction. "This could be fun, yeah?"

"Your arrogance will be your end."

"Of course it will. A snakebite isn't a very heroic way to go for a vampire. In the meantime . . ." I turned the instrument on, hearing the telltale buzz that could cause anyone near it to tremble. Its shock was jolting and powerful, sending the pain into the depth of a victim's bones if held against the skin long enough. Glancing at him, I said, "I'm not overly concerned. I've survived much worse than you."

"Dannika hasn't," he sneered, and I snapped my head in his direction. The leering grin that curled up his face spiked the rage inside me, mixing it with an emotion I hadn't felt in a long time. "She'll suffer for your failures, the same way your sister did."

I sped toward him, and Ysa yelled for me to stop. I swung, landing my fist on his jaw. The resounding crack echoed off the cellar walls.

He manipulated his jaw, twisting it and moving it back and forth the way you would expect someone to do after just being hit. But his next statement sent a chill through me, and I knew I had screwed up. "Thank you, Your Majesty," he mumbled through a mouth full of blood. He clenched his teeth in an open grin, and an audible crunch sounded. The scent of magic filtered in the air, and a red mist released from Jordan's nostrils, curling out of the corners of his mouth.

"No." Ysa shouted and ran forward, grabbing his mouth and prying it open. "He had a capsule in his tooth. Get a witch, hurry!"

The poison was running its course and had already changed the color of his irises. Black lines formed around his eyes. It was magically enhanced ricin.

"We don't have time." Rushing to him, I put my hand on his jawline, shoving it up.

Ysa grabbed me. "You can't—"

"He's going to die anyway! I need to know what he knows."

She knocked my hand away, pointing to his skin. Little black lines had replaced his veins as the poison worked its way through. "What if that kills you?"

"It won't." My fangs shot out, and I positioned myself over his neck, stabbing into his flesh and puncturing the artery.

I pulled from him, drinking greedily, and the magic I was cursed with mingled with his blood. Pulse after pulse of his racing heart drew his lifeblood into me while my power devoured him, pounding at a rate that would kill anyone who wasn't supernatural. He opened his mouth in a silent scream, and his body tensed.

Visions of the truth filled my mind.

Sleeping with Katie, using her for information to pass on. Jordan never appeared before Mathis directly. But there were others. Names of traitors. Faces of false allies. My House was blessedly skimp on those who had betrayed me, but there were more to deal with.

Jordan started to seize, his end coming soon. I clamped down on his neck, pulling more blood and more information.

Memories of hidden meetings and secrets shared with Vesperus's mole. An army, hidden in Utah. Mathis had every intention of starting another war. Taking over territory, fighting to take down entire Houses. All he needed was something to kick it off. Biding his time, he planted his spies, preparing to strike when he knew he wouldn't get caught.

Dannika's image flashed through Jordan's memories. A picture of her standing with Nova, turning almost as though she could see me looking at her. The image warbled. He didn't know what Mathis's plans for her were, but the picture in his mind charred, breaking into pieces of falling ash.

I released his neck with a pop, grunting as I took in deep breaths and tried to unravel the makings of what I had seen.

The poison had traveled the length of his body, and his head lolled forward. "You can't . . . protect . . . her," he wheezed, barely able to speak the words between his dying breaths. "She's . . . already . . . dead . . ."

His final words hung in the air, as potent as the poison he'd used to end his life.

Fear.

That was the emotion I was no longer acquainted with. Not since the Great Sacrifice. But here it was, burying itself beneath my skin, taunting me with the thought of losing Danni.

I clenched and unclenched my fists, breathing hard. I tried to control my reactions while everything inside me sat on the precipice of explosion. My head snapped in Ysa's direction.

"Where is Danni?" I asked, looking at Ysa over my shoulder. She shook her head. "Find her. *Now*."

CHAPTER 19

DANNIKA

I sat next to a koi pond, stroking Nova's fur while I watched the fish glide through the water. Overcast skies spread as far as I could see, floating gently for miles, blocking out any chance of the sun peeking through.

I wasn't sure how long I'd slept in, only that I was alone when I woke up. Elias had left, which I'd suspected he would. He'd held up his end of the bargain. He'd kept me safe during my heat, and he never crossed any of the lines I'd put in place. Now he was gone. As king, he had a job to do, and the logical part of me understood that. But there was another part of me, one that felt confused and lonely when I'd realized his side of the bed was empty.

The days we'd spent between the sheets were hazy, but some of those moments shone through the fog. I pressed my legs together, shaking the thoughts from my head, but it was no use.

Echoes of my voice replayed in my mind, demanding Elias to give me relief, pleasure, and satis- faction . . . to give me everything. Images of the way his eyes looked up at me when I ground myself against his face made my pulse quicken.

My cheeks warmed at the memory of his hands pressing against my thighs, and the way his warm, wet tongue licked me from — A buzzing against the rock made me jolt in surprise, pulling me away from my erotically charged reverie.

I grabbed the phone as it vibrated, skidding across the stone. My heart skipped a beat in excitement. It was my sister's number. Four times she'd sent me a message with a date and time, but a call never came through. "Hey," I said, clearing my throat of its hoarseness.

A suspended moment passed before Adora's voice filtered through the other line. "Oh my god, you had sex."

I sputtered. "What? I did not! Why would you even think—"

"Your throat is hella scratchy. So you've either been screaming for your life, or you've been having a grand ol' time. It doesn't sound like the former."

My jaw fell open, and I looked at Nova. She snuffed loudly, turning her face in the other direction while avoiding eye contact. How could my wolf look guilty for me? Adora's laugh told me she'd heard Nova's reaction.

"It's not what you think," I started, then sighed. "Markus hasn't rejected me yet, so the bond triggered my heat."

My sister's breath hitched, no longer playfully teasing with her assumptions. She knew how serious this was and how complex things could get. "Oh shit, you're not . . . was it Markus? Please, no . . ."

"That got your attention." I chuckled. "And no, Markus was kept . . . away." Now that I'd said that, I didn't know where he was. Or if he was out yet. Did he know the entire ordeal had passed? "So I never saw him. But things have gotten slightly complicated around here."

"Yeah, we heard *all* about it." I was glad I warned them before they heard it from members of Fire and Fluorite. They would know the truth. It wasn't hard for them to figure out, especially considering Adora's presence when I was exiled. "Believe me, it continues to cause quite the uproar on this side."

I cursed under my breath. "How bad? Are you guys okay?"

"Pssh," she responded. "Nothing we can't handle."

But I heard a flicker in her voice. I knew there was something she wasn't saying. Before all of this, I had spoken to my sister every day since the moment we could talk. Even on days we'd fought, even when we'd been mad at each other—we'd never shut each other out completely. I knew her sounds, her inflections, and tones.

"Adora," I started, letting a moment pass between my words. "What aren't you telling me?"

She sighed, sending a crackle through the phone as the air hit the receiving end. "We've always been targets. You know this. It was just that we tried to fade into the background. Now we're front and center because of everything that happened. We're constantly watched. Tracked. Getting a secure line to you was hard, but I found the magic I needed on my last trip to No Man's Land. It's just . . . you know how it goes."

"Rowe?" I asked.

"Safe for now."

I squeezed my eyes shut. "Mom and Abbey?"

"They're with other members of the Inland pack right now. Just setting up potential safe houses in case . . ."

My jaw dropped. Mathis would never allow them to leave his pack. For my mom to be willing to leave our home . . . things would have to be dire. That simple act spoke volumes about the instability of their situation. Inland was the pack Abbey was from, just one of the many under the protection and rule of Fire and

Fluorite. No matter what happened, they would always be loyal to my family.

"I'm so sorry," I whispered. Guilt washed over me. My family was suffering. They were in danger because of me. I was safely tucked away in Blood and Beryl while they had become the target of Mathis and his wrath. "This is all my fault. I should have just—"

"Stop," my sister ordered, the firm and harsh set of her voice leaving no room for argument. "Don't you dare finish that sentence. There is no world that exists where this is your fault. There is no world where Mom and Abbey and I would have wanted you to accept Markus as your mate. To live that life. You deserve better than that, and if for one second you've started to believe otherwise, you've lost yourself, sister. That's not who you are."

I huffed through my nose, my eyes welling with unshed tears. "No. It's not."

"We'll manage. Have a little faith. Mom might get a little weepy at times, but she's powerful, and she knows how to survive. You're both fighters."

"So are you," I reminded her.

"Oh, I know I am," she said. "Never have been one to stay in line, have I?"

I snorted. "Must be a peacock thing."

"Pretty sure it's just a Kresley thing."

I barked a laugh, missing the back and forth between us. The silence spanned for several moments, but it wasn't uncomfortable. "You know, I think you'd like it here," I said, changing the subject. "It's a lot like home. A lot of the same trees. Similar smells. It rains about as often. It's not all that bad. Elias is going to find a way to get you all here when things settle. I promise."

"Sounds tempting. How's the *other* scenery?" she asked, and I could imagine her waggling her eyebrows. "Anybody at court worth courting?"

"I haven't looked, to be honest," I admitted. And it was true. I'd really only been focused on Elias. I knew I didn't have options, so I hadn't been looking around.

"What's he like?"

"Elias?" I asked. She hummed in response. "Not what you'd expect. On the one hand, I absolutely see where he gets his reputation from. The rumors aren't exaggerated. I wouldn't ever want to be on the receiving end of his anger. On the flip side, he's actually thoughtful and genuine. And . . . nice. I don't know what else to say. I enjoy spending time with him."

"Oh wow," Adora mused. "You have *feelings* for him. I can hear it in your voice."

And there it was. The truth.

"I . . . yeah, there's something there, I think. It's so complicated, I don't know what to do with it all." I scratched my nail against the stone wall surrounding the pond. "And then with the heat—"

"Wait. You and Elias? While you were in heat?"

Adora's shock wasn't contained as part of her question squeaked out toward the end.

"Not the way you're thinking. But sort of? Elias kept me safe through it. We didn't go all the way, though."

"Mm-hmm," she murmured, clearly not believing me.

"It wasn't like that. We set limits ahead of time, and he kept his promise. It lasted for two days. Probably would have been longer if he hadn't helped me. There may have been a good deal of screaming involved, so that's why my throat is still a little raw."

"I bet your twat is too."

"Fuck's sake, Adora," I chided, turning my head and looking around the gardens. There wasn't a person in sight, and I knew it. Otherwise, I wouldn't have been having the conversation. It didn't stop some strange feeling of embarrassment from crawling over my skin.

"What?" she asked. I could practically hear my sister shrug on the other line. I could picture her looking at her nails while she did it, twisting her lips. She'd act as though she didn't notice you watching, all while a grin would be curling up one side of her face.

"I'm not saying I wouldn't—maybe, probably— but it's all so complex with crossing feelings with responsibilities," I mumbled, my cheeks heating up. "And those feelings. What are they? Are they real or are they a result of having no options anymore because I'm, you know, mated and going to be his queen—and don't even get me started on the complexities of *that* whole thing. Plus, there's Markus—"

"Whoa, whoa, whoa," my sister interjected. "What does he have to do with anything?"

I groaned, knowing how she was going to react. "He's different here," I said quietly. "And before you get your feathers all ruffled, I *don't* want to be with him. That hasn't changed. But *he* is starting to. Once we were out of Fire and Fluorite for a little bit, I started to see a few things about him I hadn't before."

Silence. She sniffed. "Such as?"

"For as awful as Mathis was in public, he didn't go home to his family and suddenly become the doting father. We both knew who he took it out on behind closed doors. We've all seen the dead look in his mate's eyes. What about his sons? It's not news. It's just easier to think about here. It's easier to see when you look at him." I paused, inhaling deeply before letting it sink in. "Markus was his target. I don't know who he would have been under better circumstances in life, but I know it's hard to be a better human when you're raised by a monster."

"You can't be fucking serious right now," she breathed.

"I know it sounds insane, but he apologized to me, Adora. And he meant it." She snorted in derision.

"I don't care," she said flatly. "I'll never forgive him for what he's done to you. To us. I watched him break you down over and over, and we always put the pieces back together, but we were kids. We shouldn't have had to."

I pressed my lips together and exhaled. "I'm not forgiving him. I'm just letting it go. There's a difference."

"I can't."

I chuckled. "I don't expect you to. In all reality, you're my perfect other half. You hold grudges so I don't have to."

"Accurate." She huffed a laugh, and we spent a moment sharing our agreement in a contented pause. "So answer me this. Why does he complicate things with your feelings-not feelings-maybe feelings with Elias?"

"Because I see him suffering with our bond, and the last thing I want to do is actually make him suffer more." I heard an intake of breath, and I kept talking before she could interrupt me. "And before you say he deserves it—which I don't disagree with —it makes my life more difficult. I need him to accept my rejection. Jealousy isn't going to make that happen. I can't entirely tell why he's holding on to the mate bond, but if I can befriend him enough, maybe I can convince him to let me go. Then to counter that, Elias doesn't want me spending time with him. He trusts Markus about as far as he can throw him."

"Seems Elias and I have something in common," she said.

"You two would get along, actually," I commented. "You're both hotheaded and you both want to throw Markus off a cliff."

"Only because we love you," she replied, raising her voice to a chipper tone.

"Ha," I barked a laugh, shaking my head. "You do, yes. It's not like that with Elias."

"Oooh. Now I get it," Adora murmured. "There's the core of why it's complicated. You have *feeling*-feelings. But he's not into feelings."

"Pretty much. He enjoys spending time with me, but even when we talk about whatever we are, he makes it clear it's a business arrangement. So you see my dilemma," I mumbled in return, cradling the phone against my shoulder. "But it's honestly okay. This entire thing is one giant clusterfuck. Adding feelings to the mix? Nope. Not going to happen. It's better off this way."

"I know you don't actually believe that," she said. "I know you better than that. You don't get a case of feelings and think it's better for nothing to happen."

"But nothing is going to happen. So isn't it better to detach myself from the deeper part of it? Do what you would do and just enjoy the ride?"

"You aren't me," she countered. "And I don't want you to be. Why don't you just tell him?"

"Ha! Tell him I actually remember the heat and maybe some of the things I said were really me? That I wouldn't mind something more happening between us?"

"Yes. Exactly that," she deadpanned.

I considered it for a moment. What would it look like while I stammered over my words? I'd probably throw up on some priceless ancient rug made from the magical fibers of some mythological creature that no longer existed. Because that was something he would own. And it was certainly something I would find a way to damage.

What if he was receptive to my feelings, even in the slightest? I thought back to our day at the waterfall. He'd said he was willing to take some risks. What kinds of risks? Maybe it was time to be honest about it. Take a few shots of liquid courage and say it. What was the worst that could happen? I could be rejected by him, and we'd pretty much be back to the act we'd been putting on. I inhaled, steeling my spine, metaphorically anyway. I was still sitting on the wall hunched over with my back looking like a question mark.

"I'll try," I murmured. Adora cleared her throat loudly and purposefully, calling out my use of the word *try*. She hated that. "I'll talk to him. No guarantees about what words actually end up coming out of my mouth."

"As long as they're words and not you throwing up on him," she snickered.

"No promises." We both laughed, and my sister blew out a loud breath, and I knew there would be a loose strand of hair falling into her face, flying around as the air hit it. I could imagine exactly how she looked at the moment. A sudden sadness filled me, and I sighed. "I miss you, Adora."

"I miss you so much, it hurts," she replied, her voice barely more than a whisper. Abbey's warning howl sounded in the background on her end, and she cursed. Nova perked up her ears, cocking her head in question.

My moms were a mile out from the house. They always let us know when they were almost home. But the pitch she used meant they were being followed. I had no doubts Mathis had had them trailed, hoping to find something he could use against them. They would find nothing, but the idea of my family being targets made my stomach turn.

"I know that call," I said calmly, even as worry filled me.

"Not again," she mumbled. "Mathis has Andreas or Shade follow us everywhere. Like you're dumb enough to come back here and hide under the staircase."

"Will you be okay?"

"I'll be fine. The same as it always goes," she answered, but I knew what that meant. They'd try to provoke Mom and Abbey into a fight by using Adora as a punching bag. She'd take her hits, and she'd remind our moms to stay back. "Hopefully it's Shade. He pulls his punches. His son is a dick, though." For her sake, I hoped it wasn't his son. Andreas was the worst, and he seemed to enjoy it.

"Go," I whispered. "Be careful. Don't give them a reason to stay, okay? Eyes down, mouth shut. I love you. Tell Mom and Abbey too."

"Love you too." She'd sped through her words before the absence of sound on the other line filled my ear.

I tried to distract myself, squeezing my eyes to stop the emotions from leaking out. Holding the phone in one hand, I tilted my neck back, facing up to the sky. A fat drop of water landed on my forehead, then several other drops started to land around me as the clouds opened up.

The weather was fitting for the mood I was in.

Nova jumped up, shaking her body before taking off in a run for the tree line. I followed behind her, my pace slower, letting the rain mask the tears that fell down my cheeks.

CHAPTER 20

ELIAS

She's already dead.

The words played on repeat in my head. After Jordan's interrogation, I'd headed straight to our room, only to find it empty, and the bed made. No one knew where Dannika was. She'd been gone for hours, not answering her phone. I couldn't take it. After the threats that had been made, I needed to know she was safe. It took all of five minutes before I decided to send out a search party.

I paced in front of the fireplace, anxiety clawing at my throat. The repetitive echo of my footsteps measured the time, stepping in sync with every tick of the clock. Thunder rolled outside, shaking the windows, and the skies darkened further.

The earlier half of my day hadn't been so grim. She had been on my mind, just in a different way. Now all I could think about was Mathis making a move to kill her just to get back at me. I'd had put her in harm's way, and now I didn't even know if it was too late to save her.

My pocket buzzed, and I pulled it out, reading a message from Ysa.

Found her.

Turning on a heel, I rushed out of the room. Blood pounded in my head. My heart raced. Hallway. Stairwell. Another hallway. Lower-level entry.

There she stood, soaking wet, with her arms crossed, and several soldiers near her. Nova appeared to already have shaken out her coat, and she was cleaning her legs. Water was splattered everywhere, and even Ysa's clothes had been caught in the crossfire.

"Where have you been?" I demanded, storming toward her, wrapping my arms around her and pulling her into an embrace. "I've had everyone looking for you."

Danni tensed, not returning any kind of affection. "I was at the koi pond and then I just found a trail in the woods to walk for a while. Why? What is this all about?"

Several members of the guard exchanged glances. "In the rain? You've been gone for hours. Who were you with?" I asked, not answering the questions she'd asked. After releasing her, I gripped her upper arms, looking straight into her eyes. I had to know. I had to make sure she was okay. Jordan had known of traitors, and I'd sent out for them to be tracked, but there could be others. Others he hadn't been aware of.

"I wasn't with anyone. It was me and Nova." She twisted, wiggling herself free of my hold. Her eyes darted to the audience of soldiers who were around us before turning attention back to me.

"Why were you gone so long?" I looked behind her, making eye contact with Ysa. She held up five fingers. "Five *hours*, Danni. You didn't even leave a note. Why?"

"I don't know. Because I walk slow? I don't know. I didn't realize I had a curfew." Her brows furrowed, and the muscle in her jaw tightened. She scanned the room again, her heart rate picking up.

I waved everyone out, cupping Danni's elbow, then started walking. She smacked my hand away, then got ahead of me as she headed toward the staircase.

Nova ran to catch up, taking the steps up to our floor side by side with her. On the top level, Danni stomped down the hallway, then stormed into our room, practically shutting the door in my face. My hand caught it, and I followed inside before closing it.

She whirled around, her wet strands flying and slapping her in the face. "What just happened down there?"

"I needed to know you were safe." I reached forward, brushing the thick ropes of hair away.

She backed up, gesturing up and down to her body. "You can see that I am."

"You didn't answer your phone, Danni. We tried, and when we asked around, no one said they'd seen you. No one knew if you were alone or not."

She blinked several times, pulling her phone from her pocket and tossing it to me. "It died. I was talking to my sister. Magic or not, the battery needs to be charged." Clearing her throat, she motioned toward her wolf, who was resting in front of the fireplace while she dried off. "I'm never alone. I always have Nova, and we know how to take care of ourselves."

Every part of me struggled to find the right way to convey my concerns without sending her into a panic. She'd already lived so long under Mathis's cruelty. I wouldn't let him have that power over her while living here. I could protect her. I held the phone in my hand, considering the magic used to make it work. I'd just get her a better one. Taking a deep breath, I tried to calm myself. "I didn't know where you were, and you'd been gone too long. Next time, I just need to know where you're going. And with whom."

She shook her head. "You said I could roam the grounds. That I was free to explore. Don't turn this around and give me stipulations. We can agree to a lot of things, but I'm not going to let you control me."

Danni pointed toward the window. "You sent a group of soldiers to look for me so they could drag me in and stand in front of you in a public hallway while you chastised me for not leaving you a note?"

"That's not what happened. I left the room, and you were asleep. When I came back, you were gone. This has nothing to do with control." Irritation leaked into my voice at her accusation. Why would she even think I wanted power over her? I'd done nothing to convey that.

"I think we have different definitions of what it means to be controlling," she said, staring at me with a flat expression. She pressed her fingertips to her temples, rubbing in circles. "Look, I'm sorry. I have a lot on my mind. I don't want to argue about it. I just don't like feeling shamed for calling my sister and taking a walk. You were worried. Okay. You don't need to act like an overprotective Alphahole just to get people's attention on us. I know we want them to believe we're bonded, and they do. We've done a good job. We've done a lot in public to lead them to believe we're together. But this? The whole act of panicked hugging and sending a royal guard to find me? I don't know how to react to stuff like that. It was over the top, especially if we're just pretending."

She may as well have slapped me. It would have stung less than the words that had come from her mouth. The "whole act"? That was how she viewed me? My stomach tightened, and a knot filled my throat. "Is that what all of this is to you?"

Danni stared at me, her brows scrunching as she looked around. "What do you mean, 'Is that what this is to me'?" She crossed her arms, leaning to one side. "You're the one who came up with the plan to be pretend mates. It was your idea. I don't know what else to call it?"

"My idea," I repeated, nodding gently, letting it soak in. "That it was."

My nostrils flared as I exhaled through my nose. How could I have been so stupid? Was she *that* good of an actress and I just hadn't seen it before? Everything? The physical attraction and flirtation had all been part of the ruse? Like studying for a part she had to play. She was just doing the homework? I'd been gushing over her like a lovesick fool, thinking about what I could do to spend more time with her. How to make her happy. What I could do to *be* with her. If she could carelessly throw out that we were nothing more than pretend—beyond the mate story—then I'd read into all of it.

I was falling in love with a woman who didn't feel the same.

Fuck me.

My jaw tightened as I clenched my teeth, the intensity of the pressure threatening to crack them. "My apologies for the misunderstanding."

"Are we . . . good?" she asked, uncrossing her arms so she could fidget with her hands.

"We're just fine," I said, forcing myself to smile. She nodded quickly, toying with the ring that hung around her neck. Then blew out a breath as though she were preparing herself for something.

"I actually wanted to talk to you about what happened . . . when I was in heat," she said. My eyes shot to the bed where we'd been not twelve hours before. A flush crept up her neck, tinting her cheeks pink. She looked away, unable to make eye contact. "I spent some time thinking, and I, um, I said some things . . . things I wouldn't have said otherwise, and honestly, it wasn't—"

"There's no need to explain it," I said, jutting my chin out. I'd spent the better part of the day thinking about what we'd shared in bed together. Wondering if she'd felt anything from it or if the words had been at all real. But that would only happen if she felt anything between us at all—and we were just pretending. What she'd said and done while in heat had all been induced by the heat itself. I just couldn't bear to hear her say it. "It was business. Nothing more."

Her lips parted, and a small crease formed between her brows before she nodded. "Well, I guess that's that," she said softly.

"Anything else? I have somewhere to be," I said,

trying to keep my tone even. She didn't understand. There was no way for her to know what I had witnessed in Jordan's mind. The foreshadowing of her death wasn't filling her mind with poison. And I wouldn't let her carry that burden. It was what Mathis wanted. I'd go deal with it, and she'd be none the wiser.

"Elias," she started, inhaling while considering her words. She grimaced, tilting her head to the side before she gestured between us. "This doesn't feel right."

"That's because none of this is *real*," I said without thinking, mimicking the same motion she had just used to point at herself and then me. Even I heard the cruelty in my voice, and I knew she didn't deserve it. Instant regret sent a shot of adrenaline through my veins, but it was too late. I couldn't take it back. Danni's eyes widened, and her lips separated slightly. She recovered from her shock, dropping her arms to her sides. She balled her hands into fists, clenching and unclenching them. "Danni, I—"

"You're an asshole." She turned on a heel, heading for a dresser I'd put in our room just for her.

"Let me explain," I said as I followed her, my heavy footsteps sounding louder than I meant them to.

"No." She yanked a drawer open, grabbing items and tucking them into her arms. Whirling around, she pointed her finger toward me. "Get away from me. I've had enough of Markus explaining to me why he's an asshole. Do me a favor and save me from listening to the same excuses."

Indignation lit a fire in me. "Do not compare me to Markus."

"If the shoe fits, Elias." She turned, walking toward the bedroom door. After snapping her fingers, Nova jumped up, trotting to her side.

"Where are you going?" I demanded, heading in her direction.

"I'm going to take a long bath somewhere far away from you and this room," she said, looking at me over her shoulder. "Want me to leave you a note?" Before I could answer, she slammed the door, knocking over the unlit candles that sat on a table near the exit.

I pounded my fist on the wooden frame, a part of me knowing that she'd heard it and I was only making things worse. That better judgment was overridden by pure emotion. Anger. Hurt. Fear. Things I didn't want to admit.

All of it was my fault. I'd put her in this situation. I'd made the deal with her. She was just another pawn to piss off Mathis. A way for me to make my life uncomplicated by some mate bond that would skew my vision and alter my priorities. Turned out having a fake mate was no different in that regard. Arguably worse because I felt something for her that I couldn't take back, and the feeling wasn't exactly mutual.

It was okay. It was the deal I'd made, and one we would live with.

For now, I had to weed out the traitors in my House and bring Mathis down. That was my endgame. I didn't know if Mathis was using Danni to instill fear so I would make a mistake. I didn't know if he wanted to try to use her against me, or if he simply wanted to kill her for his own pleasure, and in doing so, he figured it was a two-for-one deal. I'd be hurt in the end no matter what.

He wouldn't get the chance.

I would do anything to keep her safe, even if she ended up hating me for it.

CHAPTER 21
DANNIKA

Two days.

Two days we hadn't spoken to each other. Two days of leaving passive aggressive notes whenever I went to the bathroom, went for a walk, or looked for a hairbrush. Two days of me going to sleep before he came to our room in the early morning hours. Two days of ignoring each other in every way possible. Two days of what felt like hell.

I picked up a pebble between my thumb and forefinger, rolled it around, then dropped it on the ground again. Nova watched me play with the rocks, keeping me company and soothing me with her presence. The nearby waterfall's rhythmic sound filled the air with a calming effect.

In an effort to be alone and clear my thoughts, I

hiked to the waterfall. It wasn't my best idea. Looking around, it just reminded me of Elias when he'd followed me that first time. When I'd pretended I didn't know how to skip stones, hoping he'd touch me. When he'd kissed me, and I'd kissed him in return.

I couldn't understand how I'd misread the situation to such a great extent. When I looked at the tree, imagining my back up against it, him pressing into me —I wasn't making that up. That moment had felt real. He'd even said so, hadn't he? Now I wasn't sure if I'd just made it up because I wanted it to be true. Because something had happened between then and now that I had missed.

He'd embarrassed me, shamed me, and made me feel like he was putting me on a leash. I didn't think I'd overreacted, but I'd never know. It was over and done with. That wasn't even the part that hurt me the most. It was when I tried to tell him I had what Adora called "a case of the feelings" and he'd cut me off, telling me it was business. Nothing more.

I'd just wanted to say that it wasn't so terrible that some of those things came out of my mouth. I did want him. I wanted more of him. Maybe the heat had just given me the courage to say things I really felt. I'd dreamed in my haze that he'd said the same types of things, but it had been just that. A dream.

A sound on the trail startled me, and Nova turned

her head, perking her ears up. A glimmer of excitement shot through me. I'd left a note telling Elias I was at the waterfall. The hope for him to come for me was embarrassing, and I was thankful I didn't have to confess that to anyone.

Nova huffed loudly, rolling her eyes, and dropped her face on her paws.

Markus held his hand up in a mock surrender, and that ember of hope flickered out. "I come in peace," he said, almost like a question, a lopsided smile on his face.

"Did you follow me again?" I asked, sighing in disappointment.

"I did," he admitted. "I won't stay long. I just had a few things I wanted to tell you."

I frowned, waving him over. "I'm not good company right now, so I hope you're not looking for riveting conversation."

He kneeled beside me, sitting down and crossing his legs. "I've never been good company to you. Can't expect a lot in return there, can I?"

Nova watched him with suspicion, not liking his proximity to me.

I jerked my head up, meeting his gaze and taking in his form. His hair wasn't styled, but it was clean. He looked tired, but not sick. Just like he needed more rest. In a stark contrast, his skin looked healthier somehow. What threw me off guard was his eyes. They weren't pinched at the corners. They were doe-like. Sincere.

"What did you want to talk about?" I asked, unsure of what his change in demeanor meant.

"A lot," he huffed, looking at his hands, and I gestured for him to continue. "I could hear you. When you were in heat. I felt the pull . . ."

I squeezed my eyes shut, grimacing. "Are you okay?"

"I'm better than I've been for a while, actually. Maybe ever," he whispered, turning to look at the waterfall in front of us.

"That's . . . good," I started, not knowing how to have a friendly chat with my childhood bully, especially when it was about what the heat had done to us. Every time we spoke, it was contentious, and this felt anything but.

"I have you to thank for that," he said, picking up a rock and looking at it intensely.

With my elbows resting on my knees, I leaned forward more, trying to get him to look at me. "I didn't do anything . . ."

He gazed up toward the sky, nodding his head. "You did everything. Everything I couldn't. You were always the better person. You knew right from wrong, no matter what the world threw at you. I envy that."

I sat quietly, not knowing what to say. This wasn't

the Markus I knew. Whoever this was, we'd never spoken before. Nova met my gaze, angling her head toward the woods. I dipped my chin. She wanted to hunt. I was safe. She got up, and he flinched. I pressed my lips together, trying not to smile, but she snorted, not trying to hide her amusement as she trotted to the tree line. Turning back to him, I said, "Look, I don't know what you want me to say right now."

"You don't have to say anything." He shook his head. "I had a lot of time to think while I was locked up in the dungeon—"

"You were locked in a dungeon?" I hadn't even known there was one. I turned around as though I could see the estate. It was miles away, but the shock of it made me look anyway. Jutting my thumb over my shoulder, I said, "They just said you were locked away . . . from me."

Markus chuckled. "It's okay. I mean, it was a surprise at first. I'm pretty sure Ysabeau took pleasure in it." Of course she had. She wanted to drag him through the streets, and she made no attempt at hiding it. He repositioned his body to face me, and I struggled with a fight-or-flight response. Or even just a "scooch away from him" response, but I didn't move. "I'm glad they put me there. I'm actually glad I heard you."

"I wasn't in control." *Lies*, my subconscious whispered. My cheeks flushed, and I was sure they were turning red. "I was . . ." *Enjoying every minute of it*, that voice reminded me. Ugh. Stupid feelings. I sighed deeply, hating the words that were about to come out. "It wasn't meant to hurt you."

"It helped me." My lips parted at the admission.

"It helped you?"

He nodded. "It opened up my mind. Hearing your call, and the pull of the heat. It was clarity. Proof. I could see us for what we *really* are."

Oh, no. My heart rate sped up, and I felt the color drain from my face. I'd let my guard down. I was alone, and he'd lured me into a trap. "No, we aren't anything."

"We're mates—"

"Stop it, Markus." I shook my head, scooting backward. Where was Nova?

"Let me finish," he said, scrunching his eyebrows and frowning.

Scrambling farther, I tried to get to my feet. To get away from him. And what did he do? Reached for me, but I hit his hand, and rolled over the ground out of range. He stood up at the same time I did.

"Dannika, what I'm saying is we're mates and we—"

"NOVA!" I screamed, patting my leg, only to find my sheath empty. The blade was imbedded in the ground between rocks where I had been boring a hole absentmindedly. *Fuck.*

Markus stepped toward me, and I heard my wolf's telltale footsteps pounding the earth. I turned to run away, pumping my legs to get into the woods and find a sturdy branch to knock over his thick head. Nova's growl sounded at the tree line, and she came barreling for him.

"Danni, I reject you!" he shouted, and I stopped dead in my tracks, sliding on the rocks. Looking over my shoulder, I saw Nova had done the same. Her head was cocked, considering Markus where he stood; his eyes squeezed shut, fists clenched, face tight into a grimace as he waited to be taken down by a giant wolf. He hadn't even shifted to protect himself, though a line of fur had exploded up his arms and neck.

He'd suppressed the natural instinct.

I was dumbfounded.

An invisible weight was lifted over my shoulders, and I felt something inside me release. A tightly wound cord that had been straining my very being snapped, freeing us from the veiled shackles our bond had created.

Gasping, I fell to my knees, lightheaded, but no longer restricted to that particular curse. Markus dropped in the same way, breathing heavily. "Are . . . you . . . okay?" he managed. "What happened?"

I nodded, exhaling through my nose. "We're not bound together anymore. The magic is gone"—I paused, taking more time to slow my heartbeat—"and it let go of us."

"I'm sorry." He panted, shaking his head. "You thought . . . You thought I was going to hurt you. I didn't mean to. I had . . . things I wanted to say. It didn't come out right."

Nova ran up to me, nudging me with her nose. There was almost a bounce in her step. She felt the release too. Running my fingers through her fur, I smiled at her, thanking her silently for coming when I'd needed her. She always would.

"Thank you," I said after my senses had settled. Markus looked stunned, probably never expecting those words to come from my mouth addressed to him. That made two of us.

"I'm sorry I didn't do it earlier," he said, glancing away. He shoved himself to a standing position, dusting off his jeans, and walked toward me. Holding out a palm, he offered to help me up. I took his outstretched hand, and for the first time, it felt like a truce. "I held on to something that wasn't there, and you suffered for it."

I wiped my hands off on my shirt. "What made you change your mind?" I asked. The reversal of his stance was so stark, it made me wonder if I was dreaming. Curiosity fueled so many questions.

"I realized it when you were in heat. That's what I was trying to say. Poorly, though, it would seem." He grimaced, running his fingers through his hair. "I could see us for what we were. We were mates, and we never should have been."

Ooooh. I winced, realizing I'd never given him the chance to finish speaking. In my mind, I'd known what he'd been going to say. My trauma had spoken for me. The past had let me believe I'd known what was going to happen.

Those traumas had protected me in many ways, even as their toxic aftermath continued to eat at me, they'd kept me guarded. But they'd also continued to harm me, letting me assume the worst in someone, even as he was trying his best.

"I thought the heat was going to make it worse," I admitted, crossing my arms as a breeze brushed over my skin, sprouting goosebumps everywhere.

"Me, too," he agreed. "It did at first. I could hear you, and I knew you were with him." I opened my mouth to explain, but he held a hand up. "It's okay. I mean, it wasn't then. I wanted to kill him. I tried to break through the door. But as the minutes turned to hours, it felt like a part of that tie between us loosened. Like you weren't there on the other side of it anymore."

I stared blankly. It had? How was that possible? "I don't understand . . ."

"I didn't either at first, but eventually it made sense. If we were truly meant to be mates, that wouldn't have happened. You aren't meant to be mine. You never wanted me, but the bond made reasoning cloudy, and I couldn't see the *why*. It was just so strong, that pull toward you. Fate couldn't be wrong, could it? That's what I kept telling myself. It took you being in heat and losing that connection slowly over days for me to realize it. None of it was ever real, but you knew that from the beginning."

"Wow. . ." I breathed, at a loss for words. It was so much more than I had even hoped for.

"Right?" he said, a small laugh escaping him. "You were willing to die rather than be with me, and even that wasn't enough for me to see it all." He crossed his arms, almost looking uncomfortable as he stood in silence for a moment. Clearing his throat, he spoke again. "Can I ask you something?"

"Sure?" I said, though I was sure it sounded like a question.

"You don't have to answer me. I've asked before . . . Why didn't you kill me? You saved me. A few times. But in the throes of the mate bond, I thought it was because deep down, you wanted to be with me. Now I understand that's not the case." He left the statement open-ended, not pushing it further.

I blew out a big breath, my cheeks expanding. I could give him that. "I didn't kill you at the commemoration because it was wrong. All of it. The way your father acted, the way he was willing to throw us both out on a whim because he thinks we've sullied the Del Reyes name, the way he wanted one of us to die—mostly me. It was all wrong. You deserved so many things, Markus, but you didn't deserve to die. You still don't. I wasn't going to let your dad win. He doesn't care about you, and he was going to prove it again that night, only I didn't know how far he'd take it. That's why I said you were in Blood and Beryl when Elias rescued us."

"You were willing to die, though. You wouldn't fight back. What would have happened if I hadn't . . . if I hadn't stopped?"

I swallowed thickly. "Then we wouldn't be here, would we? And you'd have to live with it. But I wasn't going to."

He shook his head in disbelief. "You could have died." His voice was barely a whisper. "And it would have been my fault."

"You made a choice not to kill me. So really, thank you for that. Definitely appreciated," I said. He met my eyes, snorting a small laugh. "And yes. I would have died, but I couldn't live with myself if I killed you, or anyone, without cause."

He scrunched his eyebrows, giving me an incredulous look. "How was that *not* a just cause?"

"I don't believe in killing someone unless it's self-defense, and before you say it, it wasn't self-defense. It was Mathis setting up a blood match. There was no winner, no matter the outcome. I wasn't going to be a part of it. That was my choice." I shrugged my shoulders, hoping it all made sense to him.

"You make it seem effortless."

I twisted my lips, considering him as we stood just feet apart. I felt like I could say more, and that he would hear it, so I continued, voicing thoughts I hadn't shared with anyone.

"I spent my childhood missing my father. My mom always said I was so much like him. He was fair and even-tempered. He wasn't a killer, but he punished accordingly. He was kind but fierce. They were things I didn't believe about myself, but I knew I could be that way. If he were still here, he would've been guiding me. I know what he would have wanted me to be, and it was in line with who I knew I wanted to be too. I may not be the heir to that House anymore, but I strive to embody all that it means to be a leader, even if no one sees me as one." I touched my father's ring that hung around my neck, that small reminder that he was with me.

Silence spanned between us. I couldn't believe I'd shared that with Markus, of all people. After a while, he smiled, though it didn't reach his eyes. There was a sadness to it, and it ran deep.

"I've learned a lot from you. About myself, about our life in Fire and Fluorite. Things maybe I didn't want to realize about my family, or me . . ." He turned, taking in the waterfall. "I, um . . . I know I said I wasn't going to stay, but with your permission, I'd like to remain in Blood and Beryl."

"You're asking me?" I pointed toward my chest, eyebrows rising. He nodded. "Yeah, I mean . . . I want you to make a life for yourself somewhere. Here is as good a place as any. Work doing something you like. Maybe you can find yourself a friend or two?"

He chuckled, tipping his head back. "Oh, I'm not entirely sure that will happen yet. The way everyone gave you the stink eye back home? It would appear that the tables have turned." He waved his hand, as if it weren't a concern. "I'm okay. I'm not sure I'd want to be friends with me, either."

"You *are* hard to like sometimes," I said, but a grin crept upon my face.

He dipped his chin. "So you've told me. It's something I need to work on. Amongst many, *many* other things."

He looked like a puppy that had been kicked. In all reality, he was. He'd spent his life under his father's fist. If I stepped outside of my own emotions for a moment, empathy for his experience took hold. Neither one of us had fathers, not really. At least the stories of mine were honorable, and I had a family filled with love.

I'd rather have my life than his any day of the week —the good, the bad, and the ugly. Even on my worst days, it would have been better than the life he'd lived. It didn't excuse his behaviors. He would atone for that, and for once, I believed it was possible, given time.

"I'm sorry I didn't let you finish talking earlier. I had every intention of stabbing you, or hitting you with a tree branch, and here you were, trying to do the right thing."

"For once." Markus huffed a humorless laugh and shook his head. He took my hands in his and I didn't feel the need to recoil or defend myself. Holding them firmly, he looked me in the eye. "You owe me nothing. Certainly not an apology." He pressed his lips into a tight, thin smile. "I never deserved you, Dannika Kresley. You are too good for me. For Fire and Fluorite. For any of them. Remember that."

Then he let me go.

In more ways than one.

I watched him walk away, into the trees, never once looking back. Nova came to my side, knocking her head against my arm.

I tried to remember how long it had been since the commemoration. A touch over three weeks since that fateful, cursed night.

The chains were broken now.

An overwhelming sense of freedom filled me, and I threw my arms out, letting the breeze lick my skin. Markus had rejected me. Finally. No blood had been spilled. We could move on with our lives. I looked up, checking the sun's position in the sky to gauge the time. I wanted to get home and tell Elias. Screw the fight and the notes and the ignoring each other. I just wanted to talk to him and share everything that had just happened. Describe the feeling of being let go, and the internal snap when the bond had been truly broken. I wanted him to listen.

I sighed.

None of it was business for me. Not anymore. I wanted him. I loved spending time with him. I didn't need to be rejected to know that. If anything, I just felt it more.

For the first time in my life, I felt romantic love. I knew what it meant to *be* in love with someone. It wasn't a bond decided by fate. It was genuine. It was decided by *me*, without the influence of any magic whatsoever. I couldn't keep this inside me now that I was actually free to do something with it. My stomach twisted in a knot, wondering how Elias would respond, but I had to know. I couldn't spend my life here if he wanted nothing to do with me. Now that I could make my choices, that was exactly what I was going to do.

Maybe he was just as pissed off and stupid as I had been. I'd said things I hadn't meant. He might've done the same. I held on to a thread of hope that I was right, and some unknown voice inside me said it would be the case.

"C'mon, Nova," I said, taking off at a jog on the trail back home.

I had no idea where to find him, but I knew if I left him a note, he'd see it. Except this note wouldn't be so snarky.

CHAPTER 22
ELIAS

Two days.

Two days since I'd said what was between us wasn't real. Two days that Dannika had been leaving me notes reminding me of what an asshole I'd been. Two days I'd been wishing to turn back time, but not to that moment. I'd go back to when I could have told her it was more than business. To let her know she meant more than that to me. To tell her I wanted to *choose* her as my mate.

Fuck fate.

I had a choice in who to love, and I'd done everything to screw it up.

She was angry. Rightly so. I'd scolded her in public. I'd made every effort to talk about us like we weren't a real couple. Then I'd gotten my feelings hurt when she'd played along with that? The worst of it was that I couldn't bear to hear her say that everything she'd said and done while she'd been in heat had been a lie. It had felt so real. The hunger had been forced upon her, but the connection between us? I couldn't understand how that could have been faked.

I replayed the confrontation in my head over and over. I'd missed something. There was a piece to the puzzle that was misplaced, leaving a gaping hole, the entire picture incomplete and not making any sense. If we were nothing more than a business arrangement, why did our fight break us apart so terribly? I sighed. Nothing could excuse what I'd said to her. I'd said it to make her feel as badly as I had in that moment, and it had worked. I cringed, repeating the nastiness of my words and the tone of my voice so it echoed in my memory.

Leaning back in my chair, I dug my fists into my eyes. The throbbing headache should have subsided. What good were healing powers when you couldn't stop your own head from pounding? I could regrow an eyeball, but I couldn't stop stress from needling at my brain. Nature's joke, right there.

My thoughts were ugly, asking if I'd pushed her too far. She may have been soft, but she wasn't a pushover. She wouldn't accept someone who bullied her, let alone blackmailed her. Did I even have a chance to make this right? Did I deserve that chance? Deserve *her*? Markus still hadn't rejected her. My mind toyed with me and whispered that she could still choose him. She would never, I'd argue with myself in return, but it didn't stop the noise.

It was my fault. A chasm between us of my own making. And I would do everything in my power to make it right, given time. *If she even lets you*, a voice rasped in my subconscious.

Yes. If she let me.

"Elias?" Bianca's chipper voice sounded on the other side of my office door. I called for her to come in, and she entered, halting when she took in my form. "For the love of the gods . . . have you slept? You look terrible."

My expression flattened. "It's good to see you too, Bianca."

She fixed the shock on her face, then sat down in front of me, setting the pile of folders she'd been carrying on her lap. "I didn't mean . . . It's just. Look, I call it like I see it. You look like a pile of shit."

Huffing through my nose, I said, "It matches how I feel at the moment."

"Permission to speak freely?" she asked, and I raised my eyebrows in response.

"I'm sorry, weren't you doing that already?"

"Perks of growing up with you." She grinned, lifting a single shoulder. "But seriously. Are you okay?"

I nodded. "I haven't slept much. Just a lot going on."

Twisting her lips, she considered me. "Whatever you said or did to Dannika, fix it."

Her perceptiveness caught me off guard. "I . . ."

"Don't lie to me. I've known you your entire life. Give me more credit than that," she deadpanned.

I sniffed, then turned to look out the window. "I might have said something I didn't mean in a moment of heated discussion."

"That's a very diplomatic way of saying you were a righteous asshole in the middle of a fight." Bianca cocked her head to the side, and I frowned. "Just make it right. You clearly regret it. Tell her. She's the one for you, Elias. Fate be damned, you know she is."

I snapped my head in her direction, wide-eyed. No one knew the truth except Ysa. "How?"

She rolled her eyes. "Seriously? You're like my brother, Elias. I know you. Are you really telling me you wouldn't be able to figure it out if I were pulling this same scam?"

I stared silently, considering her words. I would've noticed. I knew Bianca as well as she knew herself. I also knew her loyalty to my family was as strong as my loyalty to hers. I pressed my lips together, then dipped my chin. "Fair enough."

She nodded once. "No one knows. No one even suspects. I mean, there's Ysabeau, but you tell her everything." I acknowledged her assumptions, and she smirked. "Whatever it is with Dannika, I'm sure you can fix it. She loves you."

I barked a laugh. "You aren't as all-knowing as you think you are."

"Yes, I am," she said, her tone flat. "You're just blind to it. I've seen the way you two act when you're together. You are head over heels smitten with that shifter, and she is just as besotted as you. Maybe you can't see it, but I can. It's obvious, and it's not just the show you're trying to put on for everyone."

A knock sounded at the door, and I cleared my throat, thankful her interrogation was ending.

"Ysabeau," I said, after she came in. "Do you have—"

"Ask her," Bianca interjected, jutting her thumb in my second's direction. "She'll tell you."

"Tell him what, exactly?" Ysa asked, her words slow with caution.

"That he and Dannika are in love with each other."

Ysa turned to look at me through her dark glasses, keeping her stoic face, giving away nothing.

I frowned, nodding my head. "Yeah, she knows."

She tilted her head back, letting out a raucous laugh. "Then yes, Bianca is right. I will tell you the same thing. And you've been a moody bitch for two days now, all because you got into an argument."

Bianca grinned like a fool. "See?" She stood up, setting the files on my desk. "Dannika brings out your better nature, brother," she said softly, using the term of endearment reserved only for moments we shared that involved matters of intimacy. Never once had she used it at Court, or in public. "Don't let that go."

"I'm not sure I have a better nature," I muttered.

"True," she agreed, tilting her head to the side. "But if Ysa and I see what both of you really are when you're with each other, that means something." She walked to the door, leaving the files she'd been carrying on my desk.

I pointed to them. "What are these?"

She waved her hand in the air. "I'm the High Court liaison. I liasoned."

"Bianca," I stated firmly.

Standing in the doorway, she turned to look at me. "Correspondence from other Houses in regard to the disaster that was the commemoration hosted by our *favorite* leader at Fire and Fluorite. Read through it. It bodes well for us. It would appear Mathis's call for blood and punishment in public didn't resonate with other advisors and councils. No one is willing to make a move yet, but their interest is piqued." She winked, then left, closing the door softly behind her.

"You told her?" Ysa asked, raising her eyebrows in surprise.

"She figured it out. I didn't say a word."

Ysa shrugged. "I'm not surprised. It's Bianca. She's observant, and she's good at reading people. That's part of her job. Blood or not, she is your family. It's hard to keep secrets from her."

"It would seem so." Ysa held a single file, and I jutted my chin while I looked at it, indicating it was time for a change of topic. "What do you have for me?"

Her expression changed, and she sat in the chair Bianca had been in. "It's all the intel you asked for on Dannika and her family, and the pack that Abbey is from." She placed it on my desk, pushing it across the wood with her index finger. It sat in front of me, unopened. I toyed with the edge of the thick manila cardstock, but I couldn't bring myself to look. "Is there a problem?" Ysa asked, her brows furrowing.

I exhaled loudly. "It feels like a breach of trust to read about her life on paper like this. She told me if I was curious, I could ask her anything. Perhaps I should." I'd already made more than enough mistakes with her. How would she react if she knew I had research done on her and her family? What if there was something in this file she didn't want to tell me yet? I'd hurt her enough. I shook my head, pushing the file back to Ysa. "I can't. Not right now."

The crease between Ysa's brows deepened. "Elias," she started, but she paused. Her mouth opened, then closed, and she twisted her lips to the side. This wasn't like her. She was straightforward and didn't take time to think about her words this carefully.

"What?" I asked, finding myself annoyed.

"There's something in that file you need to know. Now."

"No, I'm not going to—"

"Listen to me. As your second," she said harshly. Her expression softened, and her voice lowered. "And as your friend. This is important."

That had my attention. I could only recall a handful of times that Ysa had played that card. None of which had ever been regarding good news. My gut tightened. I tilted my head in her direction, telling her to speak her piece.

"Danni's father," she started. "He died in the Great Sacrifice."

I blew out a sigh of relief and nodded. "I already know this. It was the night she was born."

Ysa shook her head slightly and took her sunglasses off. The look in her dark eyes stilled me. Regret. Pain. The sense of dread was overwhelming. "Did she tell you who he was?"

"No."

She closed her eyes, sighing. When she opened them, the anxiety inside only worsened. She was able to communicate entirely too much with just a simple look. "He was Scott Kingston."

I slumped in my chair, staring blankly at Ysabeau.

"No," I breathed. "But he was . . . Alpha Supreme before Mathis. He was . . ."

"Her father," she finished, reaffirming her statement. "And she was the rightful heir."

Leaning forward, I ran my hands through my hair, resting my elbows on the desk. Cradling my head, the past ran through my mind. I squeezed my eyes shut. "But her last name . . ." I trailed off. Maybe Ysa was wrong.

She tapped on the file. "Is her mother's. Mathis had the name Kingston wiped from their family. No member of any pack in Fire and Fluorite carries that surname, and no child born is permitted to have it as a first name."

I knew her father. He was a good man. A good leader. When I thought about everything I knew about Danni, it made sense. Her innate sense of decency, her tenacious spirit, her desire to keep the harmony and not hurt others, and her ability to stand her ground when necessary: It had all come from Scott. She embodied every quality I'd admired in him. He was the complete opposite of me.

And I was the reason he was dead.

Guilt consumed every inch of my being.

"Does she know?" Ysa whispered.

I shook my head. "No. I failed to mention the part where my actions caused Claudette's death and I started the war, thereby causing her father's death in turn."

"You didn't start the war, Elias. We were on the cusp of one already."

"Didn't I, though? I threw everything Claudette had worked for out the window. I knew Mathis had killed her. There was no hope for a treaty once she'd died. Mathis knew I would react, and I was too grief-stricken at the time to see it." I pounded the table with my fist, splitting the wood.

"Stop it," she chided, her features stern and hard. "It didn't matter how much Claudette and Mathis negotiated; he was never going to let Scott sign that treaty. He baited you, and how many others? He didn't care how; he was going to take over Fire and Fluorite. He was going to kill Scott, no matter what. He just needed the shroud of war to do it."

"I'm the one who gave it to him." I groaned in frustration. It explained Mathis's pure hatred for Danni. The way he'd spewed venom and called for her death had been personal, but I hadn't understood why at the time.

"You did. And if it hadn't been you, someone else was going to jump. The entire world was standing at the edge of death and destruction. No treaty was going to stop that. Evil and greed can't be caged. It knows no boundaries. No treaties. No peace agreements. It answers to no one. Look at what we've learned of Mathis. He will stop at *nothing*, and we have all the signed, magical binding papers in place. Do you honestly believe you, a single vampire—king or not—could have stopped any of it?"

"No." But it was easier for me to take that blame. If I didn't, it felt like I was dishonoring my sister's memory. Like her loss was just a causality of war, something to be explained away without taking responsibility. Like it hadn't turned my entire existence upside down when Claudette had been murdered, left headless and on display on the land that bordered Fire and Fluorite and what was now No Man's Land, the unsigned peace treaty stabbed into her heart.

"Then let it go. I did. I was supposed to go with her that night, and I didn't. Her death wasn't my fault. The fact that she died alone is, but that is something I can't change." Ysa's eyes lowered, and her voice quivered for the briefest of moments. I hadn't heard that level of sadness or vulnerability from her in twenty-four years.

I blinked rapidly, never once having considered that Ysa felt guilt over that.

"You know you would have died too," I said, watching her.

"I would have. It's a strange thing to process the guilt of not dying with her while also being thankful to still be alive." A single tear dropped from her eye, and she put her sunglasses back on.

"I actually know that exact feeling," I admitted.

"Does Danni know Mathis killed her father?" she

asked, gesturing to the file. "Because in there, it doesn't look like it. I can't be sure. Our spies could only get so much information, and anyone they spoke to wasn't keen on discussing it. Not everyone there is loyal to him, which we already knew. The complete intel on this isn't easily obtained."

I shook my head after a moment of thinking. "She hates Mathis, but I didn't get the impression she knew he'd killed her father. When she spoke of him, it was less about his death and more about his memory."

Ysa pursed her lips. "Sounds like you have a lot to talk about." Reaching into her pocket, she pulled out a folded piece of paper, reaching out to hand it over. "Danni asked me to pass this on to you."

I hesitated, but took it from her grasp. "When did she give you this?"

"On my way here. She found me while she was looking for you."

I unfolded it, expecting another smartass message telling me she was going to the pantry to eat my cookies. Or she was going to do laundry because she'd run out of socks.

I'm not in the bathroom or roaming the forest. I'm not throwing knives in the weapons training room, pretending it's your head. I'm not off raiding the kitchen again. I'm here in our room, waiting. The fireplace is lit. Dinner will be brought up at seven. I just want to talk. Please. I have so much I want to tell you.

D.

Ysa reached in her pocket and tossed me a bag. I caught it midair, then looked at it. It was a bunch of chocolate-dipped animal crackers in a pouch. I'd just had them made and had specifically hidden them in a new location. I let out a laugh, then looked up at my second, who rolled her eyes.

"I need to find a better hiding place," I muttered.

"She's a shifter, Elias. She's going to sniff out everything." I tilted my head. It was a good point.

My thoughts drifted to Dannika wanting to talk. Her note wasn't like the others had been. Not once had she signed a note. Not once had she asked to talk. She'd been short with me. Nothing but passive aggressive. She'd even left a note on top of the bed while she'd been in it, telling me she was asleep.

I'd barely slept since that day. I'd stayed in the chair by the fireplace both nights. I'd occasionally doze off, but I couldn't sleep. Not when I could hear her breathing. Smell her intoxicating scent. I wanted to talk to her. Taste her. Tell her . . . well, everything.

Ysa groaned. "What?"

I chewed on the inside of my cheek, endless bullet points of what needed to be said bouncing around in my thoughts. "I have no clue where to start."

She looked at me over the rim of her sunglasses,

then pointed to the note. "You go to your room and talk to her, you dumbass."

I narrowed my eyes. "Yes, thank you for that."

"Then what do you mean, you aren't sure where to start?" She gestured to the door. "She's telling you she wants you. Let me explain something to you as a friend, Elias. Danni is young, and the woman hasn't had a long-lasting relationship. You embarrassed her in public, then you both said some things to each other that you shouldn't have. But a woman doesn't leave passive aggressive notes for two days when she doesn't care. She isn't leaving Markus notes, and all she has wanted was for that tool to leave her alone. Maybe she isn't the best at communicating, but neither are you. Go talk to her." She looked at the file. "About everything."

"That's a shit ton for her to unpack in one conversation," I said, looking at the folder.

"I'm sure you'll figure it out." Standing up, she pushed her glasses up her nose and checked the time. "It's five-thirty. Chop chop."

"Ysa," I said, making her pause with her hand on the door. She looked at me over her shoulder. "Thank you. For all of it." She dipped her chin to the side, then exited, leaving me alone in my thoughts.

That felt like a dangerous place to be.

I owed Danni so much. An apology. An explanation. The truth. Multiple truths, it would seem. More than just the admission of my feelings for her. How could I tell her I loved her, and in the same breath, tell her my reaction to Mathis killing my sister was the reason her father died? I'd heard the pain she felt when she'd told me about him. I was the one who'd put it there. I didn't know if that was something that was forgivable.

I leaned back, turning my head to gaze out the expansive window. The sun was beginning to set over the horizon, laying a blanket of darkness over the mountains. Danni wouldn't expect me back yet. Not until seven. I had time.

I just needed to figure out how to say it all and not break her heart all over again.

CHAPTER 23

DANNIKA

Tick. Tick. Tick.

Minute by minute, the first hour crawled by.

Then the second.

The clock's hands kept moving around its face.

Nine.

Ten.

Eleven . . .

Why wasn't he here?

I looked at Nova and her eyes met mine before she looked at the door.

"Yeah," I agreed. "Let's go look for him."

He was a king. He was busy running an entire House. He was just late, that's all.

The halls were silent this time of night, but I knew vampires were working behind the scenes. This mansion was always in motion, one way or another. Elias's spicy scent was everywhere, filling my nostrils but not leading me in one particular direction.

Nova and I passed the library, but after a quick search, it was empty. We headed to the throne room, but I only found Marisa and Uriah working on something. Poking my head in, I cleared my throat.

"Good evening, Dannika," Marisa said, smiling and gesturing to the table. "Would you like to join us? It's not exciting, I'm afraid, but you're welcome to give us some input. Just some building plans for future developments on Blood and Beryl territories. I'd love to get your take on interior additions you would find useful."

I forced a polite smile. "I have to decline for now, but maybe tomorrow if you're available. I was actually wondering if Elias was in here. I had . . . something to discuss with him."

"I haven't seen him since this morning," she said, turning to Uriah. "You?"

"Afraid not. But . . ." He paused, opening a notebook that was on the table. He dragged his finger down, reading before he looked up. "He had late afternoon meetings with Bianca, Ysa, and Katie, in that order."

A touch of excitement filled me. Hopefully Katie could lead me to wherever he was.

"Thanks," I said, giving them a half wave and

leaving as quickly as I could. I didn't miss the confused looks on their faces as I practically ran out.

I walked briskly and Nova kept pace beside me, pointing her nose in the air every now and then. I knew his main office was on another level, so we trekked up the stairs in a hurry, rounding a corner without slowing down.

Crash.

I collided with a body, tumbling to the ground with a loud thud. Nova huffed loudly, nudging my arm like she was reminding me to be careful. *I know, I know. I need to slow down.* Groaning, I pushed myself up and dusted my pants off. Katie was sprawled out, papers littering the floor. She brought herself to a sitting position. "I'm so sorry," I blurted out, holding my hand out to her to help her up.

"Dannika!" she said in surprise, rushing to stand. "My apologies, milady, I should have—"

"Stop," I whispered calmly. Embarrassment crept up my cheeks, and I looked around. "I ran into you. You're not supposed to be the one to say you're sorry."

"That's not exactly how that works," she said with a nervous laugh.

"Sure it is," I retorted. "I bump into you; that's my fault. I apologize."

Katie shook her head slightly, but smiled, bending down to pick up papers. I knelt beside her, helping to clean up everything she'd been carrying. "You'll get used to it. Being royalty, I mean."

Grabbing another paper and transferring it to a pile, I looked at her. "What will I get used to? I don't understand."

"All of it, of course." She took several folders, then started putting papers back in them. "It's probably really weird to think about, but being queen means you aren't wrong. It's our job to look out for you, not the other way around. If a mistake is made, that's on us."

"That doesn't make sense." I scrunched my eyebrows. That wasn't how I'd been taught, and it sure didn't seem like Elias ran things that way. I knew I hadn't been around long, but still.

Katie pressed her lips together in a forced smile. "It's okay. It will. Blood and Beryl thrives for it. Elias has a reputation for a reason, you know?" She stood up, tucking her hair behind her ear.

I stood up with her, handing her the stack of papers I'd collected. "Yeah," I said quietly. "Speaking of Elias, have you seen him?"

"We had a meeting earlier, but he cut it short," she answered, looking slightly annoyed.

"When was that?" I asked, feeling hopeful.

"Oh, hours ago. Ended at about six-thirty," she said, tilting her head toward the front of the mansion. "Said he was cancelling his next meeting and was going to be off the estate for a while, letting off steam."

My heart sank and my stomach twisted. "His next meeting?" I repeated quietly.

"Yeah, a seven o'clock, I guess? I told him I'd cancel it for him, but he said it wasn't needed. Said there was 'no reason for him to show up' and then he left," she said, using air quotes as she held her files awkwardly. "*To blow off steam,*" she mocked. "Like women don't know what that *really* means." Scoffing, she rolled her eyes.

I let out a tiny breath of air, not gasping, but still in shock. Katie's annoyed grimace turned flat, her eyes widening and her lips parting. "Fuck, I . . . *fuck,*" she whispered harshly. "I shouldn't have said any of that. I'm just frustrated, and I've been working on something that I needed to go over with him, and he blew me off to go get, um—and that's not your fault, I just started complaining, and I shouldn't have said any of that to you." Her words spilled out, rushed, and filled with horror.

Nova licked my arm, whining ever so slightly.

I cleared my throat. "Mates don't . . . they don't step out of the relationship. The bond . . . That's not how it works," I said, trying to convince myself he wouldn't do that.

Katie's gaze softened, and she looked at me with sympathy. "You'll get used it. Being royalty," she repeated, echoing her earlier statement. "Royal mates do whatever they want. Look at Mathis. Everyone knows he fucks around even though he's mated. Elias is um, well he's hard to please. He'll be good to you, but . . . you know . . . monogamy isn't his thing. He has a reputation for that too. It's a royalty thing. It's just . . . It's just how it is," she whispered. "I'm so sorry, Dannika. I've said entirely too much, and it wasn't my place." She shook her head, sniffling and walking by me as quickly as she could. I watched her go, taking the stairs swiftly.

Looking down at Nova, I didn't know what to do. So I just walked back to our room with her by my side. No licks or nudges. No sounds. One step after the other, my feet felt like lead as an overwhelming sadness tried to pull me under.

When I opened the door, I looked at the chair by the fireplace. I moved across the room silently, and I fell back into it, letting the pain take over. I'd been sitting there like a damned fool all night. Like a loyal puppy, eagerly waiting for Elias to come home and give me affection.

I'd imagined he'd walk through the door, smiling. That he'd apologize, and I'd apologize. I could tell him that Markus had rejected me and that more than anything in this world, I wanted to be with him. To be part of his family, and for him to be part of mine. I could tell him that I loved him. And he would admit he felt the same.

I replayed our times together over and over in my mind. I swore he'd felt it too.

But he didn't.

Katie's words echoed. I knew Mathis was terrible to his mate. Everyone knew. I'd just never really thought about how it was possible. I didn't know how royalty or leaders could feel a different mate bond. But I knew Katie wasn't wrong about Mathis. I knew I wasn't accustomed to how it all worked because not only had I rejected my mate and fought against the bond, but I also wasn't heir. That had been taken from me. There was so much I didn't know, and I felt so stupid for it. So naïve.

Bianca had told me that he and Katie had been together, but it didn't work out. Now I knew why. She didn't want to be cheated on, and she didn't want to be the mistress. Elias and I weren't even real mates. That was my future with him.

He'd never even wanted a mate. No distraction. No commitment. I understood why. I just hadn't understood that everything behind the scenes was to get laid. I choked on a sob, coughing when I tried to rein it in, shaking my head violently to make the realization just go away.

Leaning forward, I put my head in my hands, fingers scraping my scalp. I grabbed and pulled, wrenching it tightly, cursing the dirty thoughts as they filtered through my mind. A growl built in my throat. Nova whined, her head nuzzling my leg from where she lay on the carpet.

I had been ostracized and ridiculed my entire life. I'd had rumors spread while people had pointed their crooked fingers at me, laughing and mocking, making sure I'd heard every vile word, but I didn't care because those people had never mattered to me.

None of that held a candle to what I was feeling now.

Anger built inside me, threatening to explode. The pressure increased, teasing and taunting, ready to tear apart the seams of my fragile existence. I'd never felt so vulnerable. Foolish. Hurt. Unlovable. *Rejected.* The combination was so sharp and raw that I couldn't contain it.

I lashed out, a guttural cry escaping my lips, sweeping my arm across the table of food that had long since gone cold. Plates clanked. Glass shattered. Water spilled over the mahogany edge of the table.

I didn't care.

He felt nothing for me.

My mouth felt dry. My face was hot. A dull and numbing ache filled my head, fogging everything except the pain. I stared at the clock again.

Tick. Tick. Tick.

Tock.

The hands aligned, pointing up, striking midnight. I couldn't stop myself. I grabbed my phone and dialed Adora's number. It rang twice before she answered. I hit the *speaker* button, then tossed it on the bed.

"What's wrong?" Her words were muffled when she answered. She was tired, but awake, probably having fallen asleep reading a book.

"I'm leaving."

My body was on autopilot, going through the motions. Opening drawers, pulling out clothes. I grabbed the backpack I'd come with and started stuffing things into it. Nova whined again. "Did something happen with Elias?" Adora asked, her voice dropping an octave.

Yes. "No."

"Liar," she said. "If you're going to run away, at least tell me what went down."

"Is your line secure?"

I heard silence, then a muffled sound "They aren't monitoring right now. Probably too late."

"How do you know?"

"I traded my jade necklace to a technopath witch to make me a scrambler, and it tells me if I'm being listened to." I squeezed my eyes shut.

"He's not who I thought he was," I said, finally answering her question. "I'll fill you in, but not right now. I'm packing my bag and then taking a car. I'm going to drive to Portland."

"You're stealing a car?" I could hear the question in her voice.

"Borrowing."

Adora whistled under her breath. "You're serious right now?"

"Dead serious."

"You can't stay in No Man's Land. You'll be a walking target," she argued. More shuffling in the background caught my attention as she spoke.

"I'm going to travel the coast. Try to make my way to Earth and Emerald. If they won't take me, hatred for Mathis and Elias declaring me his mate will at least get Gold and Garnet's attention. I'm sure they'd take me—even if it's so no one else can." Everyone wanted a pawn in their play for power. Might as well use it to my advantage.

"I have a better plan." I could hear her moving about. The sound of a zipper closing. Feet in shoes. Keys jingling. "Don't drive too fast. I'll meet you there—"

"You can't," I said, glancing at the phone as I shoved my hairbrush in. Clothes? Check. Blood vials? Check. Toothbrush? I ducked into the bathroom. Memories of the heat flashed through me. The bathtub. Crawling toward the bedroom door. Aching for him. Elias kneeling beside me, his hand between my legs . . .

She scoffed on the other line. "One, I can. Two,

Gold and Garnet are a bunch of assassins and mercenaries. You wouldn't last a week on your own. Three, I should have done this last time." She sighed into the receiver. I could hear her breathing. The faint hum of her heart. She must have it pressed between her shoulder and cheek.

"It's not safe," I grunted, zipping my pack shut. "It wasn't then, and it's not now. Mathis sucks, but he won't kill you if you don't give him reason to—"

"Fuck Mathis," Adora spat. "And while we're at it, fuck the excuses. I'm not leaving you to navigate this alone. You're my sister—my *person*—and if Blood and Beryl isn't working out, we'll find somewhere that does. Together."

I squeezed my eyes shut, angling my neck back. "What's your plan?"

"The river. Tristan will give us passage from Sea and Serpentine. It's a twelve-hundred-mile river, and there are a ton of offshoots. We can get to Earth and Emerald without an issue."

She'd had an ongoing fling with a selkie guard, and they'd meet up in Portland. Strictly a friends-with-benefits situation. If I wasn't so tense, I'd laugh that her sexcapades would end up being my way out of this godsforsaken place. The confidence in her tone was strong, and I would always trust her. She'd thought of running away before, apparently, but that was a conversation for another time.

After a few moments of silence, I released a tight breath. "Don't drag Mom and Abbey into this. Just leave them a note."

"No shit," Adora said. "Do I need to tell you don't let Markus follow you?"

"He won't, but thanks for being a smartass."

She huffed a laugh. "I love you, Danni."

I yanked Elias's nightstand drawer open, taking Ysa's truck keys and stuffing them in my pocket. A notebook sat neatly tucked under a book, and I picked it up, ripping a piece of paper from it, taking the pen beside it. "I love you too. Be safe, okay? I'll meet you in the alley next to The Salty Siren."

"See you soon, sis."

The line went dead. I glanced at the time. Ten after midnight. Emotion clogged my throat again. Water filled my eyes, hovering on the brim, threatening to spill over.

I put the pen to paper and didn't let myself think about it. To hurt about it. The words wrote themselves. I didn't have to make it long and drawn out. There was no reason to. If Elias cared, he'd be here with me. Not . . . wherever he was.

The note was simple. It was the truth. My truth, and my goodbye.

With one last look at our room, I turned to the door, refusing to let the tears fall. Wiping beneath my eyelids, I straightened my back, tossing my backpack over my shoulder. Nova treaded lightly by my side.

The ink was still wet on the page when we snuck out the side door.

The guards near the garage wouldn't question their future queen when she said she was going for a night climb to watch the sunrise. They wouldn't stop me as I left the main property. They wouldn't think to watch me veer off that road so I could get on the path leading to Portland.

And they didn't.

With the vehicle lights turned off, I sped away, glancing in the rearview mirror as the estate got smaller. Nova hunkered in the back of the truck, looking between me and the house, then she threw her head back, letting out a deafening howl.

Something inside me fractured when she did.

Maybe it was my soul.

There was nothing left of my heart to break.

ELIAS

A piercing howl rent the air, so deep and raw, I felt it in my bones.

Dannika's wolf called to me in the distance, but it echoed through the forest, bouncing its painful cry off the conifers. I spun in a circle, trying to determine the direction I needed to run toward.

Toward Danni.

Toward my future.

I was lost. I tried to call out, but my voice failed me.

Another howl, but this one was clearer, and I took off to follow it. She needed me. I was faster than any other species of supernatural. It was a gift. Damp earth squashed beneath my boots as they pounded into the ground, flinging mud as I ran.

There she was. Standing in a clearing, unmoving.

Bloody tears fell from her face, and I panicked. She was injured. Markus came out from the trees, a wicked, leering grin on his face. He tossed a dagger in front of him, catching it by the hilt. Teasing as he dragged it over her skin. And still, she was frozen. I was going to kill him. This time, she'd let me.

But the earth held me, wrapping claw-like tendrils around my legs, pulling me down. I threw my wrist out, conjuring a blade. Aiming for Markus, I hurled it with perfect precision. It sailed in slow motion; the moonlight gleaming off the steel. Then he laughed, his form evaporating and turning into Danni. My face fell, and the knife landed true, right in her heart.

The pain of watching her death tore through me, and my body jolted. I sat upright, taking in my dark surroundings. Papers were scattered all over the desktop. I hadn't slept in days, and now it'd finally caught up to me. I'd fallen asleep writing out what I wanted to say. I scrubbed my hands down my face, feeling the spot on my forehead that had been resting against the desk for entirely too long.

Fuck.

The clock read a quarter to one.

Fuck, fuck, shit, damn, fuck.

Maybe she was still awake.

I jumped out of my chair, sending it rolling into the wooden bookshelves behind me. I had to get to her. I had to explain. Tell her I was sorry.

My office door was slightly ajar. Had she come looking for me?

Running down the hallway, I came to our bedroom, and I slowed my pace on my approach. I didn't want to barge in, cracking the frame and scaring her. It wasn't the tone I wanted to set. Tilting my head side to side, I cracked my neck, then opened the door.

Our bed was empty and undisturbed, the covers pulled up neatly the way it had been all day. Embers glowed in the fireplace, but the fire hadn't been tended to for some time. Glassware, plates, and food littered the ground by the two chairs that sat in front of the hearth. Guilt ate at me. She'd had a dinner set up for us, and I'd never showed. Walking to the bathroom, I saw the door was cracked. I knocked, but there was no answer, so I went in.

Empty.

I pinched the bridge of my nose and exited, heading toward the chair. I'd messed up so badly, and I had no way of knowing how I could make it up to her. I didn't even know where she was sleeping tonight, but I didn't blame her for not wanting it to be here.

Dropping into the chair, something crunched beneath me. Reaching under, I pulled out a piece of paper and opened it. Her handwriting covered it. This was different from her previous notes. It was longer, and it looked rushed. Messy.

As I began reading it, my stomach roiled.

All I wanted was to tell you I love you. That I chose you —because we can do that, right? Make those choices for ourselves and refuse to let fate decide for us? At least I thought we could. I didn't want this to be fake. It became real to me. Maybe fate knows better. I don't know anymore. What I do know is that I can't spend a lifetime while you pretend to love me in public when I'm nothing more than a means to an end.

I won't do that to myself.

Tell them I rejected you because I'm cursed. It's a believable story.

Time froze. I read the words again. And again. The paper shook in my hands. I jumped up, running to her dresser. No bag. Drawers partially empty.

The howl was real. It had been Nova. They were leaving.

Bursting through our door, I ran down the hall-way, flying down the stairs. I bellowed for Ysa, projecting my voice to get everyone on this godsfor-saken estate in front of me.

Soldiers appeared from nowhere, at the ready. I saw my second arrive, her eyes wide and filled with confusion as she took me in.

"Danni is gone," I said, my jaw tight, holding up the note. I didn't care who saw it. I needed her back.

Ysa's expression turned hard. Turning, she shouted, "Search for her. Send word to close down borders. You—search the falls. Close off the gates, put a post at every exit. *Now.*" Guards took the orders, disappearing from the room as they sped down hallways and up other stairwells. Looking at Ysa, she read my face. "You didn't go to her? What happened?"

"I fell asleep at my desk." I shook my head, cursing myself for not just going to her the moment Ysa had handed me her note. "I was trying to think . . . I shouldn't have waited."

She shook her head, twisting her mouth. "This doesn't make sense. She left because you were late?"

"I don't know," I muttered. "Maybe she came to me? Thought I'd chosen to stay in my office for the night instead of coming to her?"

"Why would you think that?" Ysa looked at me in disbelief.

"My door was open when I woke up . . . Nova howled, but I thought it was just a dream—"

My dream. My eyes widened and my heart dropped.

"What?" she asked, her brows furrowing.

"Markus."

Ysa immediately understood, and we took off to his room. She'd placed him on the lowest level, housed with the staff and soldiers. As far away from our room as you could get, but somewhere we could keep an eye on him. Letting him live elsewhere in our territory wasn't going to happen. I banged on his door, but there was no answer. I had no intention of waiting.

Leaning back, I kicked the door in, planting my foot near the handle and breaking it off its hinges, busting the frame.

Empty.

Barren drawers left partially hanging open, and a window cracked, not fully shut.

If I had a true heart, it would have stopped.

A soldier came bursting through the door, a look of fear on his face. He shook his head, jutting a thumb over his shoulder. "Two vehicles left earlier."

I screamed in anger, punching a hole into the concrete walls.

"Which ones?" Ysa asked. "When?"

"Ysa's truck. Your Jeep." The young guard cringed as he said it. "The guard on post said Dannika was going for a night climb. She left just before twelve twenty. Markus claimed she forgot some gear, and he was bringing it to her. That was ten minutes after."

"Did anyone follow them?" Ysa yelled, but the guard shook his head.

"Bring me a witch," I growled. Every inch of me struggled to remain in control. I wanted to kill him. He was going to hurt her, and I had to stop him before he could.

"Elias, we don't know where she actually is," Ysa started.

"Then bring me Seraphina. NOW," I shouted, and

true to Ysa's form, she didn't even flinch. She looked at the soldier and jerked her head toward the exit.

"You heard him. Go," she barked.

Gripping the splintered frame of the door, I gritted my teeth.

"We'll find her," she said, trying to soothe me. I shot her a look. I didn't want to be coddled. I wanted to find my mate.

That was what she was. I had no question. She did temper my rage. She complemented me in ways I hadn't known were possible. No part of my life or my future made sense without her.

Seraphina teleported into the room, one of her many gifts, and one I was thankful for in the moment. "You've summoned me? Quite aggressively, so it would seem." She looked me up and down, considering my stance and seething anger.

"Take me to Dannika." The way I spoke made my demands clear. I wasn't asking.

Her brows furrowed. "Very well. Where is she?"

For what may have been the first time in my life, I acknowledged how completely and utterly lost I was, entirely unsure of which direction to take. My mind spun in circles, searching for answers, but there were none. I had no idea.

Ysa stepped forward when I didn't speak. "We don't know. She's disappeared, and so has Markus."

When Seraphina raised her eyebrows, Ysa added, "She's in danger."

Her features softened. "I can't take you to a place I don't know."

"A portal, then." I leveled her with my gaze, hard and unrelenting.

"The magic isn't precise, nor is it stable for long. I don't know where you'll end up, or what you'll be entering. Do you understand?" she asked, pinning me with an intense glare in return. I nodded. I didn't care if I walked into fire. "I'll need blood sacrifice—"

"Done."

She twisted her lips. "And a flesh sacrifice. Your eye, my king." I raised an eyebrow, glancing at Ysa before returning my attention to Seraphina again. "For a portal to be created to a place unknown, the magic must *see* for you. An eye to see, your blood to power, and an item of hers so the spell may find her."

"Ysa," I said, not taking my gaze from the witch. "Bring Kieran. I'll need both of you to assist me." She snapped her fingers to a soldier at the door, and he disappeared.

Reaching into my pocket, I pulled out the leather pouch filled with animal crackers, dropping it into Seraphina's extended palm. "She gave me what's inside, but the bag is hers. Will that work?"

She pressed her lips together, dipping her chin. "We shall see."

"How long? We've already wasted enough time." No one knew where they were. No one knew if Danni was safe or if Markus had already hurt her. No one knew anything.

Except me. I knew I'd fucked up.

"Your persistence won't make it happen faster," she whispered, and I opened my mouth to speak but snapped my mouth shut. "Come. We need to be outside. I need space, and for you to be quiet while I work."

I ground my teeth and nodded, following her from the room in haste with Ysa by my side.

With every footfall that sounded in the stone hallway, another second ticked by. Another minute. Two. Three.

Walking onto the expansive lawn, Seraphina paused. "Here is good."

Kieran rushed to us, using his speed to reach us in time. "Rhett said you needed me, but I'm not sure he got the message right."

"If he said you needed to help carve out Elias's eyeball, he got it right," Ysa muttered, standing next to him. Kieran's lips parted, and his brows pinched, forming a crease. He quickly schooled his features, assessing our surroundings, and then nodded.

I knew I could rely on him.

Seraphina looked at me, glancing down. "Are you ready?"

I didn't respond. Flicking my wrist, I conjured a blade. It extended from my skin, the misty magic solidifying and shaping itself into a knife.

Seraphina gestured with her hands, making a downward circular motion as though she were shaping a bowl on a pottery wheel. A mystical basin formed, shimmering as it swirled in the air.

As she whispered words unknown, the magic danced. Sparking and burning. Flames licked up and outward, beckoning for its desired form of payment. She glanced at me, speaking in her foreign tongue, and nodding that it was time.

I sliced across my forearm, cutting deep, bringing heavy amounts of blood to the surface. The demands of magic would never accept meager offerings. Not for something like this. My blood poured into the basin, and the power it held sizzled, shooting bolts of electricity around in a cyclone.

The next step would be agonizing, but I didn't care. I met Ysa's gaze, and she inclined her head in a single nod of solidarity.

I dropped to the ground, lying down, placing my arms across my abdomen. Kieran exhaled loudly, then sat on top of me, pinning my midsection with his weight. A heaviness pressed into me, but I wasn't sure whether it was him preparing to hold me down or the gravity of the unknown.

"Are you sure about this, Uncle?" he asked quietly.

"Don't ask me that again," I growled. "I'll do anything to find her."

"I meant, are you sure you don't want Ysa to hold you down? I've taken out my fair share of eyes."

Ysa cleared her throat, kneeling down by my head, settling her body, and resting on her shins. "You tortured people, Kieran. The goal here is to *not* drag this out. I need you to hold him." She gave me a once-over, then pointed to my legs. "Do I need someone else to hold you down?"

"No, get on with it. We're wasting time." I breathed heavily through my nose. Seraphina gestured for us to go ahead.

Kieran tore his shirt, then rolled up the piece of cloth. He put it in front of my lips. "Something to bite down on." I opened, and he placed it inside. I didn't know if it was going to matter.

Ysa scooted forward, placing my head between her legs like a vice, and squeezed. Kieran pressed his weight into my shoulders as he leaned into me. They looked at each other, confirming they were both ready.

"The spell is waiting, Elias," Seraphina said in a melodic voice.

"Do it!" I mumbled through the cloth.

Ysa grabbed my face on each side, and I watched the tip of her thumb come toward me in what felt like slow motion. I knew it was anything but. She had no intention of dragging this out.

The moment her finger pressed around the soft tissue of my eye, my body responded, fighting and thrashing. My fangs extended; an instant reaction to protect myself. Searing pain exploded in my face, sending the sensation to every nerve ending in my body.

I bit down on the cloth, my jaw clenching, a scream building, but I kept my mouth shut. Muffled throaty grunts were all I could let out. The pressure of her thumb increased, and so did the agony. My purpose for doing this battled internally with my instinctive response to having someone try to gouge out my eye.

"Hold him!" Ysa shouted to Kieran as I involuntarily bucked at the weight on me.

For Danni. I need to find Danni. Anything for her.

Ysa's legs tightened around my head, and she pressed her thumb in deep, scooping beneath the delicate eyeball. Excruciating pain detonated, like being lit on fire from the inside of my face. Like my skin was being flayed and burned. It reached a crescendo, and I opened my mouth, letting out a guttural roar I couldn't keep in any longer. My head pulsed, and a sickening squelch reached my ears before a dull pop sounded.

Ysa released my head, getting away from me as quickly as she could. Kieran stayed on top of me, giving me a moment to recover, making sure I didn't retaliate against my second. "FUUUUUCK!" The word extended as I screamed in anger and pain.

With my vision obscured on one side, I looked to Ysa. She held up my bloody eye, the optic nerve and extrinsic muscles attached and hanging down.

It was done.

Blood from my empty eye socket dripped down my face, and I nodded to Kieran. He got off me, holding out a hand so he could help me. I took it, bringing myself to a standing position, then walked to Ysa.

I held my hand out, and she placed my severed eye into my palm. We said nothing. No words were needed. Turning to Seraphina, I awaited her command.

After several moments, she inclined her chin, and I dropped my offering into the magic basin. Seraphina's chanting became louder, and her eyes glowed as she continued with her spell.

Ysa came to wait beside me. She handed me a clean cloth, and I wrapped the makeshift bandage around my face, covering the gaping hole, and tying it at the back of my head. The gash on my arm was already healing, but the eye would take time to grow back. Pulling a flask from her jacket, she offered it to me, and I accepted, taking several long swigs of the blood and whiskey mixture.

"Now we wait," she said quietly. I scoffed. "I know. Patience isn't your virtue."

"I don't have any virtues, Ysa." As I watched the flames grow and the clouds form overhead, the madness I held inside me roiled. "If anything happens to her, the world will know the extent of my wrath, and there isn't a being on this planet that will stop me."

CHAPTER 25
DANNIKA

I parked a mile away, taking the rest of the journey on foot. I didn't want to draw attention to myself if someone recognized Ysa's truck while I cruised up to the bar. Who knew if someone from Blood and Beryl was in Portland tonight, hiding in the dark corners of No Man's Land? If someone was willing to overlook my presence, they sure as hell weren't going to overlook the fact that I had Ysa's vehicle when she was nowhere to be found.

The hoodie I wore was pulled up, covering my hair, my backpack over both shoulders and filled to the brim.

I wasn't going back, and I'd packed everything I would need.

It was Earth and Emerald, or Gold and Garnet. I bit

my lip as Nova and I walked, wondering if Elias would be pissed off—if for no other reason than I'd backed out of our deal and it could make him look like a fool. I didn't care if he said he'd rejected me, or if I'd rejected him. Whatever he felt made him look better was fine. If he was livid, though, that meant those Houses could refuse me in fear of his retaliation. Maybe I could just find a boat and live on the water. I wrinkled my nose at the idea of never roaming in the woods again. Nova would be miserable too. I couldn't think like that. Adora and I would come up with a plan. It would work out. It always did.

I slowed my steps, hearing the faint sound of an engine coming from the forest trail. Nova paused, lifting her nose into the air, her ears twitching as well.

"You heard it too?" I whispered to her, and she met my gaze. "Go check it out, okay?"

She glanced to the woods in the distance, then looked behind me toward the concrete sidewalks and dimly lit streets. She let out a small whine, unsure. Running my fingers through the fur on her neck, I spoke to her quietly. "It's okay. I need you to lie low. I'm just going to grab Adora, then head back here. The river is that way," I said, nodding my head in its direction. "Go see what that was and make sure we aren't being followed. I'll be back here in ten minutes, then we'll go." I pressed my forehead to hers, and she huffed, turning and heading back to the forest we'd driven out of.

I stuck to the shadows, not attracting the attention of any passersby, though I realized there weren't many out and about. It was close to three in the morning, and most of the streets were quiet.

The clouds overhead drifted in wispy puffs, letting bits of the crescent moon peek through. Its Cheshire Cat grin smiled down on me, making me feel like maybe this once it would be on my side. Maybe my curse would be lifted if I just got away from this part of the world.

The Salty Siren came into view, its wooden sign swinging in a gentle breeze, making the hinges creak eerily. Glancing over my shoulder, I double-checked that I was alone and then ducked into the alley next to the pub.

I set my backpack on the ground and waited, counting the seconds.

Adora should have been here by now. It was less than an hour's drive for her, and even accounting for the time she'd need to sneak out, it didn't make sense. An uneasiness filtered through me—a warning—but I brushed it aside. I had to. I wasn't leaving without my sister.

My mind started to play tricks on me, and my thoughts ran wild. What if she was captured? Or hurt?

What if our moms woke up and she couldn't leave yet? I'd have to find a place for Nova and me to hide while we waited for her. A sound at the end of the alley reached my ears, and I breathed a sigh of relief.

"Adora," I whispered, taking light steps toward her. "You were freaking me out—"

I stopped dead in my tracks. Three forms stepped out from the shadows, and I gasped, my heart jumping to my throat.

Andreas stood, his arm wrapped around Adora's chest, holding a revolver to her head. A thin, red line on her neck dribbled blood, nothing more than a flesh wound and likely from her struggle. Her bound hands held his arm as she moved carefully in our direction. A small knife was embedded in her shoulder, the wound bleeding and soaking into her shirt.

The left side of her face was bruised and swollen, its angry purple color a stark contrast to the white cloth they'd gagged her with. Even wounded and held hostage, her eyes didn't have a lick of fear. What I saw there was pure hatred, and my stomach twisted. That look. She reserved it for only one, and he was here.

Mathis walked around them, tutting as he sauntered slowly toward me. "I told your family they weren't to have contact with you. I warned them what I would do." He gestured to my sister. "But I counted on your sister to fuck up. I knew it was only a matter of time."

Adrenaline rushed through every vein and my heartbeat pounded, while it felt like blood boiled on my insides. My nails dug into my palm as I clenched my fists. "Let her go. You can have me," I said through gritted teeth. Adora's brows furrowed at me, and she released a small grunt in frustration. Pressing the revolver harder against her head, Andreas pulled the trigger, and a small, terrifying click sounded. My breath hitched.

But no shot rang out.

Adora's eyes were squeezed closed, and she opened one. Andreas chuckled, speaking softly to my sister, just loud enough I could hear. "Six chambers. One bullet. Want to take a chance again?"

Bile rose in my throat. They just wanted to toy with us. Play with our emotions before killing us. I knew it, but there was nothing I could do about it.

"Let her go so I can have you? I already *have* you," Mathis retorted, searching behind me. "And without your dog to save you, it would seem." He smiled, his canines reflecting the light. "But I came prepared for her too." He patted his jacket near his hip, and it didn't take a genius to figure out he was carrying a gun as well.

A small growl rumbled in my throat, but he shook his finger at me. "Temper, Dannika."

I bit the inside of my cheek, hoping that stalling for time would allow me to form some sort of plan. "What do you want?" I asked, trying to steady my breathing as I flicked my eyes between Mathis and the gun barrel jammed against my sister's temple.

"I wanted my son to have a better mate," he said in disgust, taking in my form. "But fate decided he wasn't worthy of one, and then he wasn't strong enough to kill you when he should have. I told him to kill you or fuck you, and he's done neither. He does nothing but disappoint me."

I narrowed my eyes. "No, he did what he should've done in the beginning. He rejected me."

He raised a brow, tilting his head. "Well, isn't that a twist?"

"Why?" I asked, careful not to make any harsh movements as I loosened my clenched fists.

"I had hoped losing you would be his end." He shrugged. "Losing a mate is truly terrible. It tries to destroy you. Eats at you from the inside out. You wither away. Just look at your mother."

"You son of a bitch." I took a step forward—

Click.

Another empty chamber, and I froze. Adora groaned in anger and relief, her body shaking in rage and fear.

"That's two out of six," Mathis reminded me, walking toward my sister. My heart beat wildly, pounding in my temples. He stopped in front of her, and her deep loathing glare could have bored a hole through anyone else. Angling his head to the side, he made sure I was watching as he yanked the knife out of her shoulder. Beneath her gag, Adora screamed, leaning forward, blood flowing freely from the gash.

"Stop it!" I yelled, feeling utterly helpless. I ran my fingers through my hair. "Why are you doing this? You never wanted me to begin with. You've hated me. Punished me. Sicced your dogs on me. Why didn't you just let my family leave the pack and go somewhere else? You didn't want me as your son's mate."

"That's where you're wrong." Mathis clasped his hands behind his back, teetering on his heels. "You're worthless as a shifter, but having you mated to my son would've kept your family under control. All of those loyal to your father would have had no choice but to step in line. Dead would have been nice too, of course, but Markus could give me neither."

I didn't even know what he was rambling on about. My family? Loyalty? We just kept our heads down, forced to stay in a pack that barely wanted us. The Inland pack was loyal to my family because of Abbey, but they were just as quiet as we were. If none of us caused a scene, we were able to live in relative peace. Did he think we were building some secret squad to assassinate him and take over?

I held my hands out, palms facing him, trying to

show him I wasn't a threat. "Mathis, we haven't done anything. I want nothing from Fire and Fluorite. We aren't going to cause any problems. Markus rejected me, and I'm not part of your House anymore. You're free of whatever burden I am to you. I know you want to kill me. Fine. I just want you to let go of my sister. Let her leave."

"So she can run to Elias? You think I don't know what Blood and Beryl wants? What your king is trying to do? He isn't as smart as he thinks. I have people close to him." The sneer on his face was nothing but cruel. "I hear he is quite taken with you, but it's a shame you aren't mated yet. It would hurt him that much more when he realizes you're dead."

A rush of adrenaline sent a hot flash through me, and the color drained from my face, but I refused to speak a word. I had no idea how he knew, but he could read the question on my face.

"Dannika, child. If you were truly mated, Elias would be here." His eyes flicked to the pack I carried. "And you wouldn't be running away." Still, I said nothing, and he chuckled. "Did you reject him too?"

"Maybe I did," I said. My voice sounded strangled, and I couldn't hide the sadness it carried. *No, he rejected me.*

"Perhaps you know your place more than I realized," he mused. "You are nothing. You don't belong anywhere."

Adora growled at him in anger, stomping her foot.

Click.

My stomach roiled at the sound, and I choked out a sob. Turning to my sister, he splayed his hand against her shoulder, then stuck his thumb into the knife wound, pressing against it.

Adora's eyes squeezed shut, and she screamed, her body shaking as she tried to wrench herself away from the onslaught of pain.

"What the fuck do you want?" I screamed, panic and dread filling me.

Footfalls pounded far off in the distance, headed in our direction.

"Alpha," Andreas said. "Someone's coming. We can't be seen here."

Mathis quickly reached to his hip, pulling out his gun.

We were dead if I didn't do something. I took off at a sprint, knowing it was all for naught. I wouldn't stand there while he killed my sister. I refused to wait for my turn to die. I wouldn't go down without a fight, however meager a fight it would be.

Taking advantage of the moment, Adora threw her head back, knocking into Andreas's nose, busting it. Mathis turned, taking a quick shot at my sister as she dove to the side. The bullet hit, sending her spinning and crashing to the concrete. She lay unmoving and my heart was ripped from my chest.

Seeing Adora fall to the ground knocked the wind out of me. I dropped to my knees as the world came to a screeching halt. The more I gasped for air, the harder it was to breathe. I coughed once, then twice, feeling a cold chill run through my body as bright red blood splattered onto the pavement in front of me. My hand tentatively reached for my abdomen, and I felt warm, thick fluid spilling down my stomach. When I turned my gaze downward, I collapsed in shock, feeling my body go numb.

Mathis stepped over to me, triumphant as he took aim and pulled the trigger again. I didn't feel the pain—I only heard the explosion of the gunshot as it assaulted my ears. "Maybe now that you're as good as dead, whatever curse was put on me for killing your father will be lifted, and my other son can be mated to a true shifter."

"You . . ." It was all I could manage. My eyelids fluttered as I lay on the dirty street, watching Mathis and Andreas shift and run away.

I couldn't feel my legs. My arms. I didn't feel pain anymore. I just needed to let go. I closed my eyes, whispering to myself that it was okay. It was time.

"No, no, no." A hand grabbed my face, shaking it, and I tried to open my eyes to focus. Adora leaned over me, covered in blood. "Don't you dare let go, Danni. Please." She lifted her head, taking off her shirt and pressing it where I couldn't see. She looked around and screamed, "Fuck!"

"I . . . can't . . ." I said, trying to form words but not able to breathe well enough to speak.

Tears leaked from her eyes while she held my cheek. "Shh. I've got you. I'm with you. Please don't leave me," she said. I couldn't see her well anymore, and my vision swam. Another figure appeared, his outline backlit by a streetlamp and his face partially obscured.

"Markus . . ." I whispered.

My sister leaned over me, crying out from her injuries. "Get away from her," she growled, trying to protect me. "If you come any closer, I'll kill you where you stand, and I won't think twice about it."

"I'm not gonna hurt you, I swear."

Their back and forth faded in and out, but pieces of it filtered through.

"I don't trust you."

"I followed Danni tonight to make sure she was okay. Nova was bringing me to her, but then she yelped and dropped to the ground while we were running. I don't know what happened."

A moment of silence spanned between them as she hovered over me, then she nodded, leaning back. Markus looked at me. "By the gods," he said, taking in my injuries. "Keep pressure on it. We have to try to stanch the bleeding."

"Don't you think I fucking know that? That's what I'm trying to do," Adora yelled. "I need to get her a doctor. A healer. Anyone!"

"Blood and Beryl is our only hope. I'll drive."

"Nova . . ." I rasped, my eyes traveling to his face. I tried to speak again, but my lips just moved with no sound.

Markus looked down at me, resting his hand on my head. "I have her." Looking up to my sister, he said, "Are you fast?"

"Of course I'm fucking fast," Adora spat.

"Well, I don't know what kind of shifter you are! No one does. You could be a fucking panda, for all I know!"

Adora groaned. "I'm not a godsdamned panda. What do you want me to do?"

"Bring her truck here. It's parked—"

"I've been shot and stabbed, Markus," she snapped. "I can barely move this arm, let alone drive."

"Shit, I didn't . . . That's your blood too?"

"Yes, that's what happens when people get shot and stabbed!" she shouted. A little curl twinged on my lips. Even now she could make me want to smile. "You go. I'll stay here."

"I need her keys."

My sister rummaged on my body where I couldn't see, then slapped the keys into Markus's extended palm. I lost track of one moment to the next. I tried to close my eyes. Breathing was becoming more difficult. The darkness coaxed me toward the safety of her shadowy blanket, and I reached for it.

"You're not allowed to die, do you hear me?" my sister's voice whispered to me, pulling me away from the warmth the endless night offered me. "If you die, I will find a way to bring you back and kick your ass for leaving me here."

"Love . . ." I mumbled. *I love you. I love Mom and Abbey. I love Elias. Tell them for me. Tell them all.* Those were the words I meant to say, but they wouldn't come out.

Tires screeched.

A door shut.

I was vaguely aware of distorted voices and words I couldn't make out anymore.

A single tear escaped my eye, falling down my temple and into my hair. My body lifted up, and I could have sworn my soul was trying to leave the broken corporal form that lay on the wet pavement.

I blinked slowly, looking at the sky one last time. The smiling crescent moon gazed down upon me before dark, ominous clouds rolled across, blocking it from sight. She'd disappeared. I had hoped tonight she'd be on my side. Just this once.

My sister's voice called to me from a distance, but the void was quieter. Warmer. It opened its arms, and I let it envelop me.

They said I'd been born on a cursed moon, but they never said what that had looked like.

In my final hour, I saw it for what it truly was. The moon didn't pick sides.

She was always cursed, just like me.

CHAPTER 26
ELIAS

"You'll have five minutes, maybe," Seraphina said. "Any longer, and the portal will become unstable." Sweat dotted her brow as she dipped her hand in the magic basin. My blood offering coated her fingers. She touched her palms together and red, glowing magic exploded between them.

As her hands swept outward, the magic spread, twisting and forming into swirling shades of orange and crimson. She rotated her hands clockwise, above her head and below her waist, then again counter-clockwise. All the while, the portal spread, growing in size.

"Ysa, Kieran." I only needed to say their names, and they were there. While I was more than capable of killing Markus, handicapped as I was by the lack of a functioning eye, it wasn't Markus who concerned me, but the possibility that Mathis and Andreas would be on the other side as well. If they were, we'd be fending off scores of shifters, and I wouldn't let my arrogance endanger Dannika that way.

Not wanting to waste a moment of our time, I stepped through the portal.

It was like going through a window. The wind blew harder on the other side. Complete night fell over us, with only silver moonlight and two glowing orbs moving toward me. I blinked, squinting my eye. A double-bladed halberd formed in my left hand. I crouched, fingers touching the pavement.

It was only in the two seconds between stepping through and kneeling that I realized what it was hurtling my way—and there was no time to move.

Tires squealed. The scent of burned rubber permeated the air. I threw my arm up to block my body. Metal dented, then warped around me—forming a mold around my arm as I stood my ground.

The truck's weight bore down on me, but I pushed back. Acting as an impassable barricade, I met it head-first and shoved my weight forward. The wheels let out a squeak as it bounced back. Kieran ran around to the right and ripped the door off its hinges. Ysa went to the left and did the same.

Underneath the stench of shredded tires and leaking oil—blood ran heavily. And not just anyone's blood.

Danni's.

"Where is she?" I growled, the words only barely understandable when my fully elongated fangs were out on display.

"Here," Ysabeau said, standing still in front of the passenger door. On the right, Kieran had yanked Markus out of the driver's seat and had him pinned on the ground.

I ripped my arm from the mottled steel cage and went around to the side. In the front seat, a pale, feverish Dannika was strewn across Adora's lap. Her eyes were closed. Breathing labored. Blood gushed from her stomach where her sister had pressed her own shirt into a wound, trying to stanch it.

The halberd disintegrated beneath my fingers.

"Give her to me," I demanded, already reaching for my mate even as Adora hissed.

"No! You're the reason she was out here tonight."

Shame. Guilt. Remorse. They all battled next to other emotions. Anger. Rage. Possessiveness.

I *needed* to fix her.

"Please," I said quietly, struggling to speak. It didn't escape my notice that blood was openly spilling from Adora's shoulder. She had to be in a great deal of pain, but her face didn't show it. Fierce and determined, she kept her dark-blue eyes locked on me.

From the other side of the truck, Markus let out a muffled yell. "I'm trying to help her!"

Adora studied me intently, then exhaled. "Fine, but I'm not leaving her. Nova is in the back. She's going to need help being moved. When Danni is injured, so is Nova, and vice versa. Markus had to lift her into the truck on his own after we were shot." She swallowed. Hate shone in her eyes. "Fucking Mathis."

"On it," Ysa snapped as she ran around to the back to get Nova. I reached into the cab and lifted Dannika off her sister's lap as gently as I could manage. Having her in my arms felt so right. But the condition she was in was so wrong. I didn't like the ashen color in her face, or the faint beat of her heart.

I carried her toward the portal, only pausing for a moment when Kieran asked, "What do you want done with him?"

I glanced over to see him pinning a half-shifted Markus beneath his body—a blade pressed to the shifter's neck. My immediate instinct was to kill him and be done with it. Somehow, he must have played a part in this. Led her into this. But he'd been driving the truck. Adora was with them.

There was more going on here than I knew or had time to figure out.

"He helped us," Adora said, albeit grudgingly. "His shithead dad is the one who shot her. Markus got us out of there and was driving us back to Blood and Beryl."

My arms tightened around Danni. Rage licked along my veins, igniting me with fire and hatred.

Mathis had taken Claudette from me.

He *would not* take Danni too.

I nodded once. "Let him up and help Ysa with Nova."

My foot was already halfway through the portal. The clock was ticking.

I crossed to the other side, appearing back on the estate. Guards surrounded the portal. Bianca stood off to the side in sleep shorts and a T-shirt, as if she'd come directly from bed. "Get me a doctor. *Now.*"

I looked at her as I passed, but my words were for everyone. I didn't care who got me a doctor first. I wasn't asking. My feet carried me down the hall with a speed only a true master vampire would be able to match. Pulse racing, anxiety and fear nipping at my heels, I brought her back to our room, still littered with broken glass and food and all the other remnants of her hurt.

Because of me.

It didn't matter. Not right now.

I placed her on the bed, then lifted either side of her shirt and tore it down the middle, needing to assess the damage. I may not have been a doctor, but I knew a life-threatening injury when I saw one.

There wasn't one wound, but two. One had hit dead center below her sternum. The second, to the lower right side of her stomach. Dread seeped in like poison. Doubt. Despair.

Behind me, our on-staff doctor came running in. "I heard you need a doc—"

"Fix her."

I stepped to the side, letting him do his job, but I didn't go far. My eye didn't leave her as I moved to the foot of the bed. Even as Ysa and Kieran came in carrying Nova's limp body. Even as they placed her on the other side of Dannika. Even as Adora followed, along with several other nurses and doctors.

"Please, miss, we need to sew your shoulder—"

"You can sew it after I find out what's happening to my sister," Adora barked.

"My king," a nurse gasped, seeing the bloody cloth over my eye. "We need to—"

"Focus on Dannika," I growled.

Several healers stood around Danni, their hands hovering over her body. Their palms emitted a faint glow, shimmering around their fingers as they focused on her abdomen. Light was forced into her gunshot wounds, but it did nothing. They pushed further, more magic. More power. Sweat dotted their brows. One looked up, her sad eyes meeting another's gaze across from her. A pink-haired healer shook her head lightly. My hands clenched around the footboard, where I was leaned over. The wood snapped. I tossed it aside.

"Why aren't you doing anything?" I demanded.

The doctor stood between the healers, using his magic to assess her wounds. "Your Majesty . . . My king—"

"Spit it out!" Adora yelled from where she stood on his other side, swaying on her feet. I gave him a hard look, letting him know I agreed.

"She's lost too much blood," the doctor started. The room spun. The floor was pulled out from under me. I knew where this was going, but I refused to believe it. "One of the bullets went through her spleen. The other one through her pancreas. It shattered her spine. She's only lived this long because her shifter healing is trying to repair it." On the other side of the bed, Nova started convulsing. A strangled whine ripped through the air.

"No," I snapped. "There has to be something more you can do."

"I'm sorry, my king—"

"Ysa."

"I'm here," she said, standing by Nova's side where she kept a comforting hand on the wolf's fur.

"Get me another doctor. All of them. Anyone who can fix her!" My breath heaved. I turned and flipped the table, throwing it across the room. Glass rained. Silverware went flying, the metal making tinking sounds as it bounced off stone.

"Elias," she said gently.

"*Don't.*"

She sighed. "There is another option—"

"Uncle," Kieran said. "I know the body. I know what it's capable of. What it can heal from. What it can't . . ." He cleared his throat. "Dannika won't recover from this. The moment we open her up to attempt to fix it, she'll bleed out the rest of the way. She has minutes at most."

I stared into what was left of the flames, unbelieving that this was where we were.

I'd fallen in love with my pretend mate but hadn't told her. My temper had chased her away. My cruel words. My coldness. She'd reached out to me, and I'd left her waiting, thinking I didn't care and gods knew what else.

If I didn't do something now, I'd never have the chance to tell her.

"Everyone, out."

I knew what I needed to do. It was the only way. The only option.

"She's a shifter," the doctor warned. "The process will not take."

"I don't care," I said simply. "We are out of options. It's a Hail Mary. Danni's always been different. If there's even a chance . . ." I had to take a deep breath to steady myself. "I have to try."

Shifters couldn't be vampires. The times people had tried resulted in death. Always death.

But to my knowledge, there had never been a

shifter quite like Dannika. She didn't have shifter healing. Not like she should. Maybe she lacked enough magic there that it wouldn't fight the change. Maybe, just *maybe*, I could save her.

I swallowed hard.

"You can't."

The voice rang out above all others. Above the whispering. Above Bianca's quiet sobbing outside the door. Above the sounds of our arguing.

I turned. Adora kneeled at Dannika's side, gripping my mate's limp, pale hand between her two, but it was me she looked at. Me, whom she told I couldn't.

"I'm the king. You cannot—*will* not—tell me how to save *my mate*."

Adora shook her head. "I don't care if she's a vampire. She could be human. She could be a llama. I don't give a flying fuck about her species. *You* can't do it because you'll kill her. Your bite is *death*."

I blinked, assessing this woman over once more with the one eye I had. There was no way she could have known that.

No one did. Only my family and Ysa.

It was one of the most carefully guarded Laskaris secrets.

"Not if I change her." Yes, my bite was death. It allowed me to see into someone. To peel back their memories. In doing so, it killed them—unless I turned them.

My venom was poisonous. My blood was the antidote.

"Let Ysabeau," she said. "She won't lose control."

"I won't—"

"I've seen how you *crave* her," Adora snapped, fire and fury in her eyes. Where my sweet, soft, intelligent woman had a quiet strength—the little bit I'd seen of Adora told me she was anything but. "You may love her, but her blood will be honey on your lips. I don't want to toy with the one chance we have—"

I stormed across the room. "I don't know *what* you are, Adora. Dannika wouldn't say, but it's only because she loves you that I haven't had the guards remove you yet, so listen carefully." I towered over her, but she didn't shrink away. "Dannika is my mate. *Mine.* If someone is going to sire her, it's going to be me, because as much as I might want her blood, I would *never* lose control when it came to her life. I chose her. I will continue to choose her, over blood, over House, over anyone and anything that would come between us. So respectfully, Adora, I will only repeat myself once. Everyone, get the fuck out."

Her lips thinned. She rose to stand. "If you fail, I *will* kill you."

Several gasps lined the hallways. Ysa swore under her breath. "Okay, time to go—"

"If I fail, you won't need to," I said softly.

The room emptied, but not fast enough. Her heartbeat was fading. Nova had already gone still. Our time was out. It was now or never.

Ysa had to guide Adora away. Kieran followed with them. At the door, she said, "If you need me, I'll be right here."

"Empty the wing. I don't want to be disturbed *for anything*."

"Good luck," she said before closing the door shut. The sounds of people being sent away filtered through, but my thoughts had already turned away from them. From Adora and her assertions. From the fear and the panic and the desperation.

I knelt beside her, inhaling her sweet scent, oranges and peppermint, as I brushed the hair from her cheek. My lips pressed against hers one last time as I conjured a small blade. It was easy to press the blade into my wrist. Blood welled. I let it drip over her open wounds before pressing it between her lips. She didn't gag or swallow, but I heard the liquid as it dripped down her throat.

As my wrist healed shut, I bent over and licked a spot on her throat. I sucked on the smooth patch of flesh, softening it to my bite.

"I've seen how you crave her..."

My fangs pressed against her skin. Gods. The smell. The taste.

"You may love her, but her blood will be honey on your lips."

Honey was a poor comparison. More like ambrosia. Nectar of the gods. I groaned, burying my fingers in her hair.

Mine.

My shifter.

My love.

My Dannika.

It was because of that love, that protective possessiveness, that I released her. She was strong, I reminded myself. So strong. This had to work. Because if it didn't . . .

If I fail, you won't need to.

My vigil began.

CHAPTER 27

DANNIKA

A sharp pain broke through the dark fog. It started as cold. A frigid explosion so raw and deep that it burned. One spot was bad enough, but then the icy flames spread. It lit every nerve ending ablaze, ravaging my insides while it spread like a plague. An infection. A wildfire eating away at my core.

Hoarfrost settled over every inch of my body, crawling over every ounce of my flesh. It seeped into my blood, my bones, filling me with excruciating agony. But the intensity of the pain was the only thing that grounded me. It was my tether, stopping me from drifting away into nothingness.

And then it changed.

The inferno subsided, and the frost finally numbed me. The onslaught didn't end, only my reaction to it.

I started to drift once more, in and out of a space I wasn't familiar with. This time it didn't feel so terrifying or absolute. This time, it felt safe. It wasn't silent. Quiet voices drifted over me. The sound of Nova snoring. Whispers I couldn't quite make out. My mate's breathing. The rhythmic sound of his heart. The intoxicating scent of his skin . . .

I sighed. I had no mate. Markus had rejected me. The bond was broken, and we were truly free from those cruel chains. I was in a dream, or maybe hovering on the brink of death.

Yet I couldn't help feeling like it was home that wrapped its gentle embrace around me as I began to gravitate toward the darkness and silence. Like maybe there was something more than simple contentment that was keeping me guarded and grounded.

It must have just been a happy home. Warm and inviting. Comforting and safe.

Death brought forth such a beautiful dream.

One I wanted to live in a little longer before I let go.

One day passed.

Then two.

Three.

Four.

Every hour was misery. The anxiety was death by a thousand cuts, slow and growing worse by the minute.

Vampires that were made usually changed within hours. Sometimes less. Sometimes more. How quickly the venom took was the deciding factor. It either poisoned or healed, but never this.

Dannika's heart beat frantically. Faster than either shifter or vampire. Her skin heated, turning feverish to the touch. She didn't sweat. She didn't speak. She didn't move.

But she did change. Over the days, I noticed her hair growing faster. Its luster returned to an even shinier state than before. Her pallid complexion turned healthy again, glowing with an effervescence. The gunshot wounds closed shut, but the skin didn't turn smooth and flawless. It remained jagged, red, and angry, like a healing surgical incision that was merely months old.

My hands clenched into fists at the thought of her pain. I had to put a pin in it for the time being. Mathis would be dealt with after this. War or no war. He'd gone after my queen. He would die for it.

I traced my fingers over the puckered scar for the hundredth time, wishing I could turn back the clock. Wishing I could take back what I'd said and how I'd pushed her away.

I bowed my head, fingers slipping from her stomach. A warm hand grasped mine with lightning speed.

Danni shivered.

I froze. It was the first response to my touch she'd expressed. I nearly buckled and fell to my knees right then.

"Danni," I murmured, leaning in.

She groaned. Her eyelids fluttered. Fingers tightened. On the other side of her, Nova's ears twitched. The giant wolf rolled, cracking an eye open to look straight at me. Letting out a yawn, she settled her head on Danni's thigh.

"You're my mate."

Her words were soft, yet scratchy. Her throat was

dry from disuse. I searched her form, starting from her toes, checking her body to make sure everything moved, finally looking deep into the icy-blue eyes I'd feared I'd never see again.

Need coiled in my gut. Hunger like I'd only known once.

During her heat.

I swallowed. My hand cupped her jaw, my thumb brushing over her cheek. "I've been a shit mate." My voice came out as a growl. I had to dial it back. Cool the predator. Force the creature that lusted for blood and war over her attack to subside, at least for the moment.

"No," she said, pushing my hand away. I hid my flinch as she sat up. "You're my second-chance mate. My *real* one. Not pretend."

I knew. I'd known since the moment I'd bit her to save her life.

The infamous bond had snapped into place, as if every string that had grounded me had been simultaneously cut. All but her. Right at the moment when her life had hung in the balance.

The irony was not lost on me.

"It wasn't pretend," I said, sitting back. I closed my hands into fists to keep from reaching for her, even though everything in me demanded I do so. "Not for me."

"That's not what you said."

"I was angry." I sighed. "After your heat, all I could think about was you. Places I wanted to take you. Things I wanted to do *with* you . . . *to* you." A flush crept up Danni's cheeks, lighter in hue than they had been before. She pressed her legs together, no doubt feeling the effects of the bond bearing down on her as well. The magic was loud, demanding we consummate it. "But you said it was pretend, and to say I took it poorly is an understatement."

"Me? *You* said you wanted a business arrangement." Her voice had gone quiet, devoid of emotion. That hummingbird heart of hers gave nothing away.

"I know."

"You didn't want 'complicated.'"

"I know."

"You said it meant *nothing*. That *we* were nothing—"

"*I know*." Gods, this was harder than I'd thought it would be. "I got angry. I said things I shouldn't have. Things I didn't mean and—"

"Even a lie has a grain of truth in it, Elias," she said softly. Her face was downcast, her eyes focusing on her hands.

"Not always." This growing, writhing thing beneath my skin tried to break free. It was the same beast that had caused the rage that had ignited a war.

"Not always? Or not when it suits your argument?" she asked, waiting in silence for me to respond. She picked at her nails, then snapped her head up. "Where's Adora? Please tell me she's here. Mathis shot her . . ."

"She went with the healers. She's okay."

"I'd like to see her."

"You will," I said.

"*Now*," she insisted. "I want to talk to her. We won't be staying here. *I'm* not staying here. Sorry for all of this—" She motioned to herself and Nova.

"Stop," I finally snapped, unable to hold it back. "One, you're not going anywhere." Her eyes lit up with indignation that made my blood quicken. "Two, do not apologize to me. Not for this. You ran away, and I understand why."

"Then you understand why I can't be here," she shot back.

"I don't, actually. I'm trying to make this right. I'm trying to tell you I'm sorry."

"I know you are," she argued. "But I can't help and think about what happened before the mate bond told you that you wanted to be with me. Before all this happened, I had a different vision of what we were. Like some insipid girl, I was going to pour my heart out to you, tell you that Markus rejected me, and I was free of those chains. I thought for a minute, just for a minute, that you didn't mean what you'd said. Maybe emotions got the better of us both. Maybe there was a miscommunication . . . but I was wrong—about a lot of things, it would seem." She crossed her arms, turning away from me.

"No, you weren't wrong. I was." I ran my hands through my hair, tugging while my emotions raged inside my head. This was not how I'd imagined our conversation would go.

"We both were," she whispered. "You for thinking this would work, and me for thinking it was anything more than what we'd discussed." Shaking her head, she added, "I won't do this to myself. I thought I could go along with it, and I can't. I just can't. I want more than the twisted royal standards you want to live by."

I scrunched my brows. "Royal standards? What are you even talking about?"

"Don't, Elias. Just don't. Katie let some things slip —it's not her fault—but it all makes sense after I thought about it." *Katie? What did she have to do with this?* "I just deserve a chance at a better life. Maybe in Earth and Emerald, I can find it."

Her words slammed into me. "If you think I'm going to let my mate walk out on me—"

She whipped her head around, glaring at me, eyes glittering with the beginning of unshed tears. "You never wanted a mate, Elias. You said so from the very beginning. 'A true mate would be a distraction at best.' Those were your words. I replayed everything we've said and done together over and over in my head. I just felt something . . . I thought it was love. I guess I got caught up in our lies." She dropped her arms, flinging the covers off. "I thought maybe you loved me too. It was my fault for thinking otherwise."

Panic shot through me at the thought of her trying to leave. The bond flared, burning my senses, pushing against my skin. I'd never thought those conversations with her would come back to haunt me. That she could use them against me to prove her point.

"Will you just fucking *listen* to me?" I said, raising my voice.

Dannika groaned, pulling her legs over the side of the bed, and let them hang. She looked down, recognizing for the first time that she was naked. After a moment's pause and the pinkening of her cheeks, she shrugged one shoulder, albeit stiffly, then stood up. "Where are my clothes?"

"You mean the ones you were wearing when you were shot?" I pointed to the fireplace. "I burned them. I couldn't stand to see another reminder of what happened to you."

She pursed her lips, twisting them to the side while grabbing a throw blanket and wrapping it around her body, tucking it in like a towel. Turning to me, she dropped her hands to her sides. "I don't want to do this, Elias. I don't have the mental energy anymore. We both know what this is"—she gestured between us—"it's fake. Pretend."

"We both know what this is?" I repeated. How

could she blow this off? She'd said she'd loved me before the bond, but now it was so easy to just brush it aside and try to walk away? I couldn't understand how. My heart burned with desire to be by her side. My tongue craved her taste. My body hungered to be entwined with hers. Everything I'd felt before the bond had just increased tenfold. I couldn't be alone in that. "Danni, this is real. It doesn't get more real than this."

Her eyes filled with sadness, then she closed them. "'I don't want a mate that fate chooses for me.' That is what you said to me the night we met."

"We *did* choose each other. Fate just agreed with us." Exasperation filled my tone. She was so closed off, she couldn't hear the truth, and I didn't know how to make her listen.

She smiled sadly, taking a step away from me. "You don't believe that. I want you to, but you don't. I want the words you're saying to be real, but it's the bond talking. I feel it. I know it's there. If it's this strong for me, I know it is for you. But these words? They're not yours." She huffed, smirking. "Trust me. I just went through it. If the bond can make my bully grovel for forgiveness, it can certainly make you see delusions of love."

Delusions.

She wasn't listening at all.

I had to make her understand. She needed to

know. She needed to believe. But her heart was too broken, and what remained of it was shuttered, trying to protect what fragments were left.

I'd said I wouldn't let fate dictate my life. She wouldn't let it control hers, either. I knew that about her. I respected that, more than she could ever know.

My thoughts raced, and the bond pulsed, relentless and demanding, as what came next was against everything I felt at the core of my existence. The caged beast inside me clawed, doing what it could to tear me apart. It raged against the decision I'd come to, knowing it was inherently wrong.

But I had no choice.

"Dannika Kresley, I reject you."

CHAPTER 29

DANNIKA

I couldn't believe the words he'd said.

The overwhelming sense of loss was consuming. My bones ached, feeling as though they were splintering apart inside me. A high-pitched pealing echoed, drowning out all sound. The fissures that had formed on my heart split further, threatening to shatter and leave me in a pile of nothingness on the floor as the ringing in my ears turned violent. This wasn't what I wanted, and I knew it with every fiber of my being.

I loved Elias. I didn't need the bond to know that. I didn't need fate to tell me whom I belonged to. I belonged to him. I would always belong to him.

He said nothing.

I said nothing.

The tether I'd held on to wrapped around my neck

like a noose, squeezing and pulling. I let out a strangled sob, gasping for air while I clutched my chest. I
couldn't find it in me to say the words back to him. I
had to break what bound us together, but it refused to
come out because my heart knew it wasn't what I
wanted.

His brows furrowed, and he took a step forward,
but I held a hand out, backing up. Elias retreated,
clenching his fists.

"I came to you, Danni. I swear to you I did," he
started, his nostrils flaring as he exhaled harshly. "Let
me speak, *please*. I need you to hear me."

Time stilled while he waited for me to respond.
The muscles in his neck were tight with tension. His
breathing labored. His body shook with the pain and
exertion caused by the loosened chains that battled
between us. The rejection was hurting him,
commanding a reversal.

I nodded, holding back the tears that wanted to
come out.

"I know what I said to you about not wanting a
mate. About this being a business arrangement. I
know I said we were nothing. All of that? I can't take it
back. I can't. But it's not true. None of it. Not a single
word. From the moment I saw you, I was drawn to
you. I wanted you. Every day that passed, I wanted you
more. Not just in my bed. I wanted *you*. All of you.
Every day I wanted you by my side." He shook his

head, pointing his finger toward the door. "I knew that before you left. Before I told you we were nothing. Before the bond."

"Why?" I whispered.

He ran his fingers through his unkempt hair. "Because we have been communicating for shit. I was angry. You said something that hurt me, and I hurt you in return, and the moment those words came out of my mouth, I regretted them. I regret hurting you. I regret not telling you what you meant to me as soon as I realized what this really was."

"What is this to you, Elias?" My throat was raw, and my words came out husky and filled with need. When my legs began to tighten and spasm, it was hard to hold myself up. I rubbed my fingers against my palms, sliding over the sweat-slicked skin.

"Choice, Danni. Not fate. You chose me before this bond, and you wanted to tell me. I chose you, but I was so scared of losing you when Jordan made a threat on your life—"

"Who?" I asked, a crease forming between my brows.

He shook his head. "There is so much I didn't tell you. And that's my fault. I want the chance to tell you everything. When I got your note . . ." Elias paused, swallowing thickly, his eyes darting away.

"Tell me," I said quietly. "Whatever it is, please say it this time. Don't shut me out."

Sad eyes met mine, and he nodded softly. "I wanted to come to you immediately, but Ysa had just told me things about my past—your past—and I was spiraling out of control, thinking you'd never forgive me." He took a sharp breath, as though he were having second thoughts. I urged him on, inclining my head toward him while I pressed my lips together in anticipation. "I had just learned who your father really was, and that Mathis killed him. The war . . . I started it. My actions spurred the Great Sacrifice. Scott's death was my fault . . ."

Images of Mathis standing over me in the alley flashed through my mind. His confession resounded in my ears. "I know what he did," I told him, and he gave a slight headshake, but I spoke before he could interrupt me. "You can't take that blame. No matter what happened. No matter the cause of the war. Mathis killed my dad for power. You didn't do that."

He huffed a forced breath in shock. "I should have just come straight to you. I just wanted to know what to say. So I wrote it all down, but the words weren't right. It's still in my office. You can see for yourself. When Nova's howl woke me up, I thought it was a dream."

"What do you mean, her howl woke you up?" I narrowed my eyes. This wasn't the story I'd heard.

"I hadn't slept for days. I watched you every night, with the words we'd said to each other playing in my head like a broken record. The pain and guilt ate at me. I fell asleep on my desk."

"Was this before or after you saw Katie?"

He shook his head. "I never saw Katie. I don't know what you're talking about." When I said nothing, he studied my face. "You've said her name twice. *Why?*"

I shook my head, snorting a humorless laugh. I'd fallen into a trap of lies. How stupid could I be? Tall tales of a jealous ex-lover. Was anything she said even true? "I came looking for you. She mentioned you were elsewhere. Getting laid."

"She *what?*" he growled, taking several deep breaths as he seethed. "I'll deal with her later, but none of that is true. Danni, I nearly lost my mind when you were gone." His eyes turned dark, flashing with unnamed emotions. "I came apart at the seams. I shut down the borders. Sent guards to our waterfall just to see if you were there. I had a witch make a portal so I could get to you. I made Ysa cut out my fucking eyeball for the spell." He pointed to his face, then gestured wildly around the room. "You were on the brink of death, and the fear of that happening consumed me. The doctors couldn't save you. So I gave you my blood. I *changed you.* I've never made anyone before. I need you to know that. But I am not willing to live in a world where you don't exist." Elias's jaw clenched, and he stared at me with hunger . . . and truth.

Tears filled my eyes, spilling over the edge and

falling down my cheeks. Heat coursed through me, lighting up my insides, calling to him. My body knew he was the one who had made me. More than that, my heart knew he was the one made *for* me—and every part of me knew it. I opened my mouth, lips parting, but my breath hitched.

"I can't take back what you are now." Elias's eyes blazed, catching the light of the fireplace, giving him a devilish appearance. I pressed my thighs together, feeling the heat pulse at the apex of my thighs. "But I would do it all over again just to save you, even if that means I end up losing you."

"Then why did you reject me?" The words tried to suffocate me. I didn't want that. I just wanted him—more than anything—but forming coherent sentences evaded me.

"To prove to you that what's between us isn't a bond determined by fate. It's determined by *us*. I need you to understand this is real. If you reject me in return, I don't care. You are still the one for me. I choose you, Danni. I will always choose you."

A passionate thirst unlike any I'd ever known flared in my veins. Without thinking, I ran across the room toward Elias, letting the blanket fall to the floor. His eyes widened at my approach, and I threw my arms around him, bouncing off my toes and wrapping my legs around his waist as I crashed into him. He caught me, his hands splayed across my back as I pressed my lips to his, inhaling sharply and nodding against him.

He growled against me, then pulled back slightly, his eyes searching mine. I smiled, and heat filled me to the very core.

"Elias Laskaris, I choose you."

CHAPTER 30
ELIAS

My hands burrowed in her hair, snagging on the tangles and knots. Danni didn't seem to care as she kissed me with wild abandon. Her fangs roughly scraped against my bottom lip, breaking the skin. She gasped, pulling back a fraction.

"I'm sorry . . ." Her pupils narrowed, shrinking to pinpricks. Her tongue traced the edge of her teeth.

"Sharing blood between mates is powerful," I breathed, leaning in to press my lip to hers and letting it smear. I'd give her a drop, but nothing more. "You need more control before we play."

She groaned, her eyes shuttering at the taste of me. I wanted to see that look again, except with my come on her lips instead. I stiffened, my already hard cock turning heavy and painful. The bond was bad enough, drawing us together like magnets that refused to be apart. But Dannika wasn't overly experienced in this realm. I needed to know where her boundaries were.

It was going to kill me if this was a repeat of her heat.

I'd survive, but the restraint I possessed was already incredibly thin.

"What do you want, Danni?" I said, leaning in to run my tongue up the column of her throat. She tasted of salt, oranges, and peppermint. I wanted to bite her, but I was serious about her needing control. Blood was a drug to our kind. One we needed to survive, but vampire blood? It was the greatest hit she'd ever experienced. Ecstasy like no other.

I couldn't start her on that, even if I longed to experience it with her.

"Everything," she replied, fingers curling around my shirt, holding me to her.

"Boundaries, *mi amore*." One of my hands slipped from her hair, down her neck, curving with the length of her spine until it came to a stop on her lower back. I wanted to feast on her bare skin, but I had to be patient. "You know how I work. Right now, all I can think about is fucking you into tomorrow. I need your limits."

She leaned into me, eyes hazy with lust. "Don't hurt me."

My blood cooled a fraction. "Never."

"I don't like pain. I don't think dying will change that," she added. "I might not be opposed to bondage, though. Being tied up could be . . . fun."

Gods. This woman. "Anything else?"

"Touch me," she begged. "*Fuck me.*"

Her nails scraped over my back through the thin material. One hand clamped down on my shoulder, gripping the muscle in a vice-like grip. The other cupped the back of my neck, fingers latching on to the hair at the base of my skull to pull. I tilted my head back, and she arched up. Her tongue licked my parted lips, leading us into a heavy kiss.

My palm slid lower, taking a handful of her ass to press her closer.

Danni moaned, her already warm skin smoldering.

"The things you do to me," I growled, carrying her toward the bathroom.

"Tell me," she said. Demanded.

I flung the door open, and the handle burrowed into the drywall with a crack. "That first morning I woke up with you on my chest. You were so warm." My cock throbbed at the memory as I stepped into the doorless shower. "I wanted to roll you onto your back and pull those skintight jeans off you."

Lick her. Taste her. Consume her.

Danni dropped her hands to my waist, grabbing frantically for my shirt. I pressed her back against the tiled shower wall, pinning her with my hips before letting go. She wasted no time pulling my T-shirt over my head and flinging it aside.

"You didn't know me yet," she breathed. "We were still just a business—"

I smothered her words with a kiss, then flicked the shower handle. Cold water drenched my back, running down my face and neck. Danni shivered, pressing closer.

"And yet I couldn't stop myself from thinking of all the ways I could get you beneath me." I grunted. "Your heat was almost unbearable because I finally had you right where I wanted. Wanton. Needy. Begging me to fuck you—but I could only touch. Sample. Nothing more."

She shifted in my arms, pressing her wet core into the hardened bulge of my jean-clad cock. The pressure sent the beast in me spiraling.

"Show me," Danni purred. A seductive siren, not knowing the power she held. "Show me what you wanted to do."

With one hand, I hoisted her up, pushing her bare breasts into my face. My tongue whorled around one rosy-pink bud, pulling it between my teeth. Dannika hissed, her back arching. Her blue eyes were downcast, silently commanding me to keep going. Her lips parted in pleasure.

I maneuvered my free hand under her to unbutton my jeans. I shucked them down my legs, stepping out of one leg and then kicking the other away from the shower. The soaked lump of denim smacked against the tiles, then slid across the bathroom floor.

I released her nipple with a pop. Steam fogged the air. The tiles were warm when I pushed her back against the wall, angling our bodies so I could line up with her slick heat.

"Last chance, Danni," I told her. Our eyes locked as my cock nudged her opening. "There's no going back after I take you. No undoing it. You'll be my mate in every sense of the word. When you're pissed at me because I said something dumb, you can't up and leave. There will be no sneaking out to run away. No House will take you. No person will compare—"

She dropped her hips, seating herself on my cock. Those pale-pink lips parted in bliss. Her eyes rolled back. I couldn't contain my own moan as I pulled out and thrust back into her. Tight, wet heat. Friction. I needed more.

"I'm already yours." She groaned. "I chose you. Now fuck me like you own me."

Lust made her bold. Before, I'd blamed it on the heat, but maybe there'd been more of her in there during that time than I'd thought.

Wrapping my hand around the bottom of her thighs, I pulled her legs apart, unhooking her ankles from the small of my back. "Don't you fu—"

Dannika's words broke off in a delirious moan as I

thrust slowly in and out, using the added space to brush against her clit. Her legs began to tremble, muscles coiling tightly. So close . . . so close . . .

I pulled out, pausing a couple of seconds before inching back in. Her warmth was driving me fucking crazy, making me want to power into her without caring for her own pleasure. It didn't work that way.

Keeping her wants and needs at the forefront, I reined in that beast who threatened to snap.

"Please," she moaned. A breathy little sound that made my balls tighten.

"Please *what*?"

Her lips pressed together. She tried to maneuver her feet toward the wall so she could get some sort of leverage and control of the situation. I'd chosen the shower for our first coupling for a reason.

She didn't gain an inch unless I gave it to her.

"I don't know," Danni mewled.

"Tell me to come inside you," I said quietly. Her eyes opened, her cheeks turning red. Her mouth opened, then closed. I pulled out.

"Please . . ." She swallowed hard, and I lifted an eyebrow. The vulgarity of the words were throwing her. But I wanted it. That tiny submission. That little bit of Danni that only I would ever see. Her wildness. Her passion. My even-tempered little mate had a dirty side, and I needed to see it.

Just as I started to push in, she let out the words in a rush. "Please come inside me."

Gladly. "I didn't hear you," I pushed, seeing how far she'd let me go.

I fully seated myself before pulling back out. She nearly sobbed the words as she yelled, "Please come inside me."

I dropped her on my hard length and gave us both what we wanted.

Tile cracked under her back from the force of my thrusts. Her body smacked against the wet marble before lifting off it with a pop, over and over again.

Water drenched us both, but I didn't let up. Not when her legs trembled from pure need. A string pulled taut. She needed the push over the ledge, and I was going to send her flying.

"Now, *mi amore*," I commanded, using the same voice I did when addressing my Court. "Your king wants to feel you come."

Danni lost it. Her lips parted in a voiceless cry as her muscles spasmed. Her tight pussy clenched me, pulling me over the edge with her. I lost the last thread of control and pounded into her.

My mate. My Dannika.

A haze fell over me that didn't lift, even as I got my wish and filled her with my seed. We fucked twice more in the shower before tumbling into bed. Unable to get enough, Danni rode me with abandon, then got on all fours and begged me to take her from behind.

Her heat was bad.

The mate bond forming was worse. Each time we fucked seemed to pull us deeper into its grips. We were insatiable. Inconsolable.

I wasn't sure how long had passed when we finally collapsed from exhaustion, only that when we did, there wasn't a shred of doubt in me that she was my mate. I'd had her body at every angle possible. I'd tasted every inch. Painted every ounce.

She was mine. Completely. Fully.

I was utterly hers.

This was forever.

And I'd tear apart any motherfucker who tried to separate us.

CHAPTER 31

DANNIKA

Boneless.

That was my new name.

After several days of nothing but orgasms, dirty words, whispered promises, and more sex than I'd ever had in my life—I could sleep for a day. Maybe even a few. But the world was still spinning.

While Elias and I had been in the throes of the mate bond, Ysabeau had been dealing with the fallout of my near-death. My sister had been held at bay, though Nova had left partway through to see her. I was sure she'd needed a break while I'd been indisposed, and I knew she'd have lingering anxiety to make sure Adora was okay.

As impossible as it should have been, heat blossomed in my lower belly. I felt Elias's response from across the estate. We'd been together not an hour before in the bath when I'd finally pushed him out the door and told him to go work. *Do king things.*

It was strange, being able to feel him and his emotions. Not unpleasant, just different. I'd probably find it a lot weirder if I hadn't already had something so similar with Nova. I found it comforting. For most of my life now, I'd always had her. I found peace in togetherness. It was no different with a mate.

Footsteps sounded from the hallway, quiet but audible. My bedroom door opened. I knew it wasn't Elias since I could feel him. Tossing on a robe, I poked my head out of the closet. "Who is that—"

"It reeks of sex in here," Adora said, stepping around our bed and taking in the room. "No surprise, given how Nova smelled when she came to me, but gods. Y'all really went at it like rabbits."

I threw my arms around her in relief, even if I wanted her to stop talking. "You're an asshole, but I missed you."

Her petite arms wrapped around me tightly. "You had me so worried."

"Elias mentioned you threatened to kill him." I pulled back a fraction to look at her. "You played your hand in front of them. My mate's one thing, but the doctors? Anyone else who heard?"

"You were dying," Adora said simply. "My secret didn't matter when every minute counted."

I sighed, sitting on the edge of the bed. She started to follow suit, but then eyed the comforter heavily and seemed to think better of it. I took her hand in mine.

"Your secret is your life," I said. "It always matters. You need to be more careful." The strangest thing happened. I felt . . . guilt. Frustration. It didn't make sense.

Adora sighed. "It's hard sometimes. I can't change what I am, and I wouldn't want to. I'm awesome. But sometimes I wish I didn't have the *Eyes of God* power."

I gave her a sympathetic smile. "We're freaks. Always have been, always will be."

"True," my sister said. "You're arguably even weirder now. A shifter-who- couldn't-shift-turned-vampire. Do you crave blood?"

Elias's. My cheeks flamed. He wouldn't blood share. Said I had to learn control first, but that didn't mean that the scent didn't drive me wild. I'd also slipped up a handful of times when we'd been intimate. Anytime he took me and I was on his lap, the lure of his pulse became too great. Especially when I didn't have the shower drowning out my other senses.

I saw a lot of shower sex in my future.

I felt myself dampen and embarrassment heated my face. Unlike a normal vampire, whose heart beat slower, mine was unnaturally fast and skyrocketed when I had strong emotions. The faster beating meant blood pumped into my face quicker, giving me away.

In the distance, Elias's emotions shifted, focusing on me and my lust. I tried to push it down so I'd stop distracting him. Another emotion hit me. This time, it was something closer, but not as strong as my mate's.

Disgust made my stomach turn. I lifted my eyes to—

"Don't tell me blood makes you horny?" Adora grimaced. "Have you and Elias . . . You know what? Never mind. Pretend I didn't ask."

"You're grossed out."

Embarrassment. Reproach. Guilt.

"No, I just—" She broke off when I lifted an eyebrow, silently calling her out on her bullshit. "Yeah, it's kinda gross. But you're my sister and I love you, blood sucker or not. My peacock likes bugs, so I really can't judge here."

I chuckled. Something like contentment filled me. Not quite happiness, but a calmness. The slight smile on Adora's face said it all. "Given I like my steak blue rare, I can't say it's that much different. At least I can still eat. Elias said I only need one meal a day alongside a pint of blood, so it could be a lot worse."

Adora nodded. "You could be dead."

Her statement ripped the Band-Aid off the elephant in the room. I sighed. "So could you. I'm not the only one Mathis shot—or was intending to kill."

Adora shrugged one shoulder. "I was collateral damage. Not the target."

While true, it didn't make me feel any better about the situation. "What happened? Did he follow you? He said he knew you'd slip up—"

"I didn't fuck up. He was waiting for me near the house with half a dozen of his warriors, plus that bastard Andreas. They definitely knew I was going to meet you." She pushed her ombre-blue braid over one shoulder. "I had the scrambler, and no one was listening to our call. I didn't tell Mom or Abbey. I didn't even tell Rowe. I used a silencing crystal so no one could hear me. If they were questioned, I wanted to make sure they were free from culpability."

Oh, gods. Mom. Abbey. Rowe.

I didn't want them involved. Sure, my plan to run away may have been half-cocked, but it hadn't involved them. It hadn't involved anyone except Adora, who'd insisted on coming with. "What do you think Mathis will do?"

"To them?" she asked. I nodded. "Depends. I can't imagine life can get much worse for Rowe. She's human and beneath his notice, for the most part. I'd be more worried about our moms. If Mathis thinks we're dead, he probably won't do anything. When he realizes we're not, though . . ." The look she gave me was grim.

"Elias can find them. He can put together a team to extract them from Fire and Fluorite—"

"That's all well and good, but we need to find out

how Mathis knew I was going to meet you," Adora said. "If he could figure that out, he can be ready for any team Elias might send."

Ah, crap. She was right.

I gnawed on the inside of my cheek, mulling over that fact. "Okay, let's work through this. If you didn't slip up, but he was waiting for you, someone would have had to have tipped him off before I left. From the time we got on the phone to me getting in the truck, it would have only been ten minutes."

Adora nodded, pacing the length of the room, lips pursed in thought. "I was out the door in the same amount of time. Even if someone here saw you leave and told him, he shouldn't have been able to intercept me."

True. "Could someone have foreseen this?" I asked. "Elias said a witch foresaw he'd find his mate as a vampire in Blood and Beryl. Maybe one foresaw me leaving?"

Adora squinted, clearly not convinced. "You're ignoring the fact that very, *very* few witches have the power of foresight—and the ones who do are unreliable. Look at Elias's. You were a shifter. In another House."

"And now I'm a vampire in Blood and Beryl," I pointed out. "It's not impossible."

"Foresight doesn't come with a time stamp. I don't care who the witch is or how powerful. It could be the crone herself—they can't predict the *exact* minute something like that will happen." She looked out the window, shaking her head. "Someone had to have known."

I rubbed my fists into my eyes while I thought. "I don't see how. I hadn't even decided to leave until I went to find Elias and ran into—" I stopped dead in my tracks. My lips parted.

Adora tilted her head and lifted an eyebrow, prompting me to continue.

"I know how he found out."

CHAPTER 32

ELIAS

"Elias, it's her word against the Alpha Supreme's. Vesperus and Asbesta would undoubtedly vote in our favor, but do we have enough proof to sway the other Houses?"

Ysa and I had gone back and forth for hours. Note-cards and papers were strewn about the room, and we were both at our wits' end. I wanted nothing more than to call an emergency meeting of the Council. Call out Mathis and what he had done. Demand he pay for his crimes with blood. But we were lacking the one thing we needed. Iron-clad, irrefutable evidence.

"And nothing has come back from The Salty Siren?" I asked. Ysa shook her head. We'd sent teams to scour the alleys, looking for any kind of clue. Searching for any witnesses who may have been there that evening. Any cameras. The best we had was that two people had given a description of Danni walking the streets that night, and one person had seen a man with a giant silver wolf. No one had seen her sister, no one had seen Mathis, and no one had seen Andreas. "So all we have is Adora: A witness, as well as a victim."

Ysabeau sighed, tilting her head back and slumping in the chair. "And I can poke holes in that story left and right." Waving her hand aimlessly, she changed her voice as she continued. "Why would anyone believe the word of a woman who ran away from her House? Or believe the words of a woman who got kicked out of her House? Did either of them truly see their attackers? Adora could be lying in retaliation for when Mathis slapped her in public at the commemoration. Adora is just lying for her sister; of course they would be on the same side, telling the same lies."

I hit my desk with a closed fist. "He attacked my mate, Ysa. My *queen*. He can't get away with this."

She shook her head. "She isn't queen yet, and you know that'll get thrown in our faces. Even if she is made queen today, she wasn't the queen when it happened. Someone attacked her. That much is known, and no one can refute it. We have the witnesses to prove her injuries. But Mathis will claim to have never touched your mate, and he *will* have alibis. They'll all be fake, but he'll cover his tracks and you know this. Jordan is dead, Vesperus's mole is dead. We went after two spies Jordan named, and they were already dead. We have three spies we captured that are still alive, and they gave up information, but Mathis was never directly named. They always answer to someone else, and as we follow those tracks, it either leads to dead ends or that person ends up dead too. As it stands, our case is minimal at best."

"I know." I groaned, dropping my head to my desk and banging it lightly. "And we're left with the word of Dannika and Adora, two shifters originally from Fire and Fluorite, speaking out against the Alpha Supreme," I muttered, my words muffled as I was angled downward.

"If you were on the panel, would it be enough for you to vote against a House?" she asked, peering over her sunglasses.

The reality of my answer was disheartening. "No." It was an admission I loathed as I tasted it on my tongue.

"So, what would it take to sway you?" It was a good follow-up, but it required the one thing we didn't have.

"Proof."

"We're going in circles." Ysa pressed her lips together, reaching beneath her shades to rub her eyes. "And we still have to figure out what the hell that nonsense was with Katie as well."

"I haven't addressed it with her yet. I'm afraid I'm going to rip her head from her body." My limbs shook as I tried to contain the rage I felt at her name.

"I don't know what she was thinking, spouting off bullshit like that, but I doubt she expected Danni to leave and go get shot by Mathis. Beheading is a bit much, considering her crime is stupidity."

"Her stupidity almost got Danni killed," I argued. "I've already decided to remove her from Court. I never should've allowed her to stay. I knew she had ambitions to be queen at one time, but I thought she was over the fling we had. Otherwise I never would've kept her on."

She opened her mouth to respond, but a knock sounded, and she glanced at me. I shook my head. I wasn't expecting anyone. Not when I had more important things to work out.

Ysa stood, walking to the door, answering it, and speaking in low tones. Turning to me, she said, "Give me five minutes."

"Sure," I said, waving her off. She left, closing the door behind her, leaving me to toss around everything we had already discussed. I picked the information apart, piece by piece, always coming back to the same conclusion. I couldn't call the House Council to vote.

We had knowledge of the army Mathis was building, and that would certainly give the other Houses a reason to question his truth, unless they were a part of it. I also had to account for what Mathis would say he was actually doing with that army. He would expect me to bring it up, which meant he had a cover story.

An emergency meeting of that magnitude held the weight of the future, and the breakdown was impossible to figure out. Blood and Beryl would be accusing Fire and Fluorite of treasonous acts against the mated future queen. By default, neither of us could vote. We could only present our cases. The remaining five Houses would determine the outcome. I had Gold and Garnet and Sea and Serpentine. Mathis had Air and Amethyst; of that I had no doubt. But Earth and Emerald, and Spirit and Sapphire? The latter was uptight and didn't engage in the conflict between others. The former was founded on the ideals of individuals who only wanted a House for protection. They would never vote for something that could possibly bring about disagreements or war. Both Houses would need hard evidence—and I couldn't blame them for it.

Pinching between my eyes, I rubbed the bridge of my nose in a tight, circular motion, taking a moment to calm myself. There was something I was missing, but we didn't know where to look anymore.

"Elias?" Ysa said, poking her head through the door. I looked up, confused why she didn't just come in. "We have a visitor, and I think you'll want to hear what he has to say."

I raised an eyebrow, searching behind her as she opened the door.

Markus.

I stood up fast, my hands flat on my desk, my chair rolling behind me and hitting the shelves. "What do you want?" I barked. To his credit, he held his chin high. He didn't flinch or back away. "Just because you are no longer tied to my mate doesn't mean I want you around."

"Elias, listen to him," Ysa said quietly, an eyebrow raising over her shades.

I glared at him, then waved my hand.

"I'm not here to cause trouble. I'm happy Danni found her second-chance mate," he started, and I narrowed my eyes. Clearing his throat, he continued. "I never thanked you for saving my life. I know it was Danni who stuck her neck out for me—even though I didn't deserve it. She knows I'm grateful. But you made the decision to let me stay, and I owe you. You have my allegiance."

"Is this what you wanted to tell me?" I asked, looking at my second incredulously.

"No. Well, yes, but there's more." Markus put his hands behind his back, clasping them as he stood tall. I hadn't invited him to sit, and he was smart enough to not assume he was allowed to. "Danni encouraged me to explore my options in the House. Find work that suited me. Contribute to Blood and Beryl. Heal from

. . . my past. Try to be a better person. In time, I know I'll prove myself worthy of being accepted. She also suggested that I . . . date, or at least, play the field. So I have been."

I crossed my arms, wondering where his conversation was headed. "Congratulations. You're learning how to be a man, and you're getting laid. How does any of this pertain to me?"

His jaw clenched tightly, and he sniffed, but the tension loosened shortly after that. "You have another mole, and it's someone you are entirely too close to."

I shot Ysa a look and she inclined her head, removing her shades, giving me an *I told you so* look if there ever was one.

"How do you know we had a mole to begin with? That information wasn't made public."

"Because I'm sleeping with a member of your High Court," he said. Anticipation and adrenaline coursed through me, and I dipped my chin, telling him to continue. "Katie."

"You have my attention," I said, the emotions I felt making the words come out gritty and thick.

"She is the direct line feeding information to my father," he said, wasting no time getting to the point. I exhaled sharply, my brows furrowing.

"How do you know this?" My voice was dark, and so were my thoughts.

"Because I overheard her last night," he explained. I glanced at Ysa as she remained outwardly calm.

I considered him, then pulled back my chair from where it'd hit the shelves, sitting, and resting my elbows on my desktop. Still, he remained in place, not being offered to do anything but stand. "What exactly did you hear?" I asked.

"My father knows Danni is alive. I heard someone named Jordan is dead, and he gave up information before his untimely passing. I also know you found five other rats in Blood and Beryl, two of whom are also dead. The three you captured have been under the care of someone you haven't named, at least not in front of Katie." He inhaled deeply, taking a moment between unloading everything he'd learned. "You know what he's been building in Utah. He's already given orders to make it disappear and get rid of the evidence."

A crease formed between my brows. "Katie said all this in her sleep?" I made no attempt to hide my doubt. A traitor wouldn't have gotten this far by making stupid mistakes. I'd told her not to have any more overnight visitors if her sleep talking was going to be a problem.

"Of course not. I'm not allowed to stay the night, so after we were, um . . . finished, I packed up my things to leave and she went to shower. Halfway to my room, I realized I'd left my keys, so I went back. The water was turned on, and I figured maybe I'd pop back in to surprise her. Then I heard her whispering, so I listened in. She was incredibly quiet, but . . ." He pointed to his head, shifting his ear to the shape of a wolf's, large and pointed, but not changing the rest of his body. It took a lot of practice to shift individual parts. I was impressed.

"Ysa," I said, looking at her as she waited by the door. "Get Katie's phone. Anything she carries. I want it all."

Markus shook his head, his ear back to normal. "You won't find anything."

"Then how is she contacting your father?"

"Carefully," he said simply. "Under the floorboard in her room. Beneath a rug, six planks over from the reading desk, under the chair. Inside, you'll find a phone. It has one number in it."

"You looked?"

"I waited until I knew she was managing business with the High Court. I wasn't coming to you until I could give you the location."

"How'd you find it?"

He pointed to his nose, shifting his face, and a large, wolf snout took its place. He shifted back. "Sniffed it out. Smells like her shampoo."

I didn't think my mood could have darkened any further, but I was wrong. So wrong. My blood boiled. The betrayal. One of my own. Danni was still in danger, right under my own roof. "Anything else?"

"I'm pretty sure Katie's going to kill me," he added. "That would seem to be her plan. It'll be an accident, of course, but my time is coming to an end."

"Is that what this is? You want to protect yourself? Save your own skin?" I asked bitterly.

He shook his head, his lower lip pursing slightly. "Nope."

"Then why are you telling me this?"

"Are you going to kill my father?" he asked, never answering my question. Bold move.

I tilted my head, watching his features. Looking for signs of lying. Retaliation. Anger. I saw none. "What would you do if I said *yes*?"

"I'd say I want to be there when you do." There was no hesitation. He answered quickly, and with assurance.

Ysa grinned at me, her fangs peeking over her lips.

"You want to be there . . . when I kill your father. Hypothetically, of course. You do understand I can't just go around killing other leaders." *As much as I want to.* "Doesn't look good. Also, it's kind of against the rules."

He shrugged. "Then we don't get caught."

I barked a laugh. "Well, here I was trying to plan for a House Council meeting so they could vote in favor of dethroning your father. But all I needed to do was kill him and not get caught. That just solves that problem, doesn't it? I wish I'd thought of that." The dripping sarcasm had no effect on Markus's insistence.

"He won't give up. He never does. Everything he has in this life is because he took it—and believe me when I tell you that taking is something he greatly enjoys doing. The fact that Danni is alive has enraged him. She's a job left unfinished. He will come for her again."

The instinctive need to protect my mate flared to life. It was as though Markus was the one making the threat, and the fury inside me was ready to end him for suggesting that she could be taken from me. "I won't let that happen."

"Me either," he said firmly. "She deserves better than what life has given her. I want her to have that."

"It appears we agree on something," I said softly, though my voice vibrated with barely contained rage.

Ysa stepped forward, a smirk on her face. She nudged him on the arm. "Go ahead."

I looked at Markus curiously, realizing there was more to this. In the time they'd been gone, he'd probably filled her in on everything, so she likely knew what was coming. Surprise filtered through me as I understood where it was going. "You have a plan?"

A smile curled up his lips. "My father has many goals. One of which is making sure I end up dead," he said. I nodded. That much had been made clear. "So use me as bait."

I did a double take, blinking rapidly. "I'm sorry. What?"

"A trap needs to be set if we want to bring my father to his death. Neither one of us would be willing to risk using Danni as bait, and she won't allow Adora to be used." My jaw tightened as I thought of my mate bleeding out, almost dying. "Use me."

"So you can have Fire and Fluorite when he's gone?" I suggested.

His gaze softened, and he lowered his voice as he spoke, but the tone was still stern somehow. "No, I wouldn't make a good leader. I wasn't raised by one, and I have too much of my own shit to work out. Even though I knew that deep down, Danni is the one who showed me." He shook his head, never taking his eyes off me. "I belong to Blood and Beryl."

I looked at Markus, head to toe. The former shifter heir to Fire and Fluorite. Mathis's eldest son, conspiring with a king to murder his father. It was against the bylaws to outright kill any leader. It could cause a war. It was also the best way to get rid of him once and for all. To avenge my sister. To protect my mate.

I huffed a laugh, gesturing to the chair in front of my desk.

"Take a seat. I'm listening."

CHAPTER 33

DANNIKA

The first time I'd sat in the throne room, I'd felt like a fraud. A liar. I'd known deep down I wasn't supposed to be there, and I'd hated the way the anxiety had clawed at me as I'd waited for the truth to be discovered. Anticipated the moment that I would be found out.

Not today.

I was the future queen. The king's mate. This was *my* throne. Blood and Beryl was my House. This was where I belonged.

Katie was the fraud. The liar. Soon to be the outcast, and I knew I would enjoy showing her the exit.

The table and seating for members of the High Court had been removed. Standing room only. It was about to be a show, after all. One that would require an audience. Bodies filtered in, whispering in hushed tones. Many were confused, but intrigued. Something big was going to happen. They just didn't know what.

I could hear everything they said, though they weren't aware of my newer heightened abilities. Some of the High Court knew that Elias had done something to save me. They weren't aware of what lengths he'd gone. Given Katie's disloyalty, we thought it best not to share. It was known shifter-vampire hybrids didn't survive the process of being turned, and it was unlikely they'd assume that had been what Elias had done.

High-ranking officials, members of the High Court, soldiers, guards, and a smattering of those who lived and worked on the estate waited with bated breath.

Nova and I sat in silence. I was frozen in place with my elbows against the armrest. Emotions bombarded me. Anxiety. Trepidation. Excitement. Worry. My confidence wavered for a moment as the negativity threatened to drag me under. Nova nudged me with her nose, seeming to smile at me with her eyes. Elias reached over, threading his fingers through mine in reassurance. Their strength grounded me.

Marisa's hair was pulled up in a beautiful bun, accentuated with *Latin Lady* roses. Bianca came to stand by her, winking at me when she looked at Elias's hand entwined with mine. Then Katie entered, completely oblivious to what was about to happen.

Glancing up at the dais where we sat, she smiled warmly.

Fake.

Angry, bitter emotions came at me from her, and I had to hide my wince. They felt gross, like oil in my veins. She was fuming on the inside, hiding behind her sunny camouflage.

When Ysabeau entered, she held the door open wide. The chatter and musings ceased, and curious eyes shot to the entrance, waiting to see what this was all about. It wasn't every day that so many were summoned, told they were there to witness a milestone for the House.

Kieran appeared, dragging Markus in behind him. His hair was matted, and his clothes were wrinkled. Disheveled. Anger radiated from him on the surface. Dried blood marred his face from what appeared to be a cut across his cheek. A fight, perhaps. One he didn't win. Metal cuffs held him shackled at the wrists, the teal glow of magic from the steel preventing him from shifting.

Or so that was what everyone was made to think.

I felt his true emotions. Anxiety. Excitement. An overwhelming desire to prove himself.

I flitted my eyes over to Katie as he was dragged in, and she was already playing her part. Curious. Confused. Sad. No doubt she was already forming the lies she'd tell us if questioned about him.

Her acidic rage turned to interest. The irrational part cooled a degree as cold calculation set in.

Elias stood, beckoning Kieran and Markus forward.

"Markus Del Reyes," he started, speaking loudly so his voice carried throughout the throne room. "You've been brought here today to answer for your conduct."

"What conduct is that?" he spat.

"You kissed me." I slammed my fist onto the throne. "Then tried to grope me, asshole!"

"You wanted it." Gasps echoed in the room, and all eyes turned to Markus in shock. "Your head may say *no*, but the bond says *yes*. You're my mate. You've always been my mate. Not his," he said, angling his head at Elias. "You're a shifter, and you belong with a shifter. With me."

"Just because you want something doesn't mean it belongs to you." I crossed my arms, digging my nails into the skin. "You said you rejected me. You told members of this House that you were moving on. Trying to form a life here. Is everything that comes out of your mouth a lie?"

"I tried to move on." He looked down, a faint color creeping up his neck. His embarrassment slammed into me. "But you can't fight fate."

"For what? Five minutes?" I narrowed my eyes, huffing in annoyance and ignoring his real emotion so I could focus on our plan. "I stuck my neck out for you,

Markus. And this is how you repay me? You lied to me, then tried to seduce me. I don't want you here anymore. I can't trust you."

"Danni, don't do this—" Markus's eyes flashed, showing his attempt to shift. A deep rumble filled his chest. Nova barked loudly, shushing him as she stood tall. She bared her teeth, putting on quite the show.

"*Don't* call me Danni. You're still the same shithead from Fire and Fluorite. You had me so convinced," I said, shaking my head. "But that was my mistake. I never should have brought you here." I looked at Elias, and he was playing his part well. His eyes narrowed and his jaw tightened as he gripped the arm of the throne, giving my mate the appearance of barely contained rage.

"It's your call," he said through clenched teeth. "I prefer that he just die, but I want my queen to make her own decisions."

Inclining my head, I pressed my lips into a forced smile. "I won't lower myself to his father's level, but his survival is no longer my concern. Let him fend for himself." I motioned to Ysabeau, and she stepped forward. "Have the soldiers take him to the border and drop him in No Man's Land, where I should have left him. He has a backpack with personal items. He can have them too. I want no reminder of him left behind."

Ysa grinned, her fangs on full display. "With absolute pleasure."

Several guards stepped forward to handle Markus as he thrashed in defiance. "I won't stand a chance out there, and you know it!" he yelled, jerking his arms away as they tried to gain control over him.

Elias shrugged. "You're not my problem anymore."

I gestured for the guards to continue. "You made your choices, and now I've made mine."

Unable to shift, he growled threateningly as they dragged him from the throne room. The procession passed Katie, and she couldn't help herself. She left the sidelines, stepping into the path that led to the door. Standing in front of him, she shook her head, eyes filling with tears. Her bottom lip quivered, and she sharply inhaled. I suppressed the need to roll my eyes. Then she slapped him, turning her cheek to him, and walking away.

A lovely performance from a skilled actress.

Liar.

Fraud.

But we went along with it.

When Markus was gone and the doors had shut, the gasps and chatter filled the air. Soon, rumors would fly, but that was a problem for later. We had laid the foundation for our trap. Now to build on it.

Turning to look at Elias, my eyes spoke for me as I gazed at him and gave him the go-ahead for the next phase of the plan.

Katie was wiping at her eyes, though I saw no

tears. Bianca comforted her; an arm wrapped over her shoulder as they spoke in hushed tones. Elias called her name, his voice carrying above all the conversation. She looked up, and he beckoned her forward.

Sullen and in false mourning over the exile of her supposed partner, she came down the aisle, stopping in front of us. No doubt she expected sympathy and support. She kneeled; head angled to the floor as she spoke. "My king, I am so sorry. I took him as a lover, but I didn't know what he was doing."

As she rose, Elias dropped the bomb. "Katie, did you or did you not lie to Dannika, my mate and your future queen?"

Her breath hitched. "Pardon?"

"The night I was shot," I answered. "Did you lie when you said you'd had a meeting with Elias?"

She froze. Everyone in the room stood still. Eyes widened, mouths agape in shock.

Katie stammered, searching for words. "I . . . What I meant to say—"

"I'm not asking what you meant to say. I'm asking about what you *did* say," I reminded her.

Her lips separated, opening and closing like a fish out of water. "I think my words may have gotten twisted around. Confused. I had seen him. Earlier in the day. I had a meeting with him that never happened. That's all I meant." Her eyes shot to Elias, begging for confirmation, but he gave none.

"Was that before or after you told my mate that I was likely off fucking another woman?" This time, raw, unbridled anger burned in Elias. He was *pissed*.

I narrowed my eyes, fixing my hardened stare on her face, daring her to say otherwise.

"That's not . . ."

Nova cut her off with a deep, rumbling growl.

"Tread carefully, Katie," Elias warned. "I wouldn't advise calling Dannika a liar. Certainly not in my presence."

She pressed her mouth closed, nodding quietly.

Marisa stepped forward, inclining her head respectfully. "I move to have Katie dismantled as a member of the High Court, if it pleases you." Elias nodded, and she looked at her colleagues.

Uriah raised his hand. "I second." When Katie shot him a look, he shrugged, speaking to her directly. "I have no patience for drama. I make no effort to hide this." He waved his hand around, gesturing to the room. "This is drama, and it's wasting my time."

"Elias, please," she started, looking back at him on the throne. "I—"

"Stop," he barked. "You aren't banished from Blood and Beryl, but you will no longer hold a place in my Court. You've always aspired to be a queen, but you let your jealousy rule your actions. That was a mistake you can't undo, and I won't allow it to happen again. You've lost my trust, Katie." Glancing at other members of the High Court and the high-ranking officials present, he seemed to gauge their demeanor and read their expressions. Disappointment. Disgust. Shame. "And that of everyone in this room."

She turned slowly, looking at everyone, hoping someone would speak for her. Stand up for her. Say something in her defense. When she met Bianca's hurt-filled gaze, she knew the truth. No one would support her in our presence.

"What am I supposed to do?" she asked quietly.

"Bianca will find you another job within the House," Elias said, motioning to her to see that it happened.

"Perhaps one that teaches humility," I muttered loudly, intending to ignite a fire in her. Looking at her directly, I shooed her away. "You may go now. We have private matters to discuss."

Katie's hands curled into fists, and the muscles in her jaw visibly tightened. She dipped her chin, turning on a heel and walking quickly to the door. Rage and venomous hatred radiated from her.

In the darkness, in a far corner of the room, Ysa slipped farther into the shadows. With all the commotion, no one thought to look in that direction, so no one saw her disappear.

It was a bold plan. By his own choice, Markus was the bait. Katie would pass on what had just happened with him, guiding Fire and Fluorite into No Man's

Land. She'd feel abandoned and angry, ready to give everything away as quickly as possible in order to get back at me. I hoped it would work.

I had a feeling it wouldn't take much for Mathis to go after his son. His hatred knew no bounds. His desire for power was endless. His mind was clouded with single-minded goals. His rage would win.

It always did.

CHAPTER 34
ELIAS

eadlights illuminated the trees, casting us in shadows.

Nova was in position, hidden in the trees far away from our location. I stood back, leaning against the base of a trunk, Dannika tucked against my side. Her breath against my throat and the way her hummingbird heart beat quickly calmed my senses. Vengeance roared in my blood. A darker, animalistic fury pushed me to leave our spot hidden in the darkness, and hunt Mathis like a dog. To let myself unleash the carefully confined predator that lurked beneath my apathetic façade.

Dannika knew it was there. Waiting.

In the mating frenzy, I'd let him out. She was the first person to see him for what he really was in twenty-four years. Since the Great Sacrifice.

The streets had run red with blood of innocents. Only one had needed to die, and instead, so many had paid for his sins. For my vengeance.

I wouldn't do that again.

No, this time, Mathis wouldn't escape me.

Doors shut. The approaching figure's footsteps were silent. I sensed them drawing nearer, judging by the way Dannika's head tilted, ear angling outward. She was a vampire-shifter hybrid, and we didn't know the full extent of what she could do, but so far, it seemed she'd retained the best traits of both. Shifter hearing. Vampire speed. An uncanny ability to feel the emotions of others . . .

He was close.

Not a hundred yards from us, Markus paced, head in hands as if distraught. His job was to be the *pretend mate*, lost in anger at being kicked out of our House and forced away from Dannika. Bait, as he'd said in my office.

The tables had turned. Under normal circumstances I'd never have allowed someone else to even fake being Dannika's mate. Let alone the pup, who once had been. The very idea made me want to rip him limb from limb. But removing Mathis from the equation and securing her safety was paramount.

Claudette's death had been horrifying.

We'd lost a good man—a good leader—when

Mathis had murdered Danni's father in cold blood to steal his position.

She and her family had been robbed of the lives they should have had, along with so many others.

There were plenty of reasons to bring him down. But the action that put that final nail in his coffin was when he *tried to murder my mate*.

She was right that he would never stop coming for her. Hunting her. If not for what she was to me, if not because she was Scott Kingston's sole heir, then because she was simply a loose end to tie up.

Mathis stepped into the trees, half his face hidden in shadow. He had a wild look in his eyes, like a madman. My hands clenched at my sides. Dannika wrapped her fingers around my forearm, giving me a reassuring squeeze.

"Markus," Mathis called. His voice boomed, making the branches rustle. True to his word, the boy froze as if in surprise. Fear. He turned toward his father, and I suspected it wasn't all fake. "My son. My heir." He smiled cruelly. "Such a disappointment. Still waiting here. Licking your wounds because you refused to mount the bitch—"

I started to take a step forward and Dannika stopped me. Her head tilted, a small frown playing at her lips. I lifted an eyebrow in question.

"I didn't deserve Dannika. I still don't," Markus said quietly. Even in the face of his own personal nightmare, the boy was starting to stand up like a man.

Mathis doubled at the waist, letting out a raucous laugh. "I'd say she must have a tight snatch to have you both so pussy whipped, but I know the vampire never let you near her. At least in that, he had the balls to lay a claim. Unlike you."

Magic gathered in the palm of my hand. An axe. I was going to butcher the bastard for this.

Dannika gave her head a sharp jerk, shaking it once. I frowned.

What is she trying to tell me? Danni couldn't possibly have been trying to save Mathis.

She jutted her chin to the east. Toward the forest. Trees.

I might've been a master vampire, but I wasn't a mind reader. It was only when the wind changed that I caught the scent. For all my strength and speed, my sense of smell and hearing were not nearly as strong as a shifter's, so while I knew he had shifters lurking behind him in the trees, I'd missed the dozens who were sneaking through the forest.

It was more than we'd expected.

Markus gave his father a look of disgust. "I never knew how much of a sick fuck you were until she showed me. I knew the beatings weren't right, but the rest of it? The emotional abuse, the way you pitted me against everyone—my brother, my pack, my mate—I should have challenged you a long time ago."

Mathis's laughing stopped, but he kept the leering smile.

"You couldn't win a challenge against me even if I tied a hand behind my back." Mathis scoffed. "You're weak. A poor excuse for an alpha. It's the reason fate tied you to a broken shifter. It's a shame it took that for me to finally see it." He surveyed his son, as if evaluating a stud that wasn't up to par. "Better I know now. There's still time to *fix* Triton. If I can break your mother, I can do it to him. He'll suffice."

Markus turned rigid. "I won't let you touch him. You're not going to fuck up my brother like you did me."

Mathis lifted his eyebrows. "And who's going to stop me? You?"

Glancing over his shoulder, Mathis made a movement with his head, likely motioning for someone to grab Markus. Shade, his second, stepped out—followed by Andreas.

It seemed Mathis had thrown discretion out the window and was coming in full force. I'd expected warriors. Soldiers. But his second and third in command surprised me.

No matter. It worked to my advantage, and I'd slaughter them all the same.

Shade and Andreas both grabbed Markus, each

taking an arm to hold him in place. The kid let out a roar, fur erupting along his arms and spine. "I won't have to!"

Mathis continued smiling, unfazed. His eyes lifted from his son, staring straight at Danni and me despite the trees, branches, or distance.

"Hello, Elias," he sneered. Snapping his fingers, the wolves Danni had sniffed out sprang from the trees, forming a circle around us.

In the distance, a wolf yelped, and its muffled anguish was silenced before Nova let out a howl that the gods themselves must've heard.

As her call echoed to the heavens, clouds drifted across the sky. A harvest moon peeked through, casting us in a crimson glow, foreshadowing what I already knew.

Blood would be spilled on this night.

CHAPTER 35

DANNIKA

An onslaught of rage was eating at me. I knew it wasn't my own, but that didn't stop my blood from racing. My face warmed, heat rushing up my neck and into my cheeks. A headache erupted, threatening to split my skull.

The wolf nearest me growled, snapping their teeth.

I twisted, pressing my back to Elias's. Slipping a hand inside my jacket, my fingers locked around a cool, metal handle.

"What's this?" Elias mused, his voice laced with poisoned honey. Quiet and non-aggressive, yet lethal in its deceptiveness. "The big, bad Alpha Supreme needs others to fight for him?" He chuckled, a sliver of his fury leaking into the sound.

"You think I didn't know you were here? I could smell you and that bitch half a mile away. I'm not stupid enough to fight you one on one," Mathis scoffed. "Elias Laskaris, Son of the Slayer of Alexandria, Heir of the Blade Magic, King of Blood Rage." I'd never heard these titles before, but the afternoon when Bianca had told me about them having most of the Library of Alexandria in their possession came back to me. A chill skittered along my spine, raising the hairs on the back of my neck. "There is no bravery in a senseless death. A true alpha knows that."

Of course we'd expected him to catch our scent. It was the very reason we didn't bring an army with us. But how my mate managed to appear so unaffected by everything when this rage was suffocating me, I didn't know.

Elias snorted. "Says the man who sentenced his son to death for not killing the woman who rejected him." I could imagine his facial expressions when I heard the admonishment in his tone—a cocked eyebrow, a smirk on one side of his lips. "You're weak. Pathetic. That these lemmings follow you speaks to their stupidity as much as your own. You think they can protect you?" Several wolves let out more growls, their gaping mouths salivating at the possibility of ripping us apart.

Mathis smirked. "A man is only as strong as his greatest weakness. I have none. Only a fool falls in love. But you . . ." He grinned a toothy smile. "Get them."

Elias sprang forward, meeting wolves head-on. I pulled the gun from my jacket and gunshots rang through the air as I shot down Mathis' followers, just like we'd talked about. They tried to separate us, but that was the plan. Elias needed to go after Mathis. To separate *him*. Nova took down the outliers, and I would deal with whatever wolves he'd bring.

Inside, emotions rocked me like I was trapped in a boat on a stormy sea. The violent turbulence had no mercy, increasing with each passing second. That struggle helped me point at the wolf nearest and shoot. The echo of the gun firing was thunderous. It recoiled, shaking my arm, rattling my bones.

Point. Shoot.

Point. Shoot.

Point. Sh—

My hand cracked, wrist bending an angle. I didn't register what had happened immediately. The shock of the impact had made me slow, but I realized I wasn't the only one shooting.

Blood poured from a circular bullet wound in my wrist. My fingers trembled, the barrel swaying from my loosened grip.

Another clap of thunder boomed. The gun fell from my hand.

I stared at the bleeding stump where my index finger had been.

Rage thickened. Like a fog that descended, it

pulled me in, wrapping its tendrils around me. The boat I'd been in capsized in the waves. The hurricane within unleashed.

I felt Nova as she ran through the forest, leaping over logs, dodging trees. Her feet carried her like she floated on the wind. I couldn't see Elias. I'd lost Mathis. My vision was filled with fangs and fur. Claws and teeth.

Wolves leapt at me. They grabbed at my arms, my legs, any part of me they could get their maws on.

Flesh ripped clean from my bones.

My ribs cracked, then my legs gave way.

My blood scented the air, but I felt no pain.

Only rage.

It burned bright, like a beacon for my wolf. The other half of my soul.

I threw my head back and let out a howl.

If there was a god of the moon, I could have sworn they answered. Clouds rolled across the sky, blotting out all light. Nova didn't need it to see—she could feel me. Hear me. She *was* me.

Her giant, lumbering form barreled through the wolves tearing at my skin. My vampire healing was incredible, but it could only heal so much when a half dozen beasts had their teeth in you.

Just as Nova would have reached me, our skins somehow collided—then *merged*.

I had no way to explain the sensation as her entire

being went through me, *into me.* My bones cracked. Snapped. My skin sprouted fur. My fangs grew longer, sharper.

I was changing.

I was *shifting.*

My body reformed, bigger, stronger, more powerful than ever. I didn't think about the height difference. That they might as well have been dogs compared to my size. All I knew was anger. The desire to hurt and to kill overrode all empathy or reason.

I bit down on one wolf's head, severing it clean from their body, then I whipped my neck back and forth. Their carcass landed with a dull thud. I dropped its head, turning on the others.

They turned and hauled ass. Terrified and running like their lives depended on it.

It did.

But while they were as small as foxes, they weren't nearly as agile. I trampled them with my great paws, bending to pick them up by their backs and throwing them into each other. My massive form knocked into trees as I ran, uprooting them from the ground. The earth sank beneath my paws. Gunshots echoed in the distance, but they were a far-off cry. The noise barely registered as I hunted down these traitors.

I was their heir. Their alpha. They'd followed a horrible man who beat his wife and children instead of standing up to him.

Mathis was no leader. He needed others to fight his battles. He needed to murder to gain his power.

They could have changed this. Anyone could have. Shade. Andreas. The other wolves in our pack alone could have united and kept my mom in charge, but they hadn't. They'd *let* him destroy us. Destroy my family.

I would kill them all for their betrayal.

One by one, I pinned them with claws and teeth. Their bodies were little more than rag dolls for me to use. And when I caught the last one, and their bones snapped, signaling the finality of my fight—I couldn't stop.

The forest was quiet.

The carnage, incredible.

The rage, uncontrollable.

CHAPTER 36
ELIAS

I turned from the dead at my feet to look for Mathis, but he was nowhere to be found. Bodies littered the silent forest, but I knew none were Danni's. The invisible line between us existed, but the scenery didn't make sense. Trees were smashed. Overturned. Limbs, both human and wolf, haphazardly tossed about. Paw prints two feet in diameter were pressed into the dirt.

Something other than fury touched me for the first time since Mathis had shown his face.

Concern. Worry. Fear.

Where is Danni?

I wanted to go to her. To find her. A gun clicked, but I didn't bother looking. Only Mathis would stay to end this amidst whatever had happened here.

"I gotta say, I didn't see that one coming," he

called. "Scott was a *big* bastard, but his daughter . . ." Mathis let out a whistle.

Dear gods. Dannika had shifted.

Under other conditions, that might have brought me joy. But she never had before, and she only had under duress—*after* I'd changed her. That her wolf may have been the size of a dinosaur and in some kind of killing rage . . .

I needed to deal with Mathis and find my mate.

With a glance back toward where the Alpha Supreme lingered, I started walking that way. His hands on the gun tightened. "You'd do well to stay where you are."

I cocked an eyebrow. "If you think that pathetic piece of metal will stop me from killing you, you're mistaken."

Mathis squeezed the trigger, firing off a warning shot. I whipped my head to the side, only dodging the bullet by a hairsbreadth. His eyes widened.

"Fun fact about master vampires, Mathis. We're faster." I punctuated my statement with another dodge as he fired again. "Stronger. More powerful in every way."

He emptied the clip, but this time I couldn't dodge them all. One bullet sank into my shoulder, the final shot slamming into my forehead. My skull split instantly as the bullet imbedded itself into my brain. I grit my teeth as the edges of my vision turned black—

threatening unconsciousness. My legs turned stiff, brittle. My head burned like someone had stuck a hot poker through it.

Then it stopped. The magic within me pushed the metal fragments from my shoulder and head, repairing me from the inside out. Soft thuds sounded as the bullets fell to the forest floor. The wounds closed. The darkness faded. My strength returned.

Mathis looked pale.

He should have known better than to rely on a pack of wolves and a gun. Fire and beheading were the only ways to kill me.

"That includes healing." I grunted. "Fuck, you're lucky I want to find Dannika because I'd drag this out even more for shooting me in the head." His eyes widened. Hair sprouted along his arms.

Mathis's eyes filled with fury. "Shade. Andreas, kill Markus *now*."

I chuckled. One sideways glance at Shade and a single dip of my chin was all it took. He released Markus, who twisted and pulled Andreas into a head-lock. Shade stepped back, lips firm in a grimace.

"What the—" Mathis panicked, his eyes darting between his second and third.

"Shade here has been working with me for almost a decade," I said. The blade in my hand disintegrated in favor of a double-sided halberd, my preferred weapon of choice. "He saw the writing on the wall that you would be Fire and Fluorite's ruin. We came to an agreement of sorts." I twisted the halberd, and the metal sang as the dual blades cut through the air. "I got to remove your head when the time was right, and he got to put Fire and Fluorite back on track. Sounds like a win-win, am I right?"

Mathis let out a growl. "You son of a—"

I conjured a throwing knife and hurled it at his left shoulder. The blade sunk into the skin, and he grunted, not finishing that sentence. "You don't get to speak about my mother that way, or any other woman, for that matter."

Shade lifted both eyebrows, seemingly surprised by that. I ignored him. We may not have been friends, but we were allies. His family had come from Blood and Beryl, after all. His father had been a murderer I'd put down. His mother and her children hadn't been able to escape the man's reputation, even though they'd been blameless. I'd worked with Scott's father to have them transferred to Fire and Fluorite for a new start.

It had been all too easy to form a connection with Shade after Scott had been murdered. Especially when he'd known what Mathis had done to come into power.

"If you think my House will settle for this, you're wrong." Mathis growled threateningly under his breath the closer I came to him. "This will be a war that rivals the Great Sacrifice, and it will be *your* fault."

I rolled my eyes, unbothered. "No. It won't."

"Fire and Fluorite will never know what happened here," Shade said. "We'll tell them you tried to launch an attack on Blood and Beryl, and you died at the border. Elias was never here. Upon realizing it was a lost cause, your warriors fled and were sadly slaughtered. Markus's honor will be restored for fighting bravely. My son will corroborate our story, of course." He tilted his head toward Andreas, then tipped his chin toward me in confirmation.

Andreas didn't look pleased that his father had kept secrets from him, but he was smart enough to keep his mouth shut.

"Markus—" Mathis began, changing tactics when he realized neither his second nor his third were going to step in.

Markus laughed, and it was bitter. "As far as I'm concerned, you weren't murdered. You made a choice and killed yourself. Elias is just the hand finishing the job."

While his words carried conviction, he still looked away from his father's angry, red face. Like a victim conditioned to be submissive, his eyes lowered and shoulders slumped. I didn't think he had it in him to kill his father, but that was okay. He didn't have to.

He'd played his part getting him here, and that was all I needed.

Mathis tried to shift. I whirled the halberd, and the blade struck true. His face froze in a grotesque state in between that of man and wolf. Fur covered him in patches. His nose was elongated, as were his teeth. His eyes were the same, always filled with hatred.

Blood slicked my blade, falling in droplets when the magic disintegrated.

A red line blossomed across his throat. Mathis' head slid sideways.

His body fell a moment later.

Silence descended over the clearing. The last remainders of my blood rage slipped away. For so long, I'd wanted him dead. Now he was.

The reality wasn't fulfilling for my revenge, but Danni's safety meant everything to me. That Fire and Fluorite would no longer have a bounty on her life was a weight lifted from my shoulders. His death wouldn't bring back my sister or her father, but it would prevent him from taking her too.

"Stay," I commanded them. "I need to find Danni."

"I can help—" Markus volunteered. His voice cut off with a single hard look. I may not have viewed him as a threat, but I didn't like him near her. Especially when she was feeling vulnerable.

I turned for the forest and started running, following the paw prints. Whatever birds lived here had gone silent. Not a single creature scurried or chittered, likely terrified of what had taken place.

Dread soured in my gut as I took in the dead wolves. A leg here. A head there. A carcass chewed in half. Blood saturated the ground, leaving a copper tint in the air. Unappealing even to my kind. Like rotten fruit.

Deep growling indicated that I was getting close. Then I saw my mate. The harvest moon cast her eerie glow on the blinding white fur of a giant wolf.

Pure white, stained red—Danni towered over it all. Her paws were drenched in blood. She lifted up on her hind legs and slammed her feet into one of the dead wolves, grinding it to a pulp.

"Danni," I said quietly, getting her attention. Her head whipped around, those icy-blue eyes narrowing on me. I didn't lift my hand because she wasn't a dog to be tamed. She was my mate, and right now, she was borderline feral.

We vampires called it blood rage.

A thick rumbling sound came from her chest. She bared her teeth, mouth easily large enough to swallow me whole. But this was Danni. Angry, wrathful, lost in a sea of emotions she didn't know how to control; she was still *my* Danni.

"He's gone," I said, leaning against one of the few trees still standing. "I killed him."

She let out a grunt and turned, grabbing one of the

wolf sternums with her teeth to fling it across the clearing. I didn't speak wolf, but I assumed that meant she was still pissed.

"You killed the rest of them. It's over. You can let go now."

She narrowed her eyes in my direction again, tail swishing impatiently. "I'll sit out here with you all night if that's what you want. I was thinking we could go back to the estate and get cleaned up. I'd have strawberries and rocky road brought to our room."

The wolf paused, regarding me again, as if to say, *go on.*

I took a few steps toward her, stuffing my hands in my pockets.

"Then I was thinking I'd lick your pretty pussy until you came on my tongue." I paused when the wolf started for me, her size shrinking rapidly. "I like the way you taste, and after tonight, I'm ravenous—"

I broke off when the wolf dropped on all fours, bones cracking. Breaking. Reconfiguring. Danni threw her head back and Nova sprang from her chest, circling us before falling down by a tree, exhausted. Danni leaned forward, taking a ragged breath.

I got on my knees, brushing the hair away from her face.

One look was all it took for me to know whatever had brought on her bloodlust was still riding her hard.

She lunged for me, our teeth clashing as she parted her lips. I opened my own, giving in to her.

She sucked my tongue into her mouth, her arms winding around my shoulders in an unbreakable grip. Her naked body plastered itself to my front, and my cock went hard.

"Fuck me," she groaned. I paused, gripping her by the waist.

"You don't want beach sex because it's gross. I can promise the forest covered in blood won't be any better."

"I don't care," she panted. She grabbed my collar, ripping my shirt down the middle. "I still want to kill. I want to drink. I want to fuck." She licked from the center of my chest, up my neck, to my ear. "Please, help me. This isn't me."

Gods. My poor, sweet—

"Turn around," I said, voice low. A relieved whimper escaped her as she turned and basically flung herself on all fours. I undid my pants. My hard erection pressed into her slick heat. I ran my tip up and down to make sure she was ready for me. Danni let out a moan.

"Please!" Her hands clawed the earth, digging up chunks of dirt and crushing rock.

I wrapped her wild, bloodstained white hair in one hand, pulling her up. Her back touched my chest as I pushed into her.

Relief filled me. Connection. Belonging. I wasn't sure whose emotions these were, hers or mine. All I knew was that I had to have her.

To own her.

I clamped a hand around Danni's hip bone, keeping her right where I wanted so I could fuck her savagely. Raw, unfiltered sounds came from her as Danni bowed her back and spread her legs further.

"You fought bravely." I grunted, cock pulsing in and out of her tight channel. She made a noise of satisfaction in the back of her throat. "You made them pay," I continued.

Bloodlust was a delicate thing.

It had to be worked out of the system.

"You're a powerful alpha and queen in your own right." My hips slapped against her ass. "You don't need to hold on to the rage. It's madness. It will drive you insane."

"I know." Danni shuddered, her slick heat beginning to flutter. Her fists shook from how tight she was wound. "I can't stop. I. Don't. Know. How."

I slowed my thrusting, pulling out right when she bordered on coming.

"What do you want?"

"You," she groaned, pressing her ass into me.

"What of me?" I asked, rubbing my slick shaft between her ass cheeks.

"Your cock," she ground out, growing unabashed in her neediness. I loved this side of Danni.

"Where?" I grunted.

"I want you to fuck my pussy." That made two of us. "Or bite me," she continued. "Or let me bite you—"

"No biting," I said, harder than I'd meant to. Bloodlust and biting were like binge drinking while pissed off. Nothing good ever came of it.

I nipped her neck just sharp enough to make her melt for me.

"Make me come," she said, some of the aggression draining away. I filled her in one smooth stroke.

"Is that a command, my queen?" I purred. My predator was thoroughly enjoying this. Danni didn't have the upper hand, but he wanted her to think she did. He got what he wanted either way, to fuck the remaining bloodlust out with his mate.

"Yes," she breathed. "Fuck me raw and don't stop."

I gave her what she wanted. Needed.

Danni gave me everything back in return. She screamed my name when she came. Loud enough I had no doubt Markus, Shade, and Andreas heard her. Her orgasm triggered mine, and I wrapped my arms around her chest, pulling her to me as I emptied into her.

"How are we feeling?" I hedged.

"Better." Her muscles eased, most of the tension

draining away. "I can think about something other than killing, biting you, or fucking you."

I smirked, pulling out. Come slipped down her inner thighs and I resisted the urge to rub it into the flesh. Danni wasn't one for possessive males. I'd never felt possessive about someone until her. We might have to meet in the middle on that.

"My dick thinks of little else but you."

"Better be no one else," she grumbled. On second thought, maybe she *was* the same.

"There isn't," I promised, kissing the top of her head. Bliss sang through the bond. I hated to interrupt it, but if I could hear footsteps, I knew she could. I reached out and grabbed the T-shirt Danni had ripped down the middle. "You'll want to put this on."

She stood, holding the blood-and dirt-stained shirt. "I'd complain about ripping it, but I don't think that would make it much better." Still, she shucked her arms through the holes and wrapped it around her front, then crossed her arms to hold it in place. Nova watched from her resting spot, looking like she didn't give a care about what all was happening.

I followed suit, zipping my fly shut and getting to my feet. My arm dropped around Danni's waist, pulling her into my side.

Markus, Andreas, and Shade followed Ysa and Adora through the trees. Bound in glowing rope at Ysa's side was Katie, her eyes wide with fear.

Adora stopped at the edge of the clearing, sniffed once, then gagged. "For fuck's sake." She put her hand on Katie's shoulder, shoving her to her knees.

Ysabeau surveyed the trees and dead wolves, pointing at Danni. "She did this?"

I nodded once. "Blood rage."

Ysa whistled. "You'll need to train her." Danni's heart rate picked up, and I felt a flicker of anxiety. "How to control it," Ysa added slowly. She read the apprehension on my mate's face. Danni may have been capable of killing, but she wasn't a killer at heart. What had happened today would be hard enough on her as it was.

"A discussion for another time," I said, closing the topic for now. It wasn't for Shade's or Andreas's ears. "Why is she here?" I thrust my chin toward Katie.

"Got a confession, and we recorded it," Ysa said with a savage smile. I could only imagine what she'd had to do to get that. "Ten minutes with this one and Katie was happy to tell us anything we wanted to know." She tilted her head toward Adora, who was picking at her fingernails with a knife.

I looked down at Danni, who gave the slightest shake of her head. She'd tell me what was up with that sister of hers—what kind of shifter she really was and what all she was capable of. Adora showed her hand when Danni had been shot. She saw things, and I didn't entirely know how. I had my suspicions, but it was another thing to talk about later. When we didn't have an audience.

"We don't need her anymore if you got a confession," I said.

Adora inclined her head, but there was a glint of malice in her eyes. She reached down and cut the rope binding the vampire's hands. Katie jumped to her feet, not wanting to waste a second.

"Go," Adora told her, a sharp tone filling the command.

Katie took off, making it a solid twenty yards away until a knife sailed through the air, planting itself in the notch of her neck where her spine met her head.

Everyone turned to Adora, who shrugged. "What? I was just taking out the trash."

Danni pressed her face against my chest in a show of exasperation. Adora went to retrieve the knife, but before she took it out, my mate said, "Finish the job. It's rude to play with your food."

"I'm not gonna eat her." Adora snorted, then pointed around us. "Have you seen this place? You and Nova did a number out here. If anyone played with their food . . ."

Danni smirked. "Fine. Torture isn't ladylike. Better?"

Planting a foot in-between Katie's shoulder blades, she then looked up at her sister. "Pots and kettles, sis."

In a swift move, she grasped Katie by the hair, then

turned the knife to the side like a lever, first left, then right. A sickening crunch sounded, and Adora pulled Katie's head from her body before dropping it to the ground and kicking it like a soccer ball.

"Happy now?" she asked, flicking the blood off the blade, and then wiping it on her tunic. Nova huffed loudly, seemingly happy this was over.

"Thrilled," Danni answered.

Not for the first time, I wondered about these two. I knew Danni as my mate, but who she was with Adora was another side of her. One I also wanted to know.

Shade cleared his throat. "We need to get going. Will we be taking Markus with us?"

I looked at Markus with a disinterested glance. "That's up to him."

"I want to stay in Blood and Beryl," he said immediately. He glanced at Danni, then back to me. "But, with your permission, I'd like to transfer to a different territory. Somewhere I can start over."

I nodded. "Consider it done. Bianca will make the arrangements."

Markus lowered his head in a show of respect. He'd come a long way in a short amount of time. I knew what he'd done here tonight had mostly been for Dannika, but his desire to be his own man was what would create a lasting change.

"Very well," Shade said, awkwardly shifting. He clearly wasn't sure what to make of this scenario.

Whether it was Nova growling at them, the way Adora was eyeing Andreas like he was going to be the next one she threw a dagger at, the carnage of Dannika's wolf, or the scent in the air giving away what we'd been doing just before he'd arrived. I didn't care. "If that's all, we'll be going..."

"His body stays," I said, making both him and Andreas pause.

"Whose?"

"Mathis's. Ysabeau will be adjusting the scene to fit the story. I'll notify you when it's done. After the other Houses confirm the story, you may collect your dead, provided Dannika and Adora's moms and Rowe have been delivered to my border unharmed by sunrise."

Andreas's jaw tightened, and Shade shook his head. "Their moms are safe, but Rowe stays in Fire and Fluorite. She isn't a Kresley, and she doesn't belong to them. But I'll keep her protected."

"You can't do that," Adora ground out.

Shade looked at Adora, but it wasn't harsh. It was almost sympathetic. "I can, and I have to. We have a story we have to follow here. The Alpha Supreme is dead, and he did have followers. Supporters loyal to him. You and your family are still cast out and exiled. As far as we're concerned, your mothers escaped. But if they take Rowe? Then it looks like your family has kidnapped a non-member of your family. Human or not, she's under the protection of Fire and Fluorite, and by laws, we would respond to that act against the treaty. How will that look if I *don't* respond? Understand?"

Danni and Adora met each other's gaze, sadness filling their eyes. It was almost as if they shared an unspoken conversation.

"Promise you will keep her safe," Danni said, authority filling her tone.

"You have my word," Shade answered. "I've had your moms in hiding since Mathis abducted Adora. You'll have to pick them up. If I'm seen escorting them, our cover story is blown."

"Where are they staying?" Adora asked, standing taller despite her petite height.

"No Man's Circus," he said.

She turned on her boot, blue hair swishing behind her as she started back for No Man's Land. "She can't seriously plan on walking."

"Of course not," she called over her shoulder. "We brought a truck. I'm taking it to pick them up." She glanced back, dark blue eyes filled with secrets. "You coming?" she asked Danni.

My mate looked up at me. "Ready to meet my moms?"

"Will you allow us to stop at the Blood and Beryl embassy on the way?" I asked, taking in her practically naked body. In a quieter voice, I added, "I can't imagine that introducing myself while covered in blood, dirt, and come would go over well, love."

Pink colored her cheeks. "Good idea."

"I'm rolling both windows down on the way," Adora said. "Unless you want to ride in the back with Nova."

"Adora," Danni chastised. Her sister threw her hands up and kept walking.

I looked at Danni as we started after her. I'd made this woman my fake mate, presented her to my Court, turned her into a shifter-vampire hybrid queen—and she'd done it all, albeit while occasionally vomiting and breaking a few relics.

Now I was being introduced to her mothers.

The tables had turned.

"Not so fun when you're the one in the hot seat, is it?" Danni chuckled.

"I could think of better uses for your smart mouth."

She laughed. "Same, babe. Same."

CHAPTER 37
DANNIKA

Was it a mating ceremony or a coronation? Were they one and the same? I knew he'd told me it wasn't a big deal. But then he'd also said there was a public consummation—though he'd insisted that had been a joke. Still. My nerves were shot. How bad was this going to be?

Nova lay on the rug, asleep, snoring contentedly. I sat with my hands in my lap, my remaining fingers interlaced and twirling my thumbs in a circular motion. My wrist had healed just fine, but the finger hadn't grown back. I didn't actually know why, but I also didn't care. I had nine others. As long as I could flip someone off, my sister agreed.

Moments ticked by, and I glanced at the clock

again. It had only been thirty-seven seconds since the last time I'd looked. My neck was stiff, and I angled my head to stretch it some.

"Stop fidgeting," Adora said as she finished braiding my hair. "If you keep looking around, I'll have to start over." I blew out my cheeks, then nodded. Staring at me in the mirror, she shot me an incredulous look as I moved my head yet again. "Really?"

I smiled awkwardly and mouthed, "Sorry."

Why was I nervous? There was absolutely no reason for me to be. I didn't have reservations. This was my mate. It was the official mating ceremony of Blood and Beryl. I was being crowned queen. I'd known this part was coming, and it wasn't a lie. This was real. True. It was forever. And none of that scared me.

"You're afraid of saying personal things in public," my sister muttered with hairpins in her mouth. She carefully placed them to hold my braid in a crown around my head. I pressed my lips together, smiling and trying to hold back a laugh. She knew me. So well, in fact, that she knew I'd be anxious and wondering why I had those feelings. And somehow, she had the answer.

"I guess so," I responded in a quiet voice. "None of the other stuff scares me. I'm ready to be queen." I absentmindedly rubbed my fingers over my left forearm, where my new tattoo had healed. My marking, tying me to the Laskaris name forever. I had no regrets.

Pulling a pin from her mouth, she looked at me in the mirror, meeting my gaze. "Everyone knows this is an intimate celebration. They respect it. I doubt you'd be the first person to stutter or blush. The fact that you love him isn't news to anyone." Tucking the pin into my hair and looping more of the braid, she muttered, "Trust me. Everyone can hear how much you love him every night."

I snorted, tilting my head down, then tried to stiffen my body when she grumbled loudly. "It just feels weird to say something so private in a public space."

"I can't argue with that, but you'll be fine. You always underestimate yourself when it comes to how badass you really are." I raised my eyebrows at her. "It's true. Look at your history and what you've overcome. You fight back, even if you think you'll lose. You protect others at your own expense. You were willing to do this very thing when it wasn't even real. And sure, you would have totally vomited afterward, but now? You've got it. This is just announcing the truth, and *that* you are good at. You always have been."

"Thank you," I whispered, my eyes watering.

She winked at me, then wrapped the final piece of the braid around and tucked it in place. She stepped back, studying the work she'd done. "Damn, I'm good.

If I ever did this type of thing—which I won't—I'd want to do my hair the same way."

"You don't think you'll ever find a mate or someone you want to be with for life?"

She scoffed, furrowing her brows. "And stay tied down?" She shook her head. "My tomorrow is not guaranteed, so I'm going to get laid today. And every other day."

I burst out laughing. "Why stick to one flavor when there are so many to sample?"

"Exactly." She looked up thoughtfully. "I like an assortment of things, and no one can really give me all that I want in one simple package. So I want the variety pack." She wiggled her eyebrows.

I smiled at her in the mirror. My sister. Uniquely herself and she owned every bit of it. Adora grinned in return, tucking *Black Magic* roses around my braided crown. The deep red petals mirrored the color of blood, and the contrast against the light tones of my silver hair was striking. She hummed to herself as she moved around me, and I considered her.

I was so happy to have my family together again. I'd breathed a sigh of relief when we'd arrived at No Man's Circus and picked up our moms. They were safe, and I never again had to worry about them. They were finding their place here, but Adora seemed restless. She wouldn't admit it yet, but I watched her. I couldn't tell if it was because this was so new to her, or if it was something else, but I knew she would tell me in her own time.

"It looks beautiful," I told her, moving to stand.

She'd finished my makeup earlier, so all that was left was getting dressed. I stopped in front of the bed and stared. On one side, a simple deep-pink cotton dress with long sleeves. On the other, dark leggings and a burgundy sweater. I frowned, glancing between the two options.

"Not really what you imagined, is it?"

I shook my head. "The dress is pretty, and it's simple, which I like. When I actually wear them, I prefer something that isn't fussy. Like you." I smirked, and she huffed a laugh. "But wearing what I normally wear seems too casual, doesn't it?"

Adora shrugged. "I think you're going to be the queen and you can do whatever you want. I imagine Elias would say the same." Still, I wasn't sure, and I made no move to pick something. "Or I could show you what I made."

My sister's eyes lit up as she ran to the closet and pulled out a knitted, hunter-green sweater dress with a thick cowl. I couldn't argue how perfect it was. It combined what I felt like I should wear with exactly what I *wanted* to wear. "How did you do this? I didn't know you knitted. How could I not know that?"

"I was at home without you, and it felt like forever, so I picked it up and learned. I had Rowe, but you're my sister. I had to do something to pass the time. I can also bake now. Who knew?"

"You learned how to knit . . ." Running my fingers over the patterns she'd put into the sweater; I scrunched my eyebrows in confusion. She wasn't crafty or artsy like this.

"You're welcome, of course. And I won't take your surprise and shock at my awesomeness as a slight." She flipped her hair over her shoulder, giving me a deadpan look.

I wrapped my arms around her, pulling her tightly to me. "You're the best," I whispered.

"I know." I felt her smile against my cheek, and I chuckled.

After we let each other go, I dropped the robe and shimmied carefully into the sweater dress with my sister's help. It hugged my body perfectly, staying loose in just the right places, the length coming to a few inches above the knee. The cowl dipped around my chest and shoulders. Adora held up tall, black leather boots to finish the look, and I slipped them on.

Nova had gotten up from her nap, stretching her body before she came to stand by my side. My sister came to her, pressing her forehead against Nova's head as though they were speaking to each other silently. Then she placed a lei of the same *Black Magic* roses around my wolf's neck. I turned to look at us in the full-length mirror, and I couldn't help but smile.

This was perfect. It was me—us—and it felt right. I loved it.

"You're both beautiful, and you know it," she said, opening the door and making a motion for me to exit first. "But it's time to go. You admire yourself any longer and you'll be as vain as a peacock."

I barked a laugh, and she gave me a wide grin. We left, walking down the hallway and taking the turns to head into the throne room. I didn't even pay attention to the directions anymore. It felt like second nature.

The first time I'd taken this walk to the throne room, I'd been on the verge of throwing up. Not today. I had butterflies for different reasons, but none of them were bad.

Ysabeau stood at the entrance, looking at my attire. Tilting her glasses down, she gave me a wink of approval. "It suits you," she said. "I like it." Then she opened the doors.

Each member of the High Court was present, and my mom and Abbey stood off to the side, just a few steps away from the dais. True to form, my mother had happy tears streaming down her face while Abbey wrapped her comforting arms around her.

This was it. Somehow, I had expected more, but I wasn't disappointed in the least at the small crowd.

Elias sat on his throne, a sexy smile playing on his lips. Desire struck me, his emotion leaking into me, and a warmth bloomed on my cheeks. I shook my head slightly, trying to suppress a small laugh.

Ysa cleared her throat, nudging me forward, and I stepped up to the dais as my mate stood, turning to face me. Nova stayed by my side, sitting next to me and looking out over everyone in the room.

"My queen," Elias whispered, taking my hand and pressing his lips to the top in a soft kiss. "You look good enough to eat." He cocked an eyebrow, and I pressed my legs together.

I widened my eyes slightly and mouthed, "Stop," motioning with my eyes toward my family. My moms were *right there*. They may have pretended not to hear it, but Adora groaned in response. I pressed my lips together in a slight smile.

Marisa stepped forward as head of the High Court, dipping her chin respectfully.

"Dannika, you've been given the Laskaris tattoo to show your commitment to your House and your mate."

I held my arm out, pulling the sleeve to my elbow, extending it for all to see. Where smooth and unmarred skin had once been, now there was an intricately placed tattoo. A thick band starting at my wrist, wrapping its way up my arm, curving around until it came back to end where it began. A never-ending loop. Inside it, Celtic knotwork represented his mother, lacing around strategically placed daphne flowers all centered around an olive branch, representing his father. Rage may have run deep in his family, but they'd always aspired for peace.

A new mark had been added within the band, now integrating a crescent moon and a crown. My family. Kingston and Kresley, forever merging our family lines into the Laskarises.

"I'm yours forever, Elias," I said softly. "Bound to each other by love, not just fate."

"Elias, King of Blood and Beryl," Marisa continued, staying serious, even though I could hear a tinge of happiness in her voice, "the Laskaris tattoo on your skin has been given Danni's addition, showing your commitment to your queen and mate."

Elias's gaze was fixated on mine when he lifted his sleeve, showing the new ink incorporating my name into his.

"I choose you, Danni," he said, his tone husky. "Every day, until the end of time, every part of me belongs to you."

Emotion flooded me, and it wasn't all my own. I struggled to keep the tears from falling, and I took a shaky breath.

That wasn't so bad. It was a small crowd, and the words were minimal, said quietly to the man I loved.

Marisa clasped her hands together. "Dannika, would you please turn to face us?" I did as she requested, and I felt a knot tighten in my belly. Nova adjusted herself, almost as though she were sitting higher, raising her chin a little more. I met Adora's gaze, and she was considering Nova, almost as if to say, "Look who's preening now." Marisa stepped to the side, continuing to address me, but moving herself from the spotlight. "Dannika, Queen of Blood and Beryl, we will serve you, follow you, and protect you. It is an honor to have you as our king's mate, our leader, and our queen."

Marisa dropped to one knee, bowing her head in respect. Each and every other member of the High Court followed suit. Bianca's eyes glittered with unshed tears as she lowered her gaze, a smile on her face. My mother, Abbey, and Adora tilted their heads down as they descended. Elias stepped off the dais and knelt as well, the act surprising me. My lips parted, and I shook my head in a tight motion, momentarily letting my nerves get the best of me. He grinned, winked, then lowered his head.

Nova stood up, looking over the heads of each member of the Court, lording over everyone, like she had full expectation that this would occur. She was an alpha, after all.

So was I.

Shoulders back and chin raised, I took a deep breath, accepting the reverence. It wouldn't be so formal every day. Tomorrow, I would go back to wearing sweaters, dark jeans, and hiking boots. My hair would be down. I'd have on no makeup. I would roam the halls and raid the pantry all over again. I would just do it as a queen.

When everyone stood up and looked at me, I dipped my head in return. This was my House. My people. My family.

Bianca jumped from her spot, the excitement too much for her to handle. "To Blood and Beryl," she shouted, and the room erupted in applause.

My mom and Abbey rushed to me, pulling me into a group embrace. "I'm so proud of you, baby," my mom whispered. When she pulled back, she looked into my eyes, the fierceness of her own alpha striking in her gaze. "This is who you were always meant to be. Your father would be so proud of you."

Abbey smiled. "You carry the very best of your mom and dad, Danni. You were born to be a leader," she said softly. "I'm honored to be a part of your life."

"Abbey," I said, trying to hold back the tears as my voice wavered. I pulled her into a hug. "I couldn't have asked for a better bonus mom."

"Let's cry later. We're going to mess up your make-up," my mom said as she dabbed at my face with a tissue, wiping away the moisture.

I chuckled, sniffling and letting Abbey go. Elias came up behind me and wrapped his arms around my waist. He buried his face in the crook of my neck, partially in the cowl of the sweater. Heat bloomed in my chest as I realized he was smelling me . . . and thinking dirty thoughts.

I cleared my throat. "This wasn't as bad as I thought," I mused, trying to make conversation and get my head out of the gutter.

Adora snorted. "And you didn't even throw up," she said. "That's gotta count for something."

"What were you expecting?" Elias asked, resting his chin on my shoulder.

"I don't know. A lot of talking, a bigger audience, more . . ."

"Embarrassment," my sister said, finishing for me. I gave her a deadpan look.

"Something like that." I huffed a tiny laugh. "It's easy to say 'I love you' in public, but being crowned queen and having it called a *mating ceremony* . . . it's a little nerve-racking. I didn't know what to expect."

Elias pulled me tighter to him, his body pressed against mine, and I felt him throb against my backside. Speaking softly against my ear, he said, "Well, that part of the ceremony isn't finalized."

Heat filled my cheeks, a blush creeping over my skin. My mom pressed her lips together and looked away as she tried not to laugh. Abbey put her hand over her mouth, flicking her gaze down. Not my sister, though. She groaned loudly, then muttered under her breath. "I'm going to go for a *long* walk so I don't have to hear her finalize how much she loves him. Again."

My mom raised her hand. "I think we'll join you," she said, looping her arm through Abbey's.

My jaw dropped, and I met my sister's gaze. "Wait, can everyone really hear us going at it?" I asked, lowering my voice. "I thought you were kidding when you said that."

"Afraid not. Guess the wolf is out of the bag now," she said with a devilish grin. "Now go get some, Your Majesty." She blew me a kiss and winked, turning on a heel to walk out of the throne room with our moms.

Nova nudged my side, leaning into me while I stood there speechless, wrapped in my mate's embrace. Elias nuzzled my neck, nipping at the skin. "I like the sound of that," he murmured.

"Which one? The title or the suggestion?" I asked, turning my cheek so I could see him in my periphery.

"Both," he answered, lightly digging his fingertips into my abdomen and scrunching my sweater dress beneath his palm.

"Mm-hmm. I figured as much."

"Does it bother you knowing everyone can hear us?"

I twisted my lips, considering it for a moment. For a brief second, it had thrown me off. But I was mated. I was queen. I was a woman in love. So, no. I didn't give a damn if they heard my orgasms. I shook my head.

"Nope. I'll get them earplugs. This is my home —*our* home. And I'm going to bed." Elias chuckled into my neck, and I unraveled his arms from my waist as I pushed against him, teasing. He growled at the friction, and I walked toward the exit slowly. With one hand on the door, I glanced over my shoulder. "Are you coming, my king?"

A devilish grin crept up Elias's face, and hunger flashed in his eyes. "Not until you do, my queen."

ELIAS

The setting sun spilled warm colors over the Tiber River, casting shades of orange, pinks, and red over the water. I leaned over the balcony railing, resting my elbows on the stone.

Rome in December was a tradition, one I had been excited to share with Danni and her family. It was never a long trip, but it was one I always looked forward to. It was Claudette's favorite place in the world, and the entire compound reminded me of her. My mother would likely never leave. I didn't know what it was like to be a parent, but I knew I missed my sister, and that was all that was needed to understand Mother's connection to this place.

Danni had spent a lot of time overseeing the construction of a home on the Mt. Rainier property. Everything had to be just right. She wanted the very best for her moms, and she knew they would be more comfortable in the forest . . . and out of earshot of us. She wasn't very good at staying quiet, and I loved hearing her, so I wasn't going to encourage it.

While we had territory to tend to all over the world, the one gift that I could give her that mattered more than anything was making Mt. Rainier our home base. Vampire hybrid or not, she was a shifter first. She was different when she was buried in nature, exploring and hunting. She never needed to ask. I could see it in her eyes that the estate there was her home. My home was with her. It was simple.

"Have you seen this?" Danni asked, coming out to join me. She was holding a framed picture. I smiled at her, taking it from her hand to admire it. My mate and I were sitting by our waterfall, and she'd tilted her head onto my shoulder while she'd laughed. Nova was lying next to us on the shore, and there'd been just enough sunlight spilling through the clouds that day to shine down on us, making the water sparkle.

"I have," I said, handing it back to her. "I'm the one who sent it to her."

"I haven't even seen this picture." She held it in both hands, looking down at it. "When was this?"

"It was the day Adora came with us, and she was sitting up in the trees. She took it." I turned, leaning my back against the railing. "It was a perfect day. Look at you. You were in your element. Authentic. Beautiful. Carefree. I love seeing you in moments like that."

"Your mom has this with all the other family photos and paintings." Danni blushed, twisting her lips. "There are more too. A picture of my moms with Adora and me. One with all of us together." A touch of shyness filtered through the bond between us, amplified by her empath abilities to not only *feel* others' emotions, but to *push* hers onto them as well.

"You feel like you don't belong?" I asked, turning to face her fully.

She shook her head. "Oh, no, that's not it. I think it's just the new feeling of belonging in general. I know my place with you, with my House," she said, placing a hand on my arm gently. "But to have my entire family loved and accepted too . . . It's amazing, honestly, but it's still different."

"Well, your moms fit right in with mine," I said with a chuckle. "I don't think I've seen her this happy and engaged for a long time. Did you know Abbey is teaching her judo? And my mother is teaching both of them all about gardening and how to make limoncello."

"My mom is teaching yours how to make beer," she muttered, looking away.

"A threesome of trouble, that's what they are," Adora said, coming to join us on the balcony. Her blue hair lifted off her shoulders to dance in the wind, large sunglasses that reminded me of Ysabeau perched on her head. "Going to end up like a bunch of drunk fools by midnight."

"Well, that's great," Danni said. "I wasn't worried they'd embarrass us by telling stories about the time you licked a shoe or got into a fight with a rooster, but now I am."

"That stupid rooster had it coming. You're the one who shit in the front yard when you were three," Adora said, crossing her arms. "Wait till they get going with that."

Danni's mouth dropped, but I bit my bottom lip, trying not to laugh. "I was *three*," she whispered harshly. "And—"

"I know, I know—you wanted to fit in, and other shifters did it because they could shift." Adora shrugged, smiling. "Doesn't make it any less funny."

I couldn't stop. I bent forward, busting out laughing. "Maybe I'll go drink with them if these are the stories being told."

"You will do no such thing," Danni said, but she couldn't hide the smile. It was amusing, no matter which way you looked at it.

A piercing howl cut into our conversation, and we all looked at the cobblestone road leading to the courtyard. Ysabeau had arrived, and she always knew how to give Nova just what she wanted. With a stoic expression, she reached to the pack on her back, pulled out a freshly dead plump rabbit, then tossed it to the wolf. Nova jumped, catching it, sending a loud crunch into the air. A tiny smile made its way to Ysa's face.

"Is that . . .?" Adora said, squinting at Ysa and the person by her side.

"Markus," I deadpanned. She looked at me, lip curled up in disgust and eyebrow cocked.

"But . . .why?"

"Because Ysa found a new boytoy," I muttered.

Danni nudged me with her hip. "Because Ysa and Markus are a thing now. It suits them. She likes to be in control, and he has no desire to be." She leveled her sister with a look, then gave me the same one. "Adora, I know you've seen into his soul. You know what's in his heart, so both of you, quit being grouchy."

"No promises," she said, running her hands through her hair and tugging it over one shoulder.

"You're going to make a great addition to the Portal Watch," I commented. She'd fit right in. Confident. Headstrong. Didn't take shit from anyone.

"Wait, what?" Danni said, her face falling as she looked at her sister. I glanced at Adora, not realizing she hadn't shared that with her. "What's he talking about?"

Adora glared at me in a flat expression but turned to Danni to answer. "I asked Elias to reach out and look into the Portal Watch. I want to go there, and they've accepted me. I wasn't going to tell you until I knew for sure I could go, and we just found out, but I wanted to tell you after this trip. Didn't want to ruin the holiday."

Danni's mouth fell open slightly. "Why?"

Adora sighed. "You're safe now. Mom and Abbey are safe. I want to know what's out there for me. I want to know if I'm the last peacock shifter. Guarding and accessing the portals will allow that. I feel it," she said, putting her hand on her chest. "Something out there is calling me." She lifted a shoulder, then added, "Besides, you and Elias are trying to make a baby every chance you get. I don't need to be around for that. My delicate ears have already been traumatized."

Danni smiled, and it reached her eyes. "Even if you aren't the only one, there are none out there like you."

"I know," she said, grinning. "I'm not leaving until after we get back to Mt. Rainier, okay? And the moment I know I have a niece or nephew, there is nothing on this earth that would stop me from coming back to you."

Danni wrapped her arms around Adora, and they hugged each other tightly. "You bet your ass you will."

When they let go, Adora stepped back, smoothing out her dress. "If you'll excuse me, I'm going to go check on our mothers and see what stories have been told so far. Let's hope they don't share all of it in front of Ysa and Markus. I don't need anyone at Portal Watch hearing about the time we plucked my feathers and glued them to you when you still hadn't shifted. Not exactly queen-like for you, nor does it give me the intimidating card to play with the other guards."

I snorted, trying to imagine Adora's midnight-black peacock feathers plastered to Danni's body.

Danni looked horrified. "Go. Stop them before they start making whiskey."

Adora cackled, leaving us on the balcony by ourselves.

I walked up to Danni, slipping my arms around her waist, pulling her close to me. "I'm sorry I didn't tell you that she'd asked me about the Watch. It was in confidence."

She covered my arms with her own, then patted me. "I know. She has her reasons. I could sense something was going on. She came to you with those questions because she trusts you. That's a big step for her."

"You're incredible. Do you know that?" I kissed her neck once. Twice. Danni tilted her head, giving me more access. "Understanding. Kind."

She hummed. "Go on."

"Empathetic. Generous." I planted little kisses down her throat. "You'll be an amazing mother."

"My sister did say she would come home as soon as she knew there was a niece or nephew waiting for her . . ." She trailed off, raising an eyebrow and glancing at me from the corner of her eye.

"She did," I murmured, grazing my lips over her collarbone.

"Then let's get on that," she whispered with a seductive smile on her face.

I was more than willing to give my queen whatever she wanted, whenever she wanted. She turned in my arms, pressing her body against my chest. Her fingers laced through my hair, and she pulled me to her as a growl rumbled in my chest.

"My pleasure."

Acknowledgments

This book was a beast. We aren't just talking about the size. Between the timing, both of us having major life events that could not be ignored—and yes, the size—it was a monster to write.

Both of us went into this thinking, *it's a standalone! It will be easy.*

Narrator: It was not easy.

We have never been so wrong. As it turns out, standalones are hard because our characters still have *all* the things to say. Elias and Dannika certainly did.

We hope that you enjoyed the first book in the Immortal Vices and Virtues universe. While the process was rough—rockier than either of us hoped it would be—we are so thrilled with the story we told, and truly honored that we got to kick off this amazing shared world.

We owe so many *thank yous* to people that have supported us throughout the last few months. Our husbands for the endless support and laughs. Our kiddos for being the tiny tyrants and greatest joys they were born to be. Our moms for stepping in to help keep things running when we were slammed and had a book to write. We love all of you.

As always, a huge round of applause to Dom and Maegan for being awesome. You guys make things happen, even if our readers don't *see* it. We appreciate you both so much!

And lastly, but never least, thank you, dear reader, for buying our book! At least we hope you bought it. If you pirated it, we retract the thank you and we hope you step on a fucking Lego. We appreciate all of you who have supported us by buying and reading our books. If you recommended it to anyone, you get an even bigger thanks. Basically thank you and many air high-fives to you all. We hope that you continue to read the rest of this series and the other amazing authors that are part of it.

Until next time,

Kel & Aurelia